THE GLORY HOLE

THE GLORY HOLE

Geoffrey Newson

FREDERICK MULLER LIMITED
LONDON

First published in Great Britain 1980 by
Frederick Muller Limited, London, NW2 6LE

British Library Cataloguing in Publication Data
Newson, Geoffrey
The glory hole.
I. Title
823'.9'1F PR6064.E96/

ISBN 0–584–31074–9

Today is the Highway (and Tomorrow is the Time) *composed by Eric Andersen, reproduced by kind permission of Harmony Music Ltd, 19/20 Poland Street, London W1.*

Printed in Great Britain by Biddles Ltd, Guildford, Surrey

To my mother,
who opened the
first door

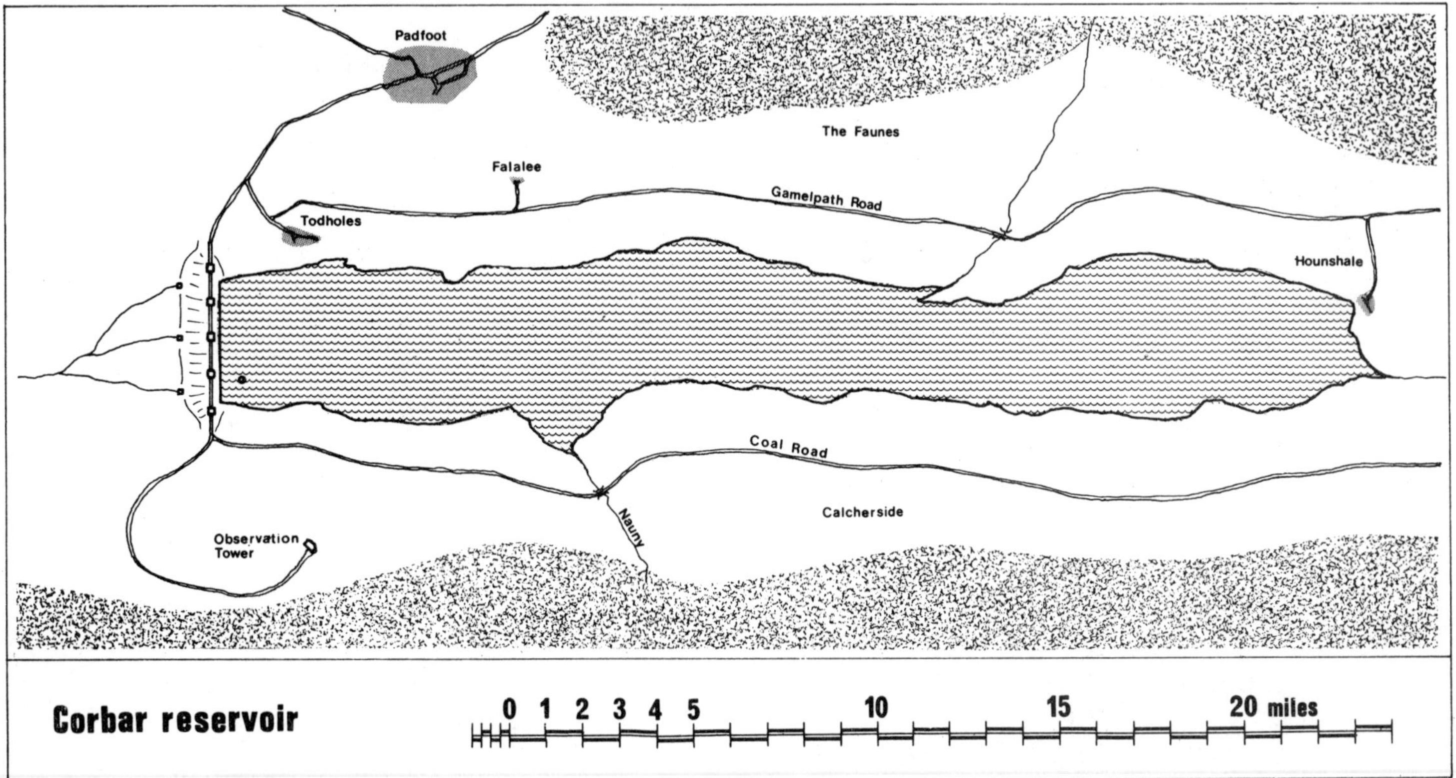

Corbar reservoir

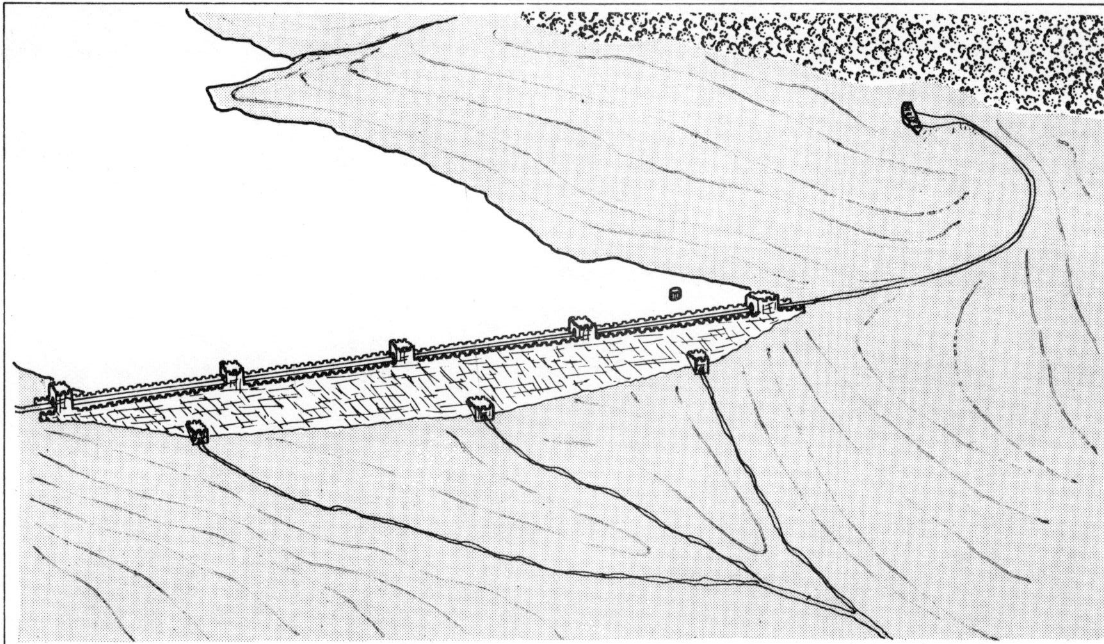

Corbar dam

0 1 2 3 miles

Part One

IMBOLC

IMBOLC *Spring – the birth of the year.*
'A renewal of the earth after
the winter sleep.'

IMBOLC

For the most of the way down the steep fellside the boy had purposefully matched the steps of the tall man ahead of him, deliberately placing his feet in the black dents in the snow left by the flockmaster's gumboots.

As the ground started to level out the man lengthened his stride and the boy found that only by making big leaps which threatened to split the crutch of his brown cord trousers could he land in the large footprints. He kept it up for a few yards before finally ending the game and instead began shuffling through the thin layer of snow, kicking up fine powdery spray before him, his hands thrust deep in the pockets of his bright red anorak.

For a moment Donald The Donald Dacre had forgotten the boy was behind him. He was staring glassily ahead unaware even that, behind him, the sun had climbed over Calcherside and was sending its warmth splashing yellow across the backs of the sheep as they descended into the valley.

Only when he heard the urgent barking of the black and white collie to his left did he shake his great bulky body to life and turned quickly to see that the boy had changed course and was making off rapidly into the distance followed by the dog.

A lamb had broken away from the flock and was bounding back up the slope towards the coal road, its black legs gathering speed as the cries of the pursuing boy became louder.

"Back boy. Rab'll get him."

He shook his head and grinned as the boy ignored him and raced determinedly through the snow with the sheep dog easily overtaking him. Still smiling, the flockmaster fumbled in the pocket of his overcoat and carefully brought out a deep bowled pipe and a leather pouch. He filled the bowl slowly, listening at the same time to the mingled sounds of the fleeing lamb, the dog and the boy. When he finally looked up, the boy was lying face down in the snow his small, short legs furiously kicking the ground behind him.

The lad was already on his feet when Donald The Donald Dacre reached him. His blue woollen bobble hat had fallen from his head and below the dark fringe of his hair his cheek was stained with mud.

"I would have caught him Grandad," he gasped, brushing the

knees of his trousers.

The old man cupped a hand against his mouth and shouted a command to the sheepdog before turning to the boy. "That's what dogs are for. Now let's have a look at you, you young callant."

He dropped his crook at his feet and bent slowly to scoop up a handful of snow. "This should do it," he said pressing the snow to the boy's face and scraping the black mud away with the heel of his hand. "We don't want your Aunt Sarah to think you've been up here playing games now do we?"

The boy screwed up his face as he waited for the shepherd to complete the repairs, relaxing only when the old man had finished. He opened his eyes to see that the lamb was standing almost at his feet, closely watched by the panting sheepdog whose jaws were leaking down into two black gullies between his paws.

"There y'are, Donny," said the shepherd. "I told you it was a dog's job. They know where to go. Sheep always make for high ground when there's trouble."

Donny fingered the tender spot on his cheek and looked up. "Will I have a bruise?" he asked hopefully.

"Shouldn't reckon so," grunted the shepherd, "This should see to it."

The boy looked quizzically at the small heap of snow in the old man's hand. "It's only snow isn't it?"

Donald The Donald Dacre raised his thick bushy eyebrows high above the broad beak of his nose which gave him an owlish look. "Only snaw is it? And you a countryman? What month is it boy?"

"It's March."

"Tail end eye" said the shepherd. "And when this sort of stuff falls round this time it's special snaw. It's what we call lambin' snaw, sent for young tups like 'im and wee callants like yourself. We get it most years just after the spring lambs have been born up on the top there. It's a kind of test. Nature's way of sorting out their weak spots right from the start. If they're tough, and most of 'em are, they'll make it all right. But if they're sickly the snaw'll kill 'em dead as stone."

The boy looked down at the bleating lamb which was anxiously scanning the flock for its ewe. "Can't you bring them in then, Grandad?" he asked.

The old man sucked on his pipe before spitting a stream of brown saliva on to the snow. "What and coddle 'em? No, boy, if you bring 'em into the shippon they'd be even worse off. They wouldn't get the chance to build up their resistance. It would be like rearing you in a greenhouse and then letting you out in the cold without a stitch on you. There are some things you have to leave to nature and lambs is one of them."

The boy's hazel eyes searched the old man's face. "But if it's bad for them why are we bringing them in now Grandad?"

"Because they've told us to," muttered the flockmaster bluntly.

He looked closely at the boy who had opened his mouth as if to make a reply but when none came the shepherd stopped to retrieve his crook and put a hand on Donny's shoulder. "Stick close to me on the way down," he said gently. "I'll be needing you when we get to the log bridge."

The sheepdog was already on its feet, nosing the lamb back to the flock, which began to move again at his approach leaving a pinchushion pattern of black circles in the snow where they had tried to burrow down to the grass beneath.

"Get'n hint," yelled the shepherd when the sheep finally settled back on course and as the sheepdog made a wide circular sweep to return to them, the three followed the flock down into the valley.

There was a bald simplicity about the farmsteads and cottages of Corbardale. The homes, like the dry stone walls surrounding them, each a personal, enclosed kingdom, were built from sturdy Cheviot sandstone. It was as if, when the childhood of Northumbria was being carved out, the Cheviots had parted, allowing a green breathing space between them where people could settle.

The sheepmen of Corbar had never made a serious attempt to compete with the landscape. The Cheviots, in their turn, had merely been persuaded from time to time to spill some of the surplus of bare rugged uplands into the valley in tidy heaps for the locals to live in.

Between the holdings were large flat areas of shielings where the hill farmers grazed their flocks in summer before selling them at the annual Haltbriggin sheep market each autumn to make way for a new season's batch on the nursery slopes. The Corbardale shielings, which stretched for thirty-two miles, spanning four miles, forming a wide rectangular basin, had never been thought of as rich grazing. Onion weathering on the mountain ridges of Calcherside and The Faunes which lined the valley on each side, had soured the soil. Summer would swell the outer skin of the sandstone, which would contract with the first bite of winter and peel away to be washed down by the heavy rainfall into the valley bottom. Consequently, the earth on the lower ground was always loose and gritty and unable to support anything other than sparse grazing for the sheep between the marshes.

The Dacres had rented the four hundred acre South Shieling for ten generations, each head of the family claiming the title of The Donald by traditional custom of a proud but declining clan. Each Dacre had jealously preserved his birthright long after their home at Falalee was left stranded firmly on English soil when the border was moved up to Berwick.

The last three Donald The Donald Dacres of Falalee, had led quiet, uncomplicated lives free from outside competition and cushioned by the weak soil from the soaring rents which tenant farmers on the more fertile plains of Durham and York to the south were being asked to pay. Donald Dacre paid his in cash, the first Monday in April each year almost as a ritual, up at the villa at Haltbriggin, to Brigadier Gillibrand who always seemed grateful even to have the land tenanted.

Donald Dacre was thinking he wouldn't be going there this year when he realised they were approaching the log bridge.

"Right now pet, you stand over there and I'll take this side," he said to Donny, pointing with his crook. "Rab'll come behind me and bring them through."

Holding the crook out as a barrier, the shepherd began whistling to the sheepdog and giving him encouraging words as the flock eased through the narrow opening.

As the leaders emerged on the other side they began fanning out in confused groups. Just when they threatened to disperse in several directions, the sheepdog, impatient to be at them, left the man and boy to funnel the remainder through before leaping into the Corbar River and swimming the twenty five feet to the other bank. Within seconds he had reduced them to a tight circle again.

"Move 'em on again Rab lad!" called the shepherd, settling into his steady step again with the boy trundling beside him. They had gone another half mile before Donny stopped and turned to The Donald.

"Are all the sheep round here ours Grandad?" he asked.

"All the ones down Todholes end are" said the shepherd, "Why d'ye ask that?"

"Because there's one over there by that round house."

The boy pointed towards a derelict stone building 200 yards away to the right. "Look, he looks as if he's trying to get inside it."

The old man followed the line of the lad's arm.

"You're right boy" he said. "It'll be one of ours right enough. Let's go and see." He waved the dog back as it began to follow them. "No, not you Rab, you stay and look after the woollies."

As they approached the building, the sheep backed only momentarily before returning to the same spot where it lowered its head and began butting at something low down on the wall.

"It's one of the ewes" said the shepherd moving towards the agitated animal. "Tan me if she 'asn't got a young 'un in there."

He peered into a narrow opening in the stone which had been almost filled in with planks of wood and the frame of a rusted bicycle. "Aye, there's one in there all right, you can hear him. Look, you try to get in there and howk 'im out Donny lad, while I try to get some of this junk shifted. You're more his size."

As the old man pulled the planks to one side, Donny squeezed easily through the gap wriggling on his hands and knees. Outside, the shepherd listened as the boy's voice came back, hollow against the walls of the building.

"I've got him Grandad. He's all right."

Inside the building Donny cradled the protesting animal in his arms and stared up towards the open roof through which the sky was glowing like a clear blue disc. He could see the remains of at least three ceilings which had been set into the smooth stone walls and between them tiny, glassless windows, some no larger than slits through which the sun was forcing shafts of bright light. The remnants of a stone staircase could be seen spiralling upwards round the walls, leading to nowhere. More than twenty feet up, above the jutting stumps of two heavy wooden beams, the biggest mystery of all: a wide stone fireplace set magically into the wall.

"Are you coming out here boy, or do I have to send Rab in to get you both out?"

The sudden appearance of the shepherd's red, beaky face through the opening gave the boy a start. He took one more look at the bare, awesome walls and scrambled back through the gap still clutching the lamb in his arms.

"Ah! There you are then. I thought you'd moved in there for good."

"It's a funny house that, Grandad," said Donny, looking at the ruined walls which stretched thirty feet from the ground. "What is it?"

"It's an old peel tower," said the shepherd, taking the lamb from the boy and pushing him back to his waiting mother. "It's what some people here used to live in, in case they were attacked."

The boy's eyes were bright against his round red cheeks. "Who'd attack people here Grandad?"

"Robbers mostly," said the flockmaster, sucking his pipe. "Reivers they were. The English reivers used to go up across the border and steal owt they could and the Scottish reivers used to come back down here and do the same."

"And did they all live in these kind of houses?"

Donald the Donald tapped his crook against the hard stone. "Those who could afford to did. They used to keep the animals on the bottom floor and live up at the top so the robbers couldn't get at them so easy."

"Were there a lot of robbers, Grandad?"

"There were indeed. They reckoned that some days when they came up over the ridge at Hounshale, the sky was red with their caps. They'd come plundering and burning and snatching till there wasn't much left to take."

"Where did the boys go when the robbers came, Grandad?"

The shepherd took his pipe from his mouth. "Up there," he said, pointing to the jagged walls at the top of the tower. "They used to mix the boiling oil to pour on the raiders. Mind you, they needed all the men they could get and if the youngsters had enough meat on their bones, they'd be down here dipping their swords with the rest of them."

"Did people get hurt then when the reivers came?"

Donald The Donald Dacre put his hand on the boy's shoulder and led him down to where Rab was waiting with the flock. "There was never a robbery where nobody got hurt son."

Rab already had the sheep army mustered and on the move when they returned to the flock.

Behind them, the man and the boy walked in silence for several minutes before Donny spoke.

"Grandad?"

"Aye boy?" said the shepherd.

"Can you stop robbers without fighting?"

"Only by having something they don't want."

"Have we got anything anybody wants?"

"Yes son, we have."

"Does that mean we'll get robbed?"

As the old man put his hand on his shoulder again, the boy deliberately evaded it and stood back waiting for an answer.

"We'd best be gettin' the sheep back," Dacre said quickly.

They had reached the narrow sike at the point where the fields started to ascend to the Gamelpath road below the Faunes before either of them spoke again.

"Grandad?"

"Aye, pet?"

"If there was robbing and fighting, I'd have been down here with you."

The Donald glanced quickly down at him and saw that the boy's face was tight and serious. "I'm sure you would boy," he said gently. "I'm sure you would."

He began digging his tall, wooden crook deeper into the snow as they climbed the higher ground. Ahead of them, he could see the peaks of the Faunes, the multi-coloured range of hills which the snow had turned into a uniform blanket of white. Together they headed for the gap where the thin, snaking mountain road would lead them to Falalee.

The twenty bulldozers hit the brow of the hill simultaneously, their warning sirens whooping like warpath Indians as they descended into Corbardale, cutting a broad black swathe through the snow.

Only when they dipped down beneath the skyline could the full force of their 120 horse-power engines be heard, a thick, throaty roaring which seemed to bounce back from the bare crags of Calcherside and reverberate through the valley.

As they advanced in formation, the chunky rubber wheels beneath their yellow painted flanks sent the snow spurting up in spirals across the name emblazoned in red letters across each vehicle. The name was Clandy.

"Get that bloody dozer up into line, Nolan. What have you got in her, lighter fuel?"

The voice was harsh, hollow, a strangely disembodied sound which gave the impression the valley itself was speaking.

It came from a yellow loudhailer jutting from the lips of a tall lean man in a fawn trench coat standing in the back of an open Land Rover parked 200 yards above the row of earth-movers. He had a black patch covering the left eye of a red, blotchy face which betrayed bad temper.

High up in the cab of the third dozer in the line, Eamonn Nolan lowered the magazine picture of the toothy, black girl in the string vest just enough to glare across at the control point.

"Pig," he muttered to the fat, grinning man squatting on the floor beside him. "What does he think this is, the May Day Parade?"

"You're still lagging behind, Nolan!" warned the voice on the loudhailer. "That is not a Clandy line!"

Nolan tossed the magazine on to the knees of the fat man and tugged at the choke. "That's not a Clandy line," he repeated, mocking the speaker in a mincing accent. "It's a bloody randy line."

As he brought the dozer level with the vehicle on his right, he saw the driver toss up his head in sympathy and give him a 'thumbs-up' sign.

Over the rise, from the direction of the Gamelpath, loomed another line of vehicles, a row of yellow 35 tonners, Cat 769s, churning up the black soil beneath their wheels as they advanced down the rigg.

"Close up those Cats!" commanded the voice from the Land Rover. "Keep it tight there!"

Apart from his mother and a few clerks in the pay pool, few men in the Clandy Group knew Joe Bamber's name. He was always The Slasher, not for any personal reasons but because he was the transport manager. His responsibility was anything that moved at Clandy's and was not on the payroll. Anyone who did that at Clandy's was always The Slasher.

Up on the ridge, the dump trucks were now beginning their assault, advancing down the slope in two lines of twenty abreast. Only one lorry, away on the far right, was breaking ranks as it deliberately took a snaking course through the unmarked snow.

The Slasher squinted at him for a moment before turning to the short man in the yellow helmet standing next to him in the Land Rover.

"Who's that joker? Can you pick him up through the glasses?"

"It looks like Dancer."

"It bloody would be," he said putting the megaphone to his lips. "Look Dancer!" he bawled down into the valley. "If I want you to make pretty patterns in the lovely snow I'll get you a reindeer and a sleigh. Now get back."

Dick Dancer flicked a finger against his long dark hair and pushed the rear view mirror on his door back into position as he grunted with annoyance. "Hang about, duckie," he said impatiently. "I was nearly finished anyway. Haven't had a bleeding comb through it all morning."

Beside him the carrot-haired man in the mate's seat giggled as he looked up. "You're wasting your time Dancer," he said. "Have you seen what the birds in this place look like?"

Dancer looked across to the high ground to his right and saw a line of four women standing motionless like a group of stern grey obelisks. The first three might have been in uniform, so alike were their dark tweed coats, each buttoned tightly beneath pale, expressionless faces.

The fourth woman alone looked as if she might be under forty. She stared silently out from behind a pair of heavy black spectacles, her lips thin and impassive. Beside her was the only male in the group. A small, round man in an oversized Crombie who was patiently holding aloft a poster which read, "Go Home Clandy".

"Christ! If they all look like them we'll all go home," said Dancer, watching them through the open window of his cab.

Until that moment he had had the impression, as the yellow army descended down the slope, that there were only Clandymen in the valley. Now he could see that beyond the four women and their tame standard-bearer there were little groups of people lined almost the full length of the route. They stretched as far as the portable cabins up on the plateau a mile away, which had been brought up for the Clandy base camp.

Most of them were standing quietly, either bemused or overawed by the procession. Only the occasional shouts of a group of small children could be heard down in the foot of the valley as they darted about throwing snowballs at each other.

In the rear mirror of Dancer's cab yet another fresh wave of Clandy hardware was appearing over the crest, a line of lean angular J.C.B. excavators, their long necks craning forward as if to peck at a track from which every blade of grass had already been eaten.

Up at the front Nolan and the light dozers were now racing over a darker patch in the valley bottom. Looking down from the cab he saw the broad wheels obliterating the tiny pin-holes left after a flock of sheep had passed.

"Go away!" shouted a pale faced young man as the line of dozers came up to him. His bottom lip trembled slightly on finding himself staring into Nolan's surprised face.

"We don't want you here!" called out the man in a shrill voice. He looked around as though trying to summon up support but found only a dozen small children behind him. For a moment he walked forward hesitantly as though undecided about what he was going to do before he heard the Slasher's voice away in the distance.

"Do not go near the machines," thundered the loudhailer. "I repeat, it is dangerous to go near the machines."

As the young man looked back in the direction of the Land Rover a snowball hit him in the back of the neck. He glared round angrily and began scraping the snow from under his shirt collar. Then suddenly he smiled and bent down to scoop up more snow from the ground. Taking careful aim he flung the snowball at the door of Nolan's cab.

"Come on chaps," he yelled "We don't need to go near their war machines. We can reach them from here."

For a moment the small boys looked uncertainly at each other as though they were debating who the 'chaps' were before they quickly decided it was an open invitation.

"Jesus, the bloody natives are fighting back!" yelled Nolan, sliding back the window before a hail of snowballs landed on the bonnet and windscreen.

The children had now rolled up their sleeves and were firing at will, giggling as their splodgy missiles landed on the bright yellow Clandy paintwork. The young man had discarded his banner now and was in the middle of them urging them on.

"Do not snowball our vehicles," commanded the man in the black patch from higher up the hill. "No snowballing. It is an offence to. . . ."

He broke off and began listening to the receiver of a small field telephone at his feet on the floor of the Land Rover. After muttering agitatedly into the mouthpiece several times he picked up the loudhailer again.

"Please do not snowball our vehicles," he called in a quieter, restrained voice. "Now please children! I know it's fun for you but snow is not fun if you're a driver."

His words seemed to have an immediate recruiting affect on the schoolchildren, who raced down from the huts, eager to join in the snowfight.

Down in the valley bottom more than forty youngsters had now formed themselves into a line as they systematically hurled snowballs in volleys. Behind them the smaller children scampered among the snow supplying them with fresh ammunition.

For a while Nolan was able to fend off the white barrage with his windscreen wipers, but the combined force and accuracy of the children's attack so completely clogged his vision that he was forced to pull out of the formation and bring the dozer to a halt.

As he stopped the engine and leapt down from the cab to clear the windscreen a cheer went up from the excited children. Behind the front line a small boy in a blue bobble hat took advantage of the temporary lull in the fighting to carve out a triumphant figure one with his finger in the snow.

It was at precisely this moment that Denzil Archbold, a silver-haired, bushy-browed man not normally given to violence passed the four ladies with their protest banner.

Archbold was Sir William Clandy's personal chauffeur. He had been released, not without some reluctance on his part, from the company Rolls in order that he might make up the round twenty on the safari truck line, a row of yellow Land Rovers, most of which were borrowed from other Clandy sites for the day.

Whether it was inspired by the children's example or merely some deep seated predatory urge the lady in the red hat may not have known. But the result was the same. She stooped down, gathered up some snow quite deliberately in her pale beige gloves and cast the missile through the open window of the nearest Range Rover, where it burst against Archbold's forehead.

Forced into driving slowly due to the tardy progress of the heavy J.C.B.s ahead of him, Archbold met the woman's stare for at least ten seconds as he gathered the snow up in his blue handkerchief. Finally he said, "You're a bitch Madam."

"Oh," said the woman, her stiff shoulders shaking with indignation. She bent down and prepared herself another snowball, the three women beside her hesitating only momentarily before following her example.

The snowball hit the window of the Range Rover before Archbold had time to raise it. Within seconds even the quiet man in the Crombie had grounded his banner and was joining the ladies in their battle.

"Please don't throw snowballs," said the loudhailer with a note of desperation. "Don't throw snow!"

Back up on The Faunes ridge the last line of Clandy hardware was entering the valley.

Already the sight of the fifteen D8s lumbering down the slope like massive war-tanks caused a stir among the crowd down in the hollow as they appeared along the skyline.

Now it was the turn of the D.9s, the biggest and most powerful bulldozers in the Clandy fleet.

Jack Fasman was leading in the first of the five giant "land-gobblers". Each of them was a mobile castle, 48 tons of yellow-painted, reinforced steel set on four-foot high caterpillar tracks which cut black tracks in the earth deep beneath the snow line.

Up on the rigg, beside the Gamelpath Road, people were pressing their gloved hands to their ears as the five 400 horse-power engines bellowed their coming to the waiting valley.

Fasman was in the last of the D.9s, furthest away from the Slasher. He was a powerfully built, heavy-gutted man who chewed gum slowly behind thick, rubbery lips which hardly moved. There was no emotion in his features as he hunched forward at the wheel, glaring at the snowfight down in the valley.

"Just plain stupid so they are. I mean, somebody could get hurt with that carry on."

Fasman had almost forgotten Gans was down there. Although there was seating room only for the driver, the plump-faced Scotsman had come along for the ride, wedging himself on the floor of the cab beside Fasman's feet. He was broad and thick-set across the shoulders, but his lack of height brought his eyes barely an inch above the bottom of the windscreen.

"Look at those kids there," said Gans pointing through the window to their right. "I mean, it's only snow but if you get enough of it, it can do damage."

Fasman ignored the finger and glanced down at Gans. "Not as much as these things can do," he said quietly.

"You're damn right," said the squatting man, "but it's not as if we're here to do damage, man, is it?"

"Have you ever seen what a D.9 can do Gans?"

"I've seen a D.8 shift a 50 ton pay-load in ten minutes flat. It looked as if it was eating it."

"Chickenshit," snapped Fasman. "Look, you see that pine forest up there? I would only have to bring the blades down, change into top and the only thing which would stop me slicing a path through the whole thing would be if we run out of gas. I'll show you, Gansie. . . ."

He pushed forward the two metal levers on his left, at the same time yanking the gear shift into top so that the blade was still descending as the giant dozer surged ahead of the others.

"Don't be stupid, man." Gans was forced back against the driver's legs by the sudden acceleration of the engine. "The Slasher'll have your balls if he sees you."

Fasman grinned at him, his lips curling to reveal a row of broken, yellowing teeth. "Him? He's too busy with his snowballs to worry about ours." He patted the gearstick affectionately as Gans scrambled back into his place at the front of the cab. "Did you know that one of these babies can turn a detached house into a car park in 15 minutes? Look, there's one down there they won't miss."

Gans held up his hand. "No, wait a minute Fasman. Hell man. . . ." His protest was too late. Fasman had already swung the massive dozer from the track and was veering off to the left with Gans clinging to the sill of the windscreen so tightly the ends of his fingers were white beneath his nails.

Ahead of them the Scotsman could see the round stone-built tower directly in the path of the dozer's tracks. He knew exactly what Fasman was about to do. He also knew there was nothing he could do to prevent him.

The tower loomed above them, grey and solid as the D.9 roared up to it.

For one moment Gans thought Fasman had changed his mind as

the giant tractor slewed suddenly to the right in response to the driver's quick hand movements on the controls. But when he saw the collision was inevitable he cradled his crew-haired bullet head in his arms and waited for the crash.

The impact, when it came, was not as fierce as he had expected. He felt only a momentary thud, followed by a dull, grating sound which seemed to come from inside the building.

When Gans looked up he saw that the broad, 16-foot blade jutting from the front of the tractor had sliced quite easily through the side of the tower, burying itself behind a fresh scar of crushed stone and mortar.

"Watch your nut, Gansie, we're pulling out."

Gans heard Fasman's hoarse, elated shout only faintly, as though it was coming from a great distance. He was staring at the base of the thick yellow shaft at the point where it was protruding from the rough weather-blenched stones in the tower wall. He wondered why there was no blood. . . .

The knife was embedded deep in the Swede's arse as he lay on the floor. Gans could see the yellowing bone handle and the grey steel shoulders of the hilt pressing firmly against the tightly stretched white cloth of the man's trousers. "There ought to be blood," he heard a voice say, and looking up he saw the face was his own; a young, flushed, pretty face with limp, protesting lips and soft fair hair curling down across his ears. It was Broomielaw, January 18, 1948. And now he was at the other end of the bar looking down at his ridiculously large boots, shiny black against the scrubbed wooden floor. Buckie was beside him and big McArthur, black like a Gorbals cat, and a knife in his hand. "I'm 18, Christ! I'm no age to kill a man," he heard himself say as the heads in the public bar turned towards him.

"Are you a man or a wee pansy, Gansie?" McArthur was saying. "The Scrob seems to think he knows. Are you going to take it from him?" On the floor the Swede had stopped struggling now. There were three pairs of hands holding him down. A nervous, ginger-haired youth was embracing his shins, another squatted behind him forcing back his arms, and his long blond hair was being pinned to the floor in two flattened hanks. "Leave it, Ken, just leave it!" Gans was saying. McArthur was still holding the knife out towards him. "Take it then. Take it and give it back to him. Maybe he has a sewing kit for you instead. Queens do the sewing you know? The kings, brother, they fight! What are you going to do, Gansie?" Gans saw himself take the knife from McArthur's hand and walk slowly across the room to where the Swede lay. For a moment he rested on one knee, fingering the short, wide blade and appearing to offer the handle to the man on the floor. Sensing the ordeal was over the Swede relaxed, all the previous tension in his face suddenly broke into a shy, almost beautiful smile which revealed his white, incredibly white teeth. "Bu-gg-er", Gans was over him now, the knife in his hand seemed to be directed down into the Swede's chest

before, at the final moment he veered away and plunged the blade into the right cheek of the man's buttocks. Only McArthur's cackling laugh behind him broke the silence. "There ought to be more blood," Gans said. He was now on his feet staring down at the unconscious Swede, the knife handle protruding from his white arse. Buckie's hand was on his shoulder. "There will be son, there always is."

"Pull it out," screamed Gans, "pull it out."

"All right Gansie, there's no panic." . . . Fasman had his left hand pressed fully down on the reverse lever. For a moment the machine seemed to shudder as though flexing itself for the effort of withdrawl, before it suddenly wrenched itself back from the tower. . . .

. . . *As McArthur's hand came up with the knife the bright red blood spurted out from the wound and began welling from the Swede's arse, staining the white cloth in an ever-widening circle. . . .*

Through the windscreen Gans watched the yellow shaft jerk back violently, hauling the steel blade with it as the whole side of the peel tower collapsed, sending the dark stone crashing into the snow.

"I told you," said Gans. His voice was quite calm now. "I told you it would bleed."

The red ball was lying on the snow in the centre of the last remaining space as the full Clandy fleet lined up in front of the wooden huts on the plateau.

With his usual military precision The Slasher had organised the vehicles into seven neat rows with a gap of five yards between each line.

Beyond the huts the crowd, which had followed the thick belt of black mud up the slope, seemed to be stunned into silence as they gazed on the might of the engineering ironware facing into the valley.

Fasman appeared not to notice the ball as he brought the last of the D.9s to take up its position in the front line. Even if he had, it was unlikely he would have stopped but for the appearance of a tall, stooping man in a battered top hat who ran, half shuffling, half skipping, into his path, holding both arms high above his head.

As Fasman brought the dozer to a standstill the man bowed slightly, removed his hat in a polite gesture and, scampering back on thin, wiry legs, picked up the ball and kicked it over to the crowd, where a small boy gratefully accepted it.

Stepping back the man waved the D.9 into the space, brandished his hat once again and turned, smiling, to find himself gazing up into the black eye patch of The Slasher.

"Playtime it is then, Tully? Or are you just taking some exercise?"

Tully placed the hat back on his head pushing it at a slanting angle before he chose to reply. "You could say that, sir. On the other hand you could be calling it a little exercise in public relations."

The Slasher scowled. "Now isn't that a coincidence Tully. You believe in public relations and this gentleman here with me earns his living in public relations."

Tully looked behind the transport manager and saw the man for the first time. He was young, fresh-faced and wearing a dark overcoat above his grey, well pressed trousers.

"You mean they pay people to publicly relate?" suggested the lean Irishman.

"Tully, we all pay this gentleman. Every week," said The Slasher waving the young man forward. "He's from the D.O.E. He wants to tag on to someone to find out what it's all about. You're elected. Now just take care of him while we get the Napoleon bit over."

"Eckersley," said the young man offering his hand as The Slasher left them. "It's my first time."

"Tully," responded the Irishman touching his hat. "Too many times."

Eckersley looked up as Fasman brought the huge D.9 to a shuddering halt beside them.

"Vicious-looking things, aren't they, when you get close to them?"

Tully took his arm and led him towards the huts. "If you think these creatures are fierce wait till you see some of the objects about to come through that door. They'd kill you with a look."

The Slasher had already knocked and had been admitted into the main hut when Tully and Eckersley took up their positions against the window. As the door opened there was an expectant swaying in the crowd as the first of the men came out. He was a small dapper man wearing calf-length brown leather boots with built-up heels which clattered against the three wooden steps as he stepped down. He paused at the bottom, his jaw moving forward uncertainly as he glanced across at the people on his right.

"Leave us alone Clandy."

The voice came from the far end of the line, near where the two policemen were standing between the spectators and the first of the Clandy machines.

If the man heard it he gave no indication of it. He adjusted his yellow helmet and looked briefly along the rows of heavy vehicles as though he was trying to scan all 140 of them in one glance. Then smoothing down the sides of his neat camel-haired overcoat he began walking briskly towards them with The Slasher following a pace behind.

Four more men in yellow Clandy helmets came down the steps immediately falling into ranks of two as the six made their way to the light dozer line on their left.

As they passed Tully and Eckersley, the man in the camel coat glared briefly at the Irishman's top hat which Tully doffed with a gentle bow of the head.

Eckersley saw that although the sideburns beneath the man's helmet were noticeably greying, the face was quite boyish looking. Only the eyes, where the lower lids seemed to be prematurely sagging across the smooth round cheeks, appeared old.

"Is that Clandy?" whispered Eckersley.

Tully spat out the wad of chewing gum he had been chasing round his mouth. "Not at all," he grunted. "That's the Shout. Fergus Bain P.M., project manager. He's to this site what your P.M. Mrs. Gwillym is to Parliament, down to everything but the knickers and we're not even sure about them."

"How do you mean, Mr. Tully?"

"Well, he's a great man for the dressing up, starting with himself. He wears so much finery no-one's ever seen what he really has underneath. He's from Edinburgh you see. It's reputed to be the only place in Britain where babies are conceived by both parents with their clothes on. Look son, are you a V.I.P.?"

Eckersley shook his head. "No, I'm only in the Environment press office."

"That's top drawer compared with most of the fellers up in those heaps," said Tully. "Follow me son, it'll be the only chance we'll ever get of being in the salutin' group."

The two men caught up the official party just as Bain and The Slasher were turning to walk down the first line of bulldozers.

Eckersley watched them move briskly down the row.

"Who's the old man behind Bain?" he whispered, nudging Tully who had just raised his hat to young Nolan in the first dozer.

"Him?" said Tully looking at the stout, elderly man who was wearing a camel-haired coat identical to Bain's. "He's Sir William Clandy. They named the whole set after him on account he owns it. He just lets the feller in front play with it sometimes."

Eckersley had taken out a notebook and was pencilling notes in it. "Is he here all the time?" he asked.

"Big Clandy only ever comes on site for two reasons," said Tully. "Either when things go right or when they go wrong. Most times they just bumble along."

"What about the thin chap in the specs?" Eckersley asked.

Tully craned his long thin neck round almost on a line with the man in the dark blue, belted raincoat ahead of them. "He's the big moneybags. You find you always need three major ingredients for a job like this. Muckshifters, money and brains. He's the E.E.C. feller from Eurobank. They're putting up half the cash."

"Which one's the brains?"

Tully smiled. "Ah, the brains. Well apparently they had as much trouble finding those as they did with the cash. So they imported them too. It's your snowman there, next to Big Clandy. Bob Liederman, the American gentleman, he's the designer for the consultants."

Eckersley glanced at the tall, slim man who was in a white safari suit and white leather boots.

"He looks a bit young, doesn't he?"

"He was a child prodigy in the dam business they say. They reckoned he built his first one in the bath before playschool using a loofah. He's older than he looks."

"And the other chap?" asked Eckersley, looking up from his pad.

Tully shrugged his shoulders. "Oh that's Caswell, he's Gus's No. Two. You'll not need a very big notebook for him."

As he spoke, the puffy red face of Caswell turned and Tully thought for a moment that he had heard him, but the group was approaching the end of the second row and Caswell followed them without a word.

"Go home Clandy," piped a woman's voice, as the official party appeared at the end of the line of vehicles before marching down the first row of dump trucks.

Eckersley noticed that once again Fergus Bain's face showed no sign of having heard the protest as his eyes darted from cab to cab. "The Shout doesn't say much," he said turning to Tully.

Tully had his top hat in his hand again, extending it in an extravagant gesture in the direction of The Goose, a grey-haired, beaky-nosed driver in the fourth cab. "We haven't reached the halfway point yet," he said. "When we do, at the end of this row, he'll turn to The Slasher and he'll say what he always says, 'Are the men in good spirits then, Slasher? Ready to get their backs into it, eh?' Wait till you see."

The young D.O.E. man was still writing his notes when the party paused beside the last dumper in the line.

Fergus Bain pulled the rim of his yellow helmet down closer to his eyebrows as he turned to face them.

"Are the men in good spirits would you say, Slasher?" he asked in a bluff over-confident voice which could not quite disguise its natural thinness.

The Slasher's voice, deep and earthy, came as a complete contrast. "When you give them the word, Gus, they'll have this place for breakfast," he said.

"Er, good, Slasher," said Bain smiling faintly at the rest of the party before moving on with short stiff steps.

Halfway down the second line of dumpers he stopped again and turned to the transport manager. "Ready to get their backs into it then, are they?" he said determinedly.

The Slasher thumped his hand against the yellow bonnet of the tipper truck in front of them. "The cavalry won't let you down," he said smiling, "I can guarantee you that much."

As the party moved off again Eckersley looked across at Tully who winked at him before both men set off in pursuit.

"It's no contest," they heard Liederman's voice say as they reached the inspecting group.

The column moved silently and quickly along two more rows of vehicles before Bain halted them at the first of the D.8s.

"They're looking good, Slasher, I must say. Very, er, chipper, eh? What do you say, Sir William?"

Sir William pushed his helmet towards the back of his head and gave him an ingratiating smile. "Certainly my boy. It makes you wonder what the infantry looks like."

By the time Tully and the D.O.E. man had caught them up again, Bain had stopped beneath Fasman's D.9 at the end of the last row.

He frowned as he looked at The Slasher. "Was this the one?" he asked. The Slasher nodded.

Bain walked bouncily round to the cab door where Fasman's face could be seen glaring down through the open window.

"I understand you were the one who er . . . collided with the peel tower in the bottom there," Bain called up.

"It was an accident."

"Fasman, isn't it? What happened Fasman?"

Fasman's dark, glowering face was unmoved. "It was the snow, wasn't it?" he said unrepentantly, "she slipped a bit coming down the slope, that's all."

Bain lowered his eyes. "Well then Fasman," he said, "be more careful in future, won't you?"

Fasman sniffed as Bain rejoined the group and headed towards The Slasher's open Land Rover parked beside the door of the main offices.

The Slasher leapt onto the back of the vehicle and offered a hand to the project manager, pulling him up beside him.

In the meantime Tully had led Eckersley over to the yellow painted door behind the loudhailer truck. "You'd better get this down for posterity," he said watching Eckersley turn a page of his notebook. "First of all he'll ask if everyone can hear him, which means they're all supposed to open up their cab windows, but most of them won't bother."

"Can all of you hear me, men?" asked Bain, making a wide sweep of their ranks with his yellow loudhailer. "Good."

"I just want to say this to all of you," muttered Tully to the young press officer.

"I just want to say this to all of you," said Bain thrusting out his jaw purposefully.

"We're all here to work," said Tully beneath his breath.

"We're here to work," said Bain, "and work damned hard. Right?"

Tully dug the D.O.E. man in the ribs causing him to look up

sourly as his pencil made a long scrawl down the page. "Now this next bit is an optional extra," he whispered. "A bit of local colour."

Bain cleared his throat and addressed the lines of silent vehicles beneath him. "Now the fact that here in Corbardale we are attempting the largest engineering feat of its kind anywhere in Britain should make no difference to our . . . er . . . resolve. I expect you to tackle it with the same determination and endeavour that you would produce for any Clandy contract whether it be a road bridge, a motorway or a housing estate.

As Bain lowered the loudhailer, waiting for the words to sink in, a stocky, bearded man over in the crowd called out, "We don't want you here!" Bain glanced only briefly at the direction of the voice before lifting the loudhailer again to his mouth.

"We're a good team," said Tully, nodding to Eckersley as he raised his fist.

"We're a good team," said Bain echoing both the words and the gesture, completely unaware that the wiry Irishman was mouthing his speech behind his back. "We've a job to do. Let's do it. Thank you gentlemen."

As Bain finished, Liederman suddenly began to applaud, a move which surprised the other members of the official party, who were put in a position of having to join in.

Some children away to the right clapped their hands, leaping eagerly up and down in front of their silent parents.

Seconds later the whole crowd moved back quickly as an obviously rehearsed signal from The Slasher brought all 140 engines roaring into life at the same time.

It happened with such suddeness and ferocity that even Sir William Clandy put his hands to his ears to escape the deafening noise.

"What was all that for?" asked Eckersley as Tully waved his top hat nonchalantly towards the shuddering parade.

"That," said Tully, "is teeth."

"What do you mean, teeth?"

"Just look at them, boy," he said. "They're like great hungry beasts waiting for a meal. And that's where they expect to get it."

He pointed down to the valley where only the Corbar river, away in the distance, and a few sparse bushes showed dark against the vast white bowl of Corbardale.

"They call that the Debateable Lands, boy. It's a fightin' valley. For centuries they've only needed to toss a sheep loose or take their foot off a sod of grass and there'd be two sides fisting over it in no time."

"Who usually wins these debates?"

Tully watched as Bain jumped down from the Land Rover, still clutching the loudhailer in his hand as he led the official party back to the offices.

As Bain passed him the Irishman doffed his top hat and bowed low.

"I'll tell you who wins, boy," he said through the side of his mouth. "The ones with the biggest mouths. Have a nice day."

As the Irishman turned to go back to his Range Rover, Eckersley called him back. "Mr. Tully!"

"Yes sir?" said Tully replacing the top hat on his head.

"Do you think they really need all this stuff for what they're going to do down there?"

Tully eyed him closely, "They'll need this and more, boy," he said softly, "because no one ever had a fight like this on their hands before in this valley. And because there's something worse than hunger in a man's belly."

"What's that?"

"Thirst boy, thirst!"

Eckersley watched him as he walked off in an odd shuffling sort of step towards the impatient vehicles, which seemed to be waiting like great beasts pawing the ground.

The tiny white-sailed dinghy was becalmed in the centre of a flat, brilliant blue ocean bathed in bright light.

A sailor on its shiny brown varnished deck could have had a clear view of the sloping sheep meadow of Hengendelly rising up to the tall crags of Calcherside, which softened into the dark green Forest of Corbar before plunging to the lower ridges of Hounshale at the end of the valley.

Behind him were the spectacular, multi-coloured rocks of The Faunes reaching for 30 miles from Hounshale Head to the small huddle of cottages at Todholes where the great white wall came out of the hillside, spanning almost the entire width of the Corbar Valley.

Rising up from the blue waters the dam dominated all, towering upwards in strong clean-cut blocks of stone to the five massive milecastles spaced along its rim, above which was the pink, urgent face of Fergus Bain.

"Gentlemen, we are going to build the biggest raintub in Europe," he said placing his small apple-bowled pipe firmly in his mouth before breathing sweet chocolate-flavoured Dutch tobacco fumes over the heads of the men seated at the board room table.

Beside him Sir William Clandy reached for a glass on the table. "Even the model makes me thirsty, my boy," he said.

Bain took his pipe from his mouth and tossed his head to one side admiringly. "Yes, they did make rather a good job of it," he said. "Your lads built it, didn't they Curran? Your up and coming earthies in the soils section, eh?"

He looked across the five foot long plaster model of the Corbar Reservoir to a grey-haired, tired-looking man at the far end of the table, who gave a faint smile before nodding agreement.

"Yes, well then," said Bain rubbing his hands together, "we're all here except . . . er. Are you sure he knew what time we were starting?"

His question was directed at his No. 2, Vince Caswell, seated next to Sir William. "He knew all right," said Caswell taking a sheet of paper from a folder. "I telexed him at Caronbrook three days ago."

Bain looked at his watch and slowly tapped the bowl of his pipe against the large white sandstone ashtray on the table as he examined the faces of the men in the room.

Starting with Caswell, most of the men on his right, with the exception of the two engineers from the Consultants, Liederman and Meyer, were Clandy men.

"Structures", the tall heavily built Jack Robson, was doodling on a large jotter beside Jack Cline, the thin faced Admin. Manager. George Steele, the technical director, was sitting next to him in serious conversation with Joe Bamber, The Slasher.

Finally there was Curran, the soils engineer, a pale untidy man slumped over the yellowing pages of a book, the cuffs of his grey herringbone jacket frayed at the edges.

For more than 15 minutes Bain had been aware of the impatient shuffling of papers on his immediate left as Bob Liederman made it obvious he was getting bored.

Liederman was tall and managed to succeed in appearing even taller by his habit of always wearing well-cut, white safari suits with white leather boots. He was thirty two but wore his short black hair in a long fringe which flopped down over his high forehead, making him look much younger.

The first three places beyond Liederman were all taken by Department of the Environment men. Young Eckersley was poised over a large note-pad and beside him were Podger and Benson, two of the Ministry's technical advisors.

Separated from them only by the short, bearded Ken Challis, the Resident Engineer, was the four-man contingent from the National Water Council and the quiet-spoken elderly representative of the Northumbrian Water Authority.

Beyond him was the empty chair at the end of the table.

"How was he supposed to be getting here Vince?" said Bain, looking again at his watch. "By train?"

Caswell threw up his hands and pulled a face. "You know what the Big Cog's like. He chooses his own methods. He could be using a broomstick for all we know."

Bain looked up as Liederman flung a batch of papers onto the table. "Do we really have to wait for this guy, Gus?" he said gathering the folders up again pointedly. "After all, it's not as though we're thin on the ground."

The project manager had a pained expression on his face. "All right, I know we're late and anxious to get on with it but we need Dando here. You explain to him Caswell."

Caswell smiled and scratched his head. "Well it's like this. Dando is the sort of halfway house in Clandy's. He's our link with the men, that's why both sides call him the Big Cog. As general foreman he's on the bottom rung of management but since he runs the Construction and Allied Workers Union, which a lot of them belong to, he's top muckshifter. And you can't move much without muck-shifters, it's as simple as that."

Liederman tossed the files back on the table and shook his head petulantly. "So we have to wait for this jumped-up sodbuster then?"

Bain took a drink from his glass of water. "Yes, I'm afraid so."

He was about to put the glass down when the green baize door at the far end of the room opened and a man's head appeared round it. "He's here, Mr. Bain."

All sixteen heads in the room suddenly looked up from the table as the door swung back with a thud against the bookcases on the pine-clad wall.

The man who came in was 6 foot 3 inches tall with a thick thatch of black hair falling over his narrow forehead. He ambled into the room with loose confident strides, eyeing up the men at the table as he peeled the heavy sheepskin coat from his massive shoulders.

Only when he had seated himself in the waiting chair did the men at the table turn their eyes away from him and look towards Fergus Bain who brushed his grey and white houndstooth check suit nervously as he stood up.

"As I was saying gentlemen," he said limply, "We are about to build the biggest raintub in Europe. The site, chosen after careful research and consideration is here, in the Corbardale Valley. It is felt that only here were the conditions perfect on geological and sociological grounds to build a reservoir large enough to meet Britain's needs for the foreseeable future."

Bain paused for a moment aware that at the other end of the table Dando was staring at him. As their eyes met the big area foreman gave him a slow, deliberate smile.

"Now we are all, I'm sure, familiar with what happened in this country in 1976, the year of the drought," continued Bain, "Crops dried up in the ground, farmers lost livestock, the price of vegetables soared in the shops and there were even emergency standpipes in some streets. In all, the drought cost Britain more than £35 million because when the rain failed we didn't have the reserves of water to meet demands, so we're here today, gentlemen, because this Government is determined that such an acute water shortage will never happen in this country again. We've been invited to build the last of the great dams, a reservoir so big that it is capable of supplying water at a moment's notice to any part of Britain which needs it.

Now, how this is going to be done will shortly be outlined to you by our American friend here, Mr. Liederman, but before that I would just like to say one thing. We in Clandy have been proud of the part we have played in re-shaping the map of Britain. For the last 50 years we have led the way in improving communications in this country by building roads, bridges, motorways. And now in face of strong competition from other construction firms in Britain and on the Continent, we have been awarded the contract for the biggest plum of all, the largest and most expensive civil engineering contract ever awarded in this country. I trust we won't be found wanting."

As Bain sat down and reached for his pipe he looked across the long table and saw that Dando was slowly applauding him but his hands were making no noise.

A sudden tug at his coat sleeve caused Bain to jump noticeably in his chair. Turning, he saw Liederman nodding towards him and he sprang quickly to his feet.

"Gentlemen," Bain said. "As I told you earlier, for the main outline of what's going on here I'd like you to listen to Mr. Bob Liederman, of Liederman and Meyer of Detroit, who are consultants for the project. Mr. Liederman."

Liederman paused a moment in his chair before standing up. When he did he had a pound note in his hand.

"Gentlemen you all know, I'm sure, what one of these is," he said holding the note up. "You don't see them for long, but you see them. It is, of course, one of your pound notes."

"It's one of mine actually," said Caswell grinning at him, "You just borrowed it."

Liederman waited for the weak laughter in the room to die down. "It's a one pound note," he said impatiently. "Now if I was to fill this board room with one pound notes, can you imagine what we would get?"

"Smothered?" suggested Caswell with a chuckle.

The American raised his hand as more laughter broke out among the seated men. "I'll tell you what we would get," he said ignoring the chunky No. Two. "Five hundred million pounds. And that, gentlemen, is the price your Government has put on the need to keep the taps of Britain flowing every day, every year. The answer they have come up with and which they will deliver, with our help gentlemen, is Aquagrid, a vast network of waterways and reservoirs supplying every town and city in Britain starting from right here in Corbardale. Now, it's a long time since I was at High School and even a little bit longer for some of you, but the only way to really get the idea across is by use of the blackboard . . . so if you'll bear with me for a moment. . . ."

The American pulled away the white sheet over the blackboard behind him, revealing a chalked outline of Britain. He waited while

Bain and Sir William moved their chairs aside.

"Right," he said picking up a piece of chalk. "Now that we've seen Gus and Sir William safely into the Atlantic we'll begin. For a start it's a crazy country, your Britain. No, don't get me wrong, the people are just fine. It's just that you all picked a crazy country to live in." He turned the chalk on its side and traced a thick line down the length of the Pennines. "For a start most of your rain for drinking and washing and feeding industry falls here on the Pennines, here, the Lake District and over here in Wales. Yet most of your people live here and here and here and here!!" He drew large circles over London, the Midlands, Manchester and South Yorkshire. "As I said, it's crazy. Now you can keep a cow anywhere, and you can plant a crop of carrots most places, but for centuries one of your main problems has been how to get a regular and reliable water supply from the places where it rains to the people who live where it doesn't. O.K. I'll admit you have your rivers. Let's see . . . you've got the Tyne up here, the Wear, the Tees and there's the Ouse here, the Trent, then there's the Mersey, the old queen the Severn and the king of course, the Thames and that's about it. But gentlemen have you ever tried to actually drink the Mersey? They tell me there's a ward in Liverpool General Hospital for people who do, and they only do it by accident. So you have loused up rivers and so you have to have nice, clean reservoirs. But where are they? Right! Where the rain is. The big ones are here in the Lake District, down here at Brennig, further down the Elan Valley, Wales again notice, and the rest are local fishponds."

Liederman looked up as the two D.O.E. men began talking among themselves.

"London," said the American pointing a finger towards them, "Is the freak in this show. I know it has large underground reserves of water directly beneath it but even then they are having to look around for more. Now what I'm coming to is this. That down in London, in Whitehall where you always imagine that all those white-bearded planners sit all day on their fat asses, they have come up with a plan to bring the water to the places where it is most needed. What you have at the moment, in effect, is hundreds of independent communities all doing private deals to use the local waterhole. It's unco-ordinated, messy and it means you sometimes get one waterhole running dry and another one full to the brim and there's nothing either community can do about it. So – what are we going to do about it? I'll show you."

Liederman picked up the chalk again and looked quickly round the faces at the table before turning round again to begin making extravagant slashes across the map with his chalk. "We're going to link 'em all up. The reservoirs, the rivers, one or two canals, overground aquaducts, underground streams, all meeting right here at Corbardale. The result, gentlemen, will be a round-the-clock, all-the-year, guaranteed piped water supply to every city, town and village in Britain, which can be topped up at the pull of a switch from the largest man-made lake ever built on this continent. That, gentlemen, is Aquagrid. Questions, gentlemen?"

Over on his right The Slasher had his pencil raised. "How long can we expect to be here?" he said.

Liederman frowned. "You can count on five years minimum," he said. "The rest of the scheme will be carried out simultaneously with the Corbar Dam, of course, but this is the meat of the job. Say five."

"What arrangements have been made regarding regular consultation between interested parties in the scheme?"

The voice from the back came from the neat, dark-suited representative from the Northumberland Water Authority.

Bain got to his feet. "It's all right Bob, I'll take this one. You'll find there will be regular monthly progress meetings involving, of course, our Board, yourselves, the National Water Council and all other bodies connected with the scheme. No doubt there will be a similar consultative meeting elsewhere through the line of the Grid."

As Bain finished, Liederman was up again. "I'd like to add, gentlemen, that the United Kingdom Aquagrid Project itself, we call it U.K.A.P., is being handled by the D.O.E. directly from London. We may expect to overlap a little but basically, all this here is our baby. She'll be enough of a handful on her own for us to look after. I'm sure you'll agree."

"Thirty-two miles! That's one hell of a lake." said The Slasher, shaking his head.

"Right. 51.5 kilometres anyway, close enough," said Liederman, picking up a sheaf of papers. "And you'll see from the statistics sheet in front of you, gentlemen, that it's 6.4 kilometres, or four miles to our English friends, at its widest point, reaching to a depth of 150 metres. In all it works out at 12,000 million cubic metres of drinking water we gotta hold back, that's one quarter of Britain's annual water needs."

He picked up a pencil and stretching across the table gave a tap on the rim of the dam wall on the model. "And that's where this baby comes in," he said, "She's the one who's got to keep our shirts dry."

"What's the pretty stuff? Brick?"

Liederman glanced down the table as Dando spoke for the first time. "Stone," corrected the American, "Hadrian stone. Quarried from some of the seams which Hadrian's military stone-masons used nearly two thousand years ago to build his great wall across Britain. The dam itself, of course, will have the normal impervious clay core but the complete outer face on the South side will be lined with white sandstone blocks and so will the top of the North face, down to a depth of fifty feet."

"It's bloody decoration," said Dando without looking up from the notepad in front of him.

Liederman was still half slumped across the table staring at the model dam. Suddenly his eyes came up over the top of the dam and glared at the big Welshman. "You might say that," he said slowly, "I don't see it that way." Straightening, he pointed to the man in the herringbone suit sitting beside Dando.

"Mr. Curran," he said loudly. "For the benefit of anyone here who might be wondering who the hell Hadrian was, could you tell us something about this gentleman?"

Curran shuffled uneasily in his seat glancing first at Liederman and then at Dando before starting to speak in a dry monotone.

"Publius Aelius Hadrianus was the first of the Roman Emperors to define the limit of the then Roman Empire. Partly because his legions were making little progress against the Northern Caledonians and partly because he wanted a visible monument to Rome's greatness he built a rampart stretching for 73 miles across the width of Britain."

"And when was that?" inquired Liederman looking directly at Dando.

"Oh, in AD 122," replied Curran airily.

"And how long did it last?"

"Something like two centuries in its entirity. Much of it, of course, still exists."

Liederman drew his breath as he smiled smugly at Dando.

"Exactly. And we know perfectly well why, gentlemen," he said. "It lasted because it was something more than just a wall. It was a celebration of the achievements of the Roman Empire, which lasted, I might remind you, more than a thousand years. The same will be true of the Corbar Dam. It will be a celebration of what we in our Western civilisation can do with a technology that has already taken us to the borders of space itself. The Wall was their monument, the Corbar Dam will be ours. A monument to. . . ."

"Liederman and Meyer," said Dando under his breath.

". . . a monument to Western achievement, a magnificent demonstration of what the free world can achieve with the help of the close communion of its greatest brains."

"What would be the cost of a normal dam?" Dando asked.

"What do you mean, normal?" asked Liederman.

"I mean a normal earth dam, Mr. Liederman. Faced with riprap."

Liederman looked directly at the D.O.E. men. "You have all the estimates for the Corbar part of the U.K.A.P. operation in front of you. It's £142 million. Without the Hadrian stone facing the cost would come down by about £2½ million, a mere drop, I suggest, gentlemen, in the sort of ocean we're building."

Liederman raised his hand as a murmur of voices spread round the table. "Gentlemen, there is another reason why U.K.A.P. has decided to face the dam in Hadrian stone. It's on account of the conservationist lobby. As you know, they have been harping on for months about the possibility of us lousing up the area and disfiguring the landscape. I've met many of these people. They're a spunky lot and they're also jealous of what they've got up here. They even regard the tourists up on the Roman wall as rubbernecking interlopers. But we will be building them a new wall, in some ways even grander than the original. And if we do that we won't be taking anything away from them, we would be giving them something they could be proud of."

"Right. If there are no more questions gentlemen," said Bain springing swiftly to his feet.

"There are," said Dando without looking at him.

Bain pouted nervously as he faced the Welsh foreman. "What do you want to know about then Mr. Dando?"

"The bunce," said Dando, sucking his pencil. "Special conditions payments and bloody bonus."

"Well we haven't actually gone into any special. . . ."

"We just did," said Dando smiling.

"How do you mean?"

Dando shot a quick glance towards Liederman. "Well, we can hardly get more special than a two thousand year-old pipe dream can we?

"It's all in the book." He opened a leaflet he was holding in his hands. "Here we are, Clause 27. . . . 'If conditions on the site are abnormal and deviate from the standards usually accepted on engineering contracts, that is to say special, negotiations may be entered into with the management for a special conditions payment.' It's there in the bible and we all believe what we read in the bible, don't we gentlemen?"

"That's only the C.A.W.S. bible," snorted Caswell.

"Which, as I think we all agree, is the gospel according to what goes on at Clandy sites," said Dando with a thin smile.

Bain licked his lips and looked for support from Sir William Clandy who was examining his nails. "What are you getting at, Griff?" he asked finally.

Dando pushed the leaflet back across the table and sat back in the chair. "Well now, if we've decided to start on the real business," he said smiling at Liederman, "We know now who wants the fancy Roman trimmings and why. But who's going to cut the stone and build the bloody thing?"

The project manager looked across at Liederman, who sprang to his feet again. "The blocks will be cut on the site itself, most of the stone will come from the quarry at Baskey's," he said, sitting down immediately.

"That's just what I mean," said Dando. "And so we come to the fellers you've missed out."

Bain threw him an anxious glance. "What do you mean?"

Dando stood up, aware that every eye in the board room was on him. From where Bain was standing the big Welshman's body seemed to take up most of the far wall as he stretched his arms like a wrestler preparing for a bout. "The men," he said. "The muckies! Look, we've sat here and listened to what the Government wants and what the Board's going to do with the help of the water authorities and the consultants and the bloody Romans. I've been waiting to hear just one word about the people who are actually going to get their hands dirty. The men who are going to build this thing when all the chat stops. Now these fellers are muckshifters and they don't mind you calling them that. If you want my opinion they are the best muckshifters you can get at the money anywhere. But if you pay peanuts you'll get monkeys. Look, they're not Roman stonemasons, some sort of elite corps that can design and build anything you throw at them. If they're going to be stonemasons they'll do it. But it'll cost you. They'll want extra."

"Like a toga allowance," suggested Caswell. The fat No. Two's grin faded as Dando glared at him.

"We'll come to the clothing allowance next, Caswell," said Dando through closed teeth. "In fact right now, if you like."

He strode down to the blackboard between Bain and Liederman and turned to face the men at the table.

"There's one thing this pretty map doesn't show," he said, "The kind of place we're going to be working in." He picked up a piece of chalk and stabbed a cross beneath London. "It's not Sussex where we built the flyover, where you could be in your shirt sleeves till Christmas." He marked another cross on the West Country. "It isn't glorious Devon where one of the boss comics even wore a pith helmet when we built the bonny motorway for the tourists. No. This time we're here," he said stabbing a cross over the Corbar Valley. "In Northumbria. On the roof of England where the summers are wringing wet, the winters'll freeze the balls off you and you've got bogs up to your thighs if you step in the wrong place. Those are the sort of special conditions I think we ought to be thinking about, Sir William."

Having made his point Dando threw the chalk towards the blackboard and walked noisily back to his seat.

It was Bain who broke the silence, his lower jaw moving slightly as he faced Dando.

"What do you think we ought to do about it then, Griff?"

Dando gazed up at the ceiling before fixing his eyes on the project manager. "A good clothing allowance would be a start," he said. "Something to keep out the kind of weather we can expect up here."

"Overalls you mean and boots. . . ."

"And the rest," said Dando.

"What do you mean?" asked Bain.

"Underwear," said Dando looking up sharply as Caswell spluttered into his water. "You see, in these sort of conditions, the muck doesn't just settle gently on your boots. It eats in everywhere, your shirt, your vest, right through to your skin."

"And what you're saying then," said Bain, "is that whatever you wear next to your skin needs to be maintained or regularly replaced, is that what you're saying?"

"For openers, yes."

"Watch him," said Caswell, whispering behind his cupped hand to Bain who had sat down again. "There's more behind this than drawers."

Hearing Caswell's remark, Sir William leaned forward in his chair and spoke quietly but directly to Dando. "Look my boy," he said. "I'm sure you'll agree we may need to make allowances for a lot of people's underwear before this job's finished. Now, if there is a case for allowances, special or clothing, I'm sure it can be put at a more appropriate time."

Bain stood up again, bouncing back partly on his heels. "Yes Sir William," he agreed. "We'll discuss that matter after this meeting then, Griff, if you'll kindly see me later. Now if there are no further questions?" He looked down the two rows of faces turned towards him. There was only one move from the table and Bain turned to see the upstretched hand of "Structures" Robson.

"Yes, what is it, Structures?" he asked wearily.

"I don't want to play the devil's advocate, Gus," he said almost shyly, "But has anyone said anything about what's going to happen to the people?"

Bain glared at him impatiently. "What people?"

"The ones who are going to lose their homes."

Bain was about to reply when Liederman stood up beside him. "Gus, do you mind if I handle this one? We have been doing quite a bit of work on it."

Liederman nodded as the project manager offered him the floor. He scratched his head as he turned to the men. "I'm grateful someone has brought this one up," he said. "Transplantation is never easy. Unfortunately, it's one of the natural hassles of the job, the bit the press always try to get their hands on when they want to wring out a few tears. You know the kind of thing, the pregnant mum with nowhere to go, the guy who has the shotgun ready to fire up your ass when you evict him. As far as it's possible to say at this stage, I can tell you this gentlemen. None of that crap's gonna happen here."

"You sound very confident Mr. Liederman," said Sir William Clandy, who was sipping from his glass as he watched the American closely.

"I am sir," agreed Liederman "You see although Corbardale's a big place there are only actually fifty-two families living on the proposed site. It's really a kinda no-mans-land, useless for any sort of real farming and too unstable for any sort of firm settlements. Most of the folk involved are forestry people and shepherds and they're gonna be taken care of real fine. Houses are already being built for them in the neighbourhood. And in any case it's not as if they're being asked to make an overnight flit. They've got plenty of time to sort of slowly wind down their operations before they move into the new council homes being provided for them."

"Thank you Bob," said Bain packing up the papers on the desk in front of him as he stood up. "And thank you gentlemen, for being here. That will be all for the present."

Bain returned to his chair beside Sir William as the men filed out through the far door. Liederman, the last to leave, was about to go when the Clandy chairman called him back.

"Mr. Liederman?"

"Yes sir?" asked the American turning to face him.

"You've met these valley people. What are they really like?"

Liederman scratched at the black fringe across his forehead. "Well sir, they're kinda tight but proud, if you see what I mean," he said. "I mean, it may not look much but they actually enjoy what they've got here. Like home, you know. But I got the distinct impression that by involving them in a sort of engineering showpiece the rest of the world will envy, then they too will be kinda . . . proud?"

"Like you, Mr. Liederman?"

"Yes sir." he said quietly. "I'm proud too."

"And behold I do bring a flood of waters upon the earth, to destroy all flesh, wherein is the breath of life. . . ."

High in his polished elm pulpit the Rev. James Churnside paused as he set the hour glass on the black wrought-iron bracket beside him and raised his eyes to the stone Norman vaulting, waiting patiently for the full impact of his text to seep into the fidgeting souls of his congregation.

By normal standards of Sunday mornings at St. Cuthbert's, Todholes, it was a well filled matins.

Despite the dip in the temperature outside, the coke stove, which had been lit at the back in the Saxon portion, beneath the squat traingular window, had succeeded in bringing many of the older parishioners to church.

They sat in their coats looking down the short narrow aisle towards the younger and more hardy members of the flock who were occupying the first nine rows of pews.

This was the part of the congregation which Jack Bennett, who was sitting with his large, fur-lined wife in the front row to the left of the Vicar, always referred to, somewhat irreverantly, as the "brass section".

The reason was not simply that the worshippers in the front had more money than the ageing and more homespun Saxons at the rear, which they did, but because the Norman set had a large brass memorial laid between them in the rough stone aisle.

Although the name of the beautifully etched knight had long since been erased by the generations of Todholes feet, the figure was generally accepted as being that of Sir Henry Hesters, the 'Flodden' Hesters.

Sir Henry, handsome, forbidding and brave almost to a fault, had earned his metallic immortality in St. Cuthbert's back in 1513, as one of the illustrious fallen of Flodden Field.

Only years later did it emerge that he had, in fact, two days prior to Flodden, fallen from his horse while taking a short cut through Furzedale when returning from visiting his mistress, the Lady Anne Braunceston. It was there that the pursuing William, the infamous "Black Braunceston" and his three sons cornered him, dispatching both the offending knight and his bull mastiff in a particularly disturbing display of savagery. So complete was their revenge, it was said, that when the pieces were brought home in three silk pillow-cases, it was impossible to decide which was Hesters and which was hound. Both were buried together, later to be gloriously separated for eternity on the floor of St. Cuddy's: Sir Henry, now wholesome and forgiving, the dog at his feet.

"God, as we well know, comes to us in many guises. And bearing many names."

The Rev. James Churnside's voice always suggested that he regarded the opening lines of his sermons as the first warning shots of a siege.

Although he was not a big man, the words seemed to generate from deep down in his large temporal belly, from where they slowly ascended, swelled by the spirit, before being hurled out through a mouth which never quite had the calibre to match the resulting salvo.

Apart from the five Challon children, who were wedged tightly between their parents in the sparsely filled centre pews, the little ones of St. Cuddy's were all strung in a line on the low stone seat along the east wall. Six small boys and beyond them, two spaces distant, one small girl.

'The weakest to the wall' was a favourite saying of the Vicar's. He used it not so much as a social comment but out of a sense of tradition.

The toddlers of Todholes had always been encouraged to occupy the wall seat because that was what it had been built for. Looking down at them from his pulpit, which he frequently did, it gave him an instant vision of Corbardale's future, as well as a clear view of the little boys' hands.

"And I would remind you all, that even the Lord God in His wisdom and understanding, sent a flood of waters only to drown the ungodly. If he could have found only twelve honest men he would not have . . ." the Vicar's voice fell almost to a whisper . . . "burned Sodom and Gomorah either".

Thrusting out his arms wide as if embracing the whole church he boomed forth again. "This is our Ark! Protected not with pitch and pine but with the faith of the people who worship here. The simple, God-fearing, ordinary people like you and me, the sick, the under-privileged, those living on fixed incomes, the pensioners, the little ones. . . ."

Even though he was now ten, Donald Dacre had never seriously objected to having to sit with the kids of Corbar on the wall seat. The "substitutes' bench" The Donald always called it, without ever really being able to explain the game.

The Donald was there in the third row of pews with Aunt Sara, although The Donald always gave her a final 'h' and chuntered when she dropped it. He smelled a bit, too, when you got close to him, not a pongy, farm smell but a tobacco-y one mostly, especially when he patted his coat pockets when he was bored.

But the main advantage of sitting on the wall seat was that it gave him a full, clear view of the silver lucies.

They were in the big pointed window in the West wall, three fat, sleek pike fish swimming round each other in a sort of triangle.

Each of them appeared to have made a lunging snap at the tail of the fish in front and missed, leaving their long jaws gasping at the effort. There were times when Donny thought the pike weren't really trying to eat each other but were displaying their sharp silver teeth purely as a gesture of strength.

It was the only window in St. Cuddy's where fish swam, a final and despairing legacy of the Delauny-Blakes before their family and its crest were submerged into the hunting Hesters by marriage. When the time came for Donny to leave the "substitutes' bench" he would miss the silver lucies.

"Now there are some who might say, perhaps even some of you here today, that parsons should not be politicians. That they should quietly busy themselves with the day-to-day spiritual needs of their neighbours. But I ask you to consider this. When such a threat appears in our midst, which deems to drown the very roots of a way of life this valley has enjoyed for centuries, who is there among us who is prepared to rise up and tell them 'Enough'. Who, I appeal, will hold up a hand and say 'Our needs are here, where our homes are and where our work is'. Our Lord told us 'To work is to pray' and surely if you attack a man's livelihood, denying him the fruits of his labour, you strike also at his soul. . . ."

Downstream of the lucies, on the West wall, Sir Piers Hesters, prone and peeling on his stone tomb, had crossed his legs below the knee, denoting that he had been on two Crusades to the Holy Land. Beside him sat Tina Padgett, a big, gamey girl who had crossed her legs in order to dab red nail polish on a hole in the hunkers of her tights. Hoisting her plaid wool skirt high up her expansive thigh, she was suddenly aware of her flesh being observed by a small, swarthy man in the opposite pew. She slowly replaced the skirt over her knees, staring at him until his sharp, needy eyes were forced to return to the Vicar.

"Larky Challon must have had someone striking at his soul full time," she murmured to the mousey-haired girl on her right. "He hasn't worked for years."

"God works in a mysterious way," said the Rev. Churnside. "I know this to be true, even of times such as we may be experiencing right at this moment. Times when it might seem the whole weight of an outside agency, which comes not in His name, is about to trample on our heritage. But even as they come, they will find we are not unprepared. We have . . . our faith. We have . . . our Ark. A symbol not only of survival but strength. Not just for our families, mine and yours, but a bulwark of resistance which will well with the tide of change until its timbers cover the width and breadth of Corbardale itself. You can rest assured that, whatever the power without, this Ark will keep its convenant within."

The Rev. James Churnside's eyes went up from the hour glass and down from the vaulting more quickly than he intended, when he realised that three people in the congregation had begun to applaud him.

He nodded down without reproach and quietly muttered "And now to God the Father, God the Son" to his neatly polished shoes. "We will now," he said, raising his brown voice to a crescendo, "sing! Hymn No. 402 in the English Hymnal."

As the Vicar left the pulpit and descended to the body of the church Donald Dacre noticed that, as if by appointment, the sun had broken through the North window above the altar and was streaming down on the Rev. James Churnside's head.

It was beaming through the translucent robes of the Hesters' "Avenging Angel", whose back was turned to the congregation, its raised sword and unseen face pointing towards Scotland, as it cast a swathe of white light along the Vicar's path to the collecting base.

When the choir, refreshed and eager, unleashed themselves into "He who would valient be", lifting the congregation with them, Donald Dacre was so overcome by the crusading urgency of it all, he forgot to sing. But as the call carried him with it in a great wave of fervour, his gaping mouth found the words, and by the time they had reached "To Be A Pilgrim" Donald's strong and vibrant treble voice was soaring high above all the others.

Even Walter Newbiggin, the churchwarden, could hear it out in the porch as he carried the small brown and white spaniel out past the open, studded door.

The dog struggled free of the man's arms, leapt the low, dry stone wall beyond the gravestones and bounded down the slope where a large yellow bulldozer was carving out a band of black, freshly turned earth across the green floor of the valley.

Finn Rafferty could still feel the sharp sting of the cold saucepan of water Teresa Kirtles had thrown over him by way of a wakening.

Sudden though it had been, it had induced a kind of jaunty swagger in his step as he strode over the brow of the hill, his brown burlap bag bouncing across his broad shoulders as he descended towards the huts of Clandy.

The snow had gone and beneath his black leather boots the grass felt coarse and thistly. A brief early shower had brought the earthworms up to the moist green surface, where they lay locked in the soft, milky mucus of their lovemaking, ready to be parted by the first drying darts of sunlight.

Even now his thick, normally ungovernable blond hair felt flat and damp against his head and there were deep morning furrows across his forehead.

Not that Finn had any personal animosity towards the widow Kirtles. "Wake me at six, with a pickaxe if need be," had he not said the previous evening with uncanny foresight? And hadn't she, with all the eagerness and enterprise of her black Northern Irish heart achieved it with sufficient force to rouse a cemetery?

No, he decided, it was the grasping nature of a universe which after trimming his wallet, should then demand that a man should report for a day's crack at 7 a.m. irrespective of having sated the night belly in the back bar of the Tup Inn.

True, the black draught of the Celt, which the Tup kept splendidly, would in itself have been balm enough for an Irishman's welcome to Corbardale.

But there had been brown draughts too and red draughts, libations of pure amber and draughts as pale as the piss of a badger.

Together they had formed a brainsplitting brew designed to induce a sleep of such mind-numbing proportions as wash ever swilled back to life in the cold of the Kirtles kitchen.

Finn smiled as he suddenly wondered whether all the rooms in Teresa Kirtles's house were so cold.

He was now approaching the tiny beck which skirted the back of the Kirtles cottage and meandered down into the valley before making a minor contribution to the Corbar river.

Although three planks had been thrown across the stream, which was little wider than a field drain, Finn ignored the invitation and leapt the dyke, losing his footing on landing on the other bank, falling heavily on his stomach against the rising ground.

For a moment he lay there laughing quietly to himself before standing up and taking a fresh bearing on the yellow huts below him.

As he regained the momentum of his earlier stride he began to sing, softly at first:

"Is the grass still growing green upon the meadow?

Is the sand still soft where tidal rivers flow?"

He stopped briefly, not to take breath as much as to lose it in a loud belch which unleashed itself in the form of a low, angry protest down in his breakfast, which was bravely attempting to repair the ravages of the evening.

"Do the railroads ever ask you where I've been?" he sang with a gusto which surprised even him.

"Do they ask you where went their lonely friend?"

Finn suddenly stopped singing and increased his pace. Ahead of him he could see the new gravel road Clandy's had cut down from the high Gamelpath road above Todholes to the base upon the plateau. More important, for the moment, he could see a small yellow Land Rover making its way down the hill travelling in the same direction as himself.

As the vehicle approached he loosed a hand from behind the cloth shoulder strap of his bag and thumbed the driver.

For a moment he thought his attempt at a hitch had failed as the truck overshot him by twenty yards before finally coming to a halt with a loud screech of brakes.

Finn ran to the open passenger window, swung his heavy bag to the ground and looked up into the cab, gasping for breath as he spoke.

"Bless you sir. You're a merciful man."

As the face inside turned slowly towards him the grin faded from Finn's lips. He immediately recognised the thick, black hair falling down the severe, square face, the wide, deep set, dark eyes glaring out above the thin, expressionless lips.

"Dando," he said.

The man in the cab made no reply as Finn looked at him.

"Well Dando, what does one say in the form of a reasonably civil greeting to an old . . . er . . . ?"

Finn opened the flap of his blue denim shirt pocket, took out a tube of mints and tossed one into his mouth nonchalently. "Unless it's to say what's a boyo from the valleys doing up here in a man's hole?"

"I'm the G.F.," said Dando bluntly.

"Yes, of course, you would be," said Finn chewing steadily without once taking his eyes from the driver's face.

"You've changed Rafferty. You're looking older."

Finn sucked the mint with his lips slightly parted. "You don't have to look in the calendar to know you'll always be older than some people."

Dando smiled thinly. "I was thinking about the coal, Rafferty," he said in a quiet, mocking voice. "They say nothing ages a man more than digging coal. It's all the dust you know. They reckon it's a killer in time."

The big Irishman grinned at him. "Well, it looks as if you haven't changed anyway, Dando. Wait till I see now." He took a step to one side so that he could see round Dando to the driver's seat where a small blonde-haired girl was peering out at him. "The wee girl's driving you, then? There's a thing now boyo."

"She's the new safari driver. She's giving me a lift to H.Q. . . ."

"Oh. H.Q. is it now then?" asked Finn with a mischievous look on his face. "That sounds grand, sure. And would your young friend be after giving a lift there to me and me trousers as well?"

"Get in," said Dando.

Finn reached for the door handle. There was ample room for the three of them across the long, front seat, but Dando immediately slammed the door shut.

"Not in here!" he snapped. "In the back, ganger."

The Irishman smiled and examined his hand after the door had been wrenched from it.

"Well Rafferty," said Dando, "I'd have thought after all this time, you and your coalies would have been used to a back seat."

Finn still had his foot on the running board of the truck. "I'll accept your hospitality Dando," he said breathing mint fumes into the Welshman's face. "Mainly on the advice of my late father, who always said, 'Never look a gift horse in the mouth.' "

He walked to the back of the truck, threw his bag up, quickly bundling himself in after it before sitting down leaving his legs to dangle over the edge. "Because if you do," he said, "it might shit on your shoes."

As the safari's engine spluttered to life Griff Dando turned his head towards the cracked perspex panel behind in the cab, fancying he heard singing coming from the back of the truck.

"Please tell them for me I still remember them.
Please tell them they taught me all I know.
Along this darkened roadway, our love will always shine.
For today is the highway and tomorrow is the time."

Only when the truck pulled up outside the Clandy huts did Finn stop singing as he hauled his bag across his shoulder, leapt down and looked at his watch. It was 7 a.m.

The yawning steel mouth of the excavator bucket reared greedily above the wall of fractured stone before plunging down to take another bite of Baskey's quarry.

As the digger moved sharply to the right, shuddering under the weight of its load before releasing the rubble into the waiting dump truck, the heavy power cable behind the machine suddenly lashed back against the legs of the cable boy, sending him sprawling to the ground.

When the boy scrambled to his feet, the driver had already come down from his cab and was standing over him, his thumbs thrust beneath a wide leather belt fastened across his straining belly.

"All right Hercules, let's go through it again," said the big man, kicking the rubber cable. "This is the cable and this, inside your jacket there, is the cableman. Now the cableman is supposed to control the cable, and not the other way around. Are you with me now?"

"I'm sorry sir. It took me by surprise again."

"Another thing," said the driver, taking a loose cigarette from his shirt pocket and lighting it, before tugging at the flap. "What colour's this?"

"Blue."

"Right. Now on a Clandy site the sirs are always in white shirts. I'm The Goose. O.K.? Where did you say you came from before you ended up here, a zoo was it?"

"A circus," said the youth.

The thin crescent-shaped mouth of the big man seemed to leap up both sides of his long nose. "Christ, what were you? The tent pole?"

The boy looked at him self-consciously. "It was nothing spectacular. I did a bit of clowning, tumbling, human pyramids, that sort of thing."

The Goose flipped his helmet to the back of his head and gave a despairing sigh. "O.K. Circus Boy, let's get some muck shifted then."

As the boy lifted the cable the Goose's narrow, beady eyes lit up as Rafferty approached.

"Finn, lad!" he yelled, thrusting out a hand, "Jesus it's been years!"

Finn Rafferty grasped the hand firmly and aimed a mock punch at the driver's sharp, pointed jaw. "Goose! It's good to see your old, pinched Fenian face. How are you doing?"

"Great boy, great. The rest of your lads are here too I see?"

"They decided to let us all out for this one," said Finn grinning. "It's a bit like emptying the jails in wartime. Well, you bugger, what's the crack like then?"

"Fierce. At least it will be now."

Finn slapped him across the arm. "Let's hope so Goose. How many fellers do you reckon we have up here?"

"About four hundred. They say it could be a thousand before

long."

"Who's the Shout?"

"Gus Bain."

"Oh Gawd. Not still the little Sun Man, all pipes and parades?"

The Goose winked at him. "Gus got married again a couple of years back to a real cracking piece. Perhaps he's changed since you last knew him?"

"If he's got wed he will have done," said Finn.

"Finn, Dando's up here too."

Rafferty lowered his eyes. "I know, I've already seen him."

"Finn?"

"Hello?"

The Goose's mouth twitched several times as though he was struggling to find the right words. "Finn," he finally said, "this time, I mean with Dando. You know."

Rafferty rumpled his hair and grinned broadly. "Don't you fret yourself! You never know, perhaps I've changed too. Who's the wee fellow with you? Is he any good?"

"Oh the maggot there? That's Circus Boy. He's good at circuses it seems. He's no cableman yet."

Finn glanced over at the lad. "What's the trouble then son?" he said quietly.

The boy kicked his boot into the ground, watching the steel toe-cap sink into the soft mud. "It's boring."

"How do you mean boy?"

He shrugged his shoulders. "Well is this all there is to it? Standing here with this thing in my hand?"

Finn looked at him without smiling. "What do you expect to have in your hand at this time of the morning? Come here son."

The boy advanced a few steps and stood gazing down at his boots.

"No, right over here. In front of me."

Rafferty waited until the boy had approached to within a yard of him until he spoke. "Now look son. What's that big yellow heap in front of you?"

Keen looked over to the digger and then back to the Irishman. "It's a 150 R.B."

"Right" said Finn, "Now, do you know what a 150 R.B. costs? I'll tell you. £80,000 quid. Do you know what its work rate is? I'll tell you again – 400 tons an hour. It also weighs 150 tons and all its power comes from that boring 3,300 volt cable between the tracks. Now what happens if one of those tracks snaps the cable? I'll tell you that too, sir. It takes two hours to fix the breakdown, we've lost 800 tons, we're after needing a new cable and a new cableman. Understand?"

"I think so."

"What's your name?"

"Michael Keen."

"Up in the cab then Michael Keen."

"What? Up there?" said Keen disbelievingly.

"Go on," ordered Rafferty, "Up! It's the only chance you'll get of being behind the controls of one of those things till we've dried out your ears, so up you go."

When the boy took his seat in the excavator and looked back the blond ganger was already behind the machine, standing beside the cable with both hands thrust deep in his trouser pockets.

"Right," bawled Finn, "You're up there, Michael Keen; you're on £150 a week and a load bonus of 10p. And I'm down here and I'm your cableman and I'm so bloody bored I don't give a damn when the cable blows and the whole show stops and there's no bunce for either of us. Now do you want Finn Rafferty for your cableman?"

Keen came down from the cab and joined Rafferty beside the driver. "I'm sorry," he said. "I see what you mean."

Finn slapped his hand down on the boy's shoulder. "Don't worry overmuch about the chap in the driving seat lad," he said, "just think about the sort of feller you'd want behind you when you're up there."

He turned to The Goose who was nodding his balding head as the boy walked briskly back to the cable.

"Who's the Blaster here then?"

"A feller called McDaid, he's up there on the shelf. Dancer's helping him."

"Dancer?" said Finn raising his eyebrows. "I wouldn't even trust him with Blue Tack. Anyway I'd better check on the next blow. Keep those dumpers fed Goose."

Up on the dolorite seam McDaid and Dick Dancer were preparing the surface for blasting.

The holes had been drilled at eight-foot intervals in a line eight feet back from the leading edge and now they were planting the gelignite sticks in each of them before connecting them with the plunger.

"I might have known you'd be here for the fireworks Finn," a Cockney voice called down as the Irish ganger approached.

Finn craned his neck up to the roof of the dolorite seam 20 feet above his head. "How the Christ did you get that job, Dancer?" he shouted, "You'll have us all in Hell yet. Where's the shot firer?"

A head popped up from just below Dancer's red sweater. "I'm here. What do you want?"

"What quant's the blast McDaid?" yelled Rafferty cupping his hands to his mouth.

"About 8000 cube yards."

"Good, that should give my lads something to get their teeth into. When will you be ready to blow?"

"Thirty minutes," shouted McDaid. "Before that you'd all better get the hell out of here!"

Finn raised his hands to his mouth again. "Can you hear me, McDaid?"

"Yeah," the voice came back.

"Well give me a hooter when you're ready and I'll make the fellers scarce. O.K.?"

As Rafferty came back, Keen was holding up the cable as though his young life depended on it. "That's it son, if you own a beast you should hold its tail. If Goose or any of the others want me for the next twenty minutes or so I'll be up seeing how the new crusher's making out."

He walked quickly over to a yellow Land Rover and drove out of Baskey's just as a second Land Rover pulled up a foot away from Keen's cable.

Almost immediately Keen heard the motors of the R.B. 150 cut out as the driver climbed down.

"Well that's another load put to bed," said the Goose slapping his hands enthusiastically. "Christ, lad. Look sharp! We've got company!"

Keen looked up as Dando stepped down from the Land Rover. A heavily muscled youth came round from the driver's side and stood beside him.

"Morning Dando," said the Goose, stuffing the cloth into his back pocket. "A grand blasting day sure. Crisp as a nut."

Dando slowly peeled off the black leather gloves he was wearing. "Is it, Goose?" he asked coolly.

"Well you see, you can get nice fine, dry days when the powder's dry and the face goes up like a dream and then, of course, there's the soft days when the. . . ."

"Who's he?" said Dando.

"The Circus Boy you mean?" said the Goose chuckling. "He's a new feller. He's the cableman."

"I can see very well what his job is. How long's he been mucking?"

The Goose's narrow eyes darted first at the boy and then at the general foreman, "Fresh today, it's his first. But then we all had to be sweet and fresh once, didn't we Griff?"

Dando avoided the Goose's eyes and looked at Keen, "Why do they call you Circus Boy?"

"I used to work in a circus, sir."

"This is your first man's job then is it?"

"They weren't exactly fairies in the circus, sir." said Keen grinning confidently.

Dando glanced at the Goose and saw he was wincing.

"Interesting," he said. "First day you say?"

"The kid's going to be O.K. Dando," said The Goose as the big foreman moved, without another word, over to where Dick Dancer was juggling with two sticks of gelignite up on the rock shelf.

When Dando was out of earshot the driver turned to Keen, "Wrong again," he said. "He's not a sir either."

"Who's he then?"

"That's Dando," whispered Goose, "the Big Cog, general foreman. He fits in just about the middle of this show. His boots are too big to be one of the men and his brain's too small to be a boss. But he makes 'em leap a bit, at both ends. Watch out, he's coming back."

"McDaid says we've another half hour before the next blow,"said Dando slowly.

The Goose nodded. "That's right."

"So we're going to have some idle hands for a while."

"There's no shortage of devils round here, sure."

Dando smiled. "I was just thinking Goose. We haven't had a christening on this job yet."

"Come off it Griff," Goose muttered. "That sort of malarky went out with the Ark."

"It happened to you, didn't it?"

"Sure but that was ages ago. They dropped it after what happened down at Preston."

"I think," said Dando blandly, "it's time we started it up again. And we've got an obvious candidate here. Haven't we Circus Boy?"

The Goose suddenly moved forward and swung Dando round to face him as the foreman turned towards the bemused Keen. "Keep your black, Welsh eyes off him Dando," he said, his thin lips tightening. "Or God help me. . . ."

Dando glared down at the driver's hand on his arm. "Easy Goose, that's not very nice, is it? And me here with a present for you."

He reached into his pocket and carefully removing the Irishman's hand from his sleeve he placed a dried mud ball, the size of an egg, in it.

"Go on then. Take it. It's yours, isn't it?" he said. "I got it from a checker you went through at Carronbrook, just after we went 40 gallons light at the fuel store. It doesn't look much of a gift for anyone but of course, it is only mud, isn't it?"

As The Goose stared silently at his hand Dando reached forward and broke the mud ball into two pieces. He took out a tightly screwed-up five pound note which he slowly unfolded, with a broad smile on his face, before placing it in his back pocket. "You were right Goose," he said. "It's only mud."

Dando had already turned to take a sweeping glance at the machines behind them when the Goose closed his fist angrily, his narrow eyes burning into the back of the G.F.'s neck as the crushed earth trickled through his fingers.

"Now then Malkin, what can we find in the amazing Clandy collection to suit a . . . circus boy?" Dando asked the broad shouldered youth beside him. "Which one's Fasman?"

Malkin pointed to where a huge yellow drag-line was parked in the centre of the quarry clearing.

Between the two heavy caterpillar tracks was a glass cockpit and, rising almost immediately in front of the driver's controls, a tall, 150-foot latticed boom. Suspended from the boom was a thick cable leading down to a steel grab, resting on the ground, its double row of metal teeth giving it the appearance of enormous jawbones.

"He's driving that," said Malkin.

Dando reached into his breast pocket and brought out a pair of black-rimmed sunglasses. Putting them on slowly he carefully surveyed the line from the top of the boom to the cable to the waiting mouth of the grab.

"She'll do just fine," he said, "for a circus boy."

He turned to Keen whose eyes darted into each man's face in turn.

"Come over here with me boy," he said "I want to show you something."

When they reached the grab bucket Dando kicked his boot against one of the eight metal teeth which formed a 6-foot jaw line below the black cavity of the machine's mouth.

"Do you know what this is, lad?" Dando asked.

"It's a dragline," said Keen limply.

"This boy, is the Clandy Dragon. And if you still read your comics you'll know what dragons do, boy. They eat things. This little beauty eats six cubic yards with every bite. That's nine tons of dolorite. Quite an appetite, isn't it?"

The Goose pushed his way between Dando and the grab. "Look Griff, if its a wee swing you're suggesting use one of the 22 R.B.s"

"But there's one big fault about this dragon, boy," said Dando, oblivious to the driver. "She hasn't any table manners. She eats anything and everything and she sometimes gets some of her food stuck in her throat and in her teeth. So we have to clean them for her, don't we? We use toothpicks. Human toothpicks. Where's your stone chisel Goose?"

"He's nothing but a kiddy, Dando. Lay off him!"

"Your chisel, Goose," repeated Dando, holding out his gloved hand.

"What's all the fuss, Goose?"

The Goose swung round and saw the bent, spiky shape of Liam Connolly at his shoulder. Behind him he could see other men gathering from the dozers.

"It's nothing," he said loudly, handing the chisel to Dando. "It's just a little game the G.F. thinks he wants to play."

As Dando accepted the chisel The Goose half covered his mouth with his hand and hissed back to Connolly, "Get Rafferty!"

Fasman had joined them now and stood beside the general

foreman.

The boy had his back to the grab as he watched Fasman nod to Dando before climbing up to his cab.

"O.K. then lad," said Dando briskly. "In you go."

Keen looked into the open jaws of the grab and then back to Dando. "What . . . you mean inside there?"

"You heard what the G.F. said. Get in. You canna clean a dragon's throat by spitting at him, can you?" The reedy high-pitched voice came from Gans who had just taken Fasman's place beside the foreman.

"Before you leave us," said Dando inquiringly, "are you a Caw? You know what a Caw is, don't you?"

"It's your union, isn't it?" said Keen.

Dando smiled at him, "You're learning lad. Yes, it's my union. Construction and Allied Workers. Are you in yet?"

Keen shook his head. "I've only just arrived," he said.

"Well I'll tell you what the C.A.W. is, kidda. Its a protection for its members. Now sometimes before we protect a new member like yourself, we like to know if he's worth protecting. Let's call it a kind of initiation, shall we?"

The boy made no reply.

"Come on sweetie. I'll give you a wee bunk up if you like," said Gans, offering him an arm.

Keen looked at the grinning Gans, the dark, impassive face of Dando beside him, examining all the faces in turn before stopping finally at The Goose, who glanced back at him for only a brief moment before lowering his head.

"It's all right," the boy said, "I'll find my own way in, thanks."

As he swung himself up into the grab between two of the great teeth, Keen was aware of something touching his arm. He looked down and saw a dirty, tightly knotted handkerchief being handed up to him. Beyond the outstretched hand was the pale, concerned face of The Goose.

"Pop this between your teeth, boy," he heard him whisper, "it'll help keep 'em in shape."

Almost immediately the two jaws of the steel grab closed behind him with a clanging sound which sent shudders along the sides of the container.

It was large enough to hold eight muckshifters, four to each side but not quite high enough for a man to stand upright in.

He could pick out at least four skull-sized rocks lying at the far end and on the floor a thick layer of fine dust, disturbed by the snapping of the jaws, was swirling through the patterns of sunlight.

Peering through the gaps between the metal teeth Keen just had time to see the sun glinting against black sunglasses before the G.F. nodded and raised a thumb to Fasman in the cab above him.

Suddenly a rapid jerk on the cable pitched him backwards. He slithered through the dust down to the end wall before the whole capsule rose from the ground, forcing him down towards the teeth. Clasping both arms around one of them he listened to the ominous rumbling of the rocks behind as they rolled down the floor of the grab and cannoned into his legs, causing him to cry out with pain.

As the grab rose quickly into the air Keen could see the upturned faces of the men shrinking beneath him until the whirring of the overhead cable stopped and the bucket came to a halt. When he looked again he could see he was suspended more than 80 feet above the quarry bed. He could see the line of excavators moving down into the valley for safety.

On the batter above the exit road, men with shovels were staring up at him and beneath him the circle of muckshifters had swollen to twice its size. Moreover, no noise seemed to be coming from them. Even the air around the hanging grab was calm, windless. At first the giant shovel began to move slowly. Only the faintest of twitches on the cable was sufficient to launch the grab three feet to one side, where it paused to gain momentum before swinging back to begin its next descent. With each plunge it swung further out into blue and cloudless sky, returning to loop again before reaching outwards, ever outwards. Inside the grab the air was now thick with an acrid dust which sucked into Keen's lungs as he gasped for breath. With each ascent the rocks came at him, juddering into his sides as he clung to the metal spar. A boulder crashed against his temple and he though he heard a kind of music. He knew the tune even before the metal tooth between his hands became a glistening silver bar suspended between two red velvet cords. The Skater's Waltz. His limbs suddenly felt a strange freedom as he stared down at the dazzling whiteness of his singlet and his slim, lithe body tapering down the sharp creases of his trousers to the bright gleam of his pumps. He was flying. Looking down he could see the faces quite clearly now. The fat, cheerful faces of old men gazing upwards, the quiet concern of the thin faced man in the top hat, the bright sticky faces of young children with ice cream dripping down their chins, mothers clutching their young babies with a fearsome wonder in their eyes. . . . Only the black sunglasses above the thin, leering lips, cast up a coldness which chilled him, because he could not see the eyes. . . . To Keen the music was becoming louder now . . . a hint of violins, softly sawing into a wide sky, which seemed to swell into trumpets and trombones and a crashing of cymbals. As the music mounted Keen found himself being thrust nearer and nearer to the bulging canvas at the roof of the tent, with the deep gaping mouths of the watchers on the ground gasping at every plunge. Finally, as though a frenzied madness had come over the orchestra, he swung upwards and outwards for the last time as the music swelled to a deafening crescendo, hurtling him through the canvas, which burst to release him into a vast, white silence. . . .

The steel grab had stopped and was hanging motionless on its cable above the excavator as the Land Rover raced into the quarry, sounding blast warnings on its hooter as the men leapt from its path.

Dando took a pace backward as the driver made a flying jump from the cab to land almost at his feet.

Finn Rafferty looked up at the suspended grab and immediately back to Dando. "All right Dando, who is it?"

Dando peeled off the black sunglasses and examined them. "Cool it, Rafferty," he said calmly. "It's not one of your coalies. You can stop your clucking."

"Get him down! Go on, get him down!"

The general foreman smiled and, looking up at the excavator's cab, gave Fasman a quick nod.

Finn waited as the grab shovel was gently lowered to within four feet of the ground before it was suddenly released, sending the capsule thudding against the quarry bed.

The ganger's face was an angry red against the white thatch of his hair. "Make him open it."

Dando nodded again to Fasman who leaned forward nonchalantly before pulling the lever which caused the grab to spring apart.

Rafferty dashed forward and saw the upturned body of the youngster slumped across the floor of the grab. "Christ! It's the boy," he said, his voice choking.

"A circus boy, you must remember," said Dando coolly. "He should be quite used to this sort of thing."

The Goose ran forward from the crowd and peered into the hole. "Has he his teeth?" he asked.

Finn peeled off his blue denim jacket and rolled up one sleeve of his shirt without once taking his eyes off Dando's face. "If he has he'll be luckier than some fellers here," he said. He began to whistle quietly to himself.

Instinctively the crowd edged backwards into a wider circle as the two men stared at each other.

Dando beckoned him forward with the upturned fingers of both hands. "Come on then Rafferty! Which one's it going to be this time? Clause Eight is it for a start? S.S.E. Striking a Senior Employee?"

"You choose," said Finn fastening a sleeve above his elbow. "You're the one with the rule book."

As Finn moved forward he felt The Goose's arms grabbing his waist. "Don't let him do it Finn," he pleaded. "He's feeding you, the kid's going to be O.K."

The ganger stopped whistling and looked back towards the grab. "Are you certain?"

"Sure I'm certain" said The Goose. "Just come over here till you see. It's just a few dents and a wee sleep on his hands, that's all."

Up on the rock face a hooter blew, sending some of the men scattering to the trucks which would take them to the half mile safety distance, further down the valley.

"I'm still waiting, Rafferty." Dando had Fasman and Gans on either side of him now.

"Oh, you're waiting to hear how the boy is?" asked the Irishman, his face softening as he turned round. "He's concussed while performing extra duties, do you have a clause for that?"

The Goose was tugging at Rafferty's shirt and pointing to his wrist. "Finn, look, I make it about two minutes to go before the blow. I don't fancy moving the lad too quickly after what he's been through."

A faint smile spread over the ganger's face. "Well there's only one thing for it," he said.

"What's that?"

"We'll have to move in with him. It's the safest place in this valley, inside one of those things."

"Try telling him that," said The Goose rubbing his handkerchief against the boy's dirt-stained face.

"Windsor! Get my Landy out of here will you?" shouted Finn to a small, thin West Indian muckshifter.

"Where the hell's Malkin?" Dando snapped as Fasman and Gans looked at him helplessly.

"Yours seems to have gone, Dando," said Finn. "Well, in that case, you can either start walking or take a chance on your skull being thick enough to stop the splinters. Or you can join us. In there!"

Liam the Liar and Nolan had already hoisted themselves into the giant grab, scrambling back to squat at the far end, quickly followed by Gans and Samson.

Fasman and The Goose were next up, the plump driver helping Samson to lift the boy across their knees as they waited for Dando and Rafferty.

For a moment the two men looked at each other before Finn waved Dando ahead of him. "Go on, in you get then," he said. "Unless there's a clause against saving your skin."

Dando lifted himself into the steel jaws and sat beside Fasman at the mouth of the grab. Finn leapt up behind him and, taking his place on the opposite side, held Keen's unconscious head on his lap.

"Hold on now," said Finn, releasing his hold on the boy for a few seconds as he reached with both hands, forcing the upper row of steel teeth down with a noisy, clanging sound.

"That's real cosy now, isn't it?" he said as the men on each side stared at each other. "Have you ever been in one of these things before, Dando?"

In the darkness, behind the thin strips of sunlight streaming through the steel teeth, he was aware Dando's eyes were on him.

But the foreman made no reply.

"I knew a G.F. once," said Finn quietly. "Big feller, quick with his fists when he needed to be. But soft in a way. He'd sub a man from his own pocket if he was short. And then lay him cold if he ever crossed him, and still fix him up with digs. They used to follow him around the country like flies. They'd get to hear he was in a place and they'd go there and start asking the way to Stan Miller like folk would ask now for the Social Security. They were still following after him when he died. And when I asked one of Miller's lads how you get to be that sort of foreman, do you know what he said? He said it was because he never once asked a man to do something he wouldn't do himself."

The Goose broke the silence, leaning forward to look into Keen's face, "Shouldn't this feller be waking up to us by now?"

Finn moved the boy's jaw slowly between his finger and thumb, "You're right," he said, giving the lad a soft tap on the cheek. "Come on, young 'un, time to get up."

As his hand slapped the boy's face a second time the hard crust of the mountain behind them burst open with a dull shudder which seemed to lift the floor of the grab.

Crouching low, the eight men covered their heads beneath their arms as they waited for the rumbling of the explosion to die away.

When the noise subsided Finn looked down and saw that Keen's eyes were wide open. "Is the show over?" he asked weakly.

"Your's is son, ours is just starting," said The Goose, slapping his hands eagerly together. "Come on lads, the golden eagle's shit on the mountain. Let's get some shovelling done."

Finn and Samson were the last to leave, the ganger gently lowering the boy down to the huge muckshifter's arms.

"You'd better put him in my Landy when it gets back," said Finn looking back down the valley to where the dumpers were bringing the men back to the rock face.

"Forget it Samson, put him in mine. I'll take him to the sick room myself." Dando said. He turned to face Finn, "You've work to do here haven't you, ganger?"

Keen lay like a limp child in Samson's arms as the big muckshifter carried him towards the returning Land Rover. In the meantime Dando had walked over to Fasman, watched closely by Gans. "What's your name again?" he asked taking off his helmet and rubbing the black sleeve of his shirt across his sweating forehead.

"Fasman."

Dando repeated the name slowly. "Yes, Fasman," he said, "well you know how to use one of these things boyo. Can you handle yourself without one?"

Fasman grinned. "No one's complained twice," he said.

"I think I can use you, Fasman. Are you game?"

Fasman took a few steps towards him before looking back to

where the podgy Gans waited with a sullen, disappointed pout on his face.

"All right," said Dando, hooking his thumb upwards, "Bring your fat friend too. We might even need him."

As Dando turned he saw that Finn Rafferty was leaving.

"Rafferty?" he shouted.

The Irishman turned and looked back.

"You'd better find yourself a fresh pair of dragon men, I've just transferred two. And while you're at it you'd better get yourself a new cableman too."

"Keen'll be back, don't worry," said Finn turning away.

"Another thing, Rafferty."

"Hello."

"Get yourself out of those soft digs of yours. They want all the unmarried muckies in the hostel, it's company policy. Move in after shift. Tonight."

"I've heard it's full to bursting up there."

Dando sniffed. "There's room," he said. "Kelly's inside again."

As Dando's Land Rover arrived Gans leapt forward and held the door open for him.

The general foreman had almost reached the truck when he swung round quickly. "If you say Circus Boy here's going to be back, that means he'll be needing a nursemaid, which is lucky for both of you, Rafferty," he said with a smirk.

"Why's that?"

"Because you're rooming with him."

Dando climbed into the passenger seat as the Land Rover moved off, taking Gans by surprise.

For a few yards the small, fat Scotsman ran behind before finally pitching himself into the back as the vehicle roared out of the quarry.

If Finn had known the drive up to Hesters Hall was going to be so long and steep he would have asked the dump truck driver to take him all the way.

The gravel path, overgrown with patches of weeds was, in fact, broad enough to take two trucks abreast, as he realised after Burkitt had dropped him off in front of the great stone lion at the main gate.

It was evident that there should have been two lions, but in the place of the partner there remained only a large stone base, against which a small, brown dog was disrespectfully urinating. Even with its missing ear and the blue moustache chalked above the snarling mouth, the surviving lion was maintaining sufficient awe and presence to ward off a similar assault.

Hauling his burlap bag across his shoulders Finn walked for more than 100 yards between the two banks of budding rhododendron bushes on either side before the path began to swing upwards into an open area of broad parkland.

Even in the fading light, Hesters Hall stood out quite clearly on the flat brow of the hill. He could pick out the high 30-foot portico with its four Grecian columns mounting up to a wide semi-circular fresco which took up almost a third of the frontage.

The portico gave the immediate impression of being too grand for the house. Without it Hesters would otherwise have been a plain, unpretentious oblong box with only the stubby, crenellated roof relieving the severity of the solid sandstone walls.

Both the portico and the sturdy undulating coping on the flat roof had been nineteenth century additions to the Hall, which had been in the Hesters family for seven hundred years.

They were the work of two separate architects, one commissioned in 1875 by Lady Blanche Hesters, wife of the Whig member for Haltbriggin, who wanted to give Hesters a more elegant Romanesque appearance.

The castellations on the roof were the fruits of Sir Ranald's designer, Berkley Hoare, who was ordered to produce a more rugged, Northern look in keeping with the traditions of Hester ancestors, the reiver lords of Corbar.

The end result was to leave the Hall looking like a foppish hybrid castle, which none of the succeeding and declining Hesters had the will or money to redress.

The original Hesters of Padfoot had come over with the Conqueror, performing a service at Senlac which resulted in both father and son being offered the Corbar Valley, after William had laid waste everything north of York.

Since nature had aniticipated him, it had never been considered remotely necessary to lay waste to Corbar and it was usually thought that to win Corbardale, the Hesters' contribution at Hastings was either a minor one or that their reward was assessed on the grounds of their being Angevin opportunists rather than pure Norman.

Despite the discrepancy of the dates, the Hester hedesmen who followed traced their ancestry deep into the roots of ancient Northumbria, claiming kinship back to the giant Colt of Corbar, a border chieftain who was said to have spawned no lesser progeny than one of the Bretwalda kings of Northumbria, three of whom became kings of the Britons.

In the valley itself, the powerful rule of the Hesters of Todholes was never seriously disputed. They were, by their own deeds and insistence, lords of Corbar. And even the doubts of later civil servants in Whitehall, which were finally resolved in a deal which permitted them the lesser status of the original baronetcy, failed to dilute the tradition.

More than eighty years after the Whitehall decision people in

Corbardale still referred to the thirty-five miles of Hesters land between Haltbriggin and Hounshale as 'The Lordship.'

Memories of centuries of heroic thieving across the Scottish border, which helped to build up the Hesters fortune, had long since mellowed to the point where even the valley folk preferred to forget the crimes and remember only the spunk of the Hesters, who carried out the raids.

It was part of the same brand of devotion and daring which had sent scores of the same and later generations of Hesters into unquestioning battle for their soveriegn in foreign service, from Sluys to the Somme and the named, yet empty shelves in the family vault beneath Todholes parish church bore witness that few Hesters died in their beds.

The last of the Hesters males, Sir Ralph, had died in his bed, however, in a sea-front hotel in Bournemouth, after surviving the Somme but not the effects of half a lifetime of Corbar winters on a chest which was never strong from birth.

He left behind a stately heap which the National Trust politely declined and the last of the Hesters breed, his daughter Latice, who was childless, and who, even had she achieved a small measure of fecundity, would have succeeded only in producing a Gillibrand.

Latice Gillibrand was now 60 and living with her husband, the Brigadier, in a white Italianate villa near Haltbriggin, neither of them wishing to reside in a draughty, crumbling, historic pile which nobody seemed to want.

True, the Army authorities, ignoring the example of the late Sir Ralph, had seen fit to use the Hall as a convalescent home for most of the Second World War, despite the notorious Corbar winters. But so many of its patients remained in the area involuntarily that the Hall became known throughout the Service as Coffin Castle, and in 1945 the unit was moved down to Hampshire.

Haltbriggin Rural District Council became the Hall's new tenants for a time, which proved to be just long enough for their new brick offices to be built in the town centre.

Throughout that time, with the exception of the main family heirlooms and those effects small enough to fit into a white Italianate villa, much of the Hesters' fittings and furnishings had remained as they were when the family was in residence.

Only when Frank and Valerie Mort, a young couple from Rochdale, opened the place as an adventure holiday home for schoolchildren did the oils and the furniture go off into storage, leaving just the fading curtains and the Army's beds.

The adventurous yet perpetually hard-up Morts lasted a bare two summers at Hesters, arriving back in Rochdale just as the Virginia Creeper around the ground floor windows was turning a warning red for the second time.

Three years later it had taken a man with all the practicality as well as the blatant humour of Vincent Caswell to stumble into Hesters on a bone-chilling February day to see the home of the heroic reivers of Corbar as a rather splendid, not to mention handy, hostel for eighty muckshifters.

There was a pair of stone Hesters lions standing guard beneath the portico on either side of Finn as he began to climb the wide steps to the front door. They seemed fitter, younger than the old guardian at the gate. For a moment Finn even thought he recognised the lion on the left. It was not so much the extended mouth, caught seemingly by the sculptor in mid roar, but the black eye patch pencilled across the beast's menacing face.

Surprised at finding the oak doors locked Finn hammered against the heavy panelling with the heel of his fist.

As he waited for an answer he flicked his finger impatiently against the column beside him and looked around guiltily as a two-foot sliver of stone fluting flaked away and fell on to the well-worn porchway.

Even though the door opened only a few inches he recognised the nose even before he saw the man.

"Open up there my man! I wish to see the Lord of the Muck," announced Finn sternly.

"Christ it's you, Finn!" yelled The Goose, dashing forward to grab his hand. "Are you in with us then?"

The Goose glanced down sheepishly at his white string vest and long johns, held up with a broad leather belt. "Sorry about the informality, old chap," he said. "It's the butler's night off – he's gone manking down at the Tup."

"Here," said Finn, tossing his bag against The Goose's chest, "Water me horse and lead me to the victuals, serf. What's all the secrecy for anyway?"

"It's for the bosses," said Goose raising a finger. "We're taking it in turns keeping a lookout for anyone from Dando up. On account of the grots."

"Are you light on the grub then?"

The Goose started laughing, "Christ no. There's too much of it. You know that tubby cook you had up there with you in Scotland."

"Tucky?"

"That's him. Well he's the new chef du Hesters you see and you've never seen anything like what he's dishing up in there. In the er . . . Great Hall," he added with a low bow. "What's happened, you see, is that Caswell says he won't know how much food to order for us on a regular basis until he's seen what we get through in the first week. So they're in there feeding their faces like nobody's business, steaks, ducks, chickens, all to get the quota ratings up, you see."

Finn pushed his fingers behind the buckle of Goose's straining belt. "You don't need much more to get yours up, Goose, do you?

What happens if the hats call in then?"

The Goose winked and tossed a thumb over his shoulder. "Your man back there's got sausage and mash at the ready, hasn't he? Reckons he can serve it up in two minutes flat, which is about the time it takes to get from the front door to the Great Hall anyway, in this place."

Finn scanned his eyes round the huge entrance hall with its dark oak-panelled walls broken on his left by the wide, uncarpeted staircase leading to the first landing.

In front of him was a long corridor leading to the room with the double doors where all the noise was coming from, and on the right there was a large stone fireplace with pine logs burning in the huge open hearth. In one of the two big red armchairs beside the fire a small grey-haired man in spectacles was reading a book.

"Yes," said Finn admiringly, "you could get a few dozens in here all right. Who's your wee guest there?"

"That's old Soils," whispered Goose. "He's here too but don't worry about him, he's all right, he's one of us already."

Finn walked over to the fireplace as the man got up and took off his glasses before reaching out a hand to him. "It's Mr. Curran, isn't it?"

"That's right," said the man smiling defensively. "I was up to see you on the O.C. job on Scotland, I believe. I remember us having to plump for the old fern beds or under the young hardwoods."

"You went for the ferns," smiled Finn, "and you were right."

"Happily," agreed Curran.

"It wasn't good coal. But there was plenty of it."

Curran smiled. "The ferns had been there longer you see. And the trees, well they're still there doing what young trees should be doing. Growing."

Finn stared for a moment at the stone fireplace in front of them, which had a large stone dog carved into a crest above the burning logs. "That's the first beast I've seen in this place that isn't a lion."

"Ah, you noticed the Hesters lions?"

"Noticed them!" exclaimed Finn, "I passed so close to their evil looking jaws they almost had my nuts off!"

Curran chuckled quietly as he put his book down on the chair. "No, our friend here, Rafferty, is a bull mastiff."

"They had dogs too, did they?"

Curran nodded. "Mainly, I suspect, because you can't take lions for walks. Not to the places the Hesters took their mastiffs anyway. They used to breed large, pure white mastiffs and take them with them anywhere they wanted to put on a show of strength. There's even a record of one of the Hesters hedesmen taking his mastiff to Agincourt to fight. The French, of course."

"For Harry, Hesters and h . . . h . . . hound dog," shouted Finn suddenly swooping his hand down to snap at the seat of The Goose's long johns. "Once more into the breeches, eh?"

The Goose leapt in the air to escape the furiously barking Finn, at the same time clutching the seat of his sagging drawers. "Pack it in now Finn," he squealed. "Finn! Look, let me show you the family portrait gallery. Curran's too shy to admit any inside information on this lot."

Finn followed the bulky dozer driver to the main staircase where on the grey, dusty walls was a succession of large rectangular empty spaces where the original oil paintings had hung. Each space had a shiny coloured magazine picture pasted in the centre of it, ranging from nude to partly clothed females.

"The first picture you will see on our right is of the 4th Duke," announced The Goose in a serious, informative tone.

He pointed to a busty blonde who was naked except for a black money box she was squeezing between her thighs as she attempted to insert a coin in it.

"The 4th Duke went with the Crusades on a saving mission and ended up saving enough to build a new wing when he returned."

Finn slapped him in the middle of the back with a resounding thump. "You're a nut, Goose," he said.

"And then we come to the esteemed and exceptionally well endowed 6th Duke," said Goose addressing a photograph of a red-haired girl who was standing naked, attempting to support a substantial pair of breasts in her inadequate fingers. "The 6th Duke also added considerably to the family chest."

"I like the look of the 7th Duke coming up," said Finn urging him forward up the stairs.

"Don't be impatient, sir," chided The Goose as he put an arm across the stairs, holding him back. "Now this, as any sensible person can see, is a lady."

"Never," said Finn staring at a blonde leggy girl with high, full-nippled breasts, sitting cross-legged on a bed.

"This is Lady Gwendoline Hesters, daughter of the unfortunate 9th Duke, who spent a lot of time in London, having come into the family after it had fallen on leaner times. But she maintained that her unfortunate position did not worry her, since she was sitting on a fortune anyway. She used to describe herself as a belted noblewoman. Frequently, in fact."

"Get down," roared Finn shoving the laughing driver down the stairs. "You're fired. You couldn't tell a Count from a cundy anyway."

Finn hauled the muckshifter to his feet, offered him an arm, indicating the way to the Great Hall with his other hand. "Shall we dine, Madam?"

Accepting, The Goose curtsied low in his long johns, and the pair walked gracefully towards the high doors, bowing briefly to the studious Curran as they passed.

As the big doors swung open a loud shout of welcome came from the left, where a group of men were sitting round the end of a huge, oak refectory table stretching almost the full length of the forty-foot room.

"Finn me old mucker!" yelled a frothy mouth from behind a pewter tankard as a dozen faces around him released a chorus of cheers and whoops.

"Most of your fellows seem to have taken over that end of the hall," said Goose.

"Perhaps they felt at home being near the family scuttle," said Finn glancing at the large brass hod in the fireplace.

He raised his arms to them producing another raucous response. He could pick out the scrawny Liam The Liar nodding across at him, glass in hand. Dick Dancer with a large, white napkin suspended beneath his chin, his long black fringed hair giving him almost a mediaeval appearance. There was Windsor Brown, the West Indian dumper driver with a fat chunk of meat on his waving fork. The white-haired Chauncy Bawn smiling into his gin glass beside the giant Samson, who was tugging at a large crust of bread. Tully was there too, a blue serviette tucked into his shirt and his stove hat pushed to the back of his head.

Down at the other end he could see Fasman and beside him, Gans, grinning from behind a large apple, and across the table from them, the ferret face of Nolan, who looked round only briefly before turning to speak to the pimply Malkin.

"I say, could we have some water do you think?" announced Dancer standing up as the gang around him cheered and thumped their glasses against the thick oak table.

"Hunt the water Finn?" yelled Liam Connolly.

Rafferty moved away, pretending not to hear them. For a moment he stared at the stone fireplace on which yet another Hesters bull mastiff had been carved beneath the wide mantelpiece.

Above it were the bare borders of a clean square, where the original painting had been replaced by a hairy gorilla.

Finally, as their cries became even more insistent, he raised his hands in surrender. "All right, all right," he bawled "But I don't have any sticks."

He had hardly got the words out before Dancer had reached over to the big joint of beef in the centre of the table, wrenched out the large carver and fork which were sticking out from the meat.

"Here you are Finn lad," he shouted, throwing the knife towards him. Finn deftly caught it before putting out the other hand to snatch the flying fork out of the air.

Facing them he slowly peeled off his brown jacket and let it sip down to his feet. "O.K. then, are you right?" he asked.

"Yes!" they roared back.

"Are you sure it's water you want?"

"Yes!" they repeated, crashing their fists on the table. "Who's got the blindfold then?" he asked as Dancer popped up beside him and fastened his napkin round Rafferty's head.

Immediately Finn thrust out the carver and fork in front of him and began walking jerkily in the direction of the shouting coalies.

As he passed along the table the knife and fork in his hands hovered in turn over the glasses in front of the men who stared up at him, watching his every move.

"Now then? Who's it going to be? Who is it has the dreaded virgin's bathwater? I'm getting a reaction!"

The fork and knife began twitching violently above Chauncy Bawn's glass as the white-haired Irishman smiled at him.

"I think we might have it," shouted Finn, kneeling down and feeling for the glass before taking a sip from it. "This has a taste of Bawn about it," he said. "That's not virgin's bathwater. It's mother's bloody ruin!"

With the gang urging him on, Finn paused directly over the almost empty whisky glass in front of Dick Dancer. The knife suddenly sprang to an upright position in his hand as Finn fingered it with a slow smile. "Dancer's night out," he said: "a bit of the hard stuff."

Moving quickly to Liam The Liar's glass, full to the brim with whisky, Finn allowed the knife to flop down lifeless in his limp hand. "Liam's downfall," he said: "too much of the hard stuff."

As the gang urged him on, Finn turned and began groping his way across the beef joint and the platters of vegetables towards Fasman's end of the table, stretching out his divining utensils in front of him as he went.

Finally he stopped opposite Nolan, who looked up at him sullenly as the knife and fork plunged down towards his glass.

Finn reached down for the glass, sniffed it, drank a mouthful and held it triumphantly above his head. "Here it is!" he cried. "The Virgin's bathwater! Sweet as a baby's breath, soft as the swish of a gymslip. And who has it?" he ripped away the blindfold, raising the glass high in his hand. "Nolan from lovely Listowel. By Christ the kings of Kerry will be weeping tonight!"

Nolan bit his lip as he glanced up at the Irish ganger towering above him. "I'm going to Mass," he said lamely.

Finn beamed down at him. "You'll have an awful burden to confess lad, with that lot under your belt and you a Clandyman."

As another roar went up around him, Finn saw the heads turn towards the kitchen door behind him.

He swung round and saw Tucky the cook waddling in with a huge, silver tray protruding from his large belly. On the tray was a pig's head decorated with a thick coating of caramel. There were two black leather gloves hanging from its mouth and a pair of sunglasses perched across its eyes.

Tucky raised the tray up to the big ganger, who leaned over and put the glasses on his own face before snatching the gloves from the pig's mouth and giving the chef a playful slap on each cheek.

Then he put on the gloves and began goosestepping down the table before returning to face Tucky, his legs slightly apart as he held his gloved hands behind his back.

"Now what can we cook up for culinary insubordination then boyo?" he said menacingly, imitating Dando's voice. "Clause 166 oblique stroke one. Shall we boil him in pure vegetable, calorie-free, non-fattening cooking oil?"

"No," yelled the coalies at the left of the table.

"Or shall we have him dipped to his nipples in best Welsh farmhouse butter and friccassied?"

"No."

"Or perhaps we should roll him up in leeks, cover him in puff pastry and serve him up as a Tonypandy toad in the hole?"

"Only if you have to eat 'im boyo," yelled Dick Dancer as the crowd around him supported their thunderous chorus of "Yes" by crashing their knives down on the table.

"Cocktails, Finn," bawled Liam The Liar from the opposite end, and the others took up the cry.

Rafferty raised his hand to silence them. "No gentlemen," he said, "Not tonight. I haven't heard any good ones lately."

Once more the tankards thumped down on the table top as the men cheered him.

"Give us 'Today', Finn," shouted Brown Windsor, pressing his hands in a downward motion to silence the whole table.

Finn looked at them as the room went quiet. "Not tonight gentlemen" he said limply, "I can't sing on an empty stomach."

The cries of "Fill it" and "Shame" passed over his head as the ganger jumped down from the table and walked across to The Goose who was chuckling to himself beside the door. "I see you haven't lost your touch then, Finn?"

"Where's the boy, Goose?" Finn asked him in a low voice. "He's not here I see."

"He's not too bad Finn. He's sleeping it off upstairs."

"Did he eat a bite?"

"No, he said he didn't fancy anything, so we thought it was best to leave him to stew through it."

"Look Goose," said Finn taking his bag from the muckshifter's hand, "I'll fix a bite and go up and see if he's all right."

"Finn," said The Goose calling him back.

"Hello sir."

"It's nothing really. Just the boy. You seem to be clucking after him like an old hen, as if he was your son or something."

"Well what's wrong with that sure?"

The Goose shrugged his narrow, sloping shoulders. "It's just that. . . ." He broke off. "Ach he's only a wee tote, but there's a smell about him."

Finn grinned at him. "I'm not planning any family at my age, feller. Christ Goose there's near on a hundred years in us, with me pushing forty and you on sixty and not a son between us."

"Well I can tell you I'm past the laying anyway," said The Goose.

"Don't you kid yourself Goose. One day you're going to hatch the golden one, just you wait. I'd hate to think of a big spread of metal like yours lying around with no one coming up pushing for it."

He walked to the table, reached over Gans' shoulder and took a chicken leg from the stacked dinner plate in front of him. "What are you doing with birds on your plate?" he said as the plump-cheeked Scotsman looked round.

"Second on the left on the first landing," The Goose called out as Finn left, raising his chicken leg behind him in acknowledgement.

Finn knocked quietly on the white-painted door before pushing it open and walking into a large, bay-windowed room which had twin beds separated by an ornate dressing table with a heart-shaped mirror.

As he threw his bag across the first bed, he saw the figure in the other one shift uneasily before turning to face him.

"Who's that?" asked the voice.

"It's all right son," said Finn softly. "You've got a new room-mate." He sat on the side of the bed and held out the chicken leg to the boy. "Have you eaten yet?"

Keen looked up at him and shook his head, revealing a large, purple bruise over his right eye which was spreading down his cheek.

"I don't fancy anything. Mr. Rafferty, isn't it?"

"Finn," said Rafferty, "Finn like a fish. With an extra nuh." He bit into the chicken leg, eyeing the boy closely as he chewed. "You didn't bust anything, did you? Split a bone or something?"

"No, I'll be all right."

"Great," said Finn. "You'll be right for helping Goose shovel 500 tons of shite before breakfast in the morning then, before you start on the real work, eh?"

"I hope so," said Keen.

"So do I," said Finn. "I was only fooling. Just you being there tomorrow will be even more important than what you do, if you know what I mean."

Keen raised his shoulders up from the elbows and looked across at him. "I think I do."

Finn unfastened the straps of his cloth bag before emptying the contents on his bed.

"Finn?"

"Hello sur," said the Irishman pushing a finger through the toe of a sock.

"They tell me I nearly got you into trouble?"

"What trouble was that now?"

"A fight?"

Finn grinned at him. "Don't credit yourself with that, son," he said. "It doesn't require any great mental exertion to get me into a scrap." He took another bite at the chicken leg. "Do you know, every New Year's Eve I make a magnificent resolution to give up fighting. And sure as luck, by teatime on the first day, some plausible bastard comes along with a good, sound sensible reason for me getting the mittens up."

Rafferty picked up the pillow on the bed and thumped it with his fist before looking at it admiringly. "That's class, young Keen," he said. "It must have been Lady Gwendoline's. Not a scrap of haystraw in it."

He looked around him at the long, pink, rose-petalled curtains on the window and the matching pink wall-to-wall carpeting which covered the large room. "Christ, we must have got the bridal suite, son," he said squeezing the lace-bordered pillow to his chest as he waltzed round the room.

"Oh how we danced on the night we were wed,
We danced and we danced for the room had no bed."

When he had finished he was standing in the centre of the room pressing the pillow to his cheek with an ecstatic smile on his face. "Did you know, young Keen, that any feller can make a bed, but you have to go to classes before they let you stuff a pillow?"

Keen, who had been laughing at the Irishman's antics, began clutching his body, wincing with a sudden pain which brought Rafferty striding over to his bed.

"Are you all right lad?" he asked, looking at the boy with concern on his face.

"It's my stomach. It feels as if an elephant's been on it."

"It'll be a shiner in the guts," said Finn pointing to the boy's black eye. "You can get those things inside as well as out, you know."

Keen relaxed again. "Do you know, Finn, for a moment when I was up there, I thought I was back."

"Home, you mean?"

"No, the circus. I could see it all vividly just like it was real."

"You must have had a right crack on the head," said Finn. "You deserved a kicked skull anyway, for telling them you came from a circus."

"Why's that?"

Finn took a cigarette from the pocket in the front of his shirt and lit it. "Well you made your first mistake of your first day by letting them know your life history. You see you're going to be the Circus

Boy all your muckshifting days now. They like to latch on something like that. It gives you a nickname and them some fun."

"I only told them what I did, Finn."

"That was too much for a start. When you come into one of these places your safest bet is to be one of those shy, tight-lipped, Gary Cooper-style, man-from-nowhere chaps. Like me. Even if you told them you were pissed against a wall they'd call you Cocky and put you on latrines. If you give them too much of your tongue round here, it's like handing them your head. And one or two of them will be after that too."

Keen raised himself to a half-sitting position on the bed. "You don't like him, do you Finn?"

"Who?"

"Dando."

Finn shrugged his shoulders. "Nobody actually likes Dando," he said. "Even his mother was a neutral."

"Where's he from?"

"Dando? Oh he was scrubbed up in South Wales in one of those great Methodist coalholes they call valleys. He was spawned during the great Repression. When he wanted a wank, his mother used to make him gargle in San Izal and march him off to sing hymns in one of their refrigerated Welsh chapels. Until he was sixteen he was afraid to say cock for fear it might crow in his hand. Then after all the bibling, his father put him to the pit, which he thought was a sort of Hell, leading only to coughing out your last days with the old men at the Miners Welfare. He ended up hating men for putting him down there and women for helping them. So he decided to put a bit of fresh air between him and home and became a L.D.K."

Keen shuffled uncomfortably in the bed. "What's a L.D.K.?" he asked.

"It's what you were when you were up there on the end of that bucket," said Finn, "a Long Distance Kiddie. That's what most of them are in this place. Men who don't like to get their feet pinned too long in one place, because they feel the only freedom left's in moving. Dando's no different to the rest in needing that."

"You don't hate him then?"

"In a way I'm even grateful to him."

"Grateful?"

Finn smiled at seeing the boy's surprise. "Well as I see it, I know what Dando is and I always know where he is. This sort of joint is not really so different from a jungle. From the outside it may look like a dirty great mess, but when you're in it you see that everything has its place. It switches about a bit each day but there's still a system about it. The big 'uns trying to eat the little 'uns and the little 'uns screwing the dwarfs. It may sound pretty barbaric to them down in the Home Counties but the system works. Are you a Southerner lad?"

Keen nodded, "Ilford."

"Don't let that out down there either," he said, "the muckies reckon they can always tell a Southerner on the site because his mouth always starts up five minutes before his brain."

He broke off and walked over to Keen. "Are you slipping off then, son?" he said quietly.

Keen squinted at him through swollen eyes. "It's catching up with me a bit," he said. "Perhaps it's because I haven't got used to your sort of people yet Finn."

Finn stared up at the rosy curtains to where yet another Hesters Bull mastiff was gazing defiantly down at them. "I think the sort of people who used to run this place would have understood muck-shifters," he said. "They might even have understood Dando. In a way they were the same kind of people. One week they were the local monsters and the next they were good old Sir Percy, chewing the balls off the thieving Scots from above the border, and the valley boys would love them for it. It's when you don't have big 'uns and little 'uns that the real fighting starts. Only then it happens inside where no one can see it. We're like the wee Hesters woman down the road boy, we're the last of the breed. But we do it because it's the last burst of living they've left us."

Keen moved in the bed. "You make muckshifters sound as if they're different to everybody else."

"Well they are," said Finn, "most of them anyway. You can't buy muckshifters, you know, that's what makes most of them special. I knew a man who was bought once. It was my uncle who bought him. You see, what happened was that this feller used to come round his garden making off with his crops so my uncle set out to do something about it."

The boy's voice sounded tired as he spoke. "Did he call in the police?"

"Not at all," said Finn. "He went out in the garden, picked out a good handful of the best vegetables he could find: carrots, leeks, greens, everything, until he had a real good soup mix and he took it round to this fellers house and gave it to him, there on the doostep. Once he'd taken the soup mix you see, it took all the go out of him. . . ."

Finn looked down at the boy and saw that his eyes had closed. But there was a twitching movement in his hands which spread rapidly to his shoulders, shaking the sleeping body into a sitting position.

"The tiger! He's trying to get out! Look!" cried Keen. "Quick! Don't let him get out!"

The Irishman pressed the boy gently back on the bed, his rough, broad hands feeling against the hot forehead.

"Don't fret when the beast shouts, Michael Keen," he said softly. "It's when they get you in there, when they turn up the heat and feed you through the bars and you wonder where all the wildness went. That's when you start worrying."

Finn pulled the blanket up to the boy's chin and saw his eyes were finally closed in a deep untroubled sleep. "Because when you're in there son," he said quietly, "you'll have to make your own tigers."

Finn had been eyeing up the boulder for several minutes with the slow, laborious care of a golfer observing the lie of a gigantic golf ball.

The large chunk of rock had fallen from the overfed jaws of Liam The Liar's tractor shovel and was lying right in the path of the dumper trucks along the South batter, as they ferried their heaped loads up to the crusher.

Finally he reached down, his bare back arched above the stone as he gathered it firmly between his arms and belly and began slowly raising it.

Suddenly something he saw out of the corner of his eye, high up on the opposite batter, caused him to straighten, releasing his burden to thud back to the earth.

Silhouetted against the skyline, more than a hundred feet above him, was a line of young girls, strung out in Indian file and walking purposefully along the coal road up on Calcherside.

They were dressed in starched white blouses and short red skirts which swayed jauntily against their hips as they bounced along behind their leader, whose long, yellow hair was flopping against the collar of her blue gingham dress as she walked.

"Jesus Christ, the bleeding Apaches are on us! Turn the wagons lads!" Finn bellowed to the portly Liam, who jumped back from the caterpillar truck, his grease gun spurting yellow gunge over his boots.

A dozen faces immediately looked towards the big ganger, who pointed to the schoolgirls as they stopped and began to group around the teacher.

"The Pennine Chain is a range of mountains which, as you know, stretches for almost the entire length of Northern England. . . ." Sara Dacre's voice was loud, almost shrill as she tried to compete with the roar of the excavators and the dump trucks beneath them in the valley. "And right here, girls, is the place where mountains meet. Where the Pennines meet the Cheviots. Now both of these ranges were pushed up during the Carboniferous Age rather like the wrinkles in a cloth stretched across a table which is continually shrinking."

"Is the earth shrinking now, Miss?" inquired a small, plump girl whose black pigtails had fallen across her full-busted blouse.

"Yes, very slightly, Sybil. But it was more noticeable when the earth was cooling from its molten state and its skin became too loose to remain flat. The result was places like this. When these mountains were first formed, of course, they still had their soft surfaces, but due to erosion the millstone grit and other hard rocks have pushed their way through to the top, and that's what we are seeing today."

"Why is it called millstone grit, Miss?" asked the thin, bespectacled girl at the back of the group.

Sara Dacre smiled at her, "Why do you think they call it millstone grit, Pauline?"

"Is it because they used it to build the dark satanic mills, Miss?"

The young teacher shook her head. "Well not exactly. It's a very hard stone and the millers used to use it to grind their corn. And even before that, they used to crush the stone to build roads and communications. . . ." She broke off as several of the girls rushed to the lip of the ridge where they began excitedly pointing down the slope.

"I think that man down there's trying to communicate with us Miss," piped a tall, coloured girl, urging the young teacher forward as the rest of the class cheered the advance of the helmeted Finn as he came pounding up the slope like an enraged stag.

Finn hit the rise with a final, grunting leap to find himself facing Form 4 of the Belljohn Boarding School for Girls, who promptly surrounded him in a giggling semicircle.

"What in Jesus' creation do you think this is!" he bawled "Open day? Have you taken off or something? Christ, look you need three things to get on this site, a helmet, and a couple of trouser legs and none of you have got nuthin'."

Sara Dacre stepped forward from the line of laughing schoolgirls. First of all we'll remember the company we're in, shall we Mr. er. . . ."

"Company to hell . . . all right . . . Rafferty. Rafferty I am. I'm from. . . ."

"We all know very well where you're from, Mr. Rafferty," said the teacher in a clipped voice, "and we're all from the Belljohn School in Padfoot and we've every right to be here."

Finn eyed her suspiciously. "Who the devil told you you could just walk right in on the job and. . . ."

"A very influencial devil Mr. Rafferty. Your Sir William Clandy. I take it you've heard of him? It was all arranged by our headmistress through his office. Our girls have been coming here for years as part of their geography syllabus and we were told we didn't have to stop just because you're playing with your bulldozers down there."

Rafferty pushed back his yellow helmet and put his hands on his hips in a gesture of resignation. "But didn't they tell you about the lids, Miss? You could get some god awful dents in your skulls if any of this stuff hits you. It would only need one heel of stone to land on your swedes and that would be your last bell. End of lesson."

"It's very thoughtful of you," Sara Dacre said, "but we are a good quarter of a mile from the quarry as well as 1200 feet above sea level and I don't think our swedes are in any imminent danger, do you? Especially since they are considerably smaller than yours."

Finn stood in stunned silence for a moment, listening to the girls tittering from all sides. Finally his dust-streaked face surrendered into a smile which almost immediately became an uncontrollable roar of laughter, shared by the girls.

Finn saw the blonde teacher was smiling too. When she smiled he noticed that although her mouth was quite small it gave her cool, assured face a softer, more vulnerable look. For a brief moment all her earlier composure had disappeared, just as if her lips had mischievously snatched a half-holiday without telling anyone.

"We ought to have you on the Clandy payroll, Miss," said Finn, "in charge of the clearances. With your use of words you could have gone round swaying these stubborn, old sheep-farmers to let us build our big tub on their land."

"All right now girls, settle down," Sara called to the girls, who had never needed an excuse for a giggle, even before Finn's interruption of the lesson. When she turned back to him her face was quite dispassionate. "No I don't think I'd have been much use to you there, Mr. Rafferty. You see, my father's one of them."

"I'm sorry," said Finn, rubbing his hand across his jaw.

"We're all sorry, Mr. Rafferty. But don't you worry your old stone face. We're doing something about it!"

"You're fightin' us then?" he inquired, raising an eyebrow.

"Some are. And some are realistic enough to accept we've already lost and they're helping to pick up the pieces."

"Like you, Miss Teacher?"

She ignored him, flicking a strand of hair away from her forehead in irritation. "Have you heard of C.A.R.E. yet Mr. Rafferty? It stands for the Corbardale Aid and Resettlement Executive."

Finn smiled and licked his lips, "It sounds a grand enough title."

"The idea's quite simple," she said. "A few of us have got together to work out ways of giving help to the people you're pushing out with your bulldozers. If you hear of anyone who needs us, perhaps you'll bear it in mind. You never know, Mr. Rafferty, you might even need us yourself one day."

"No. I mean, look lady," Finn protested. "This isn't all about pushing people into the street. We're giving them something too, you know."

Sara Dacre raised her eyebrows sharply. "Are you really, Mr. Rafferty?" she said. "You surprise me. Well that's a lesson we would all like to hear, wouldn't we girls?"

"Yes," screeched the girls almost in a single voice.

"Well go on Mr. Rafferty," she urged. "Explain what you've come to give Corbardale."

Finn looked around desperately as though hoping for rescue, before finally making up his mind to face them.

"O.K. I will," he said. "Now how much do you know already?" He pointed to a small, fair-haired girl who was pulling up one of her long, white socks. "You, Daisy May," he said. "What are those fellers doing down there, do you know?"

"Josephine," corrected the girl. "They're building a reservoir."

"A reservoir is it just?" said Finn, pushing back his helmet. "We're building the biggest bl . . . the biggest raintub in the world down there. The creature's so damned big you'll be able to turn a tap on down in Land's End and get a shave from it, well your Dads will. They've never built anything bigger and wetter than this since the sea, and Clandy's would have tendered for that if we'd been asked."

"I thought you only built motorways and things," said Josephine seriously.

"Sure and we have," said Finn, "miles of 'em because we're muckshifters. We move the earth. If you gave me enough dozers and enough men I could shift Everest for you. And I know what you're thinking. You reckon that because of the great skill in the backs of our fellers we can make motorways and big bridges and now we've come up here and anyone can make water."

As the giggles broke out again from the schoolgirls Finn raised his hands to silence them.

"Now listen," he said. "If Miss Teacher will permit me, let me tell you something about making water and make no mistake about it, it has to be made as sure as bread's baked. Now soon we'll be having more water down there than we've seen in this country. And most of it's already here. You can't see it but it's here alright."

Finn broke off suddenly and moved to the lip of the ridge. "Now come over here and tell me what is that dirty, great fence of stone down there in the South? You know what it is, don't you, Daisy May?"

"Josephine," she said. "It's Hadrian's Wall."

"So it is and who did the contract? I'll give you a clue, it wasn't Clandy's."

"The Romans built it."

"Sure, it was their supply base when they used to march the legions up north to fight the Painted People. Now listen, do you know who was the first man in a Roman Legion, the feller who was always right up at the front, away ahead of everyone else? I'll tell you. Now you might well think he was the gaffer man or the bridge-builder or some guy with a spear, but he wasn't at all. He was the water-diviner. The man with the twigs. Sometimes he would be miles ahead of the legion, and then when the boss man gave the word to camp, his job would be to find a nice, clean, underground spring so that the troops could catch a drink when they stopped. Look, I'll show you. . . ." Finn reached in his back pocket and brought out a black bone-handled knife, flicking out the broad blade with his fingers as he ran thirty yards to a thicket of bushes. He emerged within seconds, clutching a slim catapult-shaped branch, his hands carefully holding the two shorter ends.

"No it's not hazel as it might be but this is a divining stick, the great water-sniffer. They haven't changed the model since Roman times. Virgula Divina they called it. . . ." A group of girls on his left started tittering until he held up his hand in mock sternness. "All right, all right," he said, "I didn't name it. Now these pieces in my hands are the ones I get the signals from when there's water around and that long bit sticking out in front, that's the sort of antennae. It'll start twitching if it comes up with anything."

The sight of the big Irishman silhouetted against the skyline, holding the twin branches against the front of his thighs and intently thrusting the leading limb out ahead of him, had started the Belljohn girls giggling again.

Finn looked over to Sara Dacre for support. "Look, can I borrow your class for a minute?" he yelled, fingering the twigs with increasing enthusiasm.

"It depends on what you want to do, Mr. Rafferty," she called back.

"I want to take them to war, Miss Teacher," shouted Finn, "into battle." He slapped his hand loudly against his thigh. "Now I want you all to line up behind me," he called, forming them into along, stringy crocodile at his rear. "Are you right girls? Now you're the legion and I'm the diviner. You've marched sixty miles and your Roman plates are killing you and you're bursting for a drink! Off we go then!"

The seventeen girls marched along the ridge, preceded by the striding Finn, his twig going on before him like a proud, outstretched banner. Occasionally Finn called them to a halt while he made a thorough, penetrating search of the ground.

"As you can see," Finn's voice could be heard instructing his legion, "it's the simplest of nature's instruments and yet it can seek out what it's looking for from a distance of a hundred feet or more. The secret lies not only in the sensitivity of the stick but also the skill of the man who's holding it. When it feels something, it makes a move for it like a rabbit for a burrow."

It was Sara Dacre's voice which finally brought the army to a halt. "I think it's time for the legion to come home Mr. Rafferty," she called, and Finn wheeled his forces and returned them to her side.

"We found nothing," he said shaking his head. "But then some days you don't. And besides it's a bit high up here for springs.

He winked across at the tiny Josephine who was biting her lip in an attempt to keep her face straight. "When I was half Daisy May's age I was finding wells for farmers and diggin' them out for a ha'penny a foot. I remember one day missing school because I was so sure the spring was there and it was, about forty feet down. I was never more glad to see a wet shovel in my life."

Behind them a group of girls who had just gone into a private huddle suddenly broke away, laughing, from the small plump girl, who was looking daggers at them.

"What's going on there?" inquired Sara. "Has something happened?"

"It's Sybil Bates, Miss," said Josephine calmly. "I think she's got some water in her knickers."

"Well goodbye Mr. Rafferty," said Sara Dacre briskly, taking his hand, "It's been most enlightening."

As she began to herd her giggling flock down the mountain she turned round and gave him a faint smile. "Sorry we had to dash," she said. "They'll miss history."

They were nearly out of sight before Finn turned to begin making his own descent into Baskey's.

"I shouldn't worry, Miss Teacher," he murmured quietly to himself. "It's been there for a hell of a long time."

Rafferty could clearly hear the voices of the four men beneath the brightly lit back porch of the George as he turned off Padfoot's main street into the white gravelled forecourt of the hotel.

"You mean you have to join the C.A.W.S.?" young Keen was saying to the other three. "It's an official closed shop then?"

Dando was standing directly in front of him, flanked by Fasman and Gans. "No, it's not official . . . yet," said the general foreman. "But it's sort of expected, if you see what I mean."

"What's in it for me?"

Dando put his arm round Keen's shoulder. "Now that's better. There's a lot of things. Better bunce, better conditions. You're married, aren't you?"

"Only just. That's why I'm here."

"Well then," said Dando, "you'll be wanting a few extras won't you? Like going home the odd week-end to empty your skip, eh lad?"

Before Keen could reply, Fasman leaned towards him, his thick rubbery mouth almost a foot above the boy's head. "Ask about what it's like when you're not in?" he suggested with a slow smile.

Gans came creeping forward. "A laddie like you could have a real swinging time outside the Union, you know, Keen."

"Let me put it this way, boyo," said Dando. "Certain of us prefer people to be friendly and to be with us. Anything else is considered well . . . unfriendly? I think you'll find you may come to need us."

Finn rested his elbow on the stocky Gans's shoulder as he ambled into the centre of the group. "I'll tell you what this boyo needs, Dando," he said, smiling at the general foreman. "He's like me, he needs a rake of working beer."

"What's got you grinning, Rafferty?"

"I was taken by your usual pig-ignorant Welsh use of the English language," said the ganger.

"What do you mean?"

"Well didn't I just hear you say that anyone who didn't want to join you was unfriendly? Well, that's just what they used to call the wee, quivering fellers in this valley, the ones who wouldn't go up and fight the folk who swiped their sheep. They called them the Unfriends. The only difference between them and you is they were funny buggers. They only wanted volunteers."

Finn looked up and saw that The Goose had come out of the bar and was standing on the steps above them. "You're in the best bar tonight then, are you Goose?" Finn shouted up, "That's what comes of giving you a taste of the Big House life."

"Finn, the wife's here!" whispered The Goose. "Behave yourself tonight, won't you?"

"Don't I always?" said Finn, joining Keen and The Goose and walking up the steps past Dando with a cursory nod of his head. "Good night then gentlemen, you were just leaving, I hope?"

The Goose led them through to the crowded smoke-room, where a small, plump-faced woman in a grey coat was fishing into a large brown handbag to pay the barman.

"Mary Goose!" shouted Finn dashing foward to greet her with his hands outstretched. "My favourite Mrs. Muckie! How are you, Mary?"

The woman put both her arms round Finn's neck and kissed him noisily on the cheek. "Finn, you bugger, you haven't been round to see us."

"I've been held up a lot at the office," said Finn mincingly, "you know what it's like. Still buying the drinks I see?"

When she smiled he saw that the eyes were tired above the pale, puffy cheeks. "I buy them. He drinks them. We haven't changed."

"Except, Mary, that you look lovelier than ever, me darlin'. You'd be the belle of any Muckshifter's Ball."

"Get on with you, you smooth bastard," she said, as the large sharp-faced lady beside her, in a green coat with a fox-fur collar, sniffed pointedly.

"Who's your wee friend?" asked Finn, nodding towards the woman.

Mary Canavan put her hand to her lips. "Here while I tell you," she said in a low voice, beckoning him away from the counter. "That's Brigadier Gillibrand's wife. They own most of this place."

"So she's the last of the Hesters, eh?" said Finn, tugging the fringe of his blond hair as the woman glared at him.

"Dando was in, Finn."

"I met him."

"That feller! The personality oozes out of him like spit!"

"Well look, Mary," said Finn ushering her to a seat against the far wall. "Sit yourself down here and get these into you. I'll buy you another when I see your tongue sag."

"I've just had one drink bought for me. By a stranger."

"Well the next one will be a bit special then," he said gently. "It'll be from a friend."

When Finn arrived back at the low, wood-panelled bar he saw that a thin, ferrety man had joined Keen and The Goose and was holding out a glass of beer towards him.

"Christ, it's the Cock Lodger! I thought you only came out nights in the middle of the month."

"I thought you could use this, Finn," said the ferrety man. "We shifted some stuff today!"

"What was the final?"

"4,500 ton."

"That's good," said Finn gulping from the glass. "We'll shift some more if you stick around."

"Finn, lad?"

The Irishman looked round and saw The Goose at his shoulder. "Finn, I just wanted to have a wee word with you about the big feller," said The Goose, lurching slightly as he spoke. "You see, I heard a bit of what was going on out there. With Dando."

Finn saw that the big muckshifter's eyes were already glazed. "That was nothing, Goose," he said. "Dando and me were always ones for the warm words."

"Finn? Now Finn?" he muttered as he shuffled forward, his glass shaking in his hand. "Watch that feller will you? You're treating him as the Dando you knew before you went up to the Jocks. You still seem to think he's just a musclebound tearaway. But he's more than that now Finn. He held Gus Bain together on the last site, almost on his own. He rates now, Finn. Up there I mean. He's got notions. Don't underestimate him."

The ganger's long hair bounced up from his ears as he shook his head vigorously. "You're wrong, Goose," he said. "Dando's going nowhere. He hasn't got the paper badges and that's what they look for these days."

"Not any more, Finn," insisted the big driver, clutching his arm. "It's the accountants that run the show now and they only want results. Dando served the last job up two months before time and they loved him for it. It's not Dando they want, it's his results. If the accountants thought they could get this dam built quicker, using a gang of monkeys, they'd do it."

Finn looked at him over the rim of his beer glass. "Sometimes Goose," he said, "I get the impression they are doing. Anyway let's get down to the serious stuff, like seeing how the Cock Lodger's making out with the widow woman. Are you there Cock?"

As he swung round, Finn's arm brushed across Mrs. Gillibrand's elbow, causing her to spill her drink down her black glove.

"I'm very sorry madam," he said trying to flick away the gin with his hand as she retreated.

"You clumsy little man!" she said looking down at her glove.

Finn addressed her with a gleam in his eye. "Madam, clumsy I may be, but I can assure you that little I am not and I know that fellow isn't!"

"Glenys, we are leaving," said Mrs. Gillibrand, nudging the tall, bespectacled woman at her side. "As I was saying earlier, the whole neighbourhood is deteriorating!"

"They tell me," said Finn smiling freely, "that there's only one spot round here where the general tone of the region has actually gone up, and I'm living in it myself."

"Where is that?" asked Mrs. Gillibrand, deliberately skirting him to go to the door.

"Hesters Hall. Your place, madam," he said, returning her snort with a genteel bow. "I suppose having me up there almost makes me your lodger."

As the two women left, Keen came up to Finn's arm with two fresh pints in his hand. "They reckon her husband's the Chairman of the bench up at Haltbriggin," he said. "I should watch it Finn."

Finn sucked at the froth and looked at the glass appreciatively. "I'm glad to hear it," he said. "We're going to need all the good men we can get our hands on with all these mucky types flitting about sure."

"Finn, you haven't said much about Dando since . . . since that day?"

"I've been known to think of other pleasures."

"What I mean is, there's more to it than what you told me, wasn't there?" asked the boy.

The Irishman nodded. "That's happened too."

"What really went on between you two?" asked Keen.

"Just a minute," said Finn looking back as he listened to The Goose's voice bellowing angrily at the far side of the bar.

"I buy the drinks here!" Goose was shouting to a strapping six foot two inch navvy on a tightly filled donkey jacket. "When I want my wife to drink, I buy it! Not you! Not him! Not even the bloody barman! I buy it, understand?"

When Finn reached him the veins in the muckshifter's scrawny neck were jutting out like purple ropes.

"What's the trouble Goose?" he asked quietly.

"It's this big, shittin' lummox. Fancying himself as a bit of a

Romeo, sending drinks over to my wife behind my back, he was!"

Finn looked at the man slowly. "You're from Dolan's, aren't you. On the new road contract?"

"Yeah!"

"I've seen you. Are you in charity work too?"

The man held up his hand protestingly. "Look there was nothing intended, mate," he said. "She just looked neglected, that's all."

The Goose raised his fist up to his shoulder threateningly. "If there's any neglecting to be done here I'll do it," he said slurring his words. "I don't need you."

Finn grasped The Goose's arm, forcing it easily down to his side. "He's O.K., Goose, leave the feller alone."

He winked at the man in the donkey jacket and nudged his own fist playfully into The Goose's bulging stomach. "You should be ashamed of yourself, thinking of fightin' at your age. See you."

When he got back Keen had another pint waiting for him. "You're not soup mixing me are you?" he said. "If you're aiming at loosening my tongue it'll take more than a cableman's pay packet."

"No it's just that I've heard some of the other fellows yapping," said Keen, "And I wondered what the real. . . ."

"You wondered what the truth was, did you boy? All right, I'll tell you."

A look of disbelief came over the boy's face. "You will?"

"Well if I don't there's plenty of fellows round here will, and you'll get so many versions about Dando and me they'll split your mind. Here, come and take the weight off your legs."

They walked over to a small circular copper-topped table and as Keen sat down, Finn placed his chair opposite the boy and sat facing him. "You see the real daft end of the business happened at Warchester, in '74," he said. "We were on this straightforward by-pass contract and I was the general foreman."

"You were G.F., Finn?" asked Keen, staring up at him.

"Does it surprise you that much? If it does I'll stun you by telling you I got my first hat with Clandy's when I was 26, and that's a few years back. Anyway it was at Warchester I made the big mistake of going into business on my own account. What happened was that one of my four gangers came across some four-inch copper cable left by the Electricity Board. There was a good three miles of it along the line of the new road. Now when this sort of thing happens you're supposed to go running with your hand up to the Shout and say 'Please sir this must be yours.' In fact the surveyors had missed the wire when they put a price on the contract and nobody would have been any the wiser if we'd hived it off, sold it for scrap and shared the bunce. Which we did, most of it."

"You stole it then?" said Keen.

Finn gave him an old-fashioned look, "You can take your pick, son. It was either stealing something from someone who didn't know he owned it or it was private enterprise. But either way they did for it, and the three other gangers, Bawn, Liam the Liar and a fellow called O'Keefe."

Keen gave him a searching look. "Where does Dando come into all this, then?"

Finn pulled out a cigarette from the packet he was holding on the table, lit it and blew smoke out towards the crowded bar. "He was the fourth," he said.

"Well if Dando was one of your gangers, how come he wasn't done with you?"

"Because he was the only one who wasn't in on the deal. He was too cocky and amibitious. In his own mind he was G.F. about 15 years before anyone asked him. A couple of the others thought if he knew about it he might be the sort to go screaming to the management. So we didn't cut him in. He found out about it, and next thing he was off in his company car, driving up to Gus's family seat at Edinburgh, spilling the whole beans."

"Did they sack you, then, Finn?"

Rafferty pulled hard on his cigarette before stubbing it and putting it in the ashtray. "No son, they never sack you at Clandy's. They're subtler than that. They're a bit like the Hindoos. If they don't rate what you've done in this life they send you back as a mule or a flea or something. And if you make a reasonable flea they let you start climbing up the whole range of muckshifting evolution until they finally let you have a crack at being a man again. In our case they put a pin in the map and sent us up to the northernmost open-cast coal site they could find. Baldock. They call it the muckshifter's Siberia. Four years in the freeze-box working your bollocks off 12 hours a day like mechanical coalmen. The Hindoos must have had us marked down for polecats."

"Did anything happen to Dando, then?"

Finn drained his pint and slowly placed the empty glass on the table before looking at the boy. "Indeed it did," he said. "He went out and bought himself a pair of sunglasses."

A sudden shouting over to their right made both men look up.

"Don't touch me. I'll kill him, Christ if I won't! No bastard does that to me and gets away with it! Keep back there!"

Across the room Finn could see The Goose squaring up to the big Dolan's man again. Finn had almost reached him when The Goose wrenched himself free of The Cock Lodger and staggered forward again. His left arm was pawing the air as if measuring the distance to the tall man's chin. The intended blow caught Finn full on the shoulder as The Goose over-balanced and fell into his arms.

"Keep out of it, Finn!" warned The Goose, the two men's faces barely an inch apart. "So help me, I'll maim the bugger!"

"You're being a fool, Goose," murmured Finn. "Now get still

and give your head a chance. Tell me this, how long have you known Mary?"

For a moment he felt the dozer driver's body go limp in his arms but it was only for a few seconds. The next moment The Goose had him by the shirt neck, trying to push him aside as he took another swipe with his fist.

"I'll finish this," he shouted. "There's only one pair of balls goes up my stairs."

"How long, Goose?" demanded Finn, shaking the struggling Irishman by the shoulders. "How long have you known Mary?"

"What's that?" said Goose huskily, "Twenty-six years. A long time, a long time. Too long to have a young ruttin' blow-in like him feeling for her."

Finn held him back firmly. "And haven't you learned enough about her in that time to know she's not the type to go giving the glad eye round town?"

Over his shoulder Finn could see the other man watching them. He was standing perfectly still with a faint suggestion of a smile on his lips.

"I've been eyeing him up, Goose," said Finn hoarsely. "He hasn't put a wrong step to her all night."

The Goose dropped his head on his chest as though he was thinking the words over, but suddenly he hurled Finn aside with a force that almost took the ganger off his feet.

The next moment he came forward like an enraged bull, raking out his fists as Finn fought to control him. "Bast . . ard!"

Throwing his body between Goose and the stranger Finn caught a brief glimpse of Mary Goose in the seats behind them holding her hands against her face, and in front of her the calm, smiling face of the Dolan's man. . . .

The blow landed so quickly that no one in the crowded bar had time to see it.

It caught The Goose full on the point of the jaw, travelling up a mere ten inches from Finn's fist, concealed between the open flaps of his jacket.

Even before the big dozer driver slumped forward Finn had caught him, holding his sagging head against his shoulder as he glared at the inquiring faces around them.

"It's all right," he said clamly. "Nothing to worry about. I think the heat must have caught up with him. . . ."

When the Goose opened his eyes he was lying in bed propped against three pillows in the small back bedroom of their home.

He lifted his hand to press down the damp grey strands of hair down over his balding head before finally focussing his eyes on Finn and Mary standing beside the bed.

"Are you there, Finn?" he croaked.

"He's the only reason you're here!" snapped Mary.

The Goose looked up as though noticing her for the first time. He saw that her face was tight and drawn. "Are you all right, then, Mary?"

"Jesus," said Mary, fingering her forehead. "He tries to take on half the town and he asks me if I'm all right."

Finn pulled the blue eiderdown higher up the bed. "You just got a bit mixed up and tired, Goose, that's all."

The Goose screwed up his eyes. "What did I do, then, Finn?"

"Christ what did he do?" said Mary waving her arms impatiently. "You did what you've always done, Goose Canavan. You had your fists up for me again. Ever since I've known you, every pissing site we've been on, you've always tried to defend me with your fists. You've always taken the easy way out."

Finn looked at her and smiled. "Fists aren't always the easy way, Mary," he said. "It depends who's on the end of the other pair."

"It's not just the fighting, it's just that it seems to be the only way he knows to settle an argument. He goes at it like a baitin' bear. There are some men, Goose Canavan, you know, that actually talk their way out of trouble. You never learned, you skite! There's more to being a man than showing your knuckles. But you? No. You always play the big Mick, fighting for me with your fists!"

Finn took her arm gently. "Mary, you go down and make a nice warm cup of tea, hey. I think sleeping's the only way of settling his present problems."

When Finn came back down the stairs Mary Goose was standing in front of a green-painted radiator on the far side of the long, narrow through lounge. There was a print of 'The Chinese Girl' on the green-painted wall above her. She had taken her coat off and was wearing a pair of white slacks which fastened badly at the front, and she was noticeably breathing in to conceal a stomach which treatened to burst out of her white cotton blouse.

"You're a good friend, Finn," she said as he came into the room. "To Goose I mean. I'm sorry about what happened up there. Some days I don't care if the house flies out the window."

Finn grinned broadly. "When you keep a man from his fighting you need to be a good friend."

"But you talked him out of it,"

"Let's say I finally persuaded him."

"But you stopped the fighting?"

Finn picked up a brown mug from the wooden tray on the table. "Mary, I didn't stop him because he was going to fight," he said, "I stopped him because he was going to lose. Anyway he's up there snorin' like a hog now."

"He always snores like a hog."

Finn looked up from the mug. "He's a right to be knackered with all the shifting he does."

As the light from the single grey bowl lamp hanging from the ceiling cast deep grey shadows down the woman's cheeks he could see how strained she looked. "But not every night, Finn," she said, "if you see what I mean."

"It's a job that catches up with the bones quick sometimes."

"He's let himself go a lot. Since Warchester you know."

"He's carrying a lot of weight sure, specially in the front."

Mary Goose put her own mug down on the table and walked across to him. "I wouldn't know, Finn," she said. "This last year or two I've lain in bed and seen more backs than the 8th Army going through Italy. Don't worry, all of them were his."

When Finn did not reply she put her hand out and slowly pressed it against the front of Finn's blue denim shirt before looking up at him with a nervous smile.

"You've kept your shape well, Finn."

He grinned at her. "They say you can't fatten a whippet."

Taking her hand away she gave him a light jab in the stomach. "You're some whippet, Finn," she said. "I'm one to talk. A plain, old, middle-aged biddy gettin' plainer and older by the week and still serving up the murphies."

"You still have the apples there, Mary. In your cheeks. My mother had red cheeks till she was past sixty. They used to say she painted but she didn't."

"Oh, Finn," she said, slowly shaking her head. "That doesn't really help."

He reached out and touched her hair, realising for the first time how grey it had become since the Christmas she shared with the Cut Six gang up at Hagen's place in the Silent Valley. That night she had hidden the Cut's Christmas bonuses up her knickers, daring the fellers to hunt the bunce.

Then she had run, shrieking through the whole house, her face teasing and pretty as a schoolgirl's. It had been he who finally caught up with her in the kitchen, lifting her up by the ankles, squirming and shaking like an upturned doll. He remembered how she had suddenly gone still, looking up at him wistfully as he gazed at her firm young body splayed beneath him like the twigs of a spring sapling, and him with his head bursting with a strange new power. He had laughed then. The others had joined in and she, without smiling, had wriggled again, just enough to send the bulging packet sliding down from under the white elastic to a great roar of welcome.

"There's nothing a fine, bonny woman like yourself can't do, Mary," he said.

"Except ask, hey Finn?" she said, looking up at him selfconsciously. "You know, don't you, Rafferty, you bugger? I've always felt for you."

"I know you have, Mary," said Finn seriously. "We've never been short of the liking for each other."

"And we've never gone further?" she said, her lips looking for a moment as though they were about to smile, but the corners never quite lifted.

Finn took her shoulders in his hands. "I've been a long way myself, Mary," he said. "We were so far up the Highlands the fellers were courting reindeer some nights because the girls were too cold to come out. It's been a long time since I was this close to a woman. But I was always too close to you, and to Goose, for . . . anything else. Do you understand me, Mary?"

As she nodded he saw that her eyes were filling with tears as she looked away. Before he could say another word she turned back to him, lifting her head so high she seemed to have grown physically. She sniffed softly. "If you kiss me on the cheek and pat my shoulder I'll cripple you, Finn Rafferty! As sure as God I will!"

Finn bent down and took her face between his hands. "Now then Mary Goose," he murmured gently, "whatever made you think I'd want to kiss a good-looking woman like you on the cheek?"

He kissed her firmly on the mouth, feeling only the warm dampness of her crying as the plump wet cheeks pressed against his own.

Almost immediately she walked quickly back towards the Chinese Girl on the far wall. "Some people say it's all the fault of the central heating," she said airily, with her back to him.

"How do you mean?" he asked.

She turned to face him. "Well they say that when they took away the fireplaces we all got a bit mixed up. We needed a fire, they reckon, to give us something to look at, a sort of focal point. They say the telly's not a substitute because it changes too much, and nobody sits at home looking at a gas radiator."

Finn traced a pattern with his shoe in the red turkey carpet at his feet. "You've missed the old hearth, then, Mary?"

She smiled at him. "I'm not even sure it was the fire they meant," she said. "Perhaps all that most of us miss is having something which is always there and sort of burning for you without having to put a shilling in it."

He looked at her uncomfortably, as though he was inwardly searching for the right words. Finally he said "Are you sure you'll be all right, Mary?"

"I'll live, Finn, We'll all live, I suppose."

"I'll be going now."

As he walked towards the door he heard her taking several steps after him before calling him back.

"Finn?"

"Hello?" he said, turning.

"Thank you."

He nodded, staring at her for a few moments before he turned and walked out, closing the door quietly behind him.

Brown Windsor finished smoothing the last corner of the freshly filled concrete base and wiped his hands down his jeans. As he looked down, the baked-bean tin plopped almost silently onto the tacky surface.

For more than three hours he had been preparing the 10-foot square frame beside the storage sheds at Baskey's before the ready mixed concrete was poured into it to form the base of the new generator house. Despite his brown, almost black, boot-polish skin and the fact that he had never set foot in Ireland, Windsor was 'a Keady man' from Armagh.

It was a decision he had made swiftly two years earlier while standing in the work queue at a Clandy power station contract just outside Southampton where McNicolas was the Shout.

McNicholas was known to rate Keady men as the best muckshifters in the business. Windsor had noticed that all the men who'd been handed the pencil and invited to sign their names had first called out "Keady", while the others had been shunted over to a waiting group beside them.

When the West Indian's turn came, he too mumbled "Keady", answered "Patrick" when he was asked for his address since it was the only other word he heard in the queue, and so Brown, Windsor, from Patrick Street, Keady, joined the Clandy empire.

Clandy's had signed 64 Keady men before lunch that morning, some of them blacker and even more distant from the Celt than Windsor, who moved further north with each subsequent Clandy posting which took him further from Southampton and the boat to Kingston, Jamaica. He had never seriously regretted any of them.

Windsor rolled his eyes suspiciously, scanning the shed for a sight of the person who had thrown the tin, before deciding to make an attempt at retrieving it.

Perching precariously on the edge of the two-foot high wooden frame he pushed his fingers nearer and nearer to the tin until he finally managed to grasp hold of it.

Smiling at his success he tossed the can in the air, tried to catch it again and as he did so, caught his heel against the rim of the frame and fell back in a sitting position into the thick, tacky concrete.

"Piddock!" bawled a loud voice as Windsor sat in the deep, grey mush wondering what had gone wrong with the operation. He looked up and saw Finn Rafferty towering above him.

"Don't get up for me," said Finn as Brown Windsor attempted to rise uneasily. "Have you got your little book?"

The West Indian nodded, fumbled in his top pocket and produced an orange notebook and a pencil.

"Piddock," repeated Finn. "P.I.D.D.O.C.K. have you got it?"

"What's a piddock, boss?"

"You're a piddock, Windsor," said Finn. "Instant English lesson

No. One. A piddock is a little rock-borer who works slowly and occasionally attacks concrete and cement. Have you got that one down?"

Windsor nodded again, sucking his pencil before pulling a face and spitting out a stream of liquid concrete from his mouth.

"Right, the next one is savvy," said Finn, "but you won't have time to get that one down."

"Why's that boss?"

"Because savvy is what makes someone who finds himself sitting arse-deep in concrete when the Shout's on his way, suddenly scarper to the bog, Sunshine. Pronto."

There was a loud sucking noise as Brown Windsor swiftly rose up from the concrete lake and dashed towards the huts, leaving a gummy, grey trail behind him.

Finn grinned as he watched him go, before heading off rapidly towards the line of yellow dozers and dump trucks beneath the quarry face.

"Right get a move on then, my lovely muckies!" he yelled. "Shine for the Sun Man. I want to see your backs shifting so fast you'll be glowing like little sunbeams."

Bain's white Austin Princess was already moving down the gravel path from the coal road into the quarry. As it pulled up beside him Rafferty could see the dents and dirt stains on both wings brought about by heavy and constant use on the site.

Bain stepped out placing his yellow helmet on his head as he looked up at the tall ganger. "Good morning . . . er . . .?"

"Rafferty sir."

"Ah yes," remembered Bain. "That's right. Rafferty from up there." Bain scratched the side of his cheek. "Yes well, how are you and your lads finding things down here then?"

Finn sucked his teeth noisily. "Down here? Warmer, I'd say. Now we're a bit closer to the hearth."

"What are the production levels like?"

"Not bad," said Finn. "It's heaping up by the ton."

"Eight," yelled a Cockney voice from the bushes above the store huts.

Both Finn and Bain looked up just in time to see Dick Dancer's back disappearing over the rise.

"What's that all about?" asked Bain, looking at Rafferty.

"Eight more . . . er . . . loads sir," he said quickly. "Loads. He's the tally man."

"Ten," shouted a new voice up on the rise as both men glanced up again.

As Rafferty waved back in acknowledgement, Bain saw the big Irishman's face seemed to be colouring.

"What do these figures mean, Rafferty?"

"Oh, it's the pay tally, dolorite loads per minute." He looked anxiously towards the rise as the Cock Lodger showed his head. "Another two, Finn!"

"Can you hear some sort of shooting going on?" asked Bain, noticing that Rafferty appeared to be shooing the man away, rather than waving to him.

"Shooting sir?" said Finn, raising his eyebrows innocently. "Oh that. No, they're just testing the new detonators for the next blast, I shouldn't wonder."

Satisfied with the ganger's reply, Bain looked across at the quarry face. "Well, we look as if we're going to find enough dolorite on site for our needs, I believe then, Rafferty?"

Finn took his eyes from the bushes for a brief moment. "Yes, we hit a decent dyke," he said, "and even if this one runs out there's a good chance it will continue into the forest the other side of the coal road."

"Good," said Bain. "Unfortunately it's the white sandstone we really need in massive quantities, for Liederman's facing. But I hear you've already put some ideas to Curran's geology boys?"

"Fourteen," shouted Cock Lodger from the brow of the hill.

"That's right," agreed Finn, waving Lodger down. "I've been putting out some feelers up the valley and I think you'll find all the stone we'll need."

Bain smiled. "I thought water-tracking was your forte, Rafferty. They tell me you're pretty useful with the old divining rods."

Rafferty shrugged his shoulders. "I don't think it matters what you're looking for, if you have the feel for what you want you'll find it."

The shiny, black hair of Dick Dancer appeared again up on the slope as Finn looked across at Bain, breathing deeply with relief when he saw the project manager had not spotted him. Bain had his back to him and was walking over to a Land Rover, from which Griff Dando had just stepped, when Finn made his move.

He walked rapidly over to the huts and climbed the slope above them. Descending quickly into the bushes he found Dancer waiting for him. There was a double barrelled shotgun pointing down from his hands.

"There you are," said Dancer with a wide smile on his face. "Fourteen of them."

Finn looked behind the bush where Dancer was standing and saw fourteen dead rabbits laid out in a line on the grass.

"Who the hell was supposed to be on watch for the Sun Man?" demanded Finn, walking down a line of grinning hunters, which included Cock Lodger, Liam The Liar and Tucky Burke.

"Bleedin' hell, was that him?" asked Dancer. "I didn't recognise the suit. No we thought you were going to give us the nod when he came around."

"I was trying to, you great eejits. You're bum scouts, all of you," he snarled, almost immediately adding a wink as he pressed a thumb into the ribs of one of the rabbits on the ground. "But damned good shots. They'll come in handy up at Hesters."

As he bounded down the slope and back between the huts to return to Bain and Dando, he was smiling broadly to himself.

"Fourteen eh," he muttered. "Not bad."

"Fifteen!"

He turned to see Keen grinning gormlessly at him with a large, dead hare dangling from his outstretched arm.

"Here Finn!"

"Jesus quick give it to me!" whispered Finn, glancing down to see if Bain and Dando had noticed.

They were already walking towards him as he put the hare behind his back, holding it tightly in both hands.

"Don't go now," he muttered to Keen through the side of his mouth. "I might need you."

"Ah Rafferty," said Bain, speaking even before he had stopped, "Did you get the final figure, then?"

"Yes sir," said Finn. "Four . . . no fifteen sir."

"Good going Rafferty," said Bain beaming.

Finn shot a quick glance over to Dando, wondering if he was about to say something but the general foreman merely gave him a puzzled look.

"Thank you sir," said Finn, feeling the hare's head nudging against the back of his thighs.

"Er Rafferty?" said Bain, "I was just talking to Griff here about the fact that the first of the new crushers is ready and we still have the position of quarrymaster to fill. You knew that did you?"

"Yes sir," said Rafferty clinging tightly to the hare's ears.

"Yes well now, Griff Dando doesn't know this yet, because we decided there were no obvious names to put foward. But in view of the evident keenness and thought you're putting into this operation and taking into account your private prospecting for stone, I've decided to offer it to you."

"To him?" said Dando scowling at the Irishman.

"To me?" said Finn wondering if he had heard the project manager correctly.

Bain nodded in agreement. "Well, we'll see how it goes then. What do you say Rafferty? Will you take the job?"

For a moment Rafferty was silent as he fiddled thoughtfully with the hare's ears behind his back. Finally he gulped as he looked back at Bain. "On one condition sir," he said.

Bain stared at him blankly. "What condition do you have in mind?"

"Only that I choose my own team."

Before Dando could open his mouth Bain was ahead of him. "All right, fair enough," he said. "You've got to work with them. Oh and Rafferty, we'll say no more about . . . er . . . where was that place?"

"Warchester," said Finn and Dando simultaneously as they glared at each other.

"Warchester, yes," said Bain. "Except of course, to say that you now appear to be on your way up again, Rafferty. Just how far depends on yourself. The future's in your own hands."

"Yes sir," said Rafferty, hoisting up the long, soft ears behind his back and gently nodding the hare's head as his face presented a grateful smile to the departing Bain and Dando.

"Right, Circus," said Finn to the boy. "Now get behind me, shove this fellow up your jumper and scarper while I see the Sun Man off the premises."

Relieved of the hare at last, Finn walked briskly after the two men, catching them just as Bain was getting into his white Princess.

"I've got a bit of business in Haltbriggin, Griff," Bain was saying. "Now Caswell's on his way back from London and Cline's with the N.W.B. in Hexham, so look after the shop while I'm away, old boy, will you?"

Dando nodded. Bain got into his car and after starting it, wound down the window. "I take it we'll be seeing you at the George tonight Griff?" he asked. "Just to wave the old flag a bit, eh?"

"I'll be there," said Dando.

"What was that about?" asked Finn as Bain's car moved off.

"We're throwing a bun fight for the local bigwigs," said Dando, removing his helmet. "It's hardly your scene."

"Monkey-suit job is it?"

"Right."

Dando was about to move away when Finn saw his eyes narrow as he slowly looked at him with a thin smile on his lips. "Perhaps you should be there Rafferty?" he said. "Someone at the board meeting suggested we ought to have one of the muckies from the Hall there to show the locals."

"On display, you mean?"

"See it which way you want to," said Dando tersely "Anyway you've just been elected. Be there seven thirty O.K.?"

Finn grinned and shrugged his shoulders. "You never cease to amaze me," he said.

"What's that?" said Dando.

"All the things you do for me boyo," said Finn, winking at him.

"Griff! Griff!!"

Both men turned to see Jo Tiffin running towards them leaving the door of her safari wagon swinging open behind her.

"Come quickly Griff!" she yelled as she came up to them. "There's been a big 'un. An earthslide. A lad's under it. Quick Griff, it's awful!"

Dando grabbed her by the shoulders and shook her violently.

"Now calm down! Calm down! Where is it girl?"

"A mile up the coal road. Near the culvert. Hurry Griff please."

"I'll give you a hand," said Finn, moving towards Dando's Land Rover.

"That won't be necessary," said Dando. "I'll handle it."

"All right, I'll give you a hand," said Finn catching hold of Jo Tiffin's arm as they both ran to the waiting safari.

Dando had been at the scene only a minute before Jo Tiffin halted the yellow safari beside the general foreman's Land Rover.

As he sprang out of the passenger seat Finn could see the overturned dozer lying with its twisted blade jutting up between the tracks. Behind the vehicle was a wall of fresh earth spilling down from the coal road where two muckshifters had been digging a tunnel into the mound with their shovels. Dando was standing beside them.

"Who is he?" shouted Finn.

"He was Carter," said Dando, looking towards the diggers.

"The feller's not gone yet," said Finn, running up to the mouth of the tunnel and peering anxiously inside.

"There's nothing you can do, Rafferty," said Dando flatly "He's been under there more than twenty minutes."

"Here give me that," barked Finn to one of the two muckshifters. He snatched the man's shovel from him and began taking great lunges into the soft earth, sending the soil flying back in a flurry behind him.

"It's no use Rafferty," said Dando. "You'll split him anyway if you go in mad-headed."

Without reducing his pace, Finn called back to the G.F. "Better losing a piece than the whole muckie."

He had advanced more than four feet down the tunnel when his spade suddenly struck into something hard. Scraping the soil away he uncovered part of a blue trouser leg. It had a long, bright red stain where his shovel had sliced into the man's leg.

"I've got him," he yelled back, throwing his shovel away and diving his bare hands into the soil around the man's body. "Here, help me get him out!"

Finn had almost freed the whole body when Dando crawled up behind him. Almost immediately the Irishman could feel the unstable earth above him begin to shudder.

"I'm here Rafferty," grunted Dando on his knees. "Now look, you keep this thing held up for a minute while I get him clear."

Rafferty pressed his back against the crumbling roof, forming an arch as Dando reached for the muckshifter's feet and dragging him backwards towards the light. Then slowly Finn began edging his own way to the mouth of the tunnel, which was rapidly collapsing behind him. When he was three feet away from the entrance he suddenly hurled himself out, diving through as the roof of the tunnel crashed down behind him.

When Finn picked himself up Dando was already carrying the muckshifter's body out to the men waiting below.

The general foreman laid Carter out in front of the gang and turned to face them. "Well he's out but he's a gonner" he said.

"Not yet he isn't!" said Finn, launching himself at the boy's body and landing on his knees beside Carter's head.

"Of course he's dead," said Dando glancing down at him. "Look at his mouth. He's enough earth in there to grow spuds."

Rafferty already had his fingers in the boy's mouth, scooping the soil away frantically, before turning the head on its side to reach even further into Carter's throat.

Ripping the thin shirt apart, he listened for Carter's heart before turning him on his stomach and pummelling the wet, mud-caked back with his fists.

"It's no use," said Dando.

"It must be!" shouted Finn, feverishly hammering between the jutting shoulder blades. "He's only eighteen!"

He rolled the body over again and started thrusting his hands up from Carter's belly, spreading black stains across the boy's hairless chest.

"He's dead, Rafferty," said Dando.

"Come on Carter! Come on!" yelled Finn. With a last despairing groan he grabbed the limp head and plunged his lips over the boy's mouth, sucking and blowing into the unresponsive lungs.

The men watched him writhing over the limp shape beneath him for several minutes, before he finally lifted his head from the boy's face and sat back on his knees, staring at the lifeless body on the ground.

"Finn?"

He felt Jo Tiffin's hand on his shoulder as she spoke but he didn't look round.

"Hello," he said.

She took his arm as he slowly got up before they walked back past Dando and the silent men, to where the yellow safari was waiting.

Bautista backed through the tall swing doors of the Gladstone Suite of The George, clutching his silver drinks tray protectively against his white linen jacket as the noise of the room hit him.

He was a small, sad-faced man already balding between the two shiny slabs of black hair he had neatly plastered back on either side of his centre parting. All the men in the pale, lime-panelled room, and most of the women too, were taller than him and for more than an hour they had him darting dutifully between the Gladstone and the lounge bar as he fuelled their party talk.

Turning to face them yet again he began apprehensively threading his way through the groups of guests until he reached Bob Liederman, who was deep in conversation near the French window.

"I remember the first dam I ever designed," the lean, white-suited American was saying in a loud voice. "I was seventeen at the time. It was a bath plug compared with this one, of course. It was in Mexico, part of a small-town irrigation scheme to help them grow more blackeyed peas or some crap. Anyway, these goddam Mexies. . . ."

He broke off, noticing Bautista hovering beside him. "You're not a Mexie, Bautista, are you?"

"No sir, I'm Spanish."

"Close enough!" snapped Liederman. "Anyhow, these Mexies just sat down one morning and demanded a heat hour. Nothing to do with food breaks mind you. They just wanted to sit on their asses and grow fat on full pay. They figured that noon to 1 p.m. was for eating and one to two was for sleeping because it was too bloody hot to work. Anyway we said 'No way' and the job stopped. . . . What have you got there Bautista?"

Liederman picked up one of the glasses on the waiter's tray and tossed his head approvingly at the dark brown liquor topped with a thick layer of cream.

"Ah now, Brandy Alexander, me," he said, handing another glass to the tall, red-faced man beside him, "Scotch and water, you, Super. Now where was I? Yes, well they asked me what the heck they could do about it. I was an old seventeen at the time. So I said that if the Mexies were going to rob us of two hours sunlight a day, we ought to buy us our own sun, and by jiminy we did. We imported two dozen of the biggest arc lamps you ever saw and when the sun ran out around seven we switched on ours and made 'em keep right on out there, scratching to make up for the lost time. We finished that one three weeks ahead of schedule."

Liederman lowered his glass as a tall, striking woman broke away from the group gathered around Sir William Clandy and Fergus Bain, in front of the wide stone fireplace, and began walking towards him.

Mallowry Bain was wearing a long, low-cut scarlet dress which seemed to emphasize the smooth whiteness of her bare shoulders. As she crossed over the thick turkey carpet, tossing her long black hair behind her and glancing confidently at the other guests, Liederman caught a glimpse of the single white diamond suspended on a fine silver chain between the full mounds of her breasts. Below the full flounce of her red dress he could see she was wearing no shoes.

"May I borrow Bautista from you for a moment?" she asked even before she had reached him, smiling through her wide, slightly parted lips.

"Hey," said Liederman putting on a hurt face. "What has Bautista got that I haven't?"

"An ear, Mr. Liederman?" she suggested mockingly.

Liederman looked down at the waiter's tray. "Well just hang on there before you take him. Soils, sorry I forgot you for a moment." He took the glass of gin from the silver tray and handed it to Curran, who looked as if he had slept the night in his dinner jacket.

"Yours is the lager, John, I guess," he said, passing the glass to Cline, before finally turning to Mallowry. "He's all yours now Mallowry. We've cleaned him out."

Mallowry Bain smiled and led the waiter to the low, raised stage beyond the French window.

"Now Bautista, it's your ear for music that's concerning me," she said, bending over him and talking to the small, round bald patch on the crown of his head before realising he was staring into her breasts.

"Look I'm here," she said firmly, lifting his chin up to her face. "Now this music, I'm sure you're going to tell me he's probably the most famous classical guitarist in the whole of Spain with an unpronouncable name like. . . ."

"John Williams," said Bautista, nodding enthusiastically.

"Yes well it's very nice Bautista, except that he only seems to know Aranhuez. Put on a fresh tape, there's a love, something a bit more beaty. It'll probably take a lot to get the blood surging back in some of these cheeks but at least let's try."

Mallowry watched as the tiny Spaniard dropped to his knees and started sifting among the cassettes in the plastic box beneath the tape recorder. Then suddenly, as though she was becoming bored, she threw out her arms and began swaying gently to the music, closing her eyes with a dreamy, ecstatic look spreading over her beautiful face.

"Is this a private dance or can anyone join in?"

She opened her eyes and turned to see Griff Dando standing grinning at her. He had a glass in his hand.

"Aren't you supposed to be circulating with the locals?" she asked unsmiling.

"But you're going to be a local yourself, darling, aren't you?" said Dando. "Now you've moved into the Grange we'll be almost neighbours."

She gave him an exaggerated smile. "Mr. Dando, one can be a local without necessarily being a neighbour."

"Where have you been Mallowry? I've missed you."

"You missed me a long time ago Dando. Anyway I've been Down Under."

"Muff diving?"

"Pig," she said, stretching her lips into a perfect smile as the Rev. James Churnside passed her with a beneficent nod. "I've been doing Australia, if you must know," she said, turning back to the general foreman.

Dando raised his glass to his lips. "I'm sure Australia loved every minute of it," he said, spreading his huge hand over her forearm. "However, now you're here you'll be easy to be neighbourly to, again."

She glared down at his hand until he took it away, "Dando, you talk to women like you build your motorways. Straight, flat and obvious."

"Oh but you're one contract behind," said Dando. "We're dam-builders now, remember? Big league. Best in Europe they say, if they cut out a few of the trimmings."

"And I suppose you're going to show them how to build dams too?"

"If they really want the best of course I can show them. I could even show you."

"But you have, darling, remember?"

Dando scowled, almost biting the drink from his glass. "Yes, I was pretty bad I suppose."

Mallowry eyed him coolly, "Mr. Dando, as I recall, I didn't say you were bad. I merely said you were quick. But, of course, in bed the quick and the dead are the same."

She offered him her arm as the wilting Aranhuez switched to Tijuana beneath Bautista's nimble fingers. "Are you coming?"

He followed her without a word, to the largest group in front of the pine log fire where Mallowry pushed into a space between her husband and the Clandy chairman. "Gus, darling, your Mr. Dando's arrived all eager to tell you how to build your dam, isn't that kind of him?"

"Bring him on! He can tell me too!" said Caswell loudly, before joining in the forced laughter of the guests.

Bain transferred his champagne glass to his left hand and pulled the glowering Welshman into the circle.

"This is Griff Dando everybody," he said, looking round the group, "He's our G.F., our sort of resident Mr. Fixit. He's the, er, kind of adhesive in the middle of the Clandy team, he keeps the body and the soul together so to speak, don't you, Dando? No offence to you, Vicar, of course," he quickly added, smiling at the balding vicar of St. Cuthbert's, Todholes, "The Rev. Churnside, Mr. Dando."

Dando accepted the vicar's outstretched hand, smiling at him with clenched teeth which quickly changed to the direction of Amy Churnside, the vicar's wife, who stared up at him, open mouthed, as if overawed by the foreman's size.

"And after Mrs. Churnside we have the Brigadier, Brigadier Gillibrand, whose hand we shake extra warmly, since most of the floor of the raintub we're building belongs to him, isn't that so

Brigadier?" said Bain, starting to laugh until he saw that Gillibrand's face was quite unmoved.

Dando found himself staring into the red, blotchy features of a thin, angular man with a white stiff brush moustache who appeared to be examining him rather than meeting him.

"And Mrs. Gillibrand," said Bain nudging him towards the severe-faced woman who had a small spaniel dog tugging at the high lace ruffle round the neck of her blue taffeta eveing dress.

Bain moved Dando on towards the tall, heavily-built police superintendent who had earlier been listening to Liederman. "Someone your own size here, Dando," he said, "Police Superintendent Tyson of the Corbar and Langhope Constabulary, our local er . . . law."

The big foreman shook his hand and nodded to him before being whisked towards the superintendent's wife.

"And . . . er . . . Mrs. Tyson," said Bain, watching the two big men shake hands, "who er. . . ."

"Always ends up in the arms of the law," said Caswell, guffawing across the blank faces of the guests.

"Well Dando," said Bain, ignoring him. "You know everybody else? Sir William? Slasher? And of course, Vince Caswell."

Dando nodded to the other two briefly before walking across to the stocky, grey-haired Clandy chairman. "Sir William," he said, shaking his hand. "Are you well?"

Clandy pumped his hand enthusiastically. "Couldn't be better my boy," he said in a soft yet strong voice with only the slightest trace of an Irish accent.

Bain came between almost immediately. "There's just one thing Griff," he said. "If Sir William will permit me. Mustn't talk too much shop but I've heard you might be getting a verdict today on that new sandstone seam."

"I've got the geology boys on it right now," said Dando blandly. "They're ringing me here."

"What it is, Sir William," said Bain, turning to the Clandy chairman, "is this. Although there seems to be an average to good payload up at Baskey's, we're going to need that and more before this job's finished. And one of the muckies up there thinks he's found a new seam. It's that big, blond chap we were talking to this afternoon isn't it?"

"Rafferty," said Dando.

"Yes that's the man," said Bain turning to the guests. "You see, this chap Rafferty who's what?, just a ganger up at the quarry, has come up with a theory that Baskey's is just part of a bigger white sandstone seam which was split in two as a result of glacial action during the Ice Age. He believes that after Baskey's settled down the rest of the seam was carried by the ice flow along the valley bed and dumped there. He's even pin-pointed a place on the map where he says we'll find it. Anyway we'll know soon, apparently." He glanced quickly at his No. Two as the group went silent. "Caswell?"

"Well now Brigadier did you ever hear the one about the Irishman who wanted to take up water skiing?" said Caswell, rubbing his podgy hands together. "He's still looking for a lake with a slope. . . ."

Finn Rafferty opened the door of the Gladstone Suite and took three paces into the room before he stopped, glancing at the unconcerned faces of the guests as his jaw moved slowly up and down against the thick wad of chewing gum in his mouth. His hands were thrust deep into the pockets of his heavy brown overcoat which hung open at the front revealing the faded, badly-fitting dinner suit he was wearing.

"Can I take your coat sir?"

He looked to his left dropping his eyes as he spotted the little Spanish waiter who had crept up beside him.

"Do you have pass outs?" Finn asked.

"Pass out, sir?"

"Forget it."

He peeled off the coat and handed it to Bautista just as The Slasher and Latice Gillibrand came up to him.

"It doesn't have to be a special container," Mrs. Gillibrand was saying in a loud voice. "An ordinary soup bowl would do, it's just that the heat in here seems to be bothering him, his poor little tongue's nearly falling out of his head."

In his concern for the dog's welfare, The Slasher, never strong on his left side where he wore his eye patch, despite the rumour that he could see through it, almost collided with the big ganger.

"Oh it's you, Rafferty," he said lifting the eye patch slightly. "We've just been talking about you over there. Gus is making quite a celebrity out of you."

"I've seen this one before, haven't I?" said Latice Gillibrand, suddenly recognising Finn as she clutched the spaniel closer to her bosom.

"What is that?" said Finn.

"It's a dog, of course."

"What sort of dog?"

"It's a King Charles Cavalier."

And what do you call it?"

Latice Gillibrand patted the panting animal briskly on the head. "Rupert, don't we, darling?"

"Very royal," he said. "But I thought the Hesters reckoned to go in for bull mastiffs?"

Slasher tittered. "It's probably a good thing for you that you don't, Mrs. Gillibrand," he said. "It would lie a bit heavy on your, er, arm."

"And were you talking about me too, Mrs. Gillibrand?" asked Finn looking directly into her face, which had suddenly frosted over.

"Indeed I wasn't," she said. "Actually we were discussing Niagara Falls, where the Brigadier and I have just been on vacation. I suppose you've never been to Niagara Mr. er. . . ?"

"Rafferty," said Finn. "No, madam I haven't. I went to Fleetwood once but it was shut."

Latice Gillibrand sniffed. "I was just saying to Mr. Slasher here that apparently some people who go to see the falls become so mesmerised by all that water bubbling and foaming beneath them that they just sort of drop in. It's a sort of unconscious suicide, they say."

"I'm not surprised, considering some of the fancy prices these holiday places charge," said Finn casually.

"Come on Mr. – er – " said Mrs. Gillibrand, hoisting the dog closer to her neck. "All this talk of water, it's getting him anxious."

As the pair pushed past him heading for the kitchen, Finn saw Dando bearing down on him.

"God, Rafferty what have you come as?"

Finn looked down at the bulky serge jacket which was hanging from his shoulders like a well-used rug as it followed a straight line for a couple of feet before billowing out into wide black bell bottoms at his feet. He licked his fingers and rubbed them against the left lapel, where the suit's last tenant, Dick Dancer, had left egg stains from his brother's wedding.

"I'm wearing it for a friend," said Finn finally.

"He must be paying you."

"I was wondering. . . ."

"Rafferty, come and get yourself over to Gus Bain, if that thing will follow you. It seems he needs a flag-waver to impress the locals, and he thinks your rock find will do it."

"I've heard nothing yet."

"Nor've we. Pavey's ringing later."

As they walked towards the main group Dando looked across at him. "What were you wondering about just then?"

"I was wondering about your suit too." said Finn.

Dando glanced down briefly before glaring at him. "What do you mean?"

"I was wondering if they had them in men's?" said Finn.

"So he asked this Irish squaddie," Caswell was saying in a loud voice, " 'What's a Royal Enfield?' and the Irishman stuck his finger in his mouth, thought for a moment and said 'Is it the place where the Queen keeps her chickens?' "

Bain cut short the polite but lukewarm laughter of the guests by seizing hold of Rafferty as he approached and pulled him into the circle.

"Now here's the chappie I was telling you about," he said. "This is our man Rafferty. Let them have a good look at you then,

Rafferty."

Finn stood awkwardly in the middle of the group as their faces turned towards him. Bain drained his glass and pointed to the big ganger. "Now let's get this right, Rafferty. You're the man who believes there's more sandstone below Baskey's than we think we know about, aren't you?"

"That's close," said Rafferty.

"And you reckon we'll find it at a point along the route of this sort of glacial conveyor belt, do you?"

"You will," said Finn staring impassively into Bain's face. Bain smiled. "As you can see, Rafferty's the man with all the answers."

"Perhaps he can answer mine then," said Caswell.

"What's that?" asked Bain.

"Who's his tailor?" said Caswell, beaming as the guests in the group began to laugh.

Dando held up his hand to silence them. "Don't mock the workers, please. The construction industry's no different to the fashions industry. Everything comes round again in its turn. Perhaps, if you wait long enough, even Rafferty's suit?"

Bain joined in the second burst of laughter before raising his own hand. "Actually Griff's quite right you know. About fashions in building changing. We started with stone, at least our cavemen ancestors did; we moved on to wood, iron, steel, reinforced concrete, the lot, and now thanks to our American friend over there we are back to the age of stone again."

"With our own purpose-built stone-age man to go with it," smiled Dando, toasting Finn with his glass.

"No we mustn't embarrass Mr. Rafferty," said Bain, drawing the Irishman into the line of laughing guests beside him. "After all he's the man we've chosen to look after our Hadrian stone empire, isn't that right Griff?"

Dando smiled. "He's the man you've chosen, Gus," he said.

"Yes, well . . . good," said Bain. "Well I wonder where that waiter is?" He looked up as a large, broad-shouldered man joined the group. "Ah, here's Structures. Structures everybody, is the agent who looks after the building of everything except the dam. Our Mr. Robson, home-grown here in Northumbria. You wanted to meet Structures, didn't you, darling?" he said turning to Mallowry. "I sometimes think that if Mallowry was The Shout she'd pick the men by the pound."

Mallowry Bain accepted the massive agent's hand. "How do you do? Do you know, you even look like Structures?"

Caswell chuckled into his glass. "He looks like the tower of Pisa some nights."

"No what I mean is, he looks sort of, purpose-built, for the job," said Mallowry.

"Wimpey's did him," roared Caswell, looking round for some

response from the guests.

Mallowry smiled sympathetically at the embarrassed Robson. "I think that, even when you're all removed from your natural surroundings, it's possible to guess what you do. You're an easy one, vicar, even the way you're holding that plate gives you away. The Brigadier over there, well he could lead me into battle any time. No. Two looks like a No. Two and Mr. Rafferty here, you can tell he's in earth-moving because he's brought his work with him."

Catching hold of Rafferty's hand and stroking it teasingly she added "Here look . . . under his finger nails."

Finn drew his hand away quickly and stretched both hands out in front of him with the nails pointing upwards. "This, scarlet lady, is mud from a dead muckshifter's mouth!"

Bain was at the Irishman's side before he could say any more. "Yes it was damned unfortunate, that business, Rafferty," he mumbled. "I didn't want to say too much about it tonight, not with all this going on."

Suddenly aware that the guests were listening to him, Bain turned to them, "We had this . . . er . . . unfortunate spot of trouble at the site today. There was this earth batter just above the dam, it must have been packed solid for a thousand years and all of a sudden it sort of lurched into the valley and one of our dumper drivers was under it. Dead, I'm afraid."

Finn looked directly into Bain's eyes. "He had half the mountain in his mouth when we got him out."

Bain winced. "Yes, so I heard. Has anyone been round yet?"

"There's nowhere to go round to," said Finn bluntly. "His Dad was released himself two years ago and his Mam went up when he was a kid. There's no one else, his home's here."

Noticing that their conversation had drawn all the smaller groups in the room round them, Bain sucked on the apple-bowled pipe in his hand and cleared his throat.

"Yes, well we all tend to be gypsies in this profession. No real home to go to. Our home town is where we stand. When we arrive in a place like Corbar, we're newcomers obviously, just like we were in the early days on the previous site. But I like to think it doesn't take us too long to become a real part of the local scene. That's why I encourage the men to meet the local people as much as they can. On our notice board at the site offices you'll find posters for the local dances and whist drives, even your garden fête, vicar, because we in Clandy like to think we're very much part of the community too. Of course we may live a little faster than some of the villagers. We may even appear to drive a little faster on occasions. . . ."

Dando spotted the wink Bain directed at Tyson and nudged Rafferty in the ribs. "In other words lay off the radar traps."

". . . Perhaps we may even drink the odd extra pint or two," continued Bain, "but then its thirsty work building dams; but basically we're just like you. We don't want to take over anything that's yours. We simply hope you'll ask us to share your pleasures too. . . ."

"Like your women," whispered Dando to Rafferty.

Bain was warming to his audience, his words coming out with a confidence which suggested he had learned them by heart. "I always feel that we in Clandy like to think of ourselves as being rather like those American spaceship people they used to have on television. . . ."

Dando groaned. "Christ not bloody Star Trek again."

". . . If you remember, they had a sort of non-interference policy. It meant that they always tried to leave a place that much better than it was when they arrived there and certainly never worse. We hope to do much the same thing here in Corbar. We feel we are in a position to provide the area with an amenity which will be enjoyed for many generations of your valley people and we hope that, in return, you can offer us your friendship and your support."

Bain knew that the cream of Corbar would clap, just as Bowland and Stevenage had applauded before them, and when they did, the carefully rehearsed nods and smiles were ready for them. When the applause died down he turned to Mallowry. "Do you know where Bautista is? He's a hell of a long time with those drinks?"

"Who do you want to drink to, darling?" she asked.

Finn was already raising his glass. "How about to absent friends?" he said acidly, "coupled with the name of the wine waiter."

When Bautista came through the swing door with his full drink tray he noticed the Clandy hosts and their guests had once again split up into small groups around the room.

From behind the broad back of Structures he could hear the vicar's voice addressing the small flock in front of the wide stone fireplace.

"I must admit you're going to make a certain contribution to employment in the area," said the vicar. "To work is to pray they tell us."

"In that case I must have been on my knees all my life, vicar," said Structures, stepping back to allow Bautista to pass the drinks round.

Ignoring the remark, the Rev. Churnside lifted a finger above the rim of the glass. "But we also know that when the lion lays down with the lamb it is usually to eat him."

Structures shook his head. "It's a muckle deal, I'll grant you. But it's because we're so big we're able to do a canny lot for a place like Corbar."

"What kind of things?" inquired a voice at his side. It was Cyril Coates, a thin, white-bearded man who had come to represent Haltbriggin District Council.

"Well amenities and things," said Structures. "We gave them a new community hall at Bowland and a playing field at Glanford when we built the M62. That was an interesting one. Soils, you did that one, didn't you? Come and tell them about it."

Curran, the small, grey-haired soils engineer who had appeared to be using his large gin and tonic as a protective screen, was suddenly forced into the action.

"Yes well it was a sort of two-way benefit," said Curran drily. "You see, when you dig out a motorway you always have to find somewhere to dump the surplus muck and I noticed on this one, there was a school almost on the edge of the site which had a large crater beside the playing field. It looked as if it had once been a quarry and the Corporation had used it for a tip. Well I went to see the Governors and offered to fill it for them free, level it and soil and seed it at the same time. Within a year they had a brand-new football field."

"And they got this sports field completely free?" asked the bearded councillor from Haltbriggin.

"It wasn't that easy giving it away," said Curran, taking another sip from his glass. "I had to meet the local education committee three times before they'd accept it. I think they couldn't believe they were getting something for nothing. In the end I had to promise the field would be filled and levelled within six months, and even then one of the councillors wanted to add a penalty clause in case we didn't finish on time."

"Try us at Haltbriggin," said the councillor, chuckling. "We'd eat your hand off, man."

Immediately behind the councillor, Bob Liederman had found a new audience in his wife, the Brigadier, Mallowry Bain and Dando. "No it isn't the wage structure, Dando, it's the attitude," Liederman was saying. "Over here you seem to prefer to go down collectively rather than up individually."

Dando grimmaced. "We've had our individuals and our coal barons before! They didn't work! Practically everything we have we've got through unity."

"Or unions."

"If you like. A bunch always fills the boss's office better than one chap with his hand out."

Liederman's eyes narrowed. "Perhaps there have been too many hands out and not enough work?"

"Say who's going to open this dam anyway?" said Pearl Liederman, breaking the momentary silence.

Bob Liederman's wife had a round, frothy face like a milk drink and blonde hair to match. "Well, I mean do you hire a V.I.P. for a kinda 'I name this dam, Corbar Water, may God bless her and all that'?"

Brigadier Gillibrand gave a dry cough as he put his hand to his mouth. "Well, in ships, my dear, it's usually carried out by the wife of the owner or designer."

"Is that so. Really?" said Pearl, gazing up at her husband.

"I think you'll find it's much too big a boat for that, Mrs. Liederman," said Mallowry Bain quietly. "I imagine they'll thumb through Debretts this time and stop somewhere around Page One."

Pearl Liederman shrugged her shoulders. "Oh well, never mind, I guess I'll be too busy anyway, probably, back home in the States. We have two children back there. In high school, you know? Do you have any children, Mrs. Bain?"

Mallowry smiled sweetly. "Our masters don't believe in high schools any more so I decided there was no need for me to have any. Now if you'll excuse me, I can see Mr. Rafferty looking lost over there. I'd better rescue him."

Finn Rafferty was at the far end of the room with a whisky glass in his hand, gingerly tracing out a pattern on the thick red carpet with his worn patent-leather shoes. He raised his head as Mallowry approached.

"You're not prospecting again, are you, Mr. Rafferty?" she inquired smiling.

As Finn raised his finger to his lips she could see he had been drinking heavily. "Sh . . . sh . . . lady," he said. "I've decided the designer of this carpet was a very ingenious fellow. If you keep bypassing those big blossom things and carefully tip-toe in between the leaves you finally finish up there." He waved his glass towards the door. "At the jolly old exit."

"You don't want to leave us so soon, do you, Mr. Rafferty?" said Mallowry raising her eyebrows.

"Well it's like this, if they had such a thing as a straw less than a quarter of an inch long, I wouldn't have been here in the first place. I came on the traditional 'other ranks' ticket and I lost the draw in the mad rush for places. Actually it wasn't quite as random as that. Griff Dando picked me just to get a smile out of the suit."

Mallowry touched his arm firmly. "I'm sorry about the finger nails. I didn't know. It's just that you all look so pompous in dinner jackets. As if you're trying desperately to be the same instead of showing all your interesting differences. I'm sorry about the boy, too."

Finn looked up at her. "Carter? He was just about getting the feel of being a feller. At least," he said, negotiating two more motifs in the carpet, "he discovered the exit quicker than I'm doing." He stopped and faced her. "Some of the muckies thought that this hooley shouldn't have been held after what happened. But when it comes to it no one likes stopping the job. It's an unwritten rule in muckshifting. Even after 15 pints of wallop inside you the night before, come seven o'clock you're on shift. With some of them it's almost as if they wound themselves in the bars deliberately to give themselves top weight to carry to the post."

"How long have you been with Clandy's?" she asked.

"Twenty years, come March."

"You don't look old enough."

Finn grinned at her, "I was abducted as a small child by a gang of savage muckshifters who carried me off to their camp and brought me up as one of their own. I'm still waiting for the cavalry to come."

Mallowry's laughter had drawn Griff Dando towards them but, even though she was aware he was hovering behind her, she ignored him.

"You laugh like stage people sing," said Finn, "Sort of open and enjoying it."

She lowered her eyes, which had the effect of giving her almost a demure look.

"How is it we haven't seen you around before, Finn?"

The Irishman threw the last of his whisky at the back of his throat. "Where we are we don't often rub shoulders with folk from the sharp end."

Dando was edging in between them now. "Why don't you tell her the real reason, Finn? Tell her all about living with Old King Coal and his merry old 'ole up in Scotland."

Finn gave him a pained look. "I'm sure Mrs. Bain hasn't put on a good clean frock like that to come here and listen to how we scratch for a living."

"No, not us, Finn," urged Dando. "You! You're the specialist!"

"All right then," said Finn, "Mrs. Bain, for the last four years I've been on open cast. Up in a field in the arse end of Scotland. No motorways, no bridges, just lugging out coal all day with diggers."

"I thought miners did that," said Mallowry.

"I think he wished they did," smiled Dando. "No, they get the good stuff. This was only a heap of rubbish, wasn't it, Finn?"

Finn met his glance with a hard stare. "Coal's like people. It's only as good as the juice inside the tree it came from. Too much starch and it burns like a blister, too much cellulose and it crumbles, and too much gum arabic produces a hard, dull coke when you light it. I think our lot had been gummed up for years. It was only good enough for making up the weight at the power stations. And some of it's called spittin' coal."

"What's that?" she asked.

"It's the sort that makes a hell of a lot of noise and not much heat."

Dando smiled across at Mallowry. "There you are. I told you he was an expert. Mind you, when you send a bad lad to a reformatory you'd expect him to learn something."

"What do you mean by that?" asked Mallowry.

Finn spoke before Dando could answer. "He means it was a sort of muckshifter's penal colony. It's where they send the bad boys."

"There you are, he even admits it. . . ."

"Dando," said Mallowry with a cool smile, "belt up." She turned to Finn "And are you a bad boy, Mr. Rafferty?"

"They tell me so."

Hmm . . ." she murmured. "Interesting."

As Dando attempted to take the empty glass from her hand, Mallowry kept a tight hold of it and shook her head.

"So that little ploy didn't work very well for you, Dando, did it?" she said.

"How do you mean?" he asked.

"Well, if you knew me, Griff, which you don't, you'd also know that I never judge a man by where he's been. Only what he's doing."

"What are you doing, spending all your time with the block Irish anyway," said Dando petulantly. "You're preaching to the converted with him. He's like a stick of Irish rock, if you cut him in half you'd find Clandy printed all the way through him."

Mallowry smiled, "I wonder what we'd get if we cut you in half, Griff," she said, "perhaps a sort of Welsh leek?"

"My dear Mallowry," said Dando tersely. "I was merely suggesting that since we have to have these kinds of nights you might be better chatting up someone useful, like the vicar. Someone who can do us a bit of good. He's reputed to be the biggest conservationist around here since the wise virgins."

"And why could the vicar possibly do me any good?"

"Because this is our missionary shift. He has his turn on Sundays. We need to soften up the natives so we don't have too many long knives in our backs while we're doing the job. We're no different from him. His lot used to do it with beads and Bibles, Clandy's do it with large brandies and vol-au-vents. It's the big sweetener we have before every major Clandy production, didn't Gus explain it?"

Mallowry tossed back her hair. "Gus is much too busy trying to explain himself. But if you want my explanation for it, have you ever considered, Mr. Dando, that, for once, it might have nothing to do with politics or in-fighting, or petty scheming and that, sometimes, people just like to get together for a nice, friendly, civilised piss-up?"

As soon as she had said it Mallowry realised she had been speaking so loudly that Amy Churnside had heard her, and that at least four of the faces in Liederman's group in the corner were turned towards her.

Bautista rescued her by arriving with five drinks and a notepad on his tray. "Gentlemen and lady," he said bowing slightly to Mallowry. "A telephone call for Mr. Dando, a Mr. Pavey."

"That'll be the stone boys," grunted Dando, snatching a drink from the tray which Bautista was holding out towards Mallowry. "See you."

As Dando followed Carlos to the exit, he could hear the booming voice of the Rev. James Churnside speaking to Structures away on his right.

"And you mean to say that two or three steel rods fastened with S-bends could guarantee the tower another hundred years of life? Quite remarkable."

Dando gave a quick thumb-up sign to the big man and walked from the room.

Behind him Mallowry Bain was persuading Finn Rafferty into missionary service. "Come Mr. Rafferty," she said brightly. "I suppose we'd better go and sweeten somebody."

As they reached the fringe of the main group in the centre of the room, the red-faced Caswell was talking to Tyson.

"No, not a D.9, Super," laughed Caswell. "If we used a D.9 to carve out a new bunker for you it would be through to the Pacific in ten minutes. No, a little D.3 would chew one of those out quite nicely. By the way how many chaps do you have in this area?"

"Well it's always been a very quiet patch, Corbar. About three I think, and the odd panda. But we've been asked to step up the complement a bit now that you're here."

"Not too many I hope, Super?"

"Depends how busy you chaps keep us, I suppose. I know there won't be a rush for postings here, it's not exactly one of the fleshpots of Britain."

Caswell nodded. "I know what you mean, but look, Super, if you or the lads are ever at a loose end, you know you have our clubhouse here. Drinks, snooker, darts, that sort of thing. You'll always be welcome, you know that. Off duty, of course. Don't want to be accused of leading your fellows off the old straight and narrow, do we?"

Mallowry Bain felt a light arm at her waist and turned to see Sir William Clandy smiling at her.

"Mallowry, my dear, I've hardly seen you all evening. Come over to the eats table and tell me which of those lovely pastries are safe for an old sagging figure like mine."

As he walked her slowly over to the buffet table he took a quick look over his shoulder. "Another good reason is that Caswell's such a terrible bore. Not that I need any excuses to have you to myself," he whispered, giving her a gentle nudge.

"Didn't you choose him?" she asked with a look of surprise.

"Not at all, my dear," he said brusquely. "I choose the Number Ones. Number Ones choose their own Number Twos and I'm afraid they always seem to do it using the same system as American presidents have of selecting their vice-presidents. They seem to pick either slow plodders or bumbling idiots, on the basis that in doing so they make themselves look sharp in comparison. In a way it seems to work. I suppose the man who is always having to look over his shoulder can't always see the job in front of him clearly."

Mallowry put on a hurt expression. "I hope the same system doesn't apply when choosing wives."

"Certainly not my dear," Sir Williams said with an assuring smile. "Gus, for instance, needs a strong woman behind him. Well you know what I mean, capable, a femme du monde shall we say? They tell me some firms go so far as to interview the wives before employing the husbands. We don't, but if I'd seen you first I would have given him a job, anyway."

"What was Gus like, Sir William?" said Mallowry. "I mean before I knew him?"

Big Clandy took a careful bite from a canape and looked down at the remaining portion between his fingers. "Quite delicious," he murmured approvingly. "My dear, you must remember that although my name is on practically everything you see out there for miles, the way of the world changes for us all. Today we have all sorts of people with slide rules and computers and . . . all ready to work out who's doing what well and who isn't. The same sort of people probably worked out that I'd put in sufficient mileage to qualify for being a kind of muckshifting knight, which sounds fancy, but these old hands have known their blisters would you believe?"

Mallowry took his hand, pressing her fingers into his palm. "I can still feel them."

Without releasing his hand Sir William looked over to where Bain was in conversation with the Brigadier. "I can remember the first time I ever put Gus in charge of a contract. It was a bridge in Yorkshire. Not a large bridge but it was in a National Park so it had to look as if it had grown there naturally, and there was a lot of trouble with glacial clay which kept shifting like a jelly. When it was finished I spotted something which hadn't been on the plan. On one of the stones at the base of an arch someone had chiselled out 'This bridge was built by Fergus M. Bain' and it gave the date. Of course he took some ribbing from the lads but he was right to do it. It was a bloody good bridge. He must have been only about twenty-four at the time. I remember him telling me later that when he was a boy his father had taken him to see the railway bridge at Menai and he had seen Robert Stephenson's name on it. He thought it had been rather like an artist signing his name to an original canvas, and he thought that if a man wanted to express himself and it was good enough to look at, he shouldn't be afraid to put his name to it. Fortunately there are still a few people who can get satisfaction out of building something other people need."

Taking a small ginger biscuit from a plate Sir William examined it closely. "It's only when you lose your sense of satisfaction or grow old like me and lose your teeth that you open your mouth not to bite," he said, replacing the biscuit on the plate, "but only to smile. And now if you'll forgive me, my dear, I'll go and smile at a few more faces."

As Sir William moved away Mallowry ambushed the flagging Bautista as he made his way through the guests with his tray. "Come and feed Mr. Rafferty before he wears a hole in the carpet," she said beckoning him over.

Finn was back at the far end of the room doing a balancing act on one foot, taking care not to spill a single drop of the Scotch in his glass.

"Still trying to puzzle it out, Mr. Rafferty?" said Mallowry breezily as he arrived with the waiter. "Look, have a rock bun or something. It will give you a more solid base."

"How about a sausage?" said Finn, straightening before searching the outstretched plate.

"Salchicha?" said Bautista, handing him a sausage on a stick.

"It's sausage," corrected Finn as he took it from the waiter. "I used to have a friend once, back in Clooney, who never used to go on any journey without a bag of boiled sausages. If he walked to Dorkin, which was about four miles away, he would say it was a six-sausage journey because it would take that long to eat them. Ballyreavey was eight sausages, Braniel was twelve. It got that even without a map you could tell how far a place was away by the number of sausages Patsy bought at the butchers."

Finn held up the small cocktail sausage in front of him in a sudden gesture of admiration. "Patsy always said you could go a long way on a sausage."

Mallowry raised her eyebrows teasingly. "How far would you expect to get with that, Mr. Rafferty?"

As their eyes met their sudden laughter was immediately drowned by a noisy outburst from beneath the chandelier. Moving forward Finn saw that the whole room seemed to be laughing and their eyes were turned towards him.

Dando had returned and was standing beside Bain with a smug grin in his face. "I've just had the geologists' report on your new sandstone seam, Rafferty," he said. "The one at the end of the amazing glacial drift."

"Well it was there wasn't it?" said Finn, tight-lipped.

"It was there all right! Just where you said it would be and do you know what it was? It was coal! Grade Five rubbish they reckoned. You couldn't even burn your bra on it."

Once again the group seemed to erupt into laughter. Through the cigar smoke Finn could see the two chins of Caswell wet and quivering, the bearded councillor from Haltbriggin slapping his sides, the vicar guffawing rather grandly and the Brigadier slowly rocking from side to side, his giggles sounding almost like a cough behind his hand. Only Mallowry and the somnolent Curran appeared unmoved by the revelation.

"Ah well, we can always build the dam out of Hadrian's coal," quipped Caswell, eager to keep the mood flowing.

"Rafferty looks as if he doesn't know whether to be downcast or open cast," laughed Dando.

"Perhaps we could mine it during one of our slack periods," suggested Caswell, producing another burst of laughter.

Stifling her laughter, Latice Gillibrand asked "How much is the price of a bag these days?"

Mallowry Bain smiled sweetly at her. "It depends if you marry them or not. If you do, it used to be 7s 6d. Old money, of course."

It was Fergus Bain who broke the silence. "I wonder if you've heard about the Irishman whose wife gave birth to triplets. He's still looking for the other two men . . . the other two . . . er . . . men. . . . And then there was the. . . ."

Mallowry was not listening to him. Noticing the empty space beside her for the first time, she had walked to the centre of the room, her eyes following the pattern of the carpet all the way to the door, which was still swinging. . . .

Part Two

BELTANE

BELTANE *Summer* – 'A time of feasting and song, greeting the return of the Sun.'

BELTANE

"And Noah sent forth a raven. . . ."

The Rev. James Churnside slowly turned over his hour glass, and raised his large, bespectacled eyes to the vaulting.

There were times when some of the Sunday morning congregation at St. Cuddy's felt he should have fixed his hour glass after his customary pause for inspiration, a feeling that, had he been offering his services in more temporal fields, he might arguably have been accused of time-wasting.

At moments he almost appeared to be quietly and deliberately sleeping on the job but, in fact, he was merely fueling the inner flames which were about to be released in roaring fires of faith.

"And Noah sent forth a raven. . . . Now you may ask yourselves, and you would be perfectly correct to do so, why a raven? Why not a thrush, a chaffinch, a simple starling? Why indeed, not a stork?"

"They were all round at Larky's house," muttered Dick Dancer to Michael Keen, who was sharing the compulsory Clandy church shift with him. Keen grinned as he glanced across at the Challons, whose five swelling children seemed to be pushing them wider apart by the week.

"The raven," explained the Rev. James Churnside, "is a bird of great strength. Guardian of the Tower of London. Keeper of our most noble traditions. But the raven is also an inquisitive bird. Nosey, if you like. It likes to know what is happening on its own patch. In its way the raven is continually asking questions. It also demands answers. . . ."

"Who had nine letters and scored a hat trick in the Blackpool–Bolton cup final?" whispered Donald Dacre to the small boy beside him on the end of the first row of the choir stalls.

"How would I know, I wasn't there!"

Donald jabbed him in the ribs with his elbow. "You don't know anything, Titch," he said bossily, his clear hazel eyes blazing from a face which was beginning to fill out into broad, handsome features. He nodded gratefully as the ginger boy on his other side leaned over and murmured something in his ear.

Picking up his pencil he wrote M.A.T.T.H.E.W.S. in the squares, staring for a moment in disbelief on discovering he still had a final space unfilled. He gave a withering glance towards the ginger boy.

"Answers," boomed the Rev. James Churnside from his pulpit. "The raven demands plain, honest answers. And why, you might well wonder, did Noah, even with his great abounding faith in the Lord, still require answers from the raven? And, of course, it is the Lord Himself who has given us that answer. 'Seek and you shall find,' he said, and that is precisely what Noah was determined to do. There is surely a need for a raven in all of us. A need for some small questioning voice which is prepared to fly out into the depths of the unknown and ask quite simply – 'what's going on?' There are I'm sure, many of you here today, residents of Corbardale, one of the loveliest valleys in our great country, who are asking that very question right now. What's going on?"

Even though most of the women in the congregation were in thin summer dresses, Tina Padgett, sitting beside the stone, sleeping Sir Piers, was wearing a loose fitting Empire line coat she had borrowed from her mother.

She was sitting with her hands clasped above her lap in a gesture which only partly concealed five of the nine months adventure she was taking into the unchartered realms of motherhood.

Looking self-consciously towards the intent row of perching Challons she noticed that only once did Larky glance back at her. When he had, it had been with the look of someone hunted, rather than a fellow traveller.

The Gillibrands in their matching houndstooth tweeds were sitting where they always sat, in the front pew to the vicar's right.

The row had always been, by tradition, the spiritual seat of the Hesters.

There were even deep gouge marks low down in the dark oak wood, where earlier ancestral Hesters were reputed to have shuffled their spurs during the sermons of vicars long dead.

Churchwarden Walter Newbiggin however, suspected it was the labour of later and much smaller Hesters, with their pen-knives.

Latice Gillibrand was gazing at the space beside the Rev. James Churnside which the older parishioners always referred to as 'Cuddy's Wall'.

A keen observer would have noticed that her eyes were usually not focussed on the stone and brass memorial plaques which covered most of the wall, rather on the one empty space beneath it which was awaiting tenancy.

The names on the plaques included Sir Athol Dunham, M.P. whose roof bequest kept the rain out, the Hon. Blanche Featherstonehaugh who paid for the new stone font after the woodworms ate the original, Ronald Hanslip of the Padfoot Hanslips, who once included the Vicar of St. Cuddy's on their monthly housekeeping accounts, and six generations of Hunting Hesters in close and awesome succession.

But whereas the Hunting Hesters had taken, the Gillibrands, in their overriding wisdom, had given.

Since in their combined ninety years at St. Cuthbert's the Gillibrands had sponsored the damp course, redecorated the porch and supplied flowers on every second Sunday, so Latice Gillibrand felt the allocation of the final place on Cuddy's Wall was a formality. Preferably, of course, for the eventual memory of the Brigadier, who was nine years her senior. And so it would have been, but for the presence in the opposite front pew of the Bennetts, Jack and Edna, who, although of Black Country extraction, had descended on both church and parish six years earlier in a fit of ferocious benevolence and belonging.

Jack Bennett had brought the fruits of his non-ferrous fortune hunting in Tipton to Corbardale, where he had dispensed charity with such a fervour that even his few friends decided it would be sated only by a knighthood.

So far his overpowering patronage had yielded only the peace prize of a J.P. and a seat on the Haltbriggin Bench.

But it was St. Cuddy's who had enjoyed most of the brunt of his benevolence. He had entirely re-equipped the ageing vestry with cupboards, shelves and even new hooks for the choirboys' coats. The small Norman chapel, thanks to his charity, was now a pink pastelled Sunday school, complete with a mural of an even pinker child Moses emerging from purple bullrushes which had parted conveniently to reveal the Nine Commandments. With the vicar's permission he had omitted "Thou shalt not commit adultery" on the grounds of it being superfluous for children so young.

Jack Bennett had also revived the former custom of personal patronage, to the extent of placing three fivers in a sealed envelope each week, writing "The Rev. James Churnside" on the outside before depositing the offering on the common plate.

Even Vicar Churnside had sensed the families' rivalry while accepting both as two welcome bidders at a kind of spiritual auction at which he held the hammer. Eager to offend neither, he had ruled confidentially to the Gillibrands that wall plaques, like places in Heaven, could not be reserved by right or tradition. The final space on "Cuddy's Wall" would therefore be allocated on a "first-go, first-served" basis. Concealing her disappointment, Latice Gillibrand nevertheless considered the Brigadier, at 73, a warm favourite since Jack Bennett was a good twelvemonth off his biblical span.

Ten rows behind the Bennetts, Fergus Bain had chosen his position in St. Cuddy's with strategic precision.

Bearing in mind the head-office directive that Clandy personnel should always blend into their environment rather than lead from the front, he had deliberately avoided the exposure of the prominent pews.

On the same reckoning he had felt that to slip unnoticed into the rear pews might have been construed as a furtive, almost reconnoitring gesture. And so he had quietly and thoughtfully ushered Mallowry into the comparative neutrality of the seats halfway up the aisle.

Unlike the three other women in the pew beside her, Mallowry Bain was hatless.

She was also considerably more beautiful than any other woman between the brass section and the ageing Saxons at the rear. The Vicar's pulpit may well have been the traditional focal point of the Church but she had become increasingly aware, over the months, that she had provided St. Cuddy's with a definite and distracting alternative.

Even the congregational males directly in front of her would frequently look up, as though pretending to admire the silver lucies in the window, before glancing back to her in brief, rationed gazes.

Although her face was entirely without make-up it seemed to free itself from all the other faces in St. Cuddy's, seeking its own splendid and lovely isolation behind the jet black smoothness of her hair.

"And so this black, beautiful bird flew forth from the Ark to ask its questions," the Rev. James Churnside was informing his congregation. "Just one lone creature attempting, at Noah's bidding, to pierce the waters of the unknown. But there are many ravens. We have them, even in this valley. And before those who would bring a great flood to this, our own special soil, can achieve their desires they may well find themselves facing a land full of ravens. All guardians of our heritage. All seeking the truth and demanding . . . er . . . adequate compensation. And this I can promise you, before one drop of water is brought to fill our lovely firmament the sky above Corbardale will be black with ravens."

His outstretched fist was up among the vaulting even before his eyes had begun their customary journey. He stared at it as it shook defiantly, almost independantly of him against the background of the ancient stonework above. Then he slowly lowered it to his side and mumbled "And now to God the Father," a prayer which petered out in an incomprehensible whisper.

"We will now sing," he announced, facing his congregation squarely, "Hymn No. 541 in the English Hymnal. Fierce rose the tempest o'er the deep, Watch, did thine anxious servants, keep."

Donald Dacre was first out of the vestry. Using his advantage of being one of the two front-line trebles who led the choir back after the vicar's blessing, he had deliberately boosted the pace to the point where the final ten yards to the vestry door had been achieved almost at the double.

There were still at least a dozen worshippers waiting to shake the vicar's hand as he dashed through the porch and down the path to the wooden lych-gate.

Finn Rafferty was perched on the stone wall, his long legs dangling down almost to the grass. "Have they finished with you then?" he grinned down.

"Did you remember the bait?"

Before he could answer Finn was aware of Mallowry Bain walking towards him leaving her husband to talk to the vicar.

"Good morning Finn," she said cheerfully, "I'm sorry we had to start without you."

"You did right! The last time I was in one of those places the fellow took every penny I had. After the things I told him he should have paid me!"

Laughing she said, "What have you got there, your lunch?"

Finn lifted up the screw-topped jam jar in his hand and scraped some of the mud from the sides.

"Indeed not," he said. "These lovely, messy little volunteers are the fishes' lunch. It's taken me half the morning on my knees behind the dozer collecting them."

He shook the jar enthusastically towards Donald. "Can you see them, Donny? All fat and juicy, you could almost get a Sunday roast out of them."

"Can we go to Charlton Pond, Finn? You said. . . ."

"Then the Charlton Pond it must be," said Finn, turning to Mallowry. "It's a good step, a two sausage journey at least, so I'll be salutin' you."

They were starting to leave when Finn saw that Sara Dacre had come out of Church and was leaning over the gate, zipping up Donald's anorak.

"What time will you be bringing him home, Mr. Rafferty?" she asked.

Finn tugged at the unruly blond cowlick across his forehead. "I think we'll let the fish decide that," he said smiling. "They've got more time than we have."

"Well don't be too late and take good care of him, won't you?"

Rafferty winked at her. "If you knew anything about men, Miss Dacre, you'd know better than to ask one man to look after another. He looks as if he can handle himself pretty well."

"You know our Mr. Rafferty then?"

Sara looked round, as Mallowry Bain spoke, as though she was seeing her for the first time. She noticed how much taller she seemed when they were standing together.

"Oh yes," she said. "We met on a mountain. Up Calcherside actually, you probably don't know it."

"Oh but I do," said Mallowry sweetly. "I quite enjoy the hills myself. . . . You seem surprised?"

Sara smiled. "No, it's just that with you being so tall, I couldn't quite picture you shinning up a mountain."

Mallowry shook back her dark hair and gave her a radiant smile. "Well, I'll admit, you're almost certainly better equipped for mountain climbing than I am. I should imagine short, neat shins would give a person quite a nice grip on the slopes."

"Of course, but then, Mrs. Bain, it can be a little bit of a disadvantage up here: being high, I mean."

"Perhaps it can also give you the advantage of being better positioned, Miss Dacre, to see where you're going?"

Finn looked down at Donald Dacre, who was tugging impatiently at his jacket. "You should be learning from this, Donny," he said. "A man may work like a dog but only a woman can behave like a cat. We're leaving."

"Mr. Rafferty! Mr. Rafferty! . . ."

"Oh Christ no!" muttered Finn.

Mallowry Bain turned to see Pearl Liederman running down the gravel path towards them. "Another of your Sunday worshippers, Mr. Rafferty?" she asked.

Pearl Liederman almost hurled herself at the gate. "Mr. Rafferty? We flew Concorde you know? Going home you know? I told you we were going to fly Concorde. And it was the most marvellous. . . . We were at Heathrow at 1300 hours and at 1610 hours, your time, we were actually on the runway at Kennedy. Three hours ten minutes. Wasn't that really something?"

Finn yawned and hoisted his fishing rod over his shoulder. "Mrs. Liederman," he said tiredly, "I wouldn't have thought the fact that you can fly half way round the world in three hours ten minutes was nearly as important as what you do when you get there. See yous."

As he moved off with Donald he was aware that all three women were staring at him open-mouthed. . . .

Rafferty and the boy had walked only a short distance down the lane, when they saw the girl coming towards them.

At first Finn thought she was a schoolgirl, so small did she seem in her yellow flowered dress and white ankle socks, but as she came nearer he saw that it was Jo Tiffin.

The girl seemed hardly to have noticed him as she came up to them. "Jo Tiffin, isn't it?" he asked.

As she turned her face to him he saw she had a large poppy bruise on her left eye.

At first he ignored it. "Have you been out using the sun then," he said before realising that the girl was close to tears.

"Donald lad," he said, pointing his finger up the lane to a heap of stone away in the distance. "Would you shake yourself off down that road and find me a big, round stone and bring it back. It's got to be a good one, mind, as near round as you can find it, O.K.?"

As the boy sped away Finn turned to Jo, who was crying softly beside him. "Now then, wee girl," he said quietly, "I suppose it's no use asking you if they've switched you onto dozers?"

"He hit me, Finn," she said, blowing on a small white

handkerchief.

"I can see he did, was it the first time?"

She sniffed and shook her head.

"You're living with Dando now, aren't you?"

Jo wiped her nose and tucked her handkerchief in her sleeve. "For him, it seems," she said. "Most of the time anyway."

"Now how can that be?"

"He comes up when he needs me, mostly after closing time."

"And the eye?"

Jo brushed a strand of wispy blonde hair across the bruise. "You should expect a few knocks in this job," she said. "You told me that yourself, Finn."

Finn held her shoulders and looked closely at the bruise. "I didn't mean this sort, girl," he said.

"I think Griff worries about the job," she said, "and it's hard to blame him for that."

"Griff Dando worries about Griff Dando, girl, nobody else."

"But if he does worry so, you'd think he'd sort of need somebody."

"He needs as much as you're prepared to give him, which I suspect is still a lot. Am I right?"

She looked up at him and nodded as she fumbled at her sleeve again.

"Well, Jo Tiffin," said Finn firmly, "all I can say to you is this. You know who I am, you know where I am and if you need an extra face in things, just shout. And wherever you go, go smiling, all right?"

He pinched her cheek gently, watching the smile flicker briefly across her face before she turned to go.

As she walked away Finn looked down and saw a large round stone being offered to him by the urgent-faced boy.

"Why did you need a stone like this, Finn?" he asked, looking up.

Finn reached down and accepted it. "Because it's a very special stone, son."

"There's nothing special about a stone."

"Would you say that now?" said Finn. "And have you seen inside it?"

"No, of course not."

"There you are then," said Finn smiling. "Not many people have. That's why it's so special. But if you were to break a special stone like that open, you'd find the biggest secret of the world inside it."

"What's that?" asked Donny.

Finn handed the stone back to him and put his hand against the boy's back, edging him up the lane. "The secret of what goes on in a woman's mind, son," he said.

They walked in silence down the lane for more than half a mile before Donald finally got his question into his mouth.

"Do you ever go to church, Finn?"

The Irishman shrugged his shoulders. "Only on occasions of great desperation. Like a relative getting married or released or some such nonsense."

"Have you ever been to our church?"

"No. Oh they'd let me in, if that's what you're thinking. It's just that when the labels were handed out they put me down for the other lot, the Maries, but I didn't keep up the payments. The goods were all right, I just didn't like the small print."

Finn stopped suddenly and pointed up the track ahead of him. "Do you see what I see boy? Look, bait!"

Donald held up the jar of worms he had been carrying. "But we've got the bait here."

"Oh no," said Finn, "that's bait for fish. Up there is bait for fellers."

With the boy running to keep up with him, Finn bounded towards the big overhanging tree, red with apples, which looked to be bursting its way out of a cottage garden. Soaring up with both arms outstretched he came back to earth in a shower of leaves and fallen fruit.

"There she is," he said, rubbing an apple the size of his fist against the seat of his jeans before taking a swift, noisy bite out of it. "A beauty. Me mammy always used to say 'If you see an apple, eat it.' "

He was still grinning as the heavy wooden yardbrush struck him across the shoulders. He swung round to see a large stern-faced woman struggling with the latch of the gate to reach him.

"Vandals!" she shouted. "You should know better, a man your size! What do you think you're doing?"

"Christ, run!" hollered Finn to the boy, who was fixed to the spot in amazement.

It was a good two hundred yards before Finn and the boy dared to look back at the woman. She was standing sentinel, yardbrush in hand, beside the gate. Finn watched her for a moment, his face reddening with mischief before taking another crunch out of the apple.

"Did you get one for me?" asked Donald.

"You're an apple man too, are you?" said Finn seriously, before breaking into a wide grin and dipping his hand down the open neck of his shirt. "Here you are then," he said, throwing him an even larger apple. "You didn't think I'd stick me neck out for one, did you now?"

Donald caught the fruit with his free hand. "I never knew my mother long enough to know what she thought. About apples I mean."

Finn saw that his young face was strong-looking, determined. "Yes I heard," he said. "They were both released, they said."

"They were in a plane, you know?"

"Yes I know. But you've got Sara now haven't you?"

"Yes but she's only an aunt."

Finn raised his eyebrows. "Only an aunt, is she? Let me tell you, Donald Dacre, I've known some aunts in my day who would leave some parents standing."

"Did your mother have any more children like you Finn?"

The Irishman laughed. "Look lad, I may have been down on my knees doing the daft things like scraping the mud for wee worms so that you can go scouting for fish but I'm not still in the short trousers you know. Still, I see what you mean. And the answer's a ginormous yes. She had so many children that some weeks she used to limp with them." For a moment his eyes seemed to cloud over and the boy could see he was thinking hard but suddenly his face lit up in a flash. "And then she used to shoo us all out with a big brush, to go scouring the trees for apples."

"I think I would have liked your mother," said Donny.

"Oh she had all the words, all right," said Finn as they walked on. "Her trouble was she didn't have any apple trees. You see, if all the people in all the world went around eating all the apples, the people who owned the trees would have nothing to sell. That's why they had to be so tight with the fruit in the Garden of Eden."

"But the vicar always says the Lord will provide."

"Maybe He does, but it's a matter of interpretation. Now take the time when He said He was going to give the Jews the Promised Land. So off they all went to spend forty years in the shaugh and what happened when they got there? 'There it is' He said. 'It's all yours!' Then He read them the small print, which said they had to fight for it because it belonged to somebody else. And that's just about been the way it's been ever since."

"Do you believe in God, Finn?"

Finn finished his apple silently before tossing the core up and kicking it high into the air. "I suppose He's not bad, as bosses go," he said finally. "But I wonder about his labour relations at times."

"How do you mean?" asked the boy.

"Well you see, most people think of Jesus being up there in Heaven and thinking lovely thoughts, but how many ever stop to think about that feller Judas up in Heaven? That's if he ever made it. I can see the fellow looking down at this place and saying 'Now let me see if I've got you right, again, Lord. You went down there to try to save everybody on that little ball of stone down there. Right? And I was picked to be on the team for a game for which the result had already been worked out. Right? Every move had been planned before any of us got there. You knew it was me who was going to split on you. You even knew I was going to kiss you, because you knew the rules better than we did. Yet as soon as it happened I was bad news. The rest ended up saints and I finished up as a one-man necktie party. Yet, if it hadn't been for me, you wouldn't have saved anybody. So what puzzles me is, if we are all playing the same ball game, why was I the only loser?' And Jesus, he turns to Judas and He says 'Because it was my ball.' Mind you, He was a good Christian man for all that. He talked a lot of sense too."

Finn quickened his step as they approached a five-bar gate, between the dry stone walling on the right of the dust track.

"Is this it?" asked the boy, looking across the field.

"Charlton Pond it is," shouted Finn, scrambling over the gate and setting off down the slope to where the lake lay like a great silver disc in the hollow.

Looking back he saw the boy's eyes bright and wide, between the bars of the gate. "Well, are you coming?" called Finn, waving him down.

"Yes, I'm coming."

"Come on then," yelled Finn. "Don't keep us waiting! Today, Donald Dacre, I'm going to make you a man of fish!"

Donald scrambled over the wooden gate, impatiently hauling the two fishing rods after him, and leapt the final three bars down to the ground, falling over in his eagerness. He picked himself up and began running towards the big, beckoning man who was striding to the water's edge.

The yellow silk Clandy banner on the bonnet of the Rolls Corniche was hardly moving on its silver staff as the vehicle glided silently to a halt beside the low-roofed operations hut.

The wind had dropped and Archbold had optimistically rolled back the sun roof for the five-mile drive from the Grange to the site.

Sir William, who was sitting at the rear beside Fergus Bain, turned with a withering look as Archbold opened the door. "Not me first, you fool," he snapped. "See to Mrs. Bain."

Mallowry ignored the chauffeur's exaggerated offer of an arm and stepped down from the car in a dazzling white catsuit which, in the sunlight made her seem to glow against the black gravel beneath the office steps.

Liederman and Dando were standing at the open door, watching them arrive.

"Watch your back," Dando muttered quietly to the American. "The Kingmaker's come."

Clandy appeared not to notice them as he emerged, staring at the new, white Jaguar X.J.6 in the project manager's car space, before smiling at Bain.

"I see your parcel has arrived then, Gus?" he said.

Fergus Bain's face pinked with excitement as he saw the car for the first time. "Has it really?" he said disbelievingly. "I've been waiting nine months for this!"

Big Clandy took Mallowry's arm, following him as the project manager raced ahead of them. "Come along my dear, we'll go and help Gus open his present."

Bain was already running his hands along the wing of the car and attempting to look at it from all sides at once when they reached the vehicle.

"Good Lord, she really is a beauty, Sir William!" he enthused without taking his eyes from the car.

"Yes, well we decided to chose it to match your lovely Mallowry," chuckled Clandy looking across at Bain's wife.

"Fast, low and expensive," muttered Dando to the ogling Liederman.

Gus Bain was now at the driving wheel, easing his shoulders blissfully against the black upholstery of the driving seat. Pressing a button on the black leather centre console he waited for the window to slide smoothly and slowly down before thrusting his head out towards them. "She's got 150 on the clock," he called out excitedly.

"It looks rather pricey for muckshifting, doesn't it?" inquired Mallowry calmly.

"It's pricey for anything," said Sir William, "But then we can't have our kings running around the place in dog-carts, can we? They don't all get them, you know? Actually it was all worked very pleasantly for us by that nice Mr. Marx. To each according to his ability and that sort of thing. I'll have to explain it to you."

He tapped against the car window, causing Bain to look up reluctantly. "Gus there's no need for you to stay while I explain our peculiar laws of automobility to your good lady. You run along and busy yourself in the shop, there's a good chap."

As Bain left them Big Clandy patted the near-side wing above one of the white-walled tyres. "He liked it, didn't he? And so he might. He's the only Clandy man this side of London who can expect an X.J.6 on the firm. But then he's the only project manager we've ever had who's at the sharp end of a £500 million contract. Now below him come the Granadas. The agents get them, Number Two, Structures . . . people like that. The sub-agents get Cortinas, and finally we have the Escorts: those go to the senior supervisory staff.

"Like Dando and the other foremen?" said Mallowry.

Sir William scratched his cheek. "Not quite like Dando," he said "He's in the Cortina group. But then, of course, Dando is . . . well, Dando. Now I know what you are going to say my dear, of course it's class distinction, but it wouldn't do for every beast in the pack to be the same size. The result would be chaos, if they were.

Besides, it doesn't do any harm if one of the Escort gentlemen should happen to fancy a bit more power under his pedal."

Mallowry smiled, "What does he have to do. Bite the arse off a Cortina driver?"

Big Clandy smiled. "Only, my dear, if he can catch one. By the way, Mallowry, was Gus all right? Last night, I mean? He seemed to be up half the night."

Mallowry lowered her eyes. "It's nothing serious. He was restless, that's all."

"But does he need to see anybody?"

"No I don't think so. He's not a great sleeper."

Sir William offered her an arm. "Neither is our chairman, my dear. But he's a very old man. Come, we'll join the others."

Dando met them at the door with a large green folder under his arm. "Oh, I was just fixing some coffee for you, Sir William, I expect you are ready for some."

Clandy glanced across to Mallowry. "I'm sure we both are, aren't we?"

"I'll have it sent to Gus's office," said Dando, snapping his fingers towards Jo Tiffin, who was hovering beside the switchboard room door. "Give us two minutes, then serve."

Bain, Caswell and Structures were already in the room, listening to Liederman, when they entered.

"And this goddam vicar said you must remember that although you've bought the pasture, you don't own the flock. Well I felt like saying, 'Look we've got enough black sheep of our own to worry about, without stealing yours.' "

Bain rose as Clandy came into the room. "Have a pew over here, Sir William," he said. "We were just having a discussion about the party. I think, on the whole, it went reasonably well, don't you think? They did find Rafferty's sandstone, by the way, it was closer to the Hounshale end."

"So Rafferty was right after all?" said Clandy, turning to Dando.

Dando bit his lip before answering him. "Let's say he was right at the wrong time," he said.

"Yes, well," said Bain. "Er, by the way, Bob, a party from the E.E.C. wants to come over next month to have a look at your model and whatever we have on site to interest them. They're mainly from West Germany, I think, and France. Will you be all right?"

Liederman shrugged his shoulders. "Bring 'em all on, I say. After all they're picking up the tabs."

"Yes, I suppose they are really," said Bain. "Now you, Griff: are the men going to be happy with the new hourly rate? Now we've got the weather with us I'd like to think we can really get the old backs into it for the next few months."

A quiet tap on the door was followed by Jo Tiffin carrying a small tray of coffee cups. Dando waited until she had served them all and left the room before he spoke. Remaining on his feet he said, "Muckshifters are a bit like flowers, Gus, they need the sun on their backs to bring the best out."

Caswell sniggered. "Yes but pansies don't go down to the pub when it rains."

Dando stared at him unsmiling. "They'll work all right. In all weathers, all conditions, if the bunce suits them. You see the price for a job like this is usually fixed on a beautiful spring day, something like today when the greens are running well, the model looks pretty on the table and everyone's in their shirt sleeves. After six Martinis and a pretzel they are convinced every day's going to be like this, but most industries don't work that way. If a docker unloads tapioca one day and lamp black the next, the rate goes up. The dirtier the cargo the better the brass, and it makes sense."

Clandy placed his cup on the table in front of him. "What you're saying then, Mr. Dando, is that we should tap the barometer every day and the lower the mercury falls the higher the wages should be on that day?"

"No, I wouldn't cut it quite so fine as that," said Dando. "But we know that by all the averages the job's bound to be tougher in certain months of the year, and we could take those months into consideration. They're not soft, by a long way, but when you hit months like Jan. and Feb. a little extra bunce wouldn't harm the production figures."

Caswell looked at Dando with a tired expression on his flabby face. "Perhaps we can get it past the P.I.B. as a muckshifters' mitten allowance. Better still, we could issue them with free wool so that they could knit their own Balaclavas."

Sir William's eyes met Dando's for a moment across the rims of their coffee cups. "Well, its's an . . . er . . . interesting idea, Griff. Have you any facts and figures to go with?"

"Yes, it's all in here, Sir William," interrupted Dando as he produced the green file from beneath his chair.

"I'm sure it is, my boy. Well let Mr. Bain have it will you and we'll go through it sometime. And now I must shoot off back to civilis . . . back to London." He got to his feet. "Now, Gus, you're taking that exquisite girl of yours round the site this morning, I believe? So look after her and don't forget your helmet, Mallowry my love. It can get a bit hairy out there at times."

Fergus was up fractionally ahead of the others. "Yes, she's picked the hairiest too. She wants to see the quarry."

As they walked out to the waiting Rolls, Dando and Jo Tiffin appeared behind them. Dando was holding out a white helmet which the girl had just fetched from the safari truck.

"I've got you a lid," he said offering it to Mallowry.

Mallowry took the helmet and placed it apprehensively on her head. "I hope it looks better than it fits," she said glancing across at Big Clandy.

"You look charming, my dear," he said, kissing her cheek. He shook hands only with Bain. "Goodbye then, Gus, I'll be seeing you next week down in London. Look after the old shop."

"Goodbye sir," said Gus, watching the Rolls begin the ascent up the freshly gravelled track. When it was almost out of sight he turned to Mallowry. "Right dear, we'd better make a start. I've got the R.E. for lunch. Dando, perhaps you'd like to come along with us?"

Dando hesitated for a moment. "I'd better get The Slasher to have a look at the safari first, she's a bit dickey."

"Never mind that, we'll go in mine," said Bain walking towards the white Jaguar.

Dando quickly caught him up, "You're not going up there in that, are you? She's hardly got the wrappers off!"

"You know Dando, you worry too much," said Bain, opening the passenger door for his wife. "The coal road's as flat as a pancake all the way to Baskey's."

The Jaguar eased past the line of huts before turning to join the dirt road along the valley bottom. On their left for most of the way was a three mile stretch of black earth, flattened by the dozers.

Bain took his unlit pipe from his mouth and waved it towards the line of the dam. "This is where it will all be happening in a few months' time, darling. Each time those scrapers pass over that strip they dig a bit closer down to the bedrock so that when they're finished we'll have something to build this thing on. We should be driving the piles in by May."

Ahead of them two dumper trucks were approaching them, side by side as one attempted to overtake the other. Dando leaned forward from the back seat. "I should watch out for these two cowboys, Gus. They're not ours, they're with the sub-contractors. I wouldn't like you to forget the rule of the road with those fellers."

Gus glanced back at him. "I'm hardly likely to forget it in this, am I?" he said before immediately having to move out onto a grass verge to avoid the advancing vehicles.

As they passed within inches of the leading lorry, Mallowry saw the face of the driver grinning down at them from his cab.

"Now this, darling, is the coal road," said Gus matter-of-factly as he turned the white Jaguar left to begin the eight-mile stretch to the quarry.

"Why do they call it the coal road?" she asked. "There are no mines here are there?"

"Not big ones. Just a small drift mine up at the quarry, but it was big enough when it was opened to supply most families round here. A family called Baskey used to run it. They built this road, fortunately for us. We've improved on it, of course, but we still use some of the old slag to surface it."

As the car picked up speed along the narrow track the wheels occasionally lurched into rain puddles which sent spurts of black water up the wings and across the windows.

Two miles out they came alongside a small yellow traxcavator at the side of the road. Standing next to it was a tall, thin man in a black velvet top hat, who was stopping to light a cigarette.

"Stop here a minute, Gus, will you?" said Dando, reaching for a window winder which wasn't there. "How do you get this thing down?"

As Bain released the window for him Dando thrust his head out. "Tully! What sort of a mess do you call this?"

Tully finished lighting the cigarette before walking slowly over to the car. "What would you be having in mind sor?" he asked casually.

"Well look at it, man! The road's dished for about a mile! You could get a punt up it! All haul roads have to be crowned, you know that, don't you? It's a bloody disgrace, man!"

The ganger looked wearily up the track in the direction of the quarry. "Now isn't that a thing. Our great minds must be on the same wavelength, Mr. Dando. That's just what we're after doing here. And if you'll look beside my sleeve here, you'll see our little traxcavator here for that very purpose.

Dando scowled. "While you're at it, Tully, get that winrow shifted too! It's heaped so high at the sides in some parts we'll have a swimming pool if it rains again."

Tully raised his hat and bowed towards the car. "It's all under elegant control sor," he said, "and good day to you too."

As Dando brought his head back into the car Bain pressed the window button and smiled briefly at the lanky ganger before re-starting the vehicle.

"I remember when Big Clandy used to bark like that," he said. "He used to drive an old Lagonda round the site in those days and he had a rule of setting off round every haul road at 8.30 each morning with the needle at 50. If he felt a bump on any of them, they had to do them again."

"Tully looks as if he can hardly feel his head this morning, let alone the road bumps," muttered Dando. "Anyhow we won't have to look at him much longer. I've put him out in the long grass. He's going up to the new cutter – it'll be somewhere for him to open his bottles."

Bain grinned back at him. "Old Tully's all right. He's a Methodist compared with some we've had. We had a maintenance ganger for years called Paddy Mac. He had a tremendous fight with the bottle and when he finally lost, Sir William told him that it was time for Clandy's and him to part company. He said 'But you can't do that, I've worked for you for 37 years of my life,' and Big Clandy said 'But Paddy, we paid you, didn't we?' "

Mallowry could see the line of four trucks waiting on the right-hand side of the road near the quarry entrance long before her husband leaned back in his seat to speak to the general foreman.

"Look Dando, if those heaps are going to make a habit of parking there, you'd better build them a few extra yards of road. There's hardly space to swing a cat this side."

Slowing down to pass the first of the lorries, Bain left one hand on the steering wheel as he stretched across Mallowry's body, keeping an eye on the offside wheels. Mallowry saw they had already been forced into the low piles of earth at the road edge, which was spilling gently down the steep grass slope.

Below them she could see the brown roofs of the quarry huts and the lumbering yellow dozers plunging their blades into the newly fractured face. She looked back as suddenly, ahead of them, a D.9 moved out from behind the rear truck and was slowly approaching them.

"Christ who's this?" barked Bain, slamming his foot down on the brakes. Even from inside the car Mallowry could feel the surface of the road shudder beneath the weight of the advancing dozer, yet she could feel no sense of immediate danger in the steady ponderous progress of the vehicle.

Bain put his hand on her lap. "It's all right, darling," he said. "He'll stop soon!" Moving his hand quickly back to the steering column he began giving loud blasts on the horn.

"He won't, you know!!" Dando's voice behind him was perfectly calm. "It's one of the earth shakers!"

"He can't see us, can he?" said Mallowry, who could see the shiny, worn P.V.C. on the back of the driver's donkey jacket, high up in the dozer's cab. "Look, he's reversing!"

"Hell you're right," snapped Bain, reaching across his wife again to release the door handle, "Out you go, old girl. We're not taking any chances."

Dando and Bain were already out of the car and standing back against the line of lorries when Mallowry appeared from the back of the Jaguar.

"Well come on then, Dando, do something!" shouted Bain, biting his lower lip.

The Welshman looked at him blankly. "You know neither of us can, Gus! He can't see us. But it's his road!"

The bulldozer's blade hit the white Jaguar half way up the radiator, slicing through the thin, silver struts easily, before gouging four feet off the bonnet, with a noise which to Mallowry sounded like a scream.

Dando took her arm and led her to safety between the two lorries. She saw that the eyes set deep in his dark face had a look almost of elation in them. "I'll bet you've never seen anyone kill a car before," he said in a low voice.

Noticing that Bain had not joined them, Dando called him, "Gus, you'd better come back here! There's nothing you can do out there!"

Bain walked over to them in a daze, as the blade of the D.9 crashed through the windscreen, reaching for the roof. Beneath the bonnet both of the white-walled tyres burst simultaneously before splaying out to either side as the wings collapsed over them.

"The bloody vandal," muttered Bain as the D.9 seemed to mount the car, covering the cowering Jaguar with its full weight of 48 tons.

"I suggest you tell him?" said Mallowry glancing toward the driver.

Dando shook his head. "He wouldn't hear a word love. It's Varanger, the mad Dane. Being inside one of those things when they're switched on is worse than a pop concert. He'll think he's gone over a brick."

He took a few short paces towards the advancing dozer and cupped his hands to the mouth. "Varanger! Varanger!" he bawled, staring up the road for a few seconds before running back. "It's no use!" he said. "He's got the book on his side!"

As the giant dozer lunged forward again, both front doors of the Jaguar sprang open and flapped momentarily like bizarre ears before falling to the ground. Immediately the rear doors buckled inwards under the pressure, ripping into the black leather upholstery, squeezing pieces of the seat out from the sides like pips from a lemon. The force of the mechanical beast's weight against the back axle brought the boot of the car curling upwards like the last despairing sting of a scorpion. Only then did the roaring stop.

Dando turned to Bain, who was watching the last of the petrol bleed out from the raised boot down onto the mess of flattened metal and leather. "I'm sorry, Gus," he said finally. "Look, you stay here, I'll go and give him some gyp."

The tall, gangling Dane had already jumped down from the cab of the D.9 and was standing scratching his head when Dando reached him. "I didn't see it, Griff, honest I didn't!"

"What's the damage?" asked Dando, tight-lipped.

"You can see for yourself: she's gone."

"Not the car, stupid, the dozer?"

Varanger looked puzzled. "Not a scratch on her."

Dando smiled. "Good. Right Varanger, turn white, you're being bollocked! And next time do things properly."

"What do you mean, Griff?"

"You forgot the boot!" said Dando.

"What did Griff mean by the rule of the road?" Mallowry was asking her husband, when Dando returned.

Bain looked back at Varanger, who was hovering beside the big dozer with a glazed look on his face. "Working vehicles have the right of way on any part of the site. It's the unwritten rule that anyone else, whoever they are, has to keep out of their way at all times. If anything happens you can't do a thing about it."

Dando returned and bent down among the wreckage before picking up a wing mirror which he rubbed against his sleeve before handing it to the project manager. "This is about the only thing he seems to have left you," he said, "I suppose it's yours. Varanger's a good enough dozer man, Gus. He said he just didn't see you."

Bain looked down into the mirror. "He makes a good job of demolishing a car." he said.

Mallowry glanced quickly over to him. "He wasn't just destroying a car," she said angrily.

As the bulldozer broke free Mallowry could see that Finn Rafferty, bare to the waist, had appeared from up the quarry slope and was standing with an incredulous look on his face as he held his helmet in his hand. "I see you came second then?" he called over to them.

Bain stared at the ground as Finn paced authoritatively round the flattened heap with his thumbs tucked beneath his armpits.

"Well let me see." he murmured pretentiously, "Only one owner I take it. Peanuts on the clock and I guess you keep it in a garage. The book price for one of these is around the twelve sixteen', but for that, of course, it has to be in near perfect condition and nicely looked after. I should think, in the circumstances, my best offer will have to be er . . . 12p and I'm a fair man."

Nobody spoke as Finn walked over to Mallowry who was trying to suppress a smile. "So you've come to see me and me stones, have you?"

"Well that was the original idea, before we had this little meeting with your friend up there," said Mallowry.

Finn looked at the two silent men. "Good. Well, as your husband and Mr. Dando seem to have such a lot to discuss about the relative strengths of mechanical hardware, I will personally conduct you on a guided tour of Stonesville. Is that all right with you, Mr. Bain?"

Bain seemed to see the Irishman for the first time. "What?, er yes," he said. "You go on ahead Rafferty. We'll get on the R.T. for some more transport and catch up with you later."

Fastening his helmet on his head Finn took Mallowry's arm and led her carefully over the flat slab of steel which had been a bumper bar, to the path on the opposite side of the road which led down into Baskey's.

Hearing a sudden shout behind them they both turned to see Dando looking down at them. "Get a shirt on when you get down there Rafferty," he yelled. "I don't want her to think we're all savages."

Mallowry watched the muscles moving in Finn's bronzed chest as the Irishman waved back at him with a daft smile on his face.

"Keep it off," she said. "I'm not expecting cucumber sandwiches."

Below them two 150 R.B.s were parked side by side, their caterpillar tracks motionless as their drivers chatted to each other.

A big, bald-headed driver leaned out of his cab. "We caught some flint in one of the cat tracks Finn" he explained gingerly, "Cock's been helping me to clear it."

Finn grinned, shaking his head. "Next time Samson, use your teeth, it's quicker." He turned to Mallowry "This great, straining dwarf up here is Samson, alias Jim Simpson. We call him that on account of his hair. They reckon that if he ever got it back he'd start work again."

Mallowry smiled up at the driver. "What did he call the other one?"

"Ah now," said Finn, "This gentleman is one of the most ingenious manifestations of human evolution. He has devised a method of existing in this age of savage economics without paying the rent. We call him The Cock Lodger."

As a deep belly roar came from Samson's cab the small pinched-faced driver in the second digger popped his head through the cab window "Aw, come off it, Finn," he said.

"No, we mustn't deny our talents, whichever direction they take," said Finn, "and the particular talent of Reg Fawcett the aforenamed Cock Lodger, is that he makes a science of selecting landladies who look for more in a man than his wallet. Reg always carried his rent in his trousers. Currently he's living with a widow woman in Padfoot. They reckoned that last Christmas, when she heard we were coming she hung her bed outside the back window hopin' to get a muckshifter in it and she got Reg."

Mallowry put her hand to her mouth in an unsuccessful attempt to stifle her laughter. "Stop it Finn! You're making the man blush!"

But the wiry driver was also laughing. "It's all right, Mrs. Bain," he said. "He's only jealous."

As they walked down to the huts a tall, bulky man came away from the group of men on their right and hurried towards them.

"Finn lad," said The Goose before reaching the pair, "I've just been to see the Blaster fellow and he informs me the next blow will be around two if that suits us. What do you think?"

"I think I'd better say that this ill-shod, unsavoury-looking specimen, Mrs. Bain, is The Goose," said Finn. "Now give your face a joyride and smile for the lady, Goose. Goose is my Number Two, which makes him about waist high to a leprechaun."

The Goose took Mallowry's hand, kissing it before bowing low.

"The Goose was supposedly named because his father kept geese in Ireland. But I should watch his hands just to be on the safe side. He used to be an Irish sea scout but his tent sank!"

"Finn's the great man for the old humour, missus," said the Goose gravely. "He has a tongue as quick as his fists sure."

"Now Goose," chided Finn, "you know very well I'm a man of

peace. You wouldn't want Mrs. Bain to get the idea I'm aggressive. What he means is that I sometimes have to get a rush on to defend myself."

"What about the blow Finn? Shall I tell them its O.K. for two?"

Finn looked at his wristwatch and saw it was 11.30 a.m. "Sure that'll be fine." As the man turned to go Finn called him back. "Goose, tell the lads the Sun Man's on his way so they can be shaping when he comes, will you?"

They began walking down the narrow steps which had been cut down the face of the plateau to the base of the quarry.

"You must be ready for a coffee," said Finn. "Then you can meet the rest of the muckies. The Goose's real name, you know, is Canavan, he's a descendant of the ancient Kings of Clooney and they were a pretty mean set of creatures themselves, if you like. Goose was there in Clooney when the town fathers decided that to make a comfortable living, they should all take in each others washing every week. But his old man put the mockers on it by saying that to make a profit he would have to charge next door 6p more for their washing than they charged him. Now the town fathers said it made sense so they put up their prices. They had to stop it in the end because they said they'd all become so piled with money no-one wanted to do washing any more."

Mallowry looked into Rafferty's urgent face for several seconds before beginning to laugh. "I think the Blarney Stone must have been quarried in Clooney," she said.

"Madam, living in Clooney was a very serious business, I can assure you."

As they crossed the quarry floor Mallowry looked over at the line of three tractor shovels burrowing into the loose rock overbeak.

"What's their job?" she asked, putting her hands to her ears to deaden the noise of the machines.

Finn thumped his hand against the back of one of the tractors. "These are the hungriest fellers on the site." he said. "They gulp the rock up in those dirty great face shovels and load it on to these lorries who hump it up to the primary crushers. They can take up to eight cubic yards of solid stone inside those things. Or fifteen men. One of these could gobble up the English rugby team in six seconds flat. It takes the cream of Ireland eighty minutes most years to do the same thing, so you can appreciate the enormity of the achievement."

Moving away from the three tractors they turned to face the huddle of quarry huts in front of them. "Now I'm going to do my conservation bit," he said. "What do you notice about all this?"

Mallowry looked at the huts in turn and shook her head, "They all look the same to me."

"Exactly," said Finn. "It's unique in the industry. Everything has been painted brown to gell with the surroundings. It's the first time we've had to get planning permission for the buildings as well as the land."

As he spoke, Brown Windsor, the wiry Jamaican dumper driver, came out of the tea hut with a mug of tea in his hand.

"I see what you mean," smiled Mallowry.

"It just shows how thorough Clandy's are when they do a job," grinned Finn. "The moving bit is Brown Windsor. We decided to leave him just the way we found him."

As the Jamaican came towards them Finn introduced Mallowry – "Brownie, this is Mrs. Bain. Bwana's woman. She – who – must – be – obeyed who lives with He – who – isn't – always."

Brown Windsor took her hand politely. "I'm very pleased to meet you, Mrs. Bain," he said with a slight bow.

"When the sun's in the right direction Brownie's about the fastest muckshifter on the site. If you needed planning permission for people, half of our lot would be rejects. Most of them only work from the waist down. Brownie's from a long line of cannibals. We told him he could have any job he wanted except cook."

Taking Mallowry's arm Finn led her to the half-open wooden door of the tea hut. "We'll see if we can persuade Tucky to fix us a drinkable cup of coffee."

As they walked into the steamy room Finn suddenly put his hand across her eyes, turned her round and marched her quickly out through the entrance, but not before she had noticed the walls were papered with a mass of nudes.

"Christ, I'm sorry," gasped Finn. "I'd forgotten about the gallery. We don't get many real women out here. Most of them are snaps of Brownie's aunt. He likes to put them up to remind him of home.

Mallowry looked at him with a half smile playing round her lips. "I'm surprised he ever left home," she said. "And which one of you wears the tights?"

"Tights?" asked Finn innocently.

"That pair hanging over the back of the chair in there. Who wears them?"

"Oh, those tights," he said confidently. "We all do, well most of us anyway. Winters in these places would freeze the legs off you and the lads find if they put a pair of the missus's tights on under their trousers it saves you getting a gust up the shin."

Mallowry was about to speak when she saw Brown Windsor standing beside her with a chair in each of his massive brown hands.

"I thought you might like one of these, Madam," he said quietly.

"I liked your dusky aunts Windsor," she said smiling, "or were they your girl friends?"

He grinned down at her. "Don't judge a book by its cover, Miss. They're all pink inside like Queen Victoria."

"Thank you Windsor," said Mallowry sitting down beside Finn.

"Finn . . . where do you get your tights from?"

Finn wrinkled his eyes, "I haven't got an official source if that's what you mean."

"You're not married?"

"Not at all."

Looking away from her momentarily Finn saw a small four-wheeled dumper coughing into the enclosure in front of them with a young dark-haired man at the controls. The offside rear wheel was jammed against the mudguard as it juddered against the ground.

Finn turned to Mallowry with a perfectly straight face. "Actually I'm living with someone at the moment. We share a sort of bedsitter."

"Oh, I see," said Mallowry. "What's she like?"

"See for yourself," said Finn, standing up. "She's here now. And another thing, she snores like a bronchitic pig."

Keen stepped down from the dumper and walked up to them. "Dancer asked me to let you have a look at this, Mr. Rafferty. The back end fell into a crater near the main crusher and he couldn't get the wheel off."

Finn winked at Mallowry and spread his hands out towards the young driver. "Meet my room-mate, Michael Keen. To save the taxpayers money they put us two to a room, like Pentonville. And let's have a look at what you've been up to here. Have you got a spare?"

"Yes, but we couldn't get this one off," said Keen timidly.

The Irishman crouched low to get a closer look at the twisted wheel. Then he straightened and gave it a hard kick with his boot.

"It's buckled" he said. "Did Dancer think to let the air out first?" He answered himself. "No, of course he didn't. Get me the jack, lad."

Finn jacked the wheel off the ground before reaching down to release the valve, sending a rush of air from the sagging tyre. Grasping the wheel with both hands he began hauling at it causing the whole vehicle to vibrate.

"A wrench, boy!" he gasped as he finally stood back. When the lad handed it to him, Finn was about to launch into the motionless wheel when he saw the truck lurch backwards on the uneven ground. Throwing the wrench to the ground he placed his hands beneath each side of the rear corner of the vehicle.

"Stand back, she's slipping!" he yelled. Just as he spoke the jack collapsed to the ground leaving him to take the weight of the truck in his hands.

Keen gave him an anxious look. "What can I do, Finn?"

"Now keep your drawers on, lad," he said calmly. "Just reach under there, get that jack out and set her up again."

As Keen stooped to extract the jack, the plump, grinning shape of Tucky, the tea boy, appeared behind them. He was wearing a stretched white tee-shirt with a Donald Duck motif across his broad chest which was partly concealed by the two cups of coffee on the tray.

"I'll have mine black with one lump," grunted Finn. "Stirred but not shaken. This sylph-like sprite behind you, Mrs. Bain, is Tucky. He came to us as a reject from Oxfam. Keep your eye on the biscuits while he's talking to you, he'd have the bread off the pigeons in Trafalgar Square if we ever gave him a day off."

He looked over to Keen who was still struggling with the jack. "Stick it right up, lad, and start winding! Right up, now. Just as if you were taking a bull's temperature."

Tucky handed a cup of coffee to Mallowry and advanced towards Finn with a mug in his hand. "Where would you like yours, Finn?" he asked. "Through a funnel? Or shall I stick it right up?"

"I think that's it, Finn," said Keen, taking a few paces back from the truck.

"Well we'll soon see," puffed the Irishman, slowly letting the jack take the weight of the vehicle. "Right now, where's that drink?"

Mallowry took the mug from Tucky's tray and handed it to Rafferty, who after one brief exploratory gulp, finished the rest in one mouthful.

Producing a small white handkerchief from the jacket pocket of her suit, she rubbed a smear of oil from the Irishman's hard, flat stomach, noticing that despite his efforts, only the merest trickle of sweat was running down from his thick neck through the soft blond hairs of his chest.

"You're fit, Rafferty," she said almost in a whisper.

Finn looked down at the black grease on the handkerchief before Mallowry closed her hand over it.

"You should have seen my old man," he said. "He was a shoplifter. He always said eggs were the great strength givers. He used to go out to the banties every morning, pick up an egg, crush it in his fist and eat it, shell and all. He used to eat so many eggs that when he was finally released, Mammy didn't know whether to have him fried or scrambled. Now where's that wrench?"

As Keen handed the tool to him, Finn returned again to the bent wheel and, sliding under the vehicle on his back, began tapping against the back axle.

When the hammering stopped Finn's muffled voice could be heard beneath the vehicle. "Ah! That should do it. Now she should slip off like a barmaid's bra."

Finn slid easily from under the truck and immediately began wresting the wheel from side to side before hauling it back towards him, ending up with it clutched triumphantly to his chest.

"Here she comes!" he said. "Now where's your spare, lad?"

Mallowry watched him fit the spare wheel before handing the

spanner to the young driver. "Right, she's well again, you can take her back now. While you're there, Keen, tell Dancer and the others the Sun Man's on his way and to look lively."

As Keen threw the useless wheel in the back of the dump truck and started back for the crusher, Mallowry gave Finn a quizzical look. "Why do you call Gus the Sun Man?"

Finn rubbed his hands briskly on an oil rag.

"You're a great girl for the questions," he said, "but I'll tell you. There are three things the Irish are good at, fighting, farming and shifting muck. There's nothing new about it. Nobody ever needed to invent a muckshifter in Ireland. We've been doing it since Paddy had a cave. No, the most momentous event in history was the invention of a man who didn't work with his hands. A chap who stood back, organised the others and acted on his environment from a distance. Like the sun. In the end it comes down to fellers like Chauncy Bawn who can take a D.9 to pieces and put it together again as if it was a meccano set and who knows more about this stuff we're standing on than anyone here. Then up comes the man in the Rupert Bear trousers and a handbook and tells him how to shovel shit. The way you get the respect of fellers like these is either to be able to shout louder than they do or know the job better than they do. Anything less and you're just another man in the Ruperts."

Finn threw the rag down. "Come on," he said. "I want you to meet the great Chauncy Bawn."

Chauncy Bawn was standing stripped to the waist, 30 feet up in the bowl of the primary crusher. The sun was beating on his head, blanching his already white shock of hair. As Finn and Mallowry approached him he tossed a large, jagged sliver of rock over the lip of the tower and watched it fall to the ground.

Finn waited at the bottom of the narrow ladder as the man made his way down. "Expecting a siege are you, Chauncy?" he said.

Bawn slapped his hands together, brushing away the dust. "We had a jam," he said. "But that seems to have cleared it."

"Chauncy I want you to meet Mrs. Bain," said Finn brightly. "Bawn is Irish for white you probably know. Mind you, his hair was jet black a year ago, that was before they told us how much they were going to charge for digs at Dotheboys Hall!"

"Ah it seems an awful lot for a working man but it's better accommodation than some I've known," said Chauncy.

Mallowry Bain looked at Bawn's thin, white body, "I thought you'd be a bigger man," she said. "I hear you're one of the star performers out here."

Bawn smiled. "Performers? Ah well we all are I suppose. Would you believe my mother put me to the piano when I was a boy. But these great bananas on me hands never seemed to find any comfort in the keys. Still, I'm from Clare, Mrs. Bain, and in Clare we've always produced more muckshifters than piano players so I suppose

I fitted the pattern."

"What's that noise coming from the cabin, Chauncy?" said Finn, looking towards the half open door beside the hopper.

Bawn cocked an ear, listening for a sound. "Could it be the motor starting up, do you think?"

"No, everything's dead, you can tell that!" said Finn walking over to the door. "It sounds like . . . bloody Dancer! I thought so! Here he is snoring his evil head off."

Hearing the shouts Dancer had scrambled to his feet and was in the doorway smoothing down his long, black hair as Mallowry caught up with them. She saw he was wearing a red, slim-line shirt which sharpened almost to a point at his waist above his black, skin-tight trousers and shiny leather shoes.

"Has it started up again yet, Finn?" asked Dancer looking nervously at the big ganger.

"What are you expecting, the Paso Doble? Look Dancer, if you have to catch up on your bloody beauty kip, use your own time."

Dancer held up his arms in surrender. "It was only a quick break, Finn, The crusher was kaput at the time."

"So was your dumper until I fixed it. What were you doing, going along with your head in the air thinking about some tart and ended up in the shaugh? Never mind." He turned to Mallowry with a look of resignation in his face. "Dancer, Mrs. Bain. Dick Dancer from Balham. Philanderer, palais creeper and male lead in three sets of French postcards. He's so fashion-conscious he even wears open-toed wellies in the summer. All right, trip along Dancer."

Finn watched the muckshifter run off to join Keen in the dumper truck. "He's an eight hour a day man, that one. Three of them at work, the rest asleep. I think it was Moses who said you need six hours sleep for a man, seven for a woman, and eight for a fool."

Mallowry looked at him teasingly. "I don't believe women sleep any longer than men."

"They seem to get their quota."

"Perhaps it depends how much they're allowed."

The Irishman gave her a teasing glance. "Could be," he said. "What are your sleeping arrangements then, Mrs. Bain?"

She smiled openly. "Now, who's the great one for the questions?" she said.

As they looked at each other for a moment the machinery at the base of the crusher suddenly sprang to life and the conveyor belt beside them began transporting the heavy chunks of rock to the top of the tower, where they were falling below on to the huge churning blades.

Finn pointed to a large square boulder, almost five feet across, which was on its way up the belt. "When that reaches ground level it will be in about six pieces no more than a foot wide," he said. "They'll send those off to the secondary crusher, then the tertiary, until we finally end up with gravel, like split peas, even sand if you want it that fine. The machines do most of it these days, but if you want to see a real old-time circus act we've a feller over there drop-balling it with a monkey."

Mallowry winced. "That sounds rather painful."

"Come on, I'll introduce you to Liam the Liar, a man as good as his name."

"I thought you were a bit crushing on poor Dancer," said Mallowry as they began walking behind the rows of lorries waiting beside the hopper.

"The man's a bit of a dandy but he's a good worker. He's always got an eye out for the main chance, that's his problem. They're all a pretty good bunch really. They may curse and spit and piss all over the place, but most of them have a feel for the soil and the stone. It's almost a kind of reverence with some of them, though they never admit it. These fellows are the aldermen of the earth. They've served their time with the stuff. They know just how to handle it. Mind you, you caught them all on their best behaviour today. They're all flying. It's Poet's Day."

"What's Poet's Day?" she asked.

"Every Friday's Poet's Day. It means 'Piss Off Early Tomorrow's Saturday.' Saturday is the muckshifters' Sabbath. Six days shalt thou labour says the Sun Man and on the seventh the muckies shalt do their own thing."

"And where do the muckies go on a Saturday?"

Finn leapt over a two-foot trench which The Goose was scooping out in his traxcavator for an underground electricity cable. He turned and helped Mallowry across after him.

"Our needs," he said, "are simple. We like to pore over a few chapters of Proust or maybe put down a line or two of iambic verse or perhaps make up a four for bridge. Nothing too demanding."

"And what do you do, Finn?"

The big Irishman gave her a faint smile. "My Saturdays are even less complicated. In the afternoons I usually take a book up the valley somewhere, it's cheaper than a cab. And I just sort of read and ponce around and read a bit more. Somewhere like Teg's Head, just off the mountain road up to Hounshale. It's that big round chunk of Cheviots which seems to have been sawn off to make room for the valley. There's a spot there where if the trees ever saw two people at one time they would think the Vikings were invading again."

"Will you be there tomorrow?"

Finn looked at her, noticing for the first time her eyes were a deep brown. "It's been known," he said.

Suddenly there was a loud crash behind them as a large boulder shattered into four pieces as the heavy steel ball, swinging from a chain on the end of the jib of a dragline crashed into it. Mallowry saw a hunched figure in the cab lurch to one side as the force of the impact rocked the vehicle.

"Which one's the monkey?" she inquired.

Grabbing her arm Finn led her over to the dragline. "Here's a feller who'll tell you," he said.

Mallowry could see the yellow uneven teeth of the man as he stuck his ruddy, flat-capped head through the cab window.

"Mrs. Bain wants to know which one's the monkey, Liam?" called Finn.

Liam grinned as he slipped the cap from his greying head. "I've been asking meself that for years," he said. "It ought to be me, my darlin', I don't have to come but according to the Bible it's that fierce-looking object on the end of the string there."

"He means the muckshifter's bible," said Finn. " 'Moving the Earth', the international shit-shifting handbook, but these contraptions go back so far they probably used them in Jericho. I think they keep them just to remind everybody that a bit of human skill counts for something. This feller up here is Liam the Liar. You want to believe nothing he tells you and only half what he shows you."

Mallowry stopped laughing and stared at him closely. "Are you happy here, Finn?" she asked.

Finn found himself returning her gaze. "For one who's tight with the answers you ask a devil of a lot of questions," he said. "No muckshifter will ever admit to you he's ever happy where he is. He was happy in the site before the last. The one where the blisters have blown away and he can only remember the good crack. It's easier to have a feel for yesterday."

He broke off suddenly as he saw the yellow safari truck pull up a hundred yards below them in the clearing in front of the quarry office.

"This'll be your friend come looking for you," muttered Finn, as he saw the big yellow Labrador leap down from the cab followed by Fergus Bain, who was still wearing his green check sports jacket and tie despite the heat of the afternoon.

Even in the distance Mallowry could see he was in an angry mood, taking his eyes from the ground only to glare petulantly from side to side as though expecting a reception committee to meet him.

"If you still want to know the answer to that question, Finn, I'll tell you," she said quietly. "It's back to back. Like book-ends."

Finn wrinkled his eyes, puzzled for a moment. Then his lips broke into a smile. He was still smiling as they walked quickly down the hill to meet the Sun Man.

Ellis Curran was walking more briskly than usual. Anyone who had risen as early as he had that morning and was accustomed to his slow, almost diffident movements on the site, might have detected a jaunty mood in his step.

For the last five miles he had been striding out along the west bank of the Corbar, heading busily north towards Hounshale.

Around him April had piled the green earth with patches of celandines and had begun to repopulate the bare river banks again with sand martins and water fowl, but Curran's pale, deep-sunken eyes were staring ahead with a glow of anticipation.

As he walked, an old brown haversack kept bouncing against his windproofed kagoul, a bright orange garment which only served to emphasize the bland greyness of his face.

Even on the colour photographs Clandy's publicity department did for the D.O.E. and the trade journals, Curran always came out grey. Against a stone background he sometimes looked like one of those natural history films where you had to wait for something to move before you could really be sure which was stone and which was Curran.

After thirty-seven years in the earth-moving business he had no illusions about his ability to stir the public's imagination with startling discoveries about soil. True, he had written five papers on the subject as well as demonstrating his expertise in numerous lecture rooms, but each year the faces of the trainees seemed to get younger, and Curran felt they were regarding him as part of the hardware of the industry rather than an organic contributor.

There had even been talk that towards the end of a lecture on stabilisation of boulder clay, a student waved a pencil in front of him and the class came to the conclusion that Curran had been talking in his sleep for at least ten minutes. In recent years he had become more and more interested in what could be found in the soil rather than the soil itself. While Clandy's were building a motorway near Derby, Curran had discovered the traces of a Romano–British village and had afterwards written a paper on the influence of the Brigantes on Derbyshire. The experience had persuaded the Irishman to rediscover some of the earlier dedication he had applied to earth sciences and use it in the interests of archaeology but the rewards were thinly scattered, and only occasionally did the spirit rise above the flesh.

Now he was sixty, with no family since Sinead had died, only a collection of theories he would never put into practice and an increasing tiredness. He also had piles. He knew he was long overdue the regular embarrassment of another visit to another new doctor who would prescribe yet another "This should ease it" ointment which never did. Curran regarded his piles as he regarded his government. Both were a constant source of irritation and there was nothing he could effectively do about them.

Curran had almost reached the weir when he turned inland,

skirting the ruins of the old peel tower and taking a straight course towards Bundy Mere in the distance.

A stone curlew rose from the bracken on his right, its long, downward-curving beak calling him away from its nest, but the bird need not have bothered. Curran knew exactly where he was going.

He finally stopped beside two large boulders where the land rose momentarily before sloping down to the mere. Placing his haversack carefully beside him, he removed a flat sliver of stone from the ground in front of him and with both hands began slowly scooping out the loose earth from beneath it.

Pressing down into the hole with his fingers until he felt something solid, he turned to his haversack with a contented smile on his face and brought out a small trowel, a six-inch boring tool and a handbrush. Using the trowel he began systematically removing the turf around the hole, inserting his fingers into the ground from time to time as though to give himself reassurance. When he had finished he had carved out a circular trough, two feet across, from which he scooped out the remaining earth, placing it in a pile behind him. Then he reached down and lifted a heavy, dirt-stained circular object from the hole, which he placed beside him and began brushing the earth from it with deliberate, unhurried movements.

Gradually the indentations on the black metal shaped themselves before his eyes into something which made him leap to his feet. He gave a short incoherent cry before he raised the object in a sudden gesture of triumph to the sun.

In his eagerness to explore the find from every angle Curran failed to notice that Finn Rafferty was standing in front of him.

"I saw you from the road," said Finn, his eyes fixed on the black shape in Curran's hands. "What in Jesus do you have there?"

Curran caught his arm as he held the object out in front of him. "What would you say it was?" he asked, his face beaming with excitement.

"It's some sort of shield, isn't it?"

Curran nodded and gave the black disc another rub with the sleeve of his kagoul. "It's the Eagle of Rome," he announced boldly. "The bird is back after nearly 2,000 years."

Finn examined the shield, gently feeling the rough, raised bronze in the centre of the shield where the bird with outstretched wings seemed almost to be thrusting itself forward from the flat metal surrounding it. "She's a proud-lookin' thing sure," he murmured. "Have you just this minute spotted her?"

Curran smiled. "I knew she was there yesterday. I staked her out and came back for her this morning."

Finn stared at him in disbelief. "You mean you found her yesterday and you went away and left her here all night?"

"I reckoned that since she had been out here nearly 2,000 years already, she could take one more night on her own," said Curran drily. "Besides I didn't want to rush the pleasure."

"Soils," said Finn, bringing his broad hand down with a hefty slap on the little man's shoulder, "you're a dark horse, you know that, don't you?"

Curran extricated himself and shuffled across to where he had left his haversack. After fumbling inside for a few seconds he brought out a thermos flask and a half bottle of Scotch. "What's it to be?" he offered grandly. "Coffee or a wee drop of the other?"

"At this time of the morning?" shouted Finn. "Soils, you'll be taking women out next."

Placing the shield carefully on the grass in front of him, Curran unscrewed the flask and looked at it for a moment before changing his mind and tossing it behind him. "Bugger the coffee, we'll wet the bird's head rightly," he said as Finn hit the ground laughing. "Do you know I had a feeling last night about this and I decided that if this was to turn out to be what I hoped it would be, we couldn't let the occasion pass without suitable recognition. Mind you, I'd have brought a crate if I'd known you were coming, Finn."

"Did you know it would be here or was it luck?" asked Finn, accepting a red plastic cup from Curran.

"It was a bit of both really. You see you could come out here and dig up the whole valley and not feel a fig in your fingers. But if you dig a little with your head you can narrow the odds a bit." He pointed to the cluster of rocks where he had found the shield. "Now if you look around you'll see that that spot there is just about the only loosely defendable position round here in the valley bottom. From here you can get a good view from all sides."

Finn leapt to his feet and started gazing around him, "Yes, but you'd hardly choose this sort of place to fight a battle."

Curran eased himself from the ground. "No you wouldn't, but the Romans were great ones for the rearguard actions. When they had to retreat, and they had to more and more during the last years of their time here, they used to leave behind a handful of men, sometimes as few as two or three to put up a scrap long enough for the rest of the legion to make their escape. Now if two or three fellows stood there between those rocks, there would be no telling from the north side if the whole legion was behind them lying in wait for the tribes. And by the time they discovered they were only up against a wee slurp of men prepared to fight to the death, the legion would have been halfway back to the Wall."

Lifting the heavy shield from the ground, Finn suddenly felt close to it. "What do you think happened to the fellow who owned this?"

"I'd like to think he honoured the bird," said Curran softly. "He'd have been a centurion, you know, with a shield that shape. Men will have died worse deaths since. I expect the shield fell into some crevasse in the confusion and rested there till now. Which reminds me, we've got a job to do."

He walked over to the freshly dug patch of earth beneath the rocks and began painstakingly replacing the soil he had removed.

Finn joined him. "There's hardly any need for housekeeping with half an ocean waiting to be poured on this lot," he said.

Curran was now starting on the small individual clumps of turf, placing them thoughtfully into the ground, as though remembering where each piece came from. "A good muckshifter always cleans up after him, you ought to know that, Rafferty," he said with a smile.

Rafferty dropped to his knees and began helping to repair the hole. "Let's hope Dando doesn't spot us," he said. "He'd be in two minds whether to insist on double time or to have the men out. Have you found much before?"

The old soils engineer carefully lowered a sod into the edge of the crater before patting it down firmly with the flat of his other hand. "I found a coin a couple of months back. Pius Antoninus, around AD 150 I should say."

"He was the feller who built the other wall, wasn't he?"

"Yes, the turf one up in Scotland. Sure it wasn't much of a thing. It wasn't meant to last as long as your man down here but the fact it was built indicates there was quite a lot of activity by the legions between the two places, and you can't have that amount of chaps traipsing round the place without leaving something behind."

"Did you find anything else?"

"No, no, just a few pieces of old pottery, Samian ware and stuff like that, but that stuff's ten a penny down here. I haven't found the big one yet, and I doubt if I will."

Finn sat back on his legs and threw up his hands. "Now you know more about this game than I do Soils, but, uncultured dolt that I am, I know that right at this minute there won't be hordes of people digging in their back gardens and coming up with 2,000-year-old Roman shields. And you want more? What are you after, a whole chariot?"

Curran looked at him hard. "I'm looking for a goddess, Rafferty," he said quietly.

"A what?" shouted Finn, leaping to his feet.

"A Roman goddess," he repeated. "I don't know what she looks like, where she is. I don't even know her name. But she's here somewhere."

Finn stuck both hands on his hips and faced him squarely. "Soils! Shields I can take. And Roman soldiers fighting to the death for the honour of the legion. But goddesses, damn it! Where in hell would you expect to get to grips with one of them?"

Curran was perfectly relaxed as he replied. "In a temple, of course. Where they belong. Now by the same reasoning that led me to the shield and whatever else we may find under here, there should also be, or has been, a temple here."

"I can't see how that follows," said Finn flatly.

"Well I feel it does, on account of the water."

"The water?" exclaimed Finn mockingly. "Sure we haven't got the stuff yet."

Curran bent down beneath the small blackthorn bush close by and picked up two thin branches. "Not the reservoir, Rafferty, the water that's always been here. The stuff I've seen you go looking for more than once."

"You mean the wells?"

"The wells and the springs, the wee life-giving things the Roman diviners used to douse out for the legions. Now look, I reckon that this place was one good march out for the legions on the Wall. And on the way out they would have had sufficient water with them. But coming back, this would have been just the place where they would have felt the last thirst before getting home."

"But surely they would have been following the Corbar for miles right back into camp? They could have grabbed a helmet-ful any time they wanted sure."

Curran shook his head. "Do you ever drink from big rivers Finn? It would have been riskier still with this one. The Corbar runs all the way from Scotland, and with their Roman enemies down here on the route the old Caledonians were not averse to mixing stuff in it to cause a few aches down in the Wall. No. It had to be a spring and it needed to be high up, because unless they were flitting for their lives the legions always travelled on hilly ground to reduce the risk of attack. So that narrows it down to these two slopes on either side of the valley."

Finn took the final clump of grass from Curran's hand and fitted it into the centre of the hole. "Where does the goddess fit into all this then, Soils?" he said.

"If she's here she'll be close to the spring," said Curran, "for if the Romans were ever desperate for it they would be so grateful to find water, they would set to and build a temple on the spot to whichever of their water goddesses was in favour at the time. A few years back they found a shrine to Coventina beside a well on the Wall at Carrawburgh. Now if I can find that spring on one of these slopes I might be able to come up with a new one. Perhaps you'll give me a hand one of these days?"

Finn drew in his breath. "That's a hell of a lot of slope, Mister."

"It is," said Curran, "but then we've got a hell of a lot of time to look for it."

Curran began picking up his tools and replacing them in the haversack with the thermos flask and empty whisky bottle. Finally he lifted the shield and gazed thoughtfully at it once more.

"What are you aiming to do with the bird, Soils?" asked Finn. "Send her to a museum?"

"Not if I can help it," said Curran. "Some of these things may as well stay in the soil for the number of people who go and see them. History should be lived with every day in normal surroundings. I'd like to see this placed high up on the dam itself where people can be reminded that this was the past that helped to shape all that we're doing now."

Finn handed him the small brush the engineer had thrown down in his excitement. "How are you getting back Soils?"

"On these two things inside my boots," smiled Curran.

"But it's about seven miles back there. Look, I've got the car on the top road – I'll run you home if you like."

Curran thanked him and declined. "A walk is as long or as short as what you have in your head at the time," he said. "On this particular occasion I won't even feel my feet."

For a moment Finn stood watching the small man picking his way down the hillock. A hare, suddenly surprised in its form beneath a clump of benty grass by the unaccustomed activity, broke from under the old man's feet and began racing back up the hill.

Finn picked up a stone, made to hurl it at the disturbed animal but changed his mind and, still tossing the stone from hand to hand, began walking thoughtfully towards the high wooded slopes of Teg's Head.

Finn Rafferty had been reading for more than an hour in the clearing when she came.

A rustle of branches on his right gave him just enough time to toss away the remains of his sixth cigarette over the boulder he had been sitting against before she appeared.

She was wearing a plain, dark green dress which swayed against the bare bushes on each side of the narrow path, as her long, slim legs moved effortlessly over the brown winter leaves.

Finn could see that she had swept back her hair in a green band and that there was the faintest suggestion of a smile about her full, lovely mouth as her eyes turned to him.

"If you're real," he said, "loosen your hair."

Mallowry reached her hands up slowly, releasing the band and allowing her long black hair to fall into the soft hollows of her neck. "Why did you ask that?" she said, tossing her head as she smiled at him.

Finn sprang to his feet and went to her. "Because I wanted to be sure you weren't one of Curran's goddesses. He was telling me this morning you find them in the most unlikely places."

"And your verdict?"

"Of course you are. At least, you're a class above anyone else in the place."

When she looked up at him he was smiling. It was a broad,

confident smile, the smile of a boy caught up in a huge body which seemed to be straining with power beneath his coarse, blue denim shirt and jeans. His blond hair was an untidy burst around his head and his wide cheekbones had already caught the sun, which was streaming through the unclothed branches as though it were illuminating a private forest cave.

"But this, madam, is my place," he said softly. "What do you think of it?"

"It's beautiful. Do you bring all your women here?"

"I have a special bird call. But she only comes for one thing. They have a fierce appetite, sparrows."

Mallowry smiled and moved over to the only open side of the clearing. She saw they were on a high ledge of the Faunes at a spot where the slope plunged down into the valley, where away in the distance the Corbar river could be seen winding its way between the clumps of willows and benty grass on its banks.

"So this is all yours then, Mr. Rafferty, is it?" she asked teasingly.

Finn joined her at the lip of the slope, sharing the view for a moment. "Madam, I once used to own all this," he said, spreading his arms wide, "and places so much bigger than this, that your arms couldn't grasp them. That was before people like you told me I didn't."

"Like me?" said Mallowry with a look of surprise.

"I mean the Big House folk," said Finn. "You see, when I was a kid in Ireland I used to own a great field so vast a horseman could ride for a day and not reach the end of it. And a forest so black a torch would hardly glow in it. And the river, madam, it was so fat with fish there were days when you could walk over their backs to cross to the other side. Now I thought the only thing you had to do to claim conclusive possession of these things was simply to see them first. They explained to me later, of course, that the people in the Big House owned them, all of them, and that all we owned was the shirts on our backs and little else."

"It must have been quite a shock to you," said Mallowry, walking over and picking up the book Finn had thrown aside, before sitting down.

Finn followed her. "If I ever get done for trespassing I'll base my defence on my deprived childhood," he said.

Mallowry raised her eyes above the book. "You weren't kidding me about the books, were you? It is Proust."

"I never like to disappoint anyone," he said with a wink.

She looked deep into his eyes. "I'm sure you won't," she said.

He thumped his fingers against the book cover. "It's all true, you know. Sometimes on library days you have to beat their fists from the counter to control their enormous literary appetites. You should have seen the queues down there last week for Stendhal's latest."

"Did they have girls in the Big Houses. I mean as well as books?"

"The biggest," said Finn. "They were big in every sense of the word. A schoolteacher we had there once explained the theory to me. He argued that the Big House girls were always a good three years ahead of the cottage girls physically, on account of all the fine meat, shellfish and wine they had which the others didn't. He said the rich food used to develop their organs and bits of things faster than the cornbread and murphies they were getting on the land."

Mallowry slid back on the grass cupping the back of her head in her hands. "Did they really need all that shellfish?" she murmured. "It's so beautiful here."

"There's a hornbeam in leaf down there," said Finn. "The hawthorn's all of a burst behind us and next week, did you know, the chestnuts break out."

"Finn?" said Mallowry, touching his arm.

"Every year the chestnuts come into leaf on April the 18th as though they all had little calendars stuffed up their barks."

Mallowry turned to face him, her dark hair falling across her cheek as she supported herself with her elbow. "Finn, I'm a Big House girl," she whispered.

"Did you know the last of God's things to get itself organised for the spring?" said Finn.

"You, Finn?" said Mallowry flatly.

"It's the mulberry tree. The very last tree in the forest to open its leaves after the winter."

"Do you want me, Finn?"

"Now some people, on account of this, describe the mulberry as the wisest tree of them all because it misses the late frosts and always takes a good look round before. . . ."

"Finn darling."

"On the other hand others say it shows unnatural and unnecessary caution."

"Finn," said Mallowry, slipping her fingers inside the front of his open shirt, "do you want me?"

Without looking at her Finn said in a thick, almost hoarse voice "Mallowry Bain. . . ."

The sudden fierceness of her mouth on his lips forced him back against the grass. Finn felt her reaching for the buttons of his shirt, easily prising the coarse cloth apart and releasing the full swell of his chest. He heard the swish of a shoe as it hit the hawthorn bush behind him, the other sailing past his head immediately afterwards, in pursuit.

Opening his eyes, he found himself staring at Mallowry's firm round breasts without even noticing that she had flung the green dress on the ground behind her.

Now her hands were at his denim jeans, forcing them down to his ankles in one compulsive movement, as his underpants soared into the bushes beyond the boulder. When he looked down he saw she was quite naked.

She kneeled over him, giving a sudden cry of delight. "Oh you're a Cavalier!" she said, unpeeling him as she flung herself across his body, her fingers feverishly exploring his mouth, his eyes, his thick flaxen hair. "You're lovely, lovely," she said loudly, biting at his neck as he watched his socks being pelted into the trees. She pulled his face down, thrusting her tongue into his mouth, pressing her teeth against his lips.

Finn moved towards her, only to be thrown backwards again as she invaded him, fastening him to her flesh like some desperate insect sucking from its host. He lay back as she harvested his body with great reaping sweeps of her limbs as they writhed in the green earth.

He was aware of being inescapably drawn into a fierce current, which seemed to rise and fall almost independently of him and which gave him the impression of being a distant observer. Only when he erupted and the whole land was in clash did he feel the force from within himself which raged a brief moment before shuddering into grateful oblivion.

Mallowry was already on her feet when he opened his eyes. "Are you all right, Finn?" she asked.

Finn made no movement. "I was waiting for the pillage," he said.

She slid to her knees and put her hand on his forehead. "Did I surprise you?"

"I thought I was being sacked," he said. "I feel now how Carthage must have looked."

"I needed you, Finn."

"Christ I'd hate to meet you after Lent."

"Wasn't I good for you, Finn?" said Mallowry, helping him to reach for his shirt.

"Good for me?" exclaimed Finn. "You were good for both of us. You even had a dig at my religion when you knew you had me helpless."

"I only said you were a Cavalier."

"Me Mammy wouldn't have anything of Cromwell's near the house. She said 'you'll be glad of any protection you get when those big, English women with their great ravenous, insatiable needs get their hands on you!' "

Mallowry buttoned up the last two buttons on his shirt. "You're teasing me, Rafferty," she said. "You loved it really, didn't you?"

Finn stretched out a hand. "Come here, Mrs. Bain," he commanded. "Wait a minute, would you go and field my drawers first."

When Mallowry returned with his clothes, he dressed slowly, finally pulling his blue denim jeans over his legs with a serious look on his face. When he had finished he put his arm round her. "Now, Mallowry Bain, I want to ask you, quite plainly and openly, to do a very sinful thing for me. You'll probably be so coy and shocked you'll drop on the spot."

"What is it?"

"I've always wondered what it would be like to kiss you, Mrs. Bain," he said.

Mallowry put her hands on both sides of his cheeks and moved towards him.

"Now hold on a moment," shouted Finn before removing her hands and placing each of them carefully and deliberately on his shoulders. Then drawing her gently towards him he kissed her on the lips, softly at first but increasing in pressure until the force of his mouth pinned her to the ground as she felt the warmth of his great blond head burning into her face. It was several seconds before she opened her eyes and looked up at him. "You're a beautiful, beautiful bastard, Rafferty," she gasped.

Finn's blue eyes wrinkled mischievously. "That was for taking the breath from my body before," he said. "My old man, good, plain man that he was, always said sex with a woman was a bit like papering a room. Eighty per cent of it was in the preparation.

Mallowry sat up, shaking down her black hair. "And he never met a wall which asked to be papered, you mean?"

"You could have held vespers for a monk in our place for the first sixteen years of my life. My father wouldn't have a loose word spoken within them."

"Did you like your father?" she asked, raising her long slender legs up until her chin was resting against her knees.

Finn picked a long stem of grass and began chewing it. "He was a hell of a man for his day. He was on the Council you know."

"Clooney Council?"

"Clooney Council. They tell me if he'd learned to say yes more often, his name might have been up on the board with the rest of the big shots. You see, there were only two things anyone gave a toss for in Clooney, and they were chickens and potatoes. You were either in the chicken lobby or the murphy lobby and it worked all right until they decided to lump the lot together in a sort of County Council. Anyhow Clooney was allocated just one councillor and they decided father, who was a chicken man, should be first to go along there for us. However, when he got there he found they too had a chicken lobby and a murphy lobby and the chicken men immediately grabbed him and told him he would be speaking and voting for them. So father asks 'What if I happen to agree with the murphy people once or twice and decide to vote for them?' 'Ah then,' says they, 'we'll find somebody else, for it's no part of your job.' So he took his cap and said 'and apparently common sense is no part of yours, gentlemen,' and he came home."

Mallowry watched Finn throw the stem of grass on to the ground in front of him. "Was he on the council long?" she asked.

"Not long after that. He was a tall poppy. He had to be cut

down."

Mallowry suddenly raised herself from the ground in one graceful movement and stood for a moment holding her arms above her head, before starting to walk slowly around the small clearing. Finn gazed at her, watching the sun splash against her naked body, dappling her breasts and shoulders as the shadows of the bare branches fell across her.

"Do you not like clothes?"

"I like the sun," said Mallowry, avoiding his gaze. "I like the feel of the grass, the trees, all this." She turned to face him, her eyes dark with longing. "And most of all I like you watching me. What are you thinking?"

"I was thinking how fortunate we are we don't get many trippers up here in April . . . and that I should have been up to that Big House more often when I had the chance."

Mallowry raised a hand to her hair, smoothing her fingers down the side of her face and continuing the movement over her breast and down to the side of her thigh. "What were you really thinking, Finn?"

Finn pulled a cigarette from the packet beside him and placed it in his mouth. "The Celts, you know, always used to send a naked woman ahead of them in the battle line. It was supposed to confuse the enemy. I was thinking that if they'd sent you they would never have lost."

"You made that up."

"No, I never tell lies about history."

"What were you thinking, then?"

Finn grinned. "Do you know, the best cartoon I ever saw was of Lady Godiva coming home bollock, well naked anyway, leading her horse home to her man. She had a look on her face like a poisoned pup, her thumb was pointing down and she was saying 'Coventry 0, Gillingham 2'. Wasn't that good, don't you think?"

"And you think I'm like her," said Mallowry petulantly.

"Oh no, indeed," he said. "You'd never lose 2-0 to anyone."

She sat down beside him and pressed the tips of her teeth against the inside of his raised knee. "I want you, Finn," she whispered.

"When would that be?" he asked.

"Now," she said impatiently "Just now."

When he made no reply she opened her eyes and saw that he was staring towards the valley with a strange smile on his face.

"Why are you smiling?"

He looked down at her. "Just now," he said, "the lilac is in bloom."

Mallowry pushed her fingers against his lips. "And all before my little room, And in my flower beds, I think. . . ."

He leaned over and kissed her on the cheek. "Smile the carnation and the pink." he said.

"You're a surprise a day," she said.

"Why should I be?" he said. "I told you all muckshifters go in for the books."

"But I mean it's an odd poem for an Irishman to know."

He laughed, showing his strong, even teeth. "You can blame Uncle Eamonn for that. He went off sniping for you in the First War. Not that he particularly set out to save English skins but he was a Cork man and they always did the daft things like fightin'. Anyway he came back from his second stint at the Somme with just two things, crup and Granchester."

"What's crup?" asked Mallowry.

He pointed a finger at her. "Ah, that proves you're a Big House girl," he said. "Down on the site they usually ask what Granchester is. Crup is an inflammation of the scrotum. They used to get it through being too close together in the trenches."

"So you picked Granchester."

"I had no choice. He left the book of poems in the house after he was released and he took the crup with him. Apart from 'Celtic Tales from Old Ireland', it was the only book I could get my hands round for a year. . . . I learned most of the poems by heart. Especially Granchester. I thought for years you were all like that in England."

As Mallowry turned towards him, Finn could see that her eyes were moist. "Finn," she said, "what happened just then was one of the most glorious moments of my life. It was fantastic. Finn, I just want you to love me."

Rafferty lowered his head gently and kissed her. "You haven't noticed me running away, have you? Look, have you thought for a minute about my side of things. Here's you, wife of the biggest shout on the site and me, Finn Rafferty, stoneyard ganger, Mick of the muckies – You could have stepped straight off a Christmas tree for all the sense it makes. If I have a station in the great scheme of things it's deeper than St. Pancras underground, and yet here's me quietly steeping myself in God's nature and the boss's wife suddenly takes a great lep at me, and I'm expected to take it in my stride as though I do it every waking day. . . . If wet, in the Parish Hall."

Mallowry made a sound between a laugh and a sob and kissed him on the cheek. "I'm sorry, Finn. Perhaps I'm too used to getting what I want."

"Does Gus give you what you want?"

"Gus, Mr. Rafferty, gives me a . . . a pain in the arse."

"Kinky."

"Shut up. No, he gives me a cheque book and never looks at the stubs and he gives me a kind of security and he gives me plenty of lovely, lovely time."

"They always say the second wife sits on the best lap."

"They all say it except the second wives, I suspect," she said.

"Anyway, how would you know? You've never tried it, have you?"
"No."
"No wife?"
"No lap."
She laughed. "Everybody has a lap, silly."
Finn's face was quite serious when he looked at her. "No, there you're wrong, Mrs. Bain. Only people who sit down have laps. I've found that most of the things you really need to do in life, you can do either standing up or lying down. So no lap, no wife."
"I'm one wife, no lap," she said.
"Where did you meet up with Gus anyway?"
"Give me another cigarette." Finn lit two cigarettes and handed one to her.
"It was in Bahrein three years ago," she said. "I was working as a secretary for an oil company."
"I remember, the Acobir job. A motorway contract, wasn't it?"
"Gus was project manager for it. I met him at one of those parties you throw for the locals, the sweeteners you call them? Anyway, that was the start of it."
"And now you're going back to him?"
Mallowry looked up at him quickly. "Not yet, Finn, it's not that late." She saw he had put one of his socks on and was fiddling with the laces of his shoe. "Don't put your shoes on," she said. "I don't want you to leave me yet."
Finn picked up the book for the grass beside him. "I'll read you some Brooke," he said.
She took the book from his hands and closed it. "Hold me, Finn," she whispered almost fiercely. "Hold me really close."
He reached out, drawing her smooth white shoulders into his body as his lips softly touched her eyes, her nose and finally kissed her half parted mouth.
Mallowry smiled as he broke away and lay gazing at her body. "I feel good with you, Finn," she said. "It feels almost as if I've been out here with you all my life."
She saw he was smiling too. "What are you thinking about now?" she asked him.
"I was thinking, for the best of reasons mind you, of what my old man said when I got my first car, at least my first brand-new one. He said 'I'll give you a word of advice. Never let anyone else at the controls, because a new car gets to know the feel of its owner. It knows you from the moment you sit in it and anyone else might put the thing into a state of confusion.' "
"And what does that mean, darling?"
"It means," said Finn, determinedly undoing the buttons of his blue denim shirt, "that this time I'm doing the driving."
Fifty feet below them on the wooded slope, Ellis Curran paused to readjust his haversack on his back, thinking for a moment he had

heard the teasing, muffled voice of a woman asking "Did your father ever hear of dual controls?" Finally, accepting he was completely alone, he moved off again, his eyes firmly fixed on the sheep path ahead.

Even though the two limewashed bands stretching almost the whole width of the valley, between Todholes and Calcherside, were a good hundred yards apart, Archbold drove the Range Rover meticulously along the left hand side of the flattened earth track.

Sir William Clandy, in the passenger seat, could hear the raised, angry voices of the three men even before he recognized their faces.

He had stepped down from the vehicle, assisted by Archbold, before they appeared to notice him. He heard Liederman mutter "Cool it" through his gleaming white teeth as Bain and Dando turned to face him.

"Good afternoon gentlemen," said Sir William, smiling benignly as their grunted replies came back to him. "I gather you've reached an impasse."

Bain's lower lip trembled as he spoke. "I wouldn't say that," he said before shooting a quick glance towards Dando. "It's nothing that can't be resolved calmly, I'm sure."

"Just the way you were doing it, in fact," said Clandy, who was still smiling. "Now look, I'm just a simple, old-fashioned muck-shifter with simple old-fashioned ideas. You've got your base lines, build me a dam between them, all right?"

"Right," said Liederman, tilting his helmet as he looked first at Bain and Dando before grinning to the Clandy chairman. "That's just what I said. Why stand here scratching our asses when we could be getting the show on the road?"

"So what's the hold-up?" asked Clandy.

Bain shook his head, "We're waiting. . . ."

"You're waiting?" interrupted Dando.

"Just a moment," said Clandy tiredly. "Look gentlemen, we're all waiting. But what the devil for?"

"The grout curtain," said Bain.

"Oh I see, it's one of those again, is it?" said Sir William. "To grout or not to grout. All right then, let's get it settled. What do you say Gus?"

The small project manager walked bouncily towards the centre of the two lines, just far enough away for him to need to raise his voice when he swung round to them.

"As I see it," he said, spreading his arms, "we know everything there is to know about what's going to be above ground here for the whole width of this valley. We know the height, weight, composition, the stresses which the material will have to meet. But how much do we really know about this?" He kicked the ground with his boot, sending up a series of puffs of dust as his toecap dug into the dry earth. "Before anything goes up here we need to be absolutely certain we're on ground we can trust. And a grout curtain is the only way of giving us that sort of cast-iron assurance."

"Thank you, Gus," said Sir William, before nodding to Dando, who was slowly shaking his head. "What do you say, Griff?"

Dando dug the heel of his boot into the ground in front of the returning Bain." I say that's bedrock," he said. "We've hit bottom and we've 2,900 man-hours of scraping behind us as well as the test borings to prove it. That's solid rock, as thick as Samson's skull. And if the tests show that, what's the point of going to all the expense and time-wasting of drilling 40-metre holes at 10-metre intervals and pumping liquid cement down there which will come squirting back in your face."

"There could be cracks down there; we haven't tried it yet," said Bain, frowning.

Dando ignored him and spoke to the Clandy chairman. "We've been trying grout curtains for a hundred years. No one's ever proved they've worked. To the old school they're a bit like warming the teapot: it's something we do because our mother and our granny did, so it must be good."

"It's accepted practice, Griff," protested Bain. "We allowed for it on the tender."

"It was once accepted practice to bleed muckshifters when they were sick and sometimes when they weren't. That doesn't make it right because we used to do it in the . . . olden days."

"You can't prove it doesn't work," said Bain tersely.

Dando smiled. "No, and you can't prove it does. And it's going to cost about £270,000 to follow your tradition."

"About £250,000 with the new modifications."

"And another two months' wait before we can make a start. Look! It's expensive, it's unnecessary and it'll hold up the job! I've got men sitting around waiting to lay the earth core and the first of the gravel filters is here . . . they've already been waiting three weeks for Gus to . . . for a decision to be made about this curtain."

"Eighteen days," said Bain.

"All right gentlemen," said Sir William, holding up his hands. "Don't let's get petty about this." He turned to Liederman, who had been watching the two men with a smile playing about his lips. "Bob, what's your opinion?"

Liederman scratched the seat of his white jeans and screwed up his face. "Well there's been two schools of thought about this for years, er Bill? I must admit, back in the States, some of the newer dams haven't used them. It depends on the quality of the bedrock and, as Dando says, it certainly seems rock-solid. If I were pushed I'd be inclined to. . . ."

"To get the show on the road?" suggested Sir William, eyeing him closely.

"Right," said Liederman.

Clandy looked at Bain, who lowered his eyes as he fidgetted nervously with his fingers.

"Well Gus," he said, "I'm sorry but there it is. No grout curtain. . . ." He turned to Dando, who was wrestling with a smile. "Get your men in then, Griff," he said, pausing before glancing back at Bain. "If that's all right with you, Gus."

Liederman and Dando had joined Sir William and were beginning to return to the three parked site vehicles when the Clandy chairman noticed Bain wasn't with them. He turned and walked back to where Bain was staring at the ground.

"You know there's nothing personal in this Gus, old boy, don't you?"

Bain looked up but his eyes seemed to be gazing over Clandy's head. "No," he said in a distant voice, "I don't suppose there is."

Sir William put a hand on his shoulder and began easing him forward to where Dando and Liederman were waiting. "It's just that with over £140 million of taxpayers' money being spent up here alone, we can't afford to be er. . . ."

"Personal?" said Bain, looking directly into his face.

"Exactly, my boy," said Sir William, easing him towards the others with a gentle slap in the middle of his back. "Exactly."

Finn ran down the slope from the Gamelpath road leaping the white boulders and clumps of benty grass jutting out from the steep hillside.

At times the brown burlap bag in his hand almost threatened to bring him down as it swung across the flying knees of his blue denims.

Glancing anxiously at his wrist-watch he swerved to avoid a limping woman on the sheep path in front of him before plunging into the grey-green wood which was beginning to cloak Teg's Head.

He was still running when he arrived in the clearing, his face breathless and flushed against his blond hair.

She was already there, waiting beside their stone, cool, beautiful and smiling up at him as he came.

"How long have you been here?" he gasped.

Mallowry gave a soft laugh as he tried to get his breath back. "Would you believe all week?" she said.

As she stood up Finn walked over to her, his haversack across his shoulders, and held her in his arms. "You're a lovely liar," he whispered, "but keep it up."

When they kissed, Mallowry was the first to break away. She

looked closely into his eyes as if she was searching for a change in them. "It's been a long week without you, Mr. Rafferty," she said.

"I thought the calendar had stuck, myself, around Wednesday."

"Are you here for the holidays," she asked, looking down at the haversack.

Dropping to his knees he quickly pulled back a flap of the bag and brought out two bulky parcels. "I thought you might have had a fit of the hunger you had last time so I decided this week I'd feed you first. I never did like making love on an empty stomach, not even yours."

He looked up and saw she had opened a green tartan holdall and had emptied another two paper bags on the grass.

For an instant they looked at each other and burst out laughing. He reached out and took her hands. "I'll give you thirty-three guesses what I've got in mine."

"Sausages," she said confidently.

"Right. And scallions! I had to kick Tucky's arse to get them."

Mallowry knelt down on the grass. "And I've brought beef sandwiches with horseradish sauce, tomatoes, pork pies and cheesecake," she said, before finally producing a dark bottle from the hold-all, "and supermarket Burgundy."

"And a fine Big House beverage it is," said Finn. "You must have known I wasn't going to bring the turbot."

Lifting out a square blue cloth, Mallowry began arranging the food on yellow melamine plates.

Finn saw she even had the knives and cruet to match. "That doesn't come with the firm, does it?" he teased.

She pouted her lips crossly, "Nothing you can see here comes with the firm," she said.

"Christ, we could open a restaurant up here with all this lot," yelled Finn, lifting a sausage. "Still, it is Easter. We could use a celebration, the way the job's going."

Finn picked out a yellow-handled corkscrew from the tartan bag and opened the bottle. "Let's drink to all those big spaces between the holidays," he said, pouring a beaker for her. "It'll make the bottle last longer."

He walked over to the edge of the clearing and took a long look into the valley. "I think I'll get them to change their minds," he said. "Instead of water, we'll fill the place with draught stout. Now there's a crowd-puller."

"But what would all the women do?"

Finn raised his glass, winking at her, "They could sit around and wait for all the easy fellers coming away," he said. "Did you hear that in Dublin they once found a feller dead in a vat of Guinness?"

"That must have been a nasty death."

"It can't have been so bad. Apparently he got out three times to go to the toilet!"

As Mallowry walked over to him Finn stared at her for a moment and then snapped his fingers. "I've got it!" he shouted, "You're a Red Indian."

"I'm what?" she said.

"You're a stealthy sex-starved brave! I've been trying to work out all week, who you walked like. Yes that's it! A brave! You stalk rather than walk, with long, soft strides as though you know where you're going but you don't want to disturb the grass."

"Geronimo!" she yelled, taking a leap at him and fastening her arms round his neck.

She looked up as he held her high in his arms. "If you had ever been allowed near a convent school, Rafferty, you would have seen that they teach all their young ladies to walk with their thighs rather than shuffling about on their shins as most people do. Did you know there's a man down there?"

"Down where?" said Finn, pulling the front of his shirt open and trying to peer inside.

"Down there, silly," said Mallowry, releasing herself from his arms and pointing down the slope.

"Well dang me! Their scouts are onto us already," he said. "Pass me the Clandy corkscrew, Bain, we can't afford to leave one man of them alive!"

"No, there he is, look," she said, "by those bushes."

Finn peered over the edge and gave a sigh of relief. "Saved again," he said. "It's only Curran, a good walkin' man."

"He looks as if he's lurking rather than walking. What is he, a Peeping Tom?"

Finn shook his head and smiled. "No, old Curran's one of the most incorruptible men I know. He's O.K."

"But what's he doing down there?" she asked, slipping to the ground.

"He's out looking for the past. He thinks there might be the temple of a Roman goddess somewhere around here. A big, good-looking bird like yourself. He likes Romans."

"He doesn't look very urgent for a Roman. I always imagined them marching intensely into Gaul or out of Gaul or always on the move somewhere or other."

"Curran takes his time. He's looking for an underground spring which might lead him to the goddess's place. He's asked me to help him, with the twigs."

Mallowry turned her face from the valley and looked deep into Finn's eyes. "Of course," she said. "You're the one they call the diviner, aren't you?"

"It's only a hobby sure," said Finn, "It's people like Curran who have the real gift. He can go back so far he can tell us what we're likely to do tomorrow."

"But how can bits of pottery and Roman remains teach us anything about today?"

Finn was silent for a moment. "I'll tell you," he said. "According to Curran when the Roman Empire fell there were almost as many Romans on their backs as on their feet."

"He must be older than he looks," said Mallowry. "Was there high unemployment or something?"

"No, what happened was that just before the Goths marched in and carved up the place they had a census and they discovered they had 32,000 prostitutes in the city alone."

"And how can we learn from that?"

"We can stand on our feet, for a start."

Finn saw that Mallowry's eyes were twinkling mischievously. "Were there really that many?" she asked.

'Well, apparently the Roman lads had so much money jingling in their togas from state handouts that they'd spend it on anything."

"You could have me for one of Tucky's sausages," she said, sticking her tongue out. "I've noticed you haven't offered me one."

"You're on," he said, reaching over to the bag beside the rock. When he looked back he saw she was staring at him and moving her head slightly from side to side. "What are you up to now?" he grinned.

"I was just watching the way you walk," she said, "You roll, you know, not a lot, but you definitely roll. Just like a sailor. I wonder if you can tell someone's character by the way he walks. Curran lurks, Caswell sort of falls forward, Gus struts, Dando does a kind of goose step when he's uptight, and you, lovely Finn, you roll."

While she was talking she had been edging closer towards him, ending up with her arms around his neck. She swung her head back, closing her eyes as she smiled. The sausage was in her mouth before she was aware he had moved.

"That's a sausage roll," he laughed, ducking as she reached for the salad bowl and flung it at his head.

Even before he scooped up a handful of salad from the grass, Mallowry sensed what he was going to do and ran behind the boulder. She had hardly gone a few yards when he caught up with her and pulled her to the ground.

"Not down my dress, Finn," she giggled. "I hate anything down my neck."

"There's only one chance of your getting away with it," he said, his breath coming in deep bursts as he knelt above her.

"And what's that?" she whispered as she looked up at him.

"Confucius, he say 'woman who hates lettuce down dress shouldn't wear clothes.' "

Mallowry saw his hands tremble as he reached towards her, slowly unfastening the buttons down to her waist and pulling the dress back over her shoulders. She watched his eyes darken as he gazed down at her body.

"I'm glad they never taught you to wear bras at that convent of yours," he said, his voice thickening.

"Perhaps I wasn't paying attention when they did," she whispered, raising her arm and stroking the tangle of blond hair which had fallen across his face.

"Pants away," he said slipping them down her slim legs and cradling them in his hands before hurling them on to the grass. "A hundred knickers down the lawn!"

Kneeling on the grass beside her Finn brought his hands up her breasts, sharpening the rough brown points of her nipples until they felt as if they were boring into the pads of his thumbs. Releasing them he cupped his hands over the whole of her breasts, feeling the instant response of her skin beneath his fingers as his lips sought out her waiting mouth.

"Now Finn," she urged, snatching her mouth from his lips. "Now. Please?"

Finn held her back in his arms, drinking in her deep, urging eyes, her lips half opening to give a glimpse of her white, even teeth. Then plunging his hands downwards he forced the rest of her clothes from her body until she was naked beneath him. Looking down he saw she was lying across his kneeling thighs, her back arched as she thrust the soft, downy darkness of her love-mound towards him. Releasing her he stood above her, peeling his tight blue denims from his hips as she lay on the grass making soft groaning sounds with her lips. Finally he was standing quite naked, the sun on his yellow hair soaking his huge, reddening body and bathing the clearing.

"God, you're majestic, Finn," she cried in a loud, almost choking voice as she held her arms out to him.

He came to her, violently penetrating her damp, swelling flesh with an intensity which caused her to open her mouth in a soundless scream. Above her his raunchy, bucking body seemed to be feeding on her, gorging deep between her thighs. Almost immediately she sensed a warm quickening within herself, as though her own body was burgeoning with the same urgent green thrusts of the trees around them. For a moment he lowered himself across her and she could feel the heat of his breathing against her neck as they rocked gently together awaiting the ripening. Suddenly he was back on his knees again, his hands pressing into the hollows of her hips and drawing her on to him. He was arched above her now like some great field beast, his face dark and intense as he covered her. "You're enormous in me," she sobbed, feeling as if the seasons were suddenly melding into one magnificent moment in nature, determined to engulf them both in its bursting joy. And now he was striding within her as a man mastering the earth itself, burning her, seeding her into a pounding silence. . . .

For a moment she shuddered at the chill of his leaving, but when she opened her eyes she smelled the warm fragrance of spring streaming up from the ground.

As they lay back together, Mallowry slowly slid her hand down to his damp belly. "You're beautifully, beautifully moist," she murmured.

When he did not reply she turned over to face him. "Why is it that when we are at our most alive, we're always moist," she said.

"Perhaps we're a race of failed fish," he said.

"No, it's true. It happens when we bathe, or when we laugh, even cry and when we make love. It's almost as if we need to be wet to really live."

Finn still had his eyes closed. "Sure we're mostly water ourselves," he said sleepily. "We're bound to spill a bit at times."

"When I was a girl I used to like going to Blackpool. Some days there seemed to be millions of people stretched out on the beach, all facing the sea as though they were using it as a kind of fire. If you'd suddenly taken away the sand and the sun they would have looked as though they were all sitting in front of their hearths at home."

Finn sat up and fumbled for the cigarettes in the heap of jeans on the grass before lighting two and handing one to Mallowry.

"You were lucky," he said. "We lived a long way from the sea. We always used to go to Ballybunnion for the holidays. After the first time it was almost as if they'd tied a big string to your waist and every August they'd give it a tug and pull you back. It seemed to draw small boys like a magnet, and the wee girls used to paddle in the sea in their knickers for about eighty years and then hobble up to the huts at the top of the beach to soak their tired bones in the seaweed baths. It was as though they had never left the place. I remember seeing a small boy there once who looked as if he'd just come off the holiday train, with a parent in each hand. As their feet felt the beach he broke away, his little legs going faster and faster as he ran full pelt for the sea. And when he got there he stood for a moment in his cap and his red shorts and then he suddenly thrust out both of his arms. 'I've come back, Sea,' he yelled almost to bursting. 'I've come back. Just as I said I would.' And there was the big sea out there shimmying and splashing as though it understood the promise of the boy."

There was a long silence before Finn looked over to Mallowry and saw that she had her hand across her cheek.

"Are you all right, love?" he asked her.

"Yes, for a moment I thought I was going to cry again. That was beautiful, Finn. Do you have a handkerchief in those things?" she said, taking it from him and blowing her nose quietly. "I suppose that's where you learned how to make love? Ballybunnion I mean."

Finn drew on his cigarette. "No, that's where your theory about being wet and lovely falls down, I'm afraid. Mind you, it won't be the first theory to take a nose-dive in Ireland."

"How do you mean?"

"Well, we have everything in Ireland except love. For each other, I mean. We have thousands upon thousands of lovely women and lovely men but we can't always seem to put it all together. I've seen lovely women and lovely men so close to each other and needing the union their bellies were almost breaking up. But would they actually do something about it? And it wasn't because he was stuck on the stout. You see the climate in Ireland is too damp to produce great lovers. What the country needs is one ginormous great cloche to give us a generation or two to get some warmth back into our bodies. And of course the women realise this too, when the wet mists roll in. So you're left with heaps of frustrated fellers piling out of the bars with a headful of mother and skinful of stout, and who wants them? By the time they hit a dry spell and the sap starts rising again most of the skirt's gone."

Mallowry threw her cigarette away and lay on the grass. "It sounds very sad," she said, "but you've left out the obvious exception."

"Like who?"

"You."

"I'm nothing special sure."

"You're the most masculine man I've ever had."

Finn leaned over her, his lips gently brushing the side of her cheek. "That, Mrs. Bain, depends on how many masculine men you've had."

She turned her head away. "Finn?" she said.

"Hello?"

"There have been some others you know."

"Of course there have."

"You don't mind?"

"Look, I said you came off a Christmas tree. I didn't think for a minute you'd stepped out of a safe."

"It doesn't bother you at all then? I mean that there have been more than, than Gus."

Finn sat up quickly. "Look, my only feelings about Gus are that the fellow must have good taste and he's improving in my estimation almost by the minute. And I'd feel the same about any or all of your lovers. In fact I'll drink to each and everyone of them to prove it if I can find where you left the bloody bottle."

He ran behind the boulder and reappeared pouring wine into two yellow beakers, held in one hand.

"To love," he said handing her one, "wherever you find it. And that goes for a spot of healthy lust too."

"Finn love, listen to me," said Mallowry seriously. "There is someone now."

"Someone else you mean?"

"No silly, someone I'm seeing. I've known him for some time. We talk, we get on well together but. . . ."

"If there wasn't more than one good man in the world it would be a hard day for good women," said Finn.

"Finn, you don't understand. What I mean is, what should I do?"

Finn drained his beaker and filled it again from the bottle. "Mrs. Bain," he said, "there are two things I was always taught never to do on any account. One was to take a child's game away from him and the other was to try to make up a woman's mind for her. If you really need the full benefit of my wisdom I'd say keep your lovers, provided you pack them off to the pictures on Saturday afternoons."

Mallowry held up her arms and pulled his head down until it was resting against her breasts. "Oh Finn," she whispered, "what am I going to do about you?"

Slowly sliding his head along her neck until his mouth was an inch from her ear he said, "Do you want me to tell you?"

"Please," she said. "Yes."

"You're going to look down very slowly and you're going to . . . lift your bum off my shirt so that I can put it on."

"You bugger!" she shouted, leaping up and hurling the shirt into his laughing face.

Even before he had fastened the last button, he looked up and saw that Mallowry was still standing there, staring up where greening branches of the trees were trying to grip a darkening sky. And he saw that it was raining.

The light tap on his door made Finn look up quickly and put the book he was reading face down on the bed beside him. "Come," he called loudly.

Curran's face apeared round the door as it opened slowly. "Oh you're there, Finn," he said hesitantly. "Look, I'm not disturbing your reading, am I?"

Finn jumped down from the bed. "If anything, you've rescued me, Soils," he said, looking down at the discarded book. "It was like the floor of a pigeon's loft: all shit and messages."

Curran smiled. "It's just that I've got something rather interesting to show you."

"What have you got there?" asked Finn, looking at the silver flashlight in Curran's hand as he walked towards him.

"Oh it's not here," said Curran almost shyly, "it's down in the cellars. It's not the kind of thing you could be carrying around with you, as you'll see."

The stocky soils engineer led the way down the stairs to the small door beneath the great staircase. For the first few steps the dim light above the door guided their way, until the darkness became so deep Curran was forced to switch on the torch. Turning into a low, narrow doorway he began walking so quickly, shining the light into the darkness ahead, that Finn had difficulty keeping up with him.

"Wait on a bit, Soils," he said finally. "This must be a bit special to have you racing like this."

Without slackening his pace Curran glanced back over his shoulder. "I think you'll find it is," he said eagerly.

They had travelled through the cellars for thirty yards before Curran put up his hand, signalling Rafferty to stop. As the big Irishman came up to him he shone the torch jerkily on the wall ahead, bringing the beam to rest on a stone block set within an arch which had been filled by newer stone.

"There it is," said Curran, his narrow eyes glowing above the beam of the torch. "Look, right in the centre there."

Finn stepped forward, blinking as he looked at the stone, which seemed to have the faint outline of a figure on it.

"Feel it!" urged Curran, "Put your hands against it! It's raised!"

"It looks like some sort of animal," said Finn pressing his fingers against the stone.

"It's a lion," said Curran.

Finn saw the engineer's face was trembling with excitement as their eyes met above the beam of light. "You mean like those fellers outside?"

"No Finn," said Curran. "This one's earlier. Earlier even than the Hesters. Look!" He flashed the light around the stone-walled room, revealing the traces of a small, round arched door and tall narrow slit which had been bricked in.

"This is Norman, of course. It's been here since the first Hesters moved in. Now look at the lion stone, Finn."

Rafferty squinted up at the light against the wall. "It's different, isn't it?" he said.

"Exactly. It's much older than any of the stone in this place."

"Well what does it mean then?"

"It means," said Curran, "that when this place was built they almost certainly took this decorative stone from the remains of an earlier hall on this site, probably Saxon, possibly occupied by the Colt of Corbar. The Hesters always claimed a link with him."

"Christ, that's going back some!" said Finn.

The soil engineer's eyes seemed to burn into Finn as he faced him. "It's going back right to the roots of this country," said Curran. "Northumberland has always been called the cradle of Christianity. It spread from here. But not just with prayers and bibles. For every Cuthbert there had to be a Colt of Corbar to supply the sword to go with the idea. After the Colt it was the Kings of Northumbria who marched with the faith and, after them, the Hesters, until finally their steel and the missionaries' prayers had Christianised the whole country."

"So where does this little feller fit into it all?" asked Finn.

Curran was silent for a moment as he lifted the flashlight in his shaking hand. For a few seconds the beam made darting movements over the wall before it finally shone full against the small, stone figure.

"Rafferty," he said softly, "I think we may be looking at the original Lion of England!"

Finn pressed his lips against his teeth and gave a long, low whistle. "Christ, we're famous," he said, "Does this mean we sell the whole shoot to the Arabs and go home?"

"Dear me no, Finn," said Curran, standing back with a look of horror on his face.

"Well perhaps not the oil sheiks, a dealer or someone?"

"Certainly not," said Curran.

"Why not?"

"Because it's not ours."

"That hasn't always stopped our sort in the past! Are you going to tell the wee woman up at the villa then?"

"I'm not," said Curran. "It's not hers either. Nobody owns history."

"You mean, like the bird?" said Finn.

"Just like the bird."

"So what do we do about it?" asked Finn.

"Do, Rafferty?" said Curran. "We've already done the most important part. We've found it!"

The two men walked silently in the semi-darkness until they reached the steps leading up to the great staircase. "I was just thinking," said Curran, as they climbed the narrow steps. "It must be all this history that reminded me. You and the lads are going on the King John jaunt tomorrow, aren't you?"

"The Blackbog Derby, you mean?" asked Finn.

"Yes that's what they call it now, but it was old John, you know, who started it all. It seems he called in here during one of his many trips round the country, and cutting over from Hengendelly to Todholes his horse got stuck in a bog. Apparently he was so furious because the villagers hadn't drained the marshes properly that he made them all turn out and have a race across it. But he wasn't such a bad lot really. He did give the winner a prize."

Finn stepped out into the huge entrance just as Samson and Dick Dancer came hooting through the door, leading the Friday night shift back to the Hall.

"I'll tell you one thing, Soils," he said, shaking his head, "once the Blackbog Derby starts there won't be much history in these fellers' heads."

Finn loosened the front of his shirt and squinted through the mist towards the umbrellas of the spectators, who were gathered in two groups at the end of the meadow.

He could just pick out the long, white tape being held by The Goose and the top-hatted Tully, standing some fifty feet apart at the finishing line.

"Now you say you've done this sort of lark before, then, son?" he said in a low voice to Keen, who was limbering up in a maroon tracksuit.

"I only won two school cross-countries, that's all," said Keen breathing easily.

"That sounds about twice as much as you'll need to beat this lot, then," he muttered. "Now remember what I've told you! Stick close to me and the pig's ours!"

Keen shook his head despairingly, "I've told you, Finn. Nobody can help anyone win a race once it's started."

"You've never been in this sort of race, boy," said Finn, looking down the line of entries for the Blackbog Derby.

To his right he could see Fasman looking as if he had just come off shift, with Gans beside him, packed into a tight boiler suit. The rangy Nolan was running up and down on the spot next to the carrot-haired cableman, who looked as if he could move a bit. Most of the coalies were gathered round Rafferty. Samson was hovering like a black cloud in his borrowed tracksuit beside Dick Dancer, immaculate in a white shirt and close-fitting black trousers. Brown Windsor and The Cock Lodger had their heads close together discussing, decided Finn, how they were going to split the pig in the event of a dead heat.

Finn jabbed his elbow into Keen's vest. "Right, lad. Now remember Samson's our front runner so let him get on and make the pace."

Keen looked over at the huge, bald dump truck driver, who was overbalancing even when running on the spot. "He's no chance," he said. "He'd come second in a walkover."

"You're right, boy," said Finn, "but they don't know that."

Away to his left Finn saw the Slasher raise the loudhailer to his lips and stare down the line with his good eye, before bringing his arm back to his side.

Looking up to see the reason for the delay, Finn saw that two young, dark-haired lads had joined the end of the line at the last moment. Both were wearing white singlets and white running shorts. As they crouched, waiting for the signal, Finn could see their strong calf muscles flexed and eager to start.

"Keep an eye on those two fellows, lads," said Finn, through the side of his mouth. "They could be ringers."

"On your marks then men," bawled The Slasher from his wooden beer crate. "Get set. Go!"

Keen immediately raced into the lead. Within a few strides he was too far ahead of the field even to hear the sound of Finn's groans behind him.

He had travelled only a hundred yards when one of the white-clad runners caught him up. Matching Keen's strides for a few steps, he suddenly gave the boy a violent nudge in the shoulder, sending him sprawling head-first into a bog pool.

Keen was sitting bemused in the bog when the rest of the field caught him up. Without changing pace, Finn reached out a hand and hauled the boy up beside him. "Now do you get it?" he said. "That was Samson's job, you see! Now just watch him do it!"

Samson charged forward, appearing to have the race to himself, before both white-vested runners cruised up behind him. Finn saw them both nod to each other before each shot a leg out in front of him. They hopped away laughing, as the giant muckshifter collapsed like a felled ox between them.

"Now this one won't get up, Windsor," Finn gasped to Keen as he jumped over Samson's body and the line passed him.

Keen tried to rub some of the black mud from his face.

"It's Keen," he said. "Look, you saw what they did. Why do we let them get away with it?"

"I thought you said you knew what racing was about," grinned Finn. "Sure we'll let them have their little game for a while till they tire themselves out." He shot a glance to his right. "O.K. Are you right, Windsor? And you, Lodger?"

The two men gave him a "thumbs-up" sign as they took up the lead, racing towards a wide, boggy flash which had a narrow path through it, sufficient for just three men running abreast. As Dancer and The Cock Lodger approached neither of them spotted the single white vested runner who darted up between them and pushed out both arms, sending the two of them toppling into separate patches of bog.

"You're a great man for the sack, Lodger," yelled Rafferty as he passed. "But you're going on useless on your feet."

Finn noted the darkening sky. "It's closing in quite nicely," he said, "You stay back. I'll just stretch my shins a bit."

"Where are you going, Finn?" shouted Keen.

"Huntin'," he yelled back, as he lengthened his stride and moved up behind the second of the white runners.

As he came alongside, with the rain pelting into his face, Finn touched his mud-flecked forelock. "A fine, soft day, sir," he said as he eased himself fractionally ahead of him. Just when it seemed he was about to sprint further ahead Finn stopped suddenly and bent down in front of the accelerating runner.

Unable to stop himself in time, the man careered over the Irishman's back, his dark head launching itself forward like a spear, piercing the soft earth. For a moment the white legs held an upright position, before slowly wilting to the ground.

"Dear me, I must have stumbled," said Finn, regaining his stride as he passed the unconscious lump on the ground.

At once he was aware the other white-vested runner was behind him. Humming gently to himself he allowed the man to run in his wake for 20 yards before he again stopped suddenly and lifted his boot carefully to the same height as his pursuer's crutch.

For a split second the man had a look of utter disbelief in a face which was already sinking into a soggy sleep.

"Oops, I'm sorry," said Finn, stopping briefly to apologise. Certain that the man's race was over Finn slapped his hands together, stepped back to admire his work and overbalanced, falling face-down into a field drain.

A hand reached out to drag him dripping to his feet as the new race leader joined him. "Dr. Rafferty, I presume," said a cackling voice beside him. Finn peered out from the black ooze of mud round his eyes and saw it was Brown Windsor.

"Good man, Brownie," he grunted, giving him a hefty slap on the shoulder which proved to be the final blow for the tiring little West Indian. Windsor staggered two more paces and shook his head, grinning as he slid to the ground.

Finn gave an apologetic shrug and ran over to join Keen. "That leaves just the two of us, then," he said, "and three of them."

"The last one was an own goal. But the other two were beauties."

"I had to bend my rules a bit there."

"I noticed you did," grinned Keen.

"No, not the methods," grunted Finn. "The reasoning. I normally only fight people I know. That way you can be sure of your reasons. Anything else is a fool's game – unless you're pushed."

"And what happened there?"

"I just felt pig-headed," said Finn.

He shot a glance at the three Caws looming up ominously behind them. "Now listen, son. The only thing to remember now is that when I say 'Go', you go, understand? No questions. No nothing. Just go. O.K.?"

"O.K. Finn."

Looking to his left he saw that the carrot-haired cableman had moved up alongside him, and over on the right Gans had taken up a similar position beside Keen. He knew who owned the pair of boots which was pounding up behind him. He could almost feel Fasman's breath in the back of his neck.

"Now listen, boy," said Finn, spitting mud as he whispered to Keen. "I want you to slowly move out in front of me and then do nothing till you hear the word."

Without a glance Keen increased his pace just enough to slip ahead of Rafferty. Gans lunged at him, missed, and settled for a place beside Finn.

The five men sloshed through the mud, aware of each other, waiting for the first suggestion of a move.

"I was just thinking, boys," Finn called to his two escorts. "A pig's a big animal. It can carve up a few ways." His voice dropped to a whisper. "You've heard about the arrangement then?"

"What arrangement?" said Gans.

"This one I've got with Fasman back there."

As Gans and the cableman looked back, Finn's two fists suddenly shot out in opposite directions, bursting against both men's ears as the force of the perfectly timed blows sent them cartwheeling through the air.

"Go, boy," he yelled at Keen. "Go." He plunged to his knees, making an instant back for Fasman, who came hurtling over his shoulders and landed, splayed in the mud with his face staring up senselessly as the soles of Finn's boots flew over him.

Keen broke the tape to the loud cheering of the spectators. For a few seconds he stood alone, a thin, unrecognisable, black stick before Tully stepped forward to throw a bucket of water over his face.

As the mud rolled down his cheeks Tully turned round to the V.I.P. group behind them with a paternal grin on his face.

"It's the Circus Boy," he said. "I've always had his card marked for a winner."

Bain moved out from between Dando and Caswell with an enthusiastic nod of the head. "Well done, Keen," he said.

Mallowry Bain was behind them, standing alone in a shiny red raincoat. Only a mere glimpse of her black hair was visible beneath the hood. She was staring ahead, the concern showing in her pale beautiful face until Finn came in to cross the finishing line. He was walking in casually with a black, angelic smile on his face.

"Well run, Rafferty, you were a good second."

Finn took his eyes from Mallowry's face and turned to the project manager. "Ach, there's a million of us," he said.

"We couldn't see much of it from here. Where are the rest of them, Rafferty?"

Finn looked back into the mist which was closing in fast in front of their eyes. "There won't be any," he said shaking his head. "It's a tiring course for a man sure. The boy did well. I'd say he ran an intelligent race in the end."

During the presentation of the pig, Finn stood back watching Mallowry, who was returning his gaze as though the two of them were the only people in the wet meadow. When the applause died down Finn felt, even without a word having passed between them, they had been speaking for a long time together.

As the managers returned, it was Dando who took Mallowry's arm, leading her round a small boggy patch to return to the waiting Range Rover.

"Well done, Dando," said Finn, dashing forward offering his hand to the general foreman. Dando had accepted it before he realised the Irishman had deposited a black coating of bog slime in his own hand.

"But I wasn't in the race, Rafferty," he said.

Finn gave him a black smile. "Oh no, you weren't, were you?" he said innocently. "Well in that case, boyo, you'd better wipe that lot off, then. Otherwise they might think you had a hand in it, you know."

For a moment the two men glared at each other as Mallowry looked at them in turn. She saw that only Finn was smiling.

The hot, sweet smell of the pig revolving above the beech-log fire in the Great Hall brought a look of utter contentment to Tucky's face.

He sniffed deeply as the heady wafts of burning pork floated across his nostrils before plunging his fork into the soft, melting flesh.

"She's ready! She's ripe for you, lads!" he murmured, licking his lips and swinging the spit away from the blazing logs and into the noisy, smoke-filled room.

As a plate was handed to him he carved into the animal's buttock, allowing the slices of steaming meat to fall from his knife in swift, succulent thuds.

There was a six foot five inch fairy waiting for the first helping – Samson, who was standing awkwardly in front of him dressed in ballet shoes, white tights, a stiff laced tutu and a white running singlet.

"Right, that'll be 50p then, Samson," said Dick Dancer, who was sitting at a small table. Dancer was in black tights and a black velvet waistcoat over a white shirt with large puffed sleeves down to his wrists.

"What's that for?" asked Samson, staring down at his plate.

"It's for the Circus Boy, silly," said Dancer, nodding towards Keen at the back of the queue. "Well he won, didn't he? If you dispute it you'd better get back to the bloody bog and have another crack at it."

Behind Samson, Goose Canavan already had peas and potatoes on his plate as he waited for Tucky. He too was all in white, dressed like a fairy in a row that included Brown Windsor, Chauncy Bawn and Liam the Liar.

"Cross me palm with silver," said Dancer, when the Goose arrived at the pay table.

"What's it for?" asked The Goose, digging into his pocket.

"It's for retired muckshifters," said Dancer, putting the offered note into the top of his tights and giving him change. "We're retiring to the back bar of the Tup later."

"Watch your backs, lads," muttered Liam the Liar behind them. "Here comes the Pontypool front row."

Brown Windsor looked up to see the large doors of the Great Hall open as Dando entered the room. Three paces behind him came Gans and the massive Fasman, who was carrying a shepherd's crook with squirrels' tails hanging down from a wooden cross-piece which had been nailed to it. Dando sat at the head of the table close to the kitchen door as Fasman placed the crook against the back wall before joining Gans at the back of the queue.

When Gans brought food, Dando looked towards the seats at the far end which were taken up by fairies and quarrymen. Only the carved, high-backed wooden chair at the end of the table was empty.

"Where's the King of the Fairies, then?" said Dando, stabbing his fork towards the empty seat.

"Well evidently he's not with the Queen," said The Goose scratching his thin, wattled neck and looking down the table at him, "because I see Gans is already here."

Dando ignored the laughter and glared down the table towards the big Irishman. "It's always amazed me, Goose," he said, "why a reasonable boyo like you decided to join the coalies."

Before Goose could reply, the big doors to the room swung open and Finn Rafferty came in to shouts of welcome from the fairy end, which died down to a last final plea of "Water" from Dick Dancer.

Finn walked to the back of the tall chair and raised his hands. "Gentlemen, I have an announcement to make," he said, waiting for the noise to settle. "There'll be no water tonight."

He sat down to the accompaniment of shouts and hand-claps from the muckshifters around him as Tucky appeared at his side with a full plate.

"What's all this gear for, then?" he said. "The Nutcracker Suite?"

The Goose leaned over towards him. . . . "It's a little diversion the lads have put together. We're on first, so you sit back and watch the entertainment." He signalled the other fairies. "Are you right, lads?" he asked. "Tully, have you the cat ready?"

As Tully gathered up his violin, The Goose and Dick Dancer took up their positions in front of the table with Brown Windsor. Chauncy Bawn, Liam the Liar and Keen in a line behind them.

Tully raised his bow, which was the signal for Dancer and The Goose to hold hands and begin gazing lovingly into each other's eyes before The Goose began to sing in a rough croaky voice.

"It's oh, oh, oh so fine,
When someone says 'Be Mine'
And you're his Valentine
Your whole life through."

Dick Dancer loosened the top of his black tights, disengaging his crutch, before coming in with the second verse in a high, falsetto voice. . . .

"It's oh, oh, oh so nice
Almost like Paradise
It never happens twice,
A love so true."

Behind them the chorus of fairies joined arms and swayed gently to Tully's music.

"And it's so very rare,
The love that you find there
A love that few can share,
Only a few. . . ."

"Few . . . oo, oo, oo," echoed Liam the Liar as the rest of the line waited for him to finish.

Dancer and Goose returned to the vocal attack, gazing into each others face as they sang. . . .

"It's oh, oh, oh so grand
Walking in Wonderland
When someone takes your hand
Someone like you."

Almost as a rescue attempt, the back line piped up with their final chorus, joined by the two principals.

"So if you want my love,
And need my love
And say your love is true
Then I'll be oh so good
So good for you."

The thundering applause from the table was instantly followed by a hail of bread rolls from the Dando end as the fairies tried to fend them off with their bare muscular arms. Finally they dashed back to the table with The Goose, the last to leave the firing line, turning his back to the audience and lifting his short skirt, revealing a large pair of string underpants.

They had hardly regained their seats when a young carrot-haired lad next to Gans rose to his feet and began singing a Gilbert and Sullivan tune in a clear tenor voice which silenced the whole room.

"When I was a lad and my feet were bare
My Daddy said 'You must get your share'
So I sold my shovel and I got some stocks
In Clandy till I could have bought Fort Knox.
I bought so many that the F.T. soared
And now I'm a director on the Clandy Board.
When I was a lad and the jobs were thin
My Daddy said 'You must get some in'
So I lived and I lived and I got so old
That finally they laid me on a slab so cold.
Then the angels said with one accord

'Let's make him a director on the Clandy Board'.
"When I was a lad wondering what to be
My father said 'Be just like me'
Work all day till your feet get sore
Then bandage up your wellies, man, and work some more.
So I humped and I drank and I heaved and I whored
And I won't be a director on the Clandy Board!"

The carrot-haired lad sat down to a burst of cheering and the thumping of heavy fists on the table before Dick Dancer got up fluffing out his black hair.

"Not you again, Dancer, sit down," shouted Nolan from the far end.

Dancer put up his arms, dropping the left one immediately with a squeak of surprise as Samson rammed a bread roll into his armpit. "No, gentlemen. Please gentlemen," said Dancer. "Please!! I'm not going to sing again," he said to resounding cheers. "I'm going to give you a short recitation. . . ." He paused for the boos to die down. . . . "About someone who is very dear . . . to all our hearts."

He licked his lips, looked around the table and started:

"A little bit of dogshit fell from out the sky one day.
It landed in Northumberland, not far from Whitley Bay,
And when the angels found it they thought they'd have a jest
So they said 'suppose we leave it, as a warning to the rest?' "

At the end of the table Tucky was leaning over Finn's tankard with a large enamel jug in hand. "Are you sure you've enough of this stuff, then, Tucky?" said the Irishman, "because I think we'll be needing it."

"We've three barrels of it back there," said the chubby cook, grinning. "That should be enough even for you, Finn."

Finn nodded and drained half the tankard before looking up to see that Dancer was riding the catcalls and still on his feet determined to complete his recitation.

"So they dressed it in a Burton's suit
And with no ado, or fuss,
They sat it on its arse-end
And called it Little Gus."

"Boo," roared Samson beside him with the rest of the men accepting his lead as they stood up and faced Dancer with their thumbs pointing down.

"Today," yelled Dancer in an attempt to relieve the pressure. "Let's have, 'Today', Finn."

"That's it, Finn lad," urged The Goose, slapping his arm. "Give us your party piece."

All around him the cries of "Finn" and "Today" built up into a mess of noise which mounted into a roaring and thumping of fists on the heavy oak table as Finn stood up.

Tankard in hand, the big Irishman walked over to the fireplace as Tully sawed gently into the opening bars of the music.

For a moment the room was still as Finn stood with his back to the muckshifters, his eyes staring at the great stone bull mastiff in the Hesters fireplace. Then he turned suddenly, taking five running strides across the floor before launching himself into a final leap onto the centre of the table.

"Do you see my face in the rain that's falling free?
Do you hear my voice in the whispering of the trees?
Do you taste my love in every glass of wine?
Do you touch your heart and feel the best of mine?"

Raising the tankard Finn drank deeply from it before smacking his lips loudly and waving the vessel above the heads of the men.

"Please tell them from me I still remember them.
Please tell them they taught me all I know.
Along this darkened roadway our love will always shine,
For today is the highway and tomorrow is the time."

Even though Finn could clearly see the rows of upturned faces beneath him, as their fists beat out the tempo of the music he suddenly felt strangely detached from them.

He gazed up to the rough black beams above him which fanned down to the dark oak panelling where the Hesters had once hung their images of a great age. He could see the high, deserted minstrel's gallery with its thin, finely carved slats cob-webbed in mourning for its lost singers. And over at the great fireplace where the pig oozed sweetly in death, the bull mastiff which once raced free with the hunt on Hesters' fields was still staring out, whole and seemingly indestructible in Corbar sandstone. Below him the faces of the muckshifters seemed to blend into the Great Hall, as though they had always been there. He could see The Goose in the form of a bulky, ageing knight back from the Border wars, being served old mead in a bowl by a kitchen boy in a brown leather halbard and tights, who looked like Keen. He saw the white-haired, serious Chauncy Bawn as some visiting friar feasting, in a cowl and long flowing robes. Dick Dancer was the jester in tights, half red, half yellow, trying to catch the favours of a gouty baron who was Liam the Liar and who was throwing him a half-eaten chicken leg. Samson was there too, decked out as some bejewelled lord of the manor, lifting a silver lid under which was a pair of spurs, indicating the need to return to the hunt since the Hesters' larder was empty. At the other end of the table Nolan was a young horseman, arriving back dry from the chase but still with time enough to accept the gamey smile of the serving wench before burying his face in the tankard. Fasman was recognizable only by his great bulk, his face being covered with the black hood of the headsman as he bent over a wooden block on which the face of his victim, appealing to him for the last time, was that of the weak, fubsy Gans. Only the dark, impassive face of Dando failed to meld into the pageant. Just for one brief moment he appeared to don the black, heavy armour of a medieval knight at the jousts, but when he reached for his helmet and turned to face the waiting crowd, his scowling head bore the yellow helmet of Clandy.

The roaring of the muckshifters' voices and the battering of fists against the table signalled the end of Finn's song, long before he realised it himself. He shook himself, looked down at his tankard and raised it to his lips again.

"Toasts," yelled Dancer, springing to his feet. "It's time for the toasts." As the others took up the cry Finn raised his hand to silence them. "I'll give you the first," he said. "To the Lordship of Corbar."

The fairies cheered as Finn jumped down from the table and returned to his seat. When their voices died down he heard Dando's voice from the far end.

"To the bullshit of Rafferty."

As Dancer and Windsor started booing, Finn stood behind his chair and waved his hand to quieten them. "All right. If it's time for the toasts, let's do it properly," he said. "Tucky, bring drink for Mr. Dando and myself."

As the fat cook disappeared through the kitchen door, Dando stood up and stared down the table to Finn. "I'm not getting involved in a bar-room drinking session with you, Rafferty." he said.

"A bar room, Mr. Dando!" said Finn, making a wide sweep of the hall with both arms. "Here we are in the mighty Great Hall of the Hesters of Corbar and you call it a bar room? However, I'm going to be absolutely fair with you, Griff. We're going to have one drink each. O.K.?"

"Shame," yelled Dancer, leaping to his feet.

"No," said Finn lifting his hand. "It's been a long, hard day, where some of us have been, and I think Mr. Dando and myself have only the strength to drink just one drink apiece. And here they are!"

The muckshifters followed Finn's eyes to the kitchen door, where Tucky was waddling into the hall with a large metal pail in each hand. "One bitter for you," he announced, placing the bucket on the table in front of Dando and giggling as the foam splashed down the sides.

"And for you," he said to Finn, placing the second in front of Rafferty, whose eyes were only on Dando.

A low murmuring went round the table as Finn rose to his feet. "Right, Dando," he said, staring at the black-shirted general foreman. "One toast, one drink, until we've finished. The winner gets. . . ."

"Gets what, Finn?" called Brown Windsor.

"Pissed," said Finn, plunging his face into the bucket. "Now who's going to start us?"

The Goose was first on his feet, raising his tankard high in the air before looking round the table. "Good health, long life and a choice of the girls," he cried.

"Girls," echoed the fairies. Dando and Finn glanced at each other before dipping their heads in the pails.

Nolan stood up. "Silk for you and wool for me but enough of the drink for both of us," he shouted as the Caws echoed "Us".

The faces at the table looked up as Dando rose with his bucket held firmly between his hands. "Good luck to all Welshmen and arseholes to the Irish!" he said.

"I'm Irish," protested Nolan as mixed waves of cheers and boos broke out, before Fasman leaned across the table. "Shut it, Nolan," he bawled.

At the other end Finn was on his feet hoisting his bucket chest high. "To the biggest natural hole in England!" he bawled: "Dando's mouth!"

Up went the buckets again as the fairies stamped their boots in approval.

Fasman kicked his seat back behind him as he lifted his tankard staring directly at Finn. "To Rafferty's father," he called. "May they trace him soon."

A bread roll, fresh from Dancer's fist, thudded into the wall behind the big muckshifter as the fairies' boos were countered by the Caws cheers.

"To Dando's mother," yelled Dancer, "coupled with the name of Baron Frankenstein." As the two camps split into their own rallying cries Liam the Liar stood up and asked for silence. "They tell me that Jaws went to see Dando's mother," he said, grinning through his rotten teeth. "But they told him he'd have to be accompanied by an older fish."

"Bogtrotter," shouted Gans as the men around Dando hissed their disapproval but still raised their tankards.

As the buckets came down again Finn turned to Keen beside him, "Come on, young 'un, let's have yours," he said.

"It's not really a toast," said Keen hesitantly, "just something I read."

"Oh, it's an intellectual one, is it?" said Finn. "Well let's have you up on the table so that we can all hear it."

"Up, up, up," came the cries as the reluctant Keen was hauled on to the table top before looking round nervously.

"Oh distant land, now land of mine,
'Tis not my wish that I am come.
'Tis not my good horse brings me here,
But lusty youth and nimble wit
Audacity and tavern wine!"

He raised his tankard, smiling uncertainly before the rest of the room broke out in rousing applause.

"Well said, lad," said Finn as the boy jumped down. "It reminds me of a favourite one of me father's"

He stood up and raised his bucket which was already three quarters empty, For a moment he stared into the swirling brown liquid beneath him before looking up to the faces at the table.

"To laughing eyes and lovin' limbs
To absent arms and lips that cling
To woman's warm persuasive whims
And dreams born of remembering."

He raised the bucket, drinking deeply into it as the heels of the fairies' fists rocked the table beneath him.

The Goose drained his tankard and motioned to the hovering Tucky to refill it. "Sure, Rafferty, you must have kissed the buttock bone of a saint some time," he said, shaking his head.

"To Goose and Mother Goose and all who gander at her."

The Goose's beady eyes shot across the room and saw the grotesque Fasman standing, tankard in his hand, with a slow stream of spittle running down his chin.

For a moment Finn could see the Irishman's fists harden as they twitched against the knees of his tights. But Canavan merely rose from the table, drained his ale without a word and sat down again.

"Shall I play the music now, Finn?" said Tully, pulling with his twig-like fingers at Finn's shoulder.

"To Liam the Liar and all his bastard lying brood."

It was now Liam's turn to glare down to where Gans was smirking at him through wet rubbery lips.

"All right Tully, start playing and make it lively," said Finn to the fiddler. "Give us a jig or something."

Down the table the Welshman was staring at him with glazed eyes, only occasionally looking down at the unfinished ale in his bucket. Rafferty raised his pail and faced him.

"To Griff Dando," he said in a quiet voice, "coupled with the nearest Welsh mountain sheep."

Dando made as if to lift his own bucket but, instead, leaned back in his seat and smiled thinly at the Irishman.

Tully's deftly moving fingers on his fiddle bow seemed to break into a gallop as Fasman stood up again.

"To Brown Windsor and his circus trainer," he yelled, inciting the Caws to more cheering.

"To Romeo Nolan," bawled Dick Dancer, the words coming out in a quiet hiss, "and the canteen bird who squeezes his pimples."

"To Chauncy Bawn and Dancer's arse," squeaked Gans, bringing an angry bellow from the fairies.

"To Pansy Gansy and the man of his dreams," shouted Liam as the fairies raised their legs and threshed them wildly above the table.

Gans was about to open his mouth when Dando waved him down.

The big general foreman struggled to his feet, his damp, black hair falling across his face as he glowered down the table at Finn.

"To Mallowry Bain . . . and anybody," he said, almost spitting out the words.

There was an immediate silence in the room. Finn's face was like marble as the two men glared at each other.

"Well? Was'r matter, Rafferty? Have you run out of toasts?"

All the faces turned towards the Irishman as he slowly lifted himself out of the chair, whistling gently to himself.

"No, Dando," he said, his lips blanching. "You see, I've got nothing to drink to them with. I've . . . finished!" he shouted bringing his arm in a sudden whip-like movement, sending the empty bucket sliding along the surface of the table down to the other end, where it struck the Welshman's pail, showering ale into Dando's lap.

Nolan was the first to make a move, leaping like something scalded up onto the table and hurling his full tankard into Dick Dancer's face. Immediately the chairs around him were emptied as the fairies raced to the Caws end, colliding with Fasman and Gans who, with the carrot-haired singer, had quickly formed a wedge between Finn and Dando.

Finn leapt over the bodies of Nolan and Dancer, down mauling on the floor, and found himself facing Gans, who had broken through the first wave of fairies. Gans lowered his head, ramming the Irishman's stomach before he had time to get his fists up. Straightening to conceal the pain, Finn drew a breath slowly before aiming a single hammer blow onto the crown of Gans's head, causing him to look up with a silly, glazed expression. Finn couched his left hand under Gans's jaw, almost affectionately, before hooking him to the side of the face, sending the little fat man sinking to the floor. "Goodnight Pansy," he said, tugging his blond cowlick. As he fought his way towards the end of the table he saw the giant Fasman in the corner with a bucket on his head, being twirled round by a fairy on each wrist. Nolan had broken away from the Dancer to take a flying leap onto the back of Samson, who continued powering forward, oblivious of him. Chauncy Bawn had found himself momentarily at bay as two Caws forced him back to the white mastiff at the fireplace, their bare arms coiling above him before Finn grabbed both their heads and cracked them together. He acknowledged Bawn's appreciative thumb as they slid to the floor. Ahead of him Finn saw Brown Windsor with his fists uppishily held out in front of him like an old time prizefighter as he squared up to the carrot-haired tenor. The little West Indian winced with the pain of the tenor's boot in his groin, which was followed by a fierce blow in his mouth. Before the tenor's boot could go in again, Finn grabbed a fistful of red hair and brought the face beneath it hurtling down against his bended knee. Windsor eased himself from under the unconscious man and grinned up at Finn. "Nigger-lover," he said through the blood sluicing between his big white teeth. The Goose, spotting that Finn was idle for a moment, paused generously in his personal fight with Nolan and calmly stood aside, pushing Finn between them towards Dando before aiming another punch at the young dozer driver's head. When Finn finally reached Dando's chair it was empty. He looked down and saw the big Welshman lying beneath the edge of the table. Catching hold of the coarse, black hair he jerked Dando's face up and saw that he was unconscious with drink. "You cheating bugger," he yelled as the music from Tully's fiddle mounted to a deafening crescendo. He was about to speak again when the music stopped abruptly, and, turning round, he felt a sharp blow on the top of his head which sent him sprawling to the floor. Looking up, Finn spat out a fiddle string which was lying across his open mouth. In the thick, blue haze he could see a fairy standing over him with a concerned look on its face. It might have even been the fairy who hit him. Finn didn't care. He smiled, almost a sweet smile and closed his eyes as he slipped into a deep and blissful sleep.

Mallowry Bain was waiting in the open-topped sports car when he pulled in beside her.

"Did you have to bring the red one?" he said, glancing up the road both ways.

"If you'd asked I could have painted it khaki," she smiled, "Or perhaps worn a bush in my hair?"

Finn opened the door for her, watching her slide from the car seat almost in slow motion. She was wearing a high-necked, bottle-green sweater, fawn riding breeches and long, soft leather boots.

"I'm sorry," he said. "What I meant was it's a bit. . . ."

"Shut up and kiss me, Rafferty," she said, pressing her fingers against his lips.

"Let's get in the car, shall we?"

"Chicken," she said, walking past him.

Inside the car Finn drew her to him, holding her head cupped in his hands before kssing her gently.

"Finn?" she whispered, patting his shoulder.

"Yes?"

"You forgot to draw the curtains. The neighbours might see us."

She unfastened the brown leather band from behind her head, allowing her black hair to slip down across her shoulders as she stretched her long slim legs out in front of her.

"Even when you're sitting you look as if you're lying down," he said, starting the engine. "Did you bring a handbag or anything?"

"I never use handbags."

"Your car?" Finn suddenly remembered. "Did you lock it?"
"Of course."
She put her hand on the knee of his blue denims. "Don't worry so much, Finn," she said.
Finn covered the twenty-two miles to Hounshale in barely twenty minutes. Only then did he notice the heat of the day. The sun was beating down on the squat, stone cottages in the square. It was so hot the street dogs were stretched on the narrow pavements and the shop girls were out bearing their breasts.
They turned off behind the half-timbered Plough Inn before making their descent down the winding "No Through Road" which levelled out at the white, wooden gates of the Pinkney Stud.
A small, dumpy woman in a brown jumper and jodhpurs was holding it open, waiting for a group of children to pass through on their ponies.
Finn brought the car to a halt in the gateway and leaned out of the window.
"Hello to you, Mrs. Pinkney! Is that mare of yours still playin' the waitin' game, then?"
"Hello old stick," called Hilda Pinkney briskly. "It's Mr. Rafferty, isn't it? And party? You must have felt the labour pains from down your end. The vet's with her now."
Finn looked at Mallowry and back at the round, urgent face peering in through the car window. "This is . . . er . . . Anne Jones, Mrs. Pinkney," he said. "I've brought her to see the hosses."
"Nice to have you. Both of you," said the woman loudly. "Now you two had best get straight down to the bridle suite if you don't want to miss anything."
She smiled at Mallowry, "Your Mr. Rafferty's been worstling like an expectant father this last few weeks. Anyone would think he was having the foal."
They parked the car and walked across the grey cobbled stable yard to where the third stall door was open.
Finn put his arm round Mallowry's shoulder as they entered the musty hay-strewn stall where a small, tweedy man was sitting cross-legged beside a large leather bag. He was resting in his hap the head of a panting mare whose swollen belly was heaving beneath the light of a brilliant arc lamp.
"Ah, there you are, Hankin," said the man. "Now first of all just fetch that bucket of warm water from the corner there and we'll tart the old lass up a bit."
As Finn hesitated the man took his eyes from the fretting mare and barked, "Come on, man! We haven't got all day! She'll be obliging soon!"
With a quick glance at Mallowry, Finn shrugged his shoulders, took off his blue denim top and carried the steaming bucket over to the vet.

"Will that be warm enough for her?" he asked.

"Let's see," said the vet, dipping his fingers into the bucket. "Yes that's fine. Now listen, Hankin. You've done this sort of thing before, haven't you?"

"Yes I have," agreed Finn.

"Well now, reach into that box of tricks of mine and bring out the big green bottle! Have you got it?"

"Is this it?" asked Finn, holding up the bottle.

"That's the one, boy. Now just give a quick squirt into the bucket. It's only a mild disinfectant but it helps to keep the old girl fresh. Now just take that cloth and give her a decent swabbing down at the back end, there's a good chap."

Noticing Mallowry for the first time he waved his hand. "I don't know you Miss but I'm Fairley. Veterinary surgeon. Of this parish."

"I'm Mal. . . ."

"Malvina Jones," said Finn, jerking his head up from behind the mare's buttocks.

Fairley examined her closely as he stroked the mare's ears thoughtfully. "Well madam, there's only one essential tranquilment of horsebirth I don't carry in my bag and that's a nice cup of tea. Now if you can manage to rustle one up? Especially if you put a wee spot of something in it!"

"You evidently haven't got a sugar lump in mind, Mr. Fairley. I'll see what I can do," said Mallowry breezily as she walked towards the door. She turned back and looked over towards Finn, "Will you have a drop of that too, Hankin?"

Finn scowled as she walked away.

Watching her go, Fairley reached down into his brown tweed jacket and produced a briar pipe, which he filled and lit with visible contentment.

"The great thing about horsebirth," he said, gazing down at the pipe, "or beastbirth, mulebirth or all other kinds of birth, is always to appear entirely relaxed. They watch us, you know? These creatures. They tend to take the tempo from what we do. If we start leaping around and getting into a sweat they'll do the same. But if we sit here calm, quiet and cool it relaxes old Mum here too and Junior will be out like a pea from a pod. What do you think eh Hankin?"

"I think she's shelling now," said Finn, peering up between the animal's hind legs as a sudden movement came from the red, angry-looking opening below the mare's belly.

"What!" shouted Fairley, half-rising before realising he still had the mare's head across his thighs. "It's all right old girl," he assured the horse before peering down to the other end. "What can you see Hankin?"

"The head's arriving, by Christ," said Finn, leaping up to fill his arms with newspapers from a pile in the corner.

"Reading material, Hankin?" said the vet, sucking the pipe.

"This is for the wee parcel at the end," said Finn. "Now just you sit where you are and I'll have this creature in the world in two shakes."

Finn knelt down beside the mare, at the same time unbuttoning his blue denim shirt and spreading it carefully over the coarse straw.

"Now then girl, that should make for a happy landing," he muttered. "Now push, girl! Push! Put your back into the job! Come on now!"

Over in Fairley's lap he could hear low moaning sounds coming from the mare's mouth, followed by the heavy laboured breathing of the vet as the fat, leather mountain heaved up and down below him.

"I can see the legs!" said Finn excitedly. "Come on you great lummox, shove! One more pair of those and I can start to take the weight for you."

The hind legs pushed themselves free, sending a wet spurt of mucus and blood against Finn's chest. He reached to catch hold of all four limbs, pulling them firmly towards him.

The smoke from Fairley's pipe was now coming in swift bursts as he used both hands to pamper the mare's head. Through the haze Finn caught a momentary glimpse of Mallowry returning with Mrs. Pinkney carrying a tray of mugs.

"Strength, Hankin," Fairley was saying to his briar pipe. "Moments such as this are a time for strength. Not necessarily the strength of the flesh but of the inner man, Hankin. The strength of . . . of feeling."

Finn could now see the slimy underside of the foal's belly coming to meet him as he grasped the legs, feeling the warmth of the wet hair beneath his reaching fingers.

"He's here!" shouted Finn, falling back into the straw, the struggling foal clasped across his chest in a steaming heap of hot, sticky hair. "He's here and he's brought his own lead!" he bawled, catching hold of the wet umbilical cord. "Hang on son and I'll have you free in a jif!"

He reached for the laces in his shoes, carefully tied them to the cord ten inches apart and then raised the centre of the cord to his lips and calmly bit it into two halves, wiping away the resultant gush of blood against his chin with the back of his hand.

Finn and the foal struggled to their feet at the same time, the foal being instantly grounded again by its mother, who was licking strength into its limbs with long, lunging sweeps of her tongue.

The big Irishman was grinning broadly as he emerged from the stall, his blood-stained chest and stomach glistening beneath the bright glow of the arc lamp.

"Which of you two's being born?" asked Hilda Pinkney advancing with two mugs of tea in her hands.

"The little feller," smiled Finn. "I wouldn't take a chance on your splitting my lead like that."

Fairley, who was not free of the burden of the mare's head, eyed him closely. "Yes, I was rather interested in how you did that bit Hankin," he said. "We vets have a somewhat quaint old custom up here. We use scissors."

"It's years since I was at a foaling," said Finn. "Back home we always used to do it for quickness, especially if you thought the mare might be a bit weak with her own teeth."

Hilda Pinkney handed mugs to both men as she watched the foal on the straw becoming a rich chestnut beneath the vigorous licks of its mother. "Well you've both done a good job! It's a treat to see them so well!"

"It was nothing, Mrs. Pinkney," said Fairley, smacking his lips. "Hankin here did most of the work."

"He's not Hankin! Hankin's trying to catch Thunderball again. He must have taken longer than he thought."

"But I thought. . . . Who's this gentleman, then?"

"That's our Mr. Rafferty. He's from the dam. Going to flood us in a couple of years' time, but he's doing it in a nice way, aren't you Mr. Rafferty?"

Fairley thrust out a hand for Finn to shake. "Sorry about that, Rafferty," he said. "I was told Hankin was on his way and I took it for granted you were he. I'm new too, as you must have realised. The regular vet's away."

"If the mare was prepared to accept me as Hankin," said Finn, his eyes meeting Mallowry's as he spoke, "perhaps I was."

"What a lovely thought, Mr. Rafferty," said Mrs. Pinkney, fussily picking a piece of straw from Finn's shoulder. "Now what can we get you next?"

"A big tub," said Finn.

"Of course," she said, taking hold of Mallowry's arm. "Now while Mr. Rafferty is sweetening himself you must tell me all about yourself. Doesn't it make you a bit broody, all this? Do you hope to have a family yourself?"

"Not today, thank you," smiled Mallowry.

"Oh, Mr. Fairley," said Mrs. Pinkney turning to the tweedy vet. "I take it you have met Anne Jones, haven't you? She's Hankin's, I mean Mr. Rafferty's lady friend. Such a lot of confusion. Anyway I'll see you later Mr. Fairley. Come along you two."

"Goodbye, er . . . Miss," muttered Fairley, stroking his chin pensively for a moment before walking slowly back into the stall, where there were now two pairs of deep, brown uncomplicated eyes waiting to greet him. . . .

Finn came out of the house wearing a borrowed white polo-necked sweater. Hilda Pinkney had linked arms with Mallowry again and was beaming across at him.

"I do hope it fits you all right, Mr. Rafferty," she said, "It was one of David's. He was a stout man too. Well I don't mean to say fat but broad, like, across the shoulders. Now Anne, I can call you Anne, can't I? I've got a lovely hunter for you. Cavally. He's strong but comfortable, if you see what I mean. Now what about you, Mr. Rafferty? Are you sure you won't give it a try? He never does, you know. I have a beautiful Irish mare. So quiet you could eat your breakfast on her."

Finn shook his head determinedly. "I'll feed them, muck them out and deliver them, if I have to, but I've never felt the need to shin up their backs!" he said.

"But you're missing such a lot if you don't ride, Mr. Rafferty."

"Perhaps," he said, "but I've always felt you don't have to ride horses to enjoy them."

The three crossed the stable yard and walked through a high, bow-shaped entrance into a stall where a massive black hunter was already saddled, its silk-smooth coat gleaming with each brush stroke from the hunched, mole-like man in a ratting cap.

"He is gorgeous!" purred Mallowry, breaking away from Mrs. Pinkney's arm before rushing to the hunter's neck. "A beautiful animal!"

"He's carrot mad," said Hilda Pinkney, handing her a small brown bag. "You'd better take these. I think he was spoiled by a greengrocer's daughter."

"I know the feeling well," said Finn. "I was myself once."

As the mole-faced man led Cavally out to the stable yard Mallowry slipped her boot into the stirrup and was on the animal's back in one swift movement.

"She looks well on a horse, Mr. Rafferty."

"She looks good anywhere to me," he said, grinning.

Mallowry Bain had already broken Cavally into a trot across the cobbles.

"Hey, wait for me!" he yelled, bursting into a sprint to reach her.

He caught them up at the open gate to the ten-acre meadow, where the grey of the cobbles hit a bare worn patch of earth before fanning out into the crisp greenness of the Pinkney's gallops.

Suddenly at a glance the whole bounce of the Northumbrian countryside struck him, with the silver Corbar below them threading its way through the flat green carse and the purple lips of the Cheviots towering over all.

"I'll race you down to that old tree end at the river!" he cried, starting to run.

"You haven't a hell, Rafferty!" called Mallowry, urging Cavally easily past him. She reached the dead trunk quickly, circling it along the edge of the river bank before wheeling the hunter to return to the running Irishman.

"Once!" she shouted, holding up a finger as she passed the

panting Finn and turned the horse again at the gate.

"You're balmy!" he bawled as she passed him a second time. "Two!" she cried, holding up two fingers.

"Two to you too!" bawled Finn, returning the gesture and looking back to the gate, where Mallowry was preparing for the final charge.

Finn was now only fifty yards from the finish, his legs fighting to keep up the sprint as the hooves of Cavally thudded against the hard turf behind him. Horse and rider flashed past the trunk an instant before the Irishman flopped exhausted onto the bare wood and began clutching his stomach.

"Jesus, I'm lummoxed!" he gasped.

"Three!" shouted Mallowry, reining the big horse to a halt so close to Rafferty it was snorting and dribbling down the back of his neck.

"I did it three times to your one, so I beat you fairly," she said breathlessly, her cheeks flushed against her black hair.

"Rubbish!" wheezed Finn, swabbing his neck. "He's got four legs, so I won!"

Mallowry sat down beside him, placing a patronising hand on his thigh. "You can't stick the pace, Rafferty, that's your trouble."

"I think you'd best give your fellow a rest after the shallackin' you put him through. He'll be glad when it's Thursday afternoon and the O.A.P.'s come."

"Why did you start coming to this place, Finn?"

"I like to spread myself a bit," he said, "meet a few people, see how they live. Five years would be a long time in a place like this if you didn't. The trouble with people like the Pinkneys, is that they're people we're pushing out. The Pinkney Stud is thirty-two miles from the dam wall. If it was thirty-three and spreading back that way it would have been safe, just. They're good folk. Just because you're drowning them doesn't mean you can't be civil about it."

Mallowry took a stem of long grass and put it against her lips. "It's a beautiful place they have," she said.

Finn watched her mouth move slowly against the stem. "You wouldn't think there was a fight on," he said. "For a place like this. On a day like this."

"Your Mr. Brooke would have loved it here."

"All the war poets would have," he said. "That was the big thing about them. You'd have thought down in the shit and muck of the trenches they'd have had a whole heap of homes and buildings on their brains. But they only remembered the fields. The green bits. Places like this."

Mallowry went over to put a calming hand to Cavally, who was snorting and nodding his head. "Why don't you ever ride, Finn?" she asked.

"I don't know," said Finn. "I always had a lot to do with hosses when I was a kid. You couldn't help it where I came from. I suppose it was the red stick put me off."

"What on earth was that?"

Finn looked over at Cavally, who had gone quiet in her hands.

"Well not all of them, but some of the places which had to break new horses in used to have a brazier beside the paddock with a red hot poker in it. When the hoss swung its head back to bite your leg they would show it this red poker. They didn't often touch them with it mind, because it would have roasted a sow in heaven. But after that they only had to show a stick which was painted red to keep it in its place. I used to think if you had to do that sort of thing to get a hoss to carry you it wasn't worth it."

He watched Cavally tug the bunch of grass from Mallowry's hand. "You surprised me this afternoon, you know?" he said. "For someone who rides horses so well you didn't seem too anxious to be too close to the starting of a new one."

"Perhaps I'm not really so interested in them until they get to this size," she said. "I never did like puppies and kittens and little crawly things at home. I suppose I prefer to see the finished article, they're usually less trouble. Anyway, for a building man you weren't doing a bad job of being a farmer. If you could, you'd probably pitch yourself into this place up to your ears. You'd be the bucket boy, the mucker-out, the midwife. You'd even be the stud stallion if they'd let you."

She put her arms around his neck and pressed herself against his body. "You'd make a good stallion, Rafferty, don't you think? Two buckets of bran a day and a jug of Guinness and you'd go like a dream."

Finn smiled down at her, brushing her forehead with his lips. "I'll let you be the judge of that," he said. "Now don't you think you'd better exercise that great steed of yours again before he gets cramp waiting for you. You've given him the taste and he looks as if he's waiting for more. I'll just sit here like the Olympic judge and see what sort of a show you can put on without that sprinting feller breathing down your neck."

The black flanks of the eager Cavally rippled with anticipation as Mallowry Bain leapt neatly on to his back. She drew his great snorting head almost to the cleft of her breasts before loosening the reins to allow him to move slowly forward.

Leaving the river bank she turned the horse inward, her pale beautiful face showing instant delight as the field opened up before her. Within moments she had Cavally in a powerful, free-flowing gallop, the glinting hooves of the stallion eating up the ground beneath them in long strides. Finn could not recall when he had seen anything so exhilarating. They were an orchestra carrying their music in their movement. A symphony of undulating flesh in motion, their bodies so close at times it was impossible to define which was woman and which was animal. As they hurtled past him Finn could feel the heat of their bodies, he could hear their mouths snatching at a wind which was racing past them, defying them to catch it. And the hooves drumming against the stretched green skin of the valley had a music of their own. He would remember the music, even after the musicmakers had tired. . . .

The dew had already begun to fall as Finn drove the blue Ford back along the Gamelpath Road.

For fully fifteen minutes they had not spoken a word. Mallowry was reclining in the passenger seat half-turned towards Finn, watching his rough, broad hands firmly wresting the steering wheel from side to side as the car hurtled round the narrow bends.

She had removed her leather boots and her toes were playfully toying with the calf of the Irishman's leg, only to be shaken free at each violent curve of the road.

"Do you have to drive so fast, darling?" she appealed. "It's almost as if you want the day to end."

Finn grinned across at her. "All the muckies do it," he said. "You should see us starting shift at seven in the morning."

"I'm going out to dinner tonight."

"Oh," said Finn. "Who with?"

"Ken Challis."

"I see."

"Ken Challis and Fergus Bain and Ivanhoe."

"Ivan who?"

"Ivanhoe. He's our . . . Gus's labrador. He's the only dog they've let dine at the George."

Finn glanced over at her. "The dog eats with you, then?"

"It started when Gus phoned them up with a whole list of people we were taking out and there were so many he even threw in the dog. And when we got there, there was this place laid, you see, for a Mr. Ho. They must have thought he was one of our Chinese engineers. Anyway, Gus fetched the dog out of the car and made him sit at the table so he could see the waiter's face when he asked for the order."

Finn spluttered as he held the wheel. "And did they feed the brute, then?" he asked.

"Every course, down to the peach melba," she said. "You know what labradors are like. They'll eat anything. Ivanhoe thought it was his birthday. Now you can't get him to walk past the place. I tell him 'Why can't you go and sniff a tree like the other decent dogs?' But he just walks into the George as if it's some sort of canine benevolent club."

"And they don't mind, then? The folk at the hotel?"

She smiled. "Ivanhoe has a very long lead," she said, "and it has the habit of dragging a lot of influential people and their wallets in with it."

"I love you, Mal," he said, staring at the road, "and. . . ."

"And what, Mr. Rafferty," she asked leaning over to kiss him on the cheek.

"And I haven't even got a lead," he said, winking at her.

He looked across at her and saw that she was smiling quietly to herself. "Would you keep me well fed if I had?" he said.

"No," she said, "I'd eat you myself. For afters."

"Christ, you're not getting your Big House appetite on you again?" he said, putting his foot down.

"Stop here, Finn," said Mallowry suddenly. "Just by those trees down there."

Finn pulled the car into the side of the road and looked across at her. "What's wrong?" he asked.

"Nothing," she said. "Just come here."

She reached for him, pulling his head towards her as her lips buried themselves into his mouth. Dropping her hands, she thrust them up under his white sweater as her searching fingers probed his chest. He caught hold of her hands and kissed them before looking up at her.

"No Mal, not here," he murmured. "It's too open."

"But it's getting dark," she said quickly.

"It's not that dark. The whole country'll see us."

"Nobody looks at people in cars, darling."

"Look Mal, I want you too but what if someone like Liam comes stealing past and me with my bare arse stuck up in the window?"

Mallowry cupped his face in her hands. "But it's been such a beautiful day, Finn. After, well, everything. I just couldn't take not having you."

"Yes I know," said Finn, his voice thickening. "Look I think I know of a place a bit further up."

Neither of them spoke for five miles when Finn spotted the branch road leading further up the mountain on the right and swung the car across to join it. Mallowry was first to spot the gap in the dry stone walling where a low, stone-built barn had been set back into the field.

"Christ," snapped Finn, "that's all I need!"

"What's wrong, darling?" said Mallowry as he stared angrily out of the window. She saw a grey car parked in the barn, its long boot protruding from the entrance.

"But there's no one in it," she said.

"Look at the exhaust," said Finn. "It's still warm. It can only have been parked a few minutes. They'll probably be back for it soon."

Tight-lipped he revved the engine back to life, reversed violently into the road and roared up the steep incline.

"There must be somewhere up here," muttered Finn after they

had travelled three more miles. "The place is big enough. They once provided three kings of England from this place, did you know? They were kings of Northumbria. This was our Texas before the Yanks ever thought of it. The Bretwalda they called them. They became so big up here the ponies from the south asked them to run the whole show."

"Anywhere, Finn," whispered Mallowry touching his arm, "anywhere will do. It's dark out there now."

Finn frowned at her, "Look love, you can't just stop at the side of the road as if you were having a . . . look, there's another road up to the left, we'll try there!"

Once more the blue car changed direction, crusing down a small treeless valley before accelerating up to the summit, where Mallowry pointed to a narrow lay-by at the roadside.

"Just here, Finn," she said. "It's just made for us. They must have known we were coming."

As the car stopped, Finn reached above the dashboard, took a cigarette from a pack and lit it before leaning back in his seat.

"You don't often smoke when you're with me," said Mallowry.

"I don't often charge round the country looking for a love nest," he said. "For the last ten miles I've felt like a man with the runs trying to pick the lock of the loo door. And it's so bloody hot."

Finn was taking rapid sucks from his cigarette, noticing even through the enclosing dusk that they were on top of a small knoll. Below he could see the tiny farmsteads where the evening lights were beginning to come on.

"Love me, Finn," said Mallowry as he threw the cigarette through the half-open window and drew her head towards him, kissing her lightly on the lips.

"I mean love me really, silly. How are you feeling?"

"I feel as if I'm in a goldfish bowl," said Finn bluntly. "The whole bloody world could come and look in at us here!"

"Yes but would they want to?" said Mallowry. "Who's going to notice two people loving each other in a car miles from nowhere?"

"I'm sorry Mal," said Finn, withdrawing his arms. "It has to be right, you must see that. Hell it's hot! Look you have to have some sort of security."

"But I must have you, Finn."

"And you will love, I promise," he said quietly, reversing the Ford and heading back down the hill.

"Ah, trees," he shouted as he saw the darkening shape of a copse ahead of them. "Nature's umbrellas – I think that I shall never see. . . . You get an awful lot of flies under these things you know, this time of day."

"Fuck the flies!"

"Naughty!"

"Where does that lane lead to?" asked Mallowry, pointing to a sign ahead, caught in the car's beam.

"The mind boggles," said Finn, picking up the cigarette packet and holding it against his lips. "Rafferty to control," he announced. "We are now turning right in an attempt to explore yet another avenue of love in this spectacular, breathtaking safari of desire. . . ."

"Shut up, Finn!" shouted Mallowry.

From the corner of his eye he could see she had been crying so softly he hadn't heard her but her cheeks were already quite wet. He drew her into his shoulder.

"Look love," he said gently, "I need you too. I feel . . . I feel like one of Clooney's Last XI."

"Who the hell were they?" sobbed Mallowry, dabbing a handkerchief to her face.

"A whole team of frustrated fellers, just like me right now. They got so desperate for skirt that they all put on football jerseys and paraded through the town sort of offering themselves. They even had numbers on their backs so that any bird who was as desperate as they were could take a note of them."

"You're making it up," she said.

"Not at all. I was deadly serious. And so were they. The only joker was the centre forward. He scored more times that night than he had for a twelvemonth and him with a wee woman at home."

Mallowry took his arm from her shoulder and softly bit the sleeve of his sweater as she looked up into his eyes. "We'll never find a place now. Finn. I have to be back soon. I knew we wouldn't. . . ."

"Look I promised you and I will," said Finn, returning his hand to the steering wheel and digging hard down on the accelerator. "Now just one more left turn up here and . . . right before our very eyes . . . Look, I was right."

Ahead of them the dry stone wall of the field ended, revealing a small half-concealed yard beside a low-roofed stone barn.

When they looked the grey car was still there.

Finn pulled in beside the barn, the ends of his fingers whitening against the wheel, his head slumped forward between his arms. "Christ," he said in a low voice, "we're back where we started. We must have come full circle."

When he raised his head he could see the barn in front of him in the headlights of the car. Even in the dark it all seemed so much clearer than before. He could pick out the separate styles of two mortar layers, both of which had tried to buy time for the building in their turn and both were failing. He could see the split in the rusty guttering where the rain ran brown down the weather-eaten wall. Only the thick stone jamb where a child had written in chalk seemed certain of its survival.

When he could look at Mallowry he saw that her face was strangely calm, her white, even teeth catching the reflection of the car's lights bouncing back from the building as she smiled at him.

"What can I say to you, Mal?" he asked simply.

"Do you want a woman, Finn?" she murmured as she came to him.

"Mallowry Bain," he said, "at this moment I want you so much I could burst for the needing."

Finn caught a brief glimpse of her lips, moist and widening as her face moved down his body, slowly at first and then quickening, plunging into his thighs. He felt her firm, cool fingers urgently parting the coarse denim beneath his waist, the towering surge of his flesh reaching for her open mouth and with a sharp, sudden cry, which seemed to make her whole body tremble, she drank him.

Part Three

LUGNASAD

LUGNASAD *Autumn* – 'The festival of the first fruits of the harvest.'

LUGNASAD

"And Noah sent forth a dove. . . ."

The Rev. James Churnside stared up from the high pulpit of St. Cuddy's and waited for Corbardale to clear its throat.

"And Noah sent forth a dove," he repeated, moistening his lips as though tasting the words before offering them to his waiting flock. "Earlier, of course, he had released from the ark a quite different bird. A raven. The inquisitor of birds. A creature of great strength and purpose, pure of flight, eager to go out and seek the answers after the Flood had setted over the land of Noah and his wife and his sons and his little ones. . . ."

"What happened to the raven, then, Donny?" whispered the ginger-haired boy in the second seat of the front row of trebles.

Donald Dacre was in the end seat nearest the altar, the one traditionally held by the tallest of the St. Cuddy's choir trebles. His face above the plain white surplice was thinner, more angular and from the edge of the stall a good foot of trouser leg could be seen below his black cassock. Donny looked up from his book of poems as the ginger treble nudged him. "He never came back, did he?" he said.

"And on the fortieth day Noah sent forth a dove. . . ."

The Rev. James Churnside picked up the hour glass from the black wrought-iron stand on the wall and watched the sand slowly trickling into the debit section.

Donald had already decided it was yet another typical attempt at time wasting when the vicar boomed out again.

"Time," he said, holding the hour glass aloft. "The slow, gentle passing of time. So softly and so quietly does it slip away from us that none of us can hear it. Yet there are creatures in this world of ours, little ones in the great order of life, to whom even the simple shuffling of sand could be a deafening earthquake. Which is why we must never underestimate the importance of time and the impact it has on the very smallest of our number."

In the front pew Latice Gillibrand, yawning beside the Brigadier who already seemed to be asleep behind his thick glasses, was reading the names on the plaques on Cuddy's wall. Glancing over to the pews beyond the aisle she noticed that Edna Bennett also had her eyes on the wall.

"And Noah was on the ocean forty days. Now, even in this rapidly moving age of ours, forty days is a long time in a man's life. A great deal can happen in forty days. And Noah certainly had had time to observe and absorb some of the implications of the Flood which had fallen on his land. So what had really happened? The Lord God of Israel, and your God too, I must remind you, had chosen in His wisdom to release the great waters. But only after full and frank discussions with Noah himself, who was, after all, in the midst of apparent disaster, chosen to be a beneficiary. For, as the Lord promised, only the ungodly would perish. The good, those who were prepared to live their lives in His name, would be rewarded. For them there would be lands in abundance, nurtured and enriched by the very waters which would destroy the wicked. So how was Noah to react to this gift? This opportunity of a lifetime which was to see himself and his family and his families to come sharing a good life such as they had never before known."

"He sent out for a mac," muttered Dick Dancer to Brown Windsor, both of whom were sharing a pew beneath the silver lucies with a dozen more of the Clandy muckies on the Cuddy shift. The Clandy top brass had now established a footing, appropriately enough, in the brass section and were occupying two pews behind the Gillibrands. The identical sheepskin coats of Fergus Bain and Vince Caswell were relieved by the bright red jump suit of Mallowry Bain, sitting between them in a row which included Dando, Ken Challis the R.E., 'Structures' Robson, Jack Cline and George Steele. Liederman and his wife were in the first seats of the second Clandy line with The Slasher and a managerial assortment that might have made an outsider wonder who was looking after the shop.

"He sent out a dove," said the Rev. James Churnside fluttering his outstretched palms towards his congregation. "The bird of peace. After all, he wasn't a part of God's quarrel with the rest of the world. Neither were his family. He recognised and accepted the great power being revealed by the Almighty and he did the only realistic thing he could do in the circumstances. He offered it the hand of friendship, knowing that in that acceptance only good could come of it. And the Lord in His wisdom provided for him with His great bounty. . . ."

The vicar glanced up at the rear of the church, where Harry Newbiggin, the churchwarden, had examined his pocket watch and was already beginning to shake out his blue collecting bag.

Peering at the hour glass for confirmation, the Rev. Churnside turned once more to his congregation, his voice eager and accelerating.

"And so I say unto you that the same great bounty could be yours if, like Noah, you are prepared to send out the dove of peace. To offer to Him the bird of friendship flying out from our hearts, bringing a peace and a love which passes all understanding. In the name of GodtheFatherGodtheSonandGodtheHolyGhostamen. . . . We'll now sing Hymn No. 367."

Donald Dacre was on his feet even before the first jingle of silver was heard in the churchwarden's bag. Loudly and clearly he sang, his young lungs lifting both choir and congregation into the rousing and final hymn of the morning.

"As pants the hart for cooling streams,
When heated in the chase,
So pants my heart O Lord for Thee
And Thine eternal grace."

The hazel twigs in Rafferty's hands began twitching so violently he felt for a moment he was going to drop them.

"I told you there was no need for these fellers in a place like this," he said, kicking his boot into the soft soil.

Curran licked his pencil and made a mark in the folded map he was holding.

"You can almost taste the water," said Finn. "It's all under that darker green strip coming down from Calcherside. You can even see the bushes queuing up there drinking it."

Curran followed the line of his finger up the mountainside before looking down at his map again and tracing the line on it. "Is there much under there?" he asked.

"Not necessarily," said Finn. "It could mean it just happens to be near the surface. It might be just a trickle. The big stuff isn't obvious. It can be down so deep only the head and the twigs will sniff it out." He looked at the serious, frowning brow of the soils engineer. "You're really stuck on this goddess lark, aren't you, Curran?"

Curran nodded as he smiled. "Let us say that if someone has to find her I'd prefer it was me," he said.

"Why's it so important?"

"To me?" asked Curran, raising his thin grey eyebrows. "I suppose it's because people like me don't usually make earth-shattering discoveries. Mostly it's either shepherd boys who stumble on something by accident or people with enough money to be in the right place at the right time. You see as Pharaohs go, Tut was a sort of golden nobody but even he had a lord to wake him up."

"But why not you?" said Finn. "You're an archaeologist, aren't you?"

Curran scratched his head. "Of a sort, I suppose. But in this organisation I'm just plain old Soils, the chap you like to have around when you want to know the plasticity index or the compaction requirements. You need to be right at the top or right at the bottom for anyone to pick you out in a jungle like this. I'm the chap in the middle. The badger."

"How do you mean?" said Finn.

"Well if you accept you have the elephants at one end of the animal chain and the mice at the other, the badgers come in the middle of the set-up, and because they like to nose around a bit on their own patch and they keep unsocial hours, few ever bother to take a really good look at them. They merely accept that they're there and make sure there are less of them every year."

Finn was using the thick end of the divining rod to scrape the mud from his boots. "How does a feller like me fit in to this set-up then?"

Curran smiled at him. "You, Finn? You're all right. You're not any of them. You're a water beast. A whale. The only living creature that was bigger than us when we first came ashore and the only one which is still bigger than all of us."

"He's not doing too well either, is he, from what we hear?"

"Only because he's waiting, Finn," said Curran urgently. "You see it took the whale two hundred million years to change from a fish to a mammal on dry land. But he stayed here only forty million years helping to spawn the first great carnivores. He might even have been our ancestor. And then he decided he was too big for this place so he went back to the sea. And . . . er. . . ."

"And what?"

"Nothing. I was just thinking you've got me lecturing, haven't you?"

"Go on," said Finn. "It's good listenin'."

From where they were standing Curran could see the glint of water in the distance where Hounshale Bottom had already begun to fill. "The whale, yes," he said quietly. "You see even though the whale has been back in his ocean for one hundred million years he still has the lungs he had when he left. And it's at the time when he's most human, when he sticks his neck out of the water for air, that humans cut him down. He's now got a race against time on his hands. On his time-scale it will be another sixty million years before he gets his gills back and becomes a fish again. Only then will he really be safe."

"But can he wait that long?" asked Finn.

When Curran turned to him he had a strange look in his eyes.

"Yes, I think he will, Finn," he said.

He sat down on the grass and spread the map out in front of him. "Look, I was wondering while we're here, whether you could help me a little with this map?" he said as Rafferty scrambled down beside him.

"I wouldn't have thought there was any more to put to it," said Finn peering over his shoulder, "You seem to know more about this valley than the Ordnance Survey people."

"There's something here that puzzles me," said Curran, pointing a finger to the shaded area on Calcherside. "Now, we've got these two obvious tributaries here, the Erianne and the Nauny, and these two underground streams here which you've helped me find, but what about this one up here?"

Finn bent low over the map, "There's a name there at the side but it's very small. Dutton . . . that's it, the Dutton beck up towards Hengendelly. But you can forget about that one."

"Why's that?"

"Because it's gone. They diverted it before most of us got here. Instead of going into the Corbar River, the Dutton is now neatly packed and wrapped in a polythene pipe and being sent over to the plastic forest behind here. Just like a supermarket product. Perhaps they'll have us all up on the shelves with the Dutton one day." He looked down, noticing that the soils engineer was busy with his pencil. "Are you writin' again?" he said.

Curran looked up quickly as though he had been suddenly disturbed. "Me?" he said. "I'm sorry. No, I heard what you were saying. Do you worry yourself, Finn? I mean about the future?"

Finn grinned at him through a stem of grass he was gripping between his teeth. "I was asking the same thing to a feller down at the Tup last week and do you know what he said? He said, 'The future's not what it used to be.' Now I know it sounds Irish and it was. But that doesn't mean to say it wasn't sense."

"I know the feeling well," smiled Curran.

"I wonder what the folk in our future are going to say about that great regimented heap of stones we're building for them down there."

"Liederman's eighth wonder of the world, you mean?"

Finn nodded. "It's already six foot high. I reckon if your man Hadrian could come back and see it his eyes would pop out of his wee Roman head with envy."

He glanced across at Curran and saw he was quietly smiling to himself. "What's got you giggling?"

Curran rubbed his hand across his forehead. "Hadrian would have wondered what all the fuss was about. You see he probably never saw a wall like that in his life."

Finn was puzzled for a moment. "What do you mean? He built the thing, didn't he?"

"Not at all," said Curran softly. "It's almost certain that Severus built it, a later emperor. Hadrian built a wall, all right, but it was an earth wall. It was still a major construction, a celebration of himself and his empire, but it was made of clay. It was also meant to mark the end, territorially at least, of the Roman Empire. He even erected a temple to the god Terminus at the northernmost part."

Finn drew in his breath. "It would have saved a hell of a lot of money if Liederman and the rest knew that."

"I'm sure it would, but why disillusion them. Most people believe Hadrian built the Wall anyway. It does no harm and the result's prettier. They're probably doing the right thing for the wrong reasons."

"How are they wrong, then?" asked Finn.

"Well, Hadrian was the last of Rome's three greatest emperors. Augustus and Trajan were warriors, conquerors. Hadrian was the first emperor to choose to consolidate rather than conquer. He put away the sword and replaced it with civil servants. In the end he gave the Empire the stability which destroyed it. He was an oddball as most emperors went. He was attacked once by a slave with a knife and instead of having the fellow executed on the spot he gave him a job, and the chap served him well for the rest of his life. He even had ideas of basing the western half of his Empire in Britain."

"What, up here?" said Finn.

Curran shook his head. "No, in the south, Londinium, of course. For one whole winter, Londinium was the centre of the known world because he had his court there. But we didn't work out quite as he hoped. He said that when he first arrived here he had the feeling of a Neptune more chaotic than their own. He said ours was an infinite world of waters. He believed we were the island where the Titans were banished to by the gods of Olympus, and consequently we were never at rest but perpetually lashed by inner storms and oceans which made us always choose the delights of disorder rather than those of stability. Do you know, when he was up here building his wall, he even visited a sybil, a prophetess, in a woodcutters hut, in the hope she'd give him advice."

"And she put him off the idea?"

"She did. She looked in the fire and said she saw cities abuilding and joyous throngs, but she also saw cities in flames, a captive people and the face of a woman. So he moved on. They never did explain who the woman was. . . ."

"Perhaps it was Sally the Cat, her face gets everywhere these days. So the stone wall came later, then?"

Curran nodded. "About eighty years. It was built by the African, Severus. But by then it was a gesture of desperation rather than a showpiece. The Empire had already begun to crumble. You see, under Augustus and Trajan Rome had grown great out of its remarkable individuals. Under Hadrian and Antoninus it became an ordered, protected society. The Titans were cut down, the middle classes were exterminated and the individual was sacrificed to the State. When the Barbarians came Rome looked round for the Titans to save it and there were none. But you've got me lecturing again."

Finn threw the divining twigs over his shoulder and reached for his haversack. "I think your Hadrian was right about one thing, though," he said.

"What was that?" asked Curran.

"Well, all his worries about the people down in Londinium. I'm going there, to Londinium myself this weekend and the thought even scares me to death."

"Are they too barbaric for you down there?"

Finn ran his hand through his hair and grinned boyishly.

"No, I'm not going to London for a fight. Just the opposite in fact, but we won't go into that. But even that's changed."

"What has?"

"Fightin'. Even such a good, clean, honest thing like fightin'. The Irish have had some bloody good fighters in their time, as you well know Curran. But they were athletes, out fightin' face to face openly in a field for a cause, each knowing he'd only come out of it in one piece through his own skill and strength. But what did we do to him? We had to start the long-distance war. We invented the first soldier in history who never saw the man who killed him. The other sort was brutal but there was something fair about it. You could get worked up about the kind of feller who got through one of those scraps. They even used to sing about them. And now when they need to fight they try to make all men the same size by giving them a gun. And as for the so-called fightin' Irish, what sort of song do you sing about a man who stands in a black alley and shoots an eighteen-year-old soldier in the back? Just sits and pings his bloody young life away by proxy. . . ."

Curran put a hand on his shoulder. "Who was he, Finn?"

"My sister's lad," said Finn softly. "Short Strand, Belfast '75, boom-boom-boom. R.I.P.18. They gave him the mud sandwich on his birthday."

"Did he go as English?"

"They didn't get close enough to look at his label. They shot at the suit."

"I'm sorry, Finn," said Curran. "What do you want to do now?"

"I feel like doing something daft."

"Would a drink count?"

Finn looked up at him and saw that his face was quite serious. "I thought all archaeologists were dry," he said.

Curran was already on his feet, offering a hand to the big Irishman. "Not at all," he said. "It's just that we always look dry."

As the two men walked down the hill together towards Todholes, Rafferty's voice could be heard above the low bleating of the sheep and the cries of the birds across the valley.

"Do you know, Curran, every time I come talking to you I'm convinced that when all the sense of the world was dished out on a big spoon you got the biggest dose. And I got the rest. . . ."

Finn Rafferty picked up the pen from the reception desk, winked at Mallowry and wrote "Mr. and Mrs. Clooney" on the pink registration slip.

"You make a fine, big Irish biddy," he said, nudging her with the elbow of his red, grey and white sports jacket.

"It's Room 924," said the thin, blonde receptionist without looking up.

As Finn wrote down the number he noticed the large tan suitcase at his feet was being lifted with some difficulty by an elderly, blue-uniformed porter.

"Save your back," he said, waving him away. "You just point us in the right direction."

Finn picked up the heavy case and Mallowry's small weekend case and followed the porter across the crowded foyer. They reached the lift door at the same time as a plump young man in a black dinner jacket. The man received the suitcase full in the rump, causing him to stagger forward into the even bulkier body of his friend. Even in his anger the man's eyes seemed to be glaring at the Irishman's jacket rather than his apologetic face.

Since there were already four people in the lift Finn found that even after they had all squeezed inside, there were still ten inches of his suitcase protruding through the doors.

He looked round at the faces in turn as though searching for a solution. Finally he slapped his hands together.

"Right lads," he barked. "Let's get a bit of organisation around here. Now if you come here professor?" He steered a heavy, bespectacled man beside him to the centre of the lift. "You three each move one space along. . . . And you stand there for a moment," he said, guiding the plump man in the dinner jacket to a position just outside the lift before kicking the case inside and quickly pressing the button to close the doors.

"Where's the driver, then?" he asked as they all looked at each other in silence.

"I believe he's somewhere behind you, whoever you are," said Mallowry.

Finn swung round as the little porter squeezed himself from between his back and the lift wall. "Right, start her up," he said to the man, who peered at the panel, three inches from his nose.

"Where do you all want to go?" asked the porter.

Finn leaned towards him until their faces almost met against the panel. "Do you go anywhere near King's Cross. . . ?"

"I thought you said this was a small family hotel," he said, closing the room door behind them.

Mallowry had already crossed the room and was sitting, rocking gently on the double bed away in the distance. "I thought you needed the elbow space," she said.

"It's the first room I've been in where you have to call a taxi to get to bed."

"It's the oldest hotel I could find. I thought you'd appreciate it, at your age," said Mallowry, laughing as she flung herself back against the white candlewick cover.

The full impact of the sports jacket hit Finn only when he caught a glimpse of himself in the large gilt mirror on the wall. "Did you see the way they were geared up down there?" he said. "It's like a penguins' mass. One look at me and they must think I'm fresh in!"

Mallowry swung her legs over the side of the bed. "Tell them you've just come down from the grouse shooting, darling. Checks are in this year, anyway."

When she walked across the room Finn noticed her feet were bare beneath her green trouser suit. "Did you really need the trunk?" she asked.

Finn dropped to his knees and flung open the lid of the suitcase. "It's nothing but essentials," he said, tossing the clothes out one by one. "Two jerseys to fight off the London smogs, one pair of heavy quality jeans to keep out the chills in Hyde Park, two vests and drawers, socks, wash-gear and steel-capped boots for the summer sales."

"What are those for?" asked Mallowry, pointing to the last remaining objects in the bottom of the case.

"Those," said Finn, unwrapping two vests, "are a monkey wrench and an adjustable spanner. I've never been in a hotel yet where the plumbing works. Have I missed out anything?"

"A Balaclava and at least one husky," she said. "Couldn't you have found yourself a nice little weekend case like all the other lovers?"

"I'm a practical lover," he said.

"And another thing, where are the pyjamas?"

"Windsor borrowed them. He's courting again."

"What happens if there's a fire then?"

"We'll fight it together, girl."

When he looked up after sorting his clothes into an untidy pile beside the wardrobe he saw she had quickly undressed and was standing holding a low-necked scarlet dress in front of her.

"You were wearing that dress the first night I met you," he said quietly.

"A very long time ago," she said.

"About fifty years. You were dancing in it. You were dancing almost privately. As if you were almost defying anyone to ever get close to you."

As he looked at her, Finn saw her begin to sway gently from side to side, her long dark hair falling rhythmically around a face which had dreams in it. He wondered if any of them were his dreams. And now he could hear the loud incessant beat of the music from the hotel's resident five combo behind him as he stood in the small circular dance floor in the centre of the dining tables. Mallowry was dancing alone in the red dress, in front of him, her eyes oblivious to everything else in the room.

"What are you saying, darling?"

"I said the dinner'll be getting cold," said Finn, raising his voice above the music.

For a moment she seemed not to have heard him. She stood, swaying to the music until suddenly deciding to stop and, with a toss of her hair, followed him back to the table.

They had just sat down when the waiter came. "The escallop of veal is madam or sir?" he asked.

"It's madam," said Finn. "Sir wouldn't thank garçon for veal any night of the week."

"Sir's boeuf?" inquired the waiter.

"Sor's boeuf," agreed Finn, glancing through the corner of his eye at a young man who seemed to be smiling at him from a table near the window.

"There's not really a lot of difference," said Mallowry, "they're both killed for the table."

"So they are," said Finn, reaching for his knife. "The difference is in the timing. My feller had half a life, yours didn't even get a mouth of grass before he left us."

When the waiter left them Finn held up both glasses and handed one to Mallowry. "There you are, Liebfraumilch. Good health!"

Mallowry's dark grown eyes met his over the glass. "And to you, darling."

"Do you know why I chose Liebfraumilch?"

"It's the only wine you know?"

"Right," he grinned. "Do you know what Liebfraumilch means?"

"Surprise me."

"It means the milk of a loving woman."

He raised his glass first to Mallowry and then towards a table beside the balcony where two young men were sitting.

"Why did you do that?" she asked.

Finn nodded towards the window table. "Just being neighbourly," he said. "There's a feller there who seems to be taking a close interest in the source of my loving woman's milk."

"Who is he?" said Mallowry returning the young man's smile.

"He looks as if he spends a time on his feet, wherever he is. He's bandy. With legs like that he couldn't stop a pig in a passage!"

"How do you know? You can't see his legs."

"I saw him out at the dancing."

"He looks quite nice really," said Mallowry teasingly.

"His mammy keeps him lovely," agreed Finn burying his head in the beef.

Mallowry smiled. "Now you've got that old 'Where's my stone?'

look in your face again."

Finn looked up quickly. "What do you mean?"

"The look you had when Dando told everybody at the George your stone wasn't there. All black and thundery."

"Well he was wrong, wasn't he?" said Finn.

"I would have thought Griff could be quite sophisticated at times."

"Dando sophisticated?" snorted Finn, waving his fork towards her. "Do you know his problem? He's not selective. They reckon he'd fuck a frog if it stopped hopping."

"Perhaps he'd be different in a place like this?"

Finn raised his fork again. "You wouldn't find a ram like Dando in a place like this. He'd be down with the kitchen birds. They say he's been through everything in the Clandy canteen except the menu." He broke off, realising the smiling young man was standing beside the table.

"I was wondering if you would like to dance?" he said in a soft voice.

Mallowry glanced across at Finn who was shuffling his feet beneath his chair.

When he looked up he decided the boy was even younger than he appeared to be from a distance. When he smiled, the set of his teeth between his soft lips suggested supreme confidence . . . even arrogance.

Finally Finn said, "What's your name, son?"

"Peter Downes."

"Are you a gambling man, Peter Downes?"

"I have done, yes."

Finn thrust out a hand and slapped the boy enthusiastically on the arm. "Well look, Peter Downes. How about this? You can dance with this good woman if I can sing in the band. Fair enough?"

The young man grinned at him. "All right," he said. "Thank you."

Mallowry watched him leave and reached for Finn's hand on the glass. "That was unkind," she said.

"Not at all," he muttered. "It's not charity night. I was protecting my investment. Mind you, I didn't like the way he said 'All right.' He's probably the band leader."

He raised the wine bottle above Mallowry's half-empty glass. "Have some more loving woman's milk." She shook her head.

"I was just thinking. You've never taken me to dinner before. Not for a real meal I mean? With dancing."

Finn paused before putting another forkful of beef into his mouth. "If I had we'd have had the shortest extra-marital affair on record. I can just imagine Bautista at the George announcing us arriving at the Corbar Hunt Ball. 'Mrs. Mallowry Bain, wife of the project manager of the William Clandy Group and Mr. Finbar Patrick

Rafferty, muckshifter of this parish.' They'd have us stoned against the wall."

"I know. But it would be nice to be able to go about openly."

"Look," said Finn, "the longer people up around that big hole there believe I spend most of my time thigh deep in muck and you spend your time washing Gus's socks the longer we'll be together."

As the wine waiter partially filled Finn's glass and stood back the Irishman beckoned him forward. "Fill them up and save your wrist, man." he said.

"What's your name please?"

For a moment Finn thought the waiter was speaking to him, but he realised the young, long-haired youth had returned.

"Er Finn, I mean Patrick Clooney," he said, sitting up straight in the chair.

"Well Mr. Clooney. If you go through the door over there, down the stairs and speak to Mr. Denny Grant, you're on. All you have to do is tell them what you want to sing."

Before Finn could reply the young man's hands were at the back of Mallowry's chair helping her to her feet and swiftly escorting her onto the dance area.

Finn watched them on the floor. They were together and she was alone. She was always alone when she danced, even in a crowded room. She was swaying sensually somewhere beyond even the music. Finn could see she had taken her shoes off. The boy was observing her rather than dancing. He was a few paces from her, his black bow tie tight to his throat, his young face staring at her as he moved nonchalantly on the same spot.

Loosening his shirt collar Finn peered round the dining room before calling the wine waiter to him.

"Milk," he snapped, raising his empty glass.

"Milk, sir?"

Finn handed him the empty bottle. "Milk," he confirmed, "Father's milk. The hard stuff."

"A glass of whisky, sir?"

"And a bottle with it."

"We don't. . . ."

"A bottle," repeated Finn closing a fiver into the man's hand.

When the whisky arrived he took the bottle from the waiter's hand. "Don't wear yourself out," he said. "I may need you again."

Finn was on his fourth glass when the drummer in the resident combo behind him swung the microphone to his lips and began singing "The Nearness of You".

Instinctively the dancers on the floor moved towards each other. The youth was holding Mallowry quite close now, whispering something against her neck which made her look down at him and smile.

When she looked over to where Finn had been sitting she saw his place was empty. The back of a red, white and grey check sports jacket was disappearing through the baize door.

"Are you with me now, fellers?" said Finn as he strode down through the band. "I thought perhaps we'd boost up the tempo a bit. Do you know 'Today'?"

The eyes of the fat man on the electric guitar looked him up and down suspiciously. "What's that, mate?" he asked.

Finn grinned at him. "Well it's not quite a rave-up, it's more like an Irish folk-up. Look, I'll start and you try and catch me."

He grabbed the mike eagerly and began singing at a speed so fast it took the musicians by surprise.

"Is the grass still growing green upon the meadow?
Are the sands still soft where tidal rivers flow?"

Peeling off the sports jacket he flung it to the back of the small stage, narrowly missing the buck-toothed drummer.

"Do the railroads ever ask you where I've been?
Do they ask you where went your lonely friend?"

On the floor beneath him the young man was desperately trying to match the pace Finn was setting.

"That's better," muttered Finn to the band. "It's getting to their legs now."

"Do you taste my love in every glass of wine?" he sang, reaching out to snatch a glass from a passing waiter. "Perks for the band, sir," he whispered as the waiter stared at him. "Good health!"

When he started up again Finn noticed that the combo, anticipating the tune, had not only caught him up but had now gone into a sizeable lead.

The dancers were looking only at him now as their feet appeared to go berserk beneath them. Mallowry, alone, was unsmiling, watching him with a sad, resigned look as the young man jerked like a dervish in front of her.

Finn had his tie off now and his shirt broken to a depth of four buttons, as the sweat rolled from his face. . . .

"Please tell them from me I still remember them, I think," he sang, glass in hand, not knowing or caring if he did, as the dancers laughed, clapping their hands frantically in encouragement.

When it was over the fat guitarist bent to retrieve the handmike from the Irishman's shin, so deep was the bow he was giving in response to the cries for "More" from the applauding dancers.

"Thank you very much," said the guitarist smiling at them nervously. "That's all for the moment. Thank you."

Finn looked at his public, his face glistening as he raised his arms towards them in appreciation.

Mallowry was already back at their table when he arrived with his jacket in one hand and the tie in the other.

"I thought they came on quite strong in the end, didn't you think?" he said, flopping back into the chair.

"You all did," she said coolly.

He poured some wine into her glass. "I figured they needed a change of pace. You might still have been all out there but for me."

"You make it sound as though you were doing them a favour."

Finn drank some whisky. "I can remember the civilised dances, when they used to have three dances at a time," he said. "Just three. Three waltzes, three quick steps or three fox-trots . . . then scatter. It used to take nine minutes flat. And there were good reasons for it. You could ask a bird who she was in the first, tell her what she'd like to think you were in the second, and fix her up for the long walk home in the third."

Mallowry gazed across the room as the combo started up again at a genteel pace. "You can still do that now, can't you?" she asked, avoiding his eyes.

"Not at all," he said. "These days they put a tape on and you're lucky if they switch off before the pubs close. Instead of the old nine minutes chat-up you could go through a whole relationship out there. You could meet, marry, mate, fight, scrub and school the kids all before they're ready to play 'Who's Taking You Home Tonight.' "

"Do you think you want to dance now, Finn?"

As he leaned forward he noticed that between the tables on his left, the bandy-legged youth was on his way back. "No," he said, "I want to drink."

"I thought you did very well, Mr. Clooney," said the young man, looking down as Finn emptied his glass.

The Irishman picked up the empty whisky bottle, turned it upside down and watched as only a few drops fell on the table-cloth. "Yes, not bad," he muttered. "About thirty minutes flat, I'd say."

"Aren't you dancing?"

Finn put down the bottle and eased his chair round to face him. "No," he said, "I'm drinking. The movements have been known to be similar. But if you like to twist this good lady's arm, perhaps she'll accommodate you." He turned to Mallowry. "You have got room in your excellent accommodation for a little one, haven't you darling? If you hurry you might be back in time for the waiter. They also serve. . . ."

Mallowry was already on her feet. "Come on, Peter," she said stiffly. "We'll dance."

Even in the centre of the floor she could still hear Finn's voice calling for the waiter. "Mother wants some more milk," he was shouting.

The Liebfraumilch arrived and was gratefully embraced by the impatient Finn, who also claimed the waiter's silver corkscrew before doing his own decanting into the waiting glass.

"It's the story of our time, old son," he said, tossing the implement back to the waiter. "Some get drunk, others end up with a good screw."

The waiter eyed him curiously. "Will you be wanting anything else, sir?"

"Yes," said Finn, beckoning him closer, I want that fine, big, good-looking woman down there in the red frock. But every time I get close to her a sex-crazed dwarf leaps out from the undergrowth and has his way with her. Do you know what I mean?"

"But she's with you, isn't she, sir?" said the waiter.

"Exactly Alonzo," agreed Finn, slapping the table in front of him. "You see, how can I explain it? She's . . . er . . . fresh in you know, from primitive parts. Somewhere south of Dublin. I shouldn't wonder. And I'm sort of bringing her out, introducing her to some of the great fleshpots of Europe. She is, in effect, my guest, feeding off my hospitality and enormous benevolence, at great personal cost. And inflation is hitting my business too, Alonzo, just as hard as yours."

"What is your business, sir?" asked the waiter politely.

Finn scratched his head and tugged thoughtfully at a strand of blond hair at his temple. "I'm a hairdresser," he said. "Very tricky these days you know. I was only saying down at the bloody salon last week, 'When the hair's long, the money's short and we're the first to go to the wall, Quentin, my love,' I said."

Out on the dance floor the boy had his arms linked around the back of Mallowry's waist as they moved slowly to the music.

"What was I saying again?"

"You were telling Quentin about the rising inflation, sir," the waiter reminded him.

"Yes," said Finn. "No, what I mean is, after paying good, hard-earned money to give her all this, she's down there jigging with a dwarf. And that, mind you, is after eating my dinner and drinking my wine. She drinks like a fish, you know, that's why I had to get my hands on this first while she's out there. When she gets back I'll be doing well if I even get my lips damp. And, you might well ask, Alonzo my boy, do you suppose that when I finally get the bill for all this splendiferous dining and wining, that same dancing dwarf is going to pop up out of the carpet and pay it? Will . . . he . . . Hellaslike garçon?"

The waiter looked hard at him. "I'll have to go now, sir," he said, turning away.

"Just a minute," said Finn, calling him back and handing him a pound note. "Whatever the natives say, Alonzo, I reckon you're the best value in the place."

"Thank you Peter," said Mallowry as the young man brought her back to the table.

"My pleasure."

"Just a minute," said Finn holding out the wine bottle. "Do you drink, Peter Downes?"

"No, not a lot," he said.

"Well what do you do with yourself at times when you can't join in? Like when the other fellers are shaving?"

The boy made no reply.

"Well, if you don't drink, can I get you anything else? Like a satchel or something? Or braces for your sparkling wee teeth?"

"I think your friend's waiting for you, Peter," said Mallowry. "It was a lovely dance. Thank you."

Finn poured more whisky into his glass. "Funny," he said, "If anyone had a good reason to drink, I'd have thought it would be him. He could have won the spot prize if they'd included acne." He held the bottle out towards Mallowry.

"Will you have some?"

"No thank you," she said.

"You know," he said, sucking his lips, "for a muckshifter's mistress you don't drink a deal. I've watched you. You get pissed on people. It would take some women six rakes of gin to do what you do. You're intoxicated by attention. You really come alive in places like this, don't you?"

Mallowry gave him a thin smile. "I enjoy myself, if that's what you mean."

"It isn't that simple. You enjoy being enjoyed by other people. You like to see the effect you have on others even though you know damn well all the women want to maim you and half the men want to bed you."

"Only half?" said Mallowry, raising ger eyebrows.

"The other half should be in bed themselves at this time of night, with a good Biggles."

"You're meaning Peter, of course."

"Ach he's only a kid. And to him you're just another B.O.W."

"A Bow?"

"A beautiful older woman. He knows you've got more living packed into that dress than his whole class could muster and he's flattered by your interest."

"Do you think I just might be flattered by his?"

"The difference is that you've had an extra twenty years to learn sense. Catch yourself on."

Mallowry looked across at the boy and turned to Finn frowning. "You're seeing green, Finn. I thought you said you'd never be jealous. You even said 'Keep your lovers,' remember. In fact you almost seemed relieved there were some."

"Perhaps it was because I expected to outlive them. I didn't expect to see them stretching out for ever like the seed of bloody Banquo."

"You still think there are some, then?"

"Yes . . . No . . . I don't know."

She took a cigarette from the packet in front of Rafferty and lit it nervously. "You're a bastard for even considering it," she said.

"What did you think this was then? A put-up job? Me bringing you here, setting you up with a bottle and letting you watch your old bird prove she was still attractive enough to be fancied by a young, good-looking bloke? Perhaps you thought all the dancing was just a blind anyway, just a brief warm-up before nipping up to his room for a quick bang?"

"Listen Mal. . . ."

"No, you listen," she said, stubbing out the cigarette. "How long have we known each other now? I'll tell you because you won't know it. Two years, that's how long it's been. And this is the first time we've even had a weekend together. I'm not talking about a week away, a holiday . . . ha-ha . . . no, not one miserable weekend until now. How often do I see you, Finn? Once a week, fortnight, three weeks maybe? Some months I see more of the Betterwear man than I see of you. Don't worry, he stays on the doorstep. The rest of the time I'm like an untenanted house, mooning around wondering when or if you're going to call and which bush I'm going to meet you under. And you want to make all the rules? Look Finn, do you know why I went for you? Not just because you didn't give damn what you did to keep your freedom. It was because you also didn't give a damn what other people did to keep theirs."

Finn lifted his hands above his head, smiling in mock surrender. "All right, all right, alright," he said, "I'm wrong. I'll admit that."

"You're laughing at me, aren't you?" she said.

"Lady," said Finn, "I was not laughing. Least of all at you. I was merely thinking that somehow in a strange way, that was the first time I've ever heard you talking like a wife."

Mallowry tapped her fingers on the table cloth. "You've never had a wife."

"No," agreed Finn, "but I know a feller who's got one."

"Be serious," she said. "I've always thought it strange anyway. I mean, you going on about my lovers, whoever they might be, but you never say anything about your women."

"Perhaps there weren't a heap of them."

"There must have been some, Finn?"

He grinned. "I think they were mostly the spring variety," he said, "early bloomers."

"There must have been a special one, wasn't there?"

"There was." He reached for the wine bottle and refilled his glass. "I wonder if she's filling her face with loving mother's milk in one of the fleshpots of Tipperary right now."

"Who was she, Finn?"

"Mary Anne McCluskey."

"Did you love her?"

"She was the postmaster's daughter, a clever girl, good enough to be a teacher almost."

"Did you know her long?"

"About three years. She must have been a good nineteen at the break. It was just kid's stuff really. We just went about to the dances, trips in the country and things. She was away at school half the time. Her Dad sent her private. But we were together a lot in the holidays for the folk-singing in the summer and the fishing. All pretty harmless."

"And I suppose you grew out of it."

"You could say that. I went looking for her one day. Someone said they'd seen her going up towards the plantation, the forestry place. So I scouted round a bit on the edge and couldn't see anyone until I thought I heard voices coming from inside the wood. It was like a coalhole in there, black and damp and not a splash of green in the place. There was nothing growing, not a bird in sight. Just rows of great battery trees with no arms, standing like prisoners against a wall waiting for the firing squad to shoot them. Mind you, Mary Anne McCluskey was there. Oh yes, she was there. She was there with her legs out, lying daft in a ditch with a big tinker man labouring over her."

"What did you do Finn?"

"Nothing. For two good reasons. One was that he was about six stone heavier than me. The other was an even better one. She was enjoying it. So I just stood there. The only thought in my head was that she had good college marks. And he was a big, thick Firbolg not fit to be seen in the same county as her. I remember thinking that you only need to find a man with a big enough dick to screw out the brains of a nation and you could run a whole country. A few have tried it since."

"She had a choice, Finn," said Mallowry.

Finn had his head cradled in his hands, which were twitching nervously against his long hair. "Maybe," he said. "A pity it isn't always the head that makes it."

When he looked up he saw that Mallowry had got to her feet.

"Can I have the keys, Finn?" she asked. "I'm going up to the room."

He put them on the table in front of her without a word.

She looked at the whisky bottle in his hand and saw that it was already half empty. "When your friend runs out on you, you'll know where I'll be," she said.

He watched her make her way between the tables with quick, confident steps, her black hair bouncing against her shoulders and the stares of the diners all round her. Only when the scarlet of her dress became lost among the tight crowd of people gathered near the door did he turn his eyes away and back to the whisky bottle.

Behind him the resident combo had started up again, but the loudness of the music did not disturb him any more. For the first time during the evening he felt a sense of complete calm, as though some one had taken a file to his nerve endings leaving him with a dull, but not unpleasant numbness. He looked for the boy among the dancers on the floor but he wasn't with them.

Turning sharply round to his left he saw the boy was back at his own table with his friend. Both of them were puffing manfully at large cigars, and as the boy turned his head in Finn's direction to cough, the Irishman raised his glass to him.

Finn took another drink and put the top back on the whisky bottle. The check sports jacket was in a heap on the floor beside him. He decided it wasn't such a bad coat after all. It had good clear lines about it. A little bit loud maybe, but a positive garment. It looked like a coat which had something to say. He picked it up and put it on, brushing the sleeves and lapels as he did so and tucking the bottle under his arm he made his way, with his glass, to the window table.

"Hello there Peter."

The boy looked up at the grinning, gently swaying Irishman. "Oh, hello," he said, smiling awkwardly.

"Are you having some trouble with that great weapon there?"

The youth glanced at the cigar and coughed again. "They tell me they get better after you're used to them," he said.

"That's if you live long enough," said Finn, taking the cigar from the boy's hand and examining it closely.

"What would you advise then?" asked the boy.

Without taking his eyes from the cigar Finn said, "The best advice I can give is the old Irish countryman's tip to the tourist. You shouldn't really be starting from here."

"How do you mean?"

"Well," said Finn, "if you want to smoke big cigars you must first learn to smoke little cigars."

"They were a gift from Eric. It's my eighteenth birthday, he's twenty-one," said the boy, looking across at his toothy companion.

"We wish Eric well," said Finn, drinking from his glass. "But before even Eric could reach this great maturity of his, he had to go through all the other birthdays, the rusks and the balloons and the Postman's Knock until finally, as you well see, he blossoms. You have blossomed, Eric, haven't you?"

"Yes, er. . . ."

"I once knew a feller in Ireland who said he'd devised a way of building himself up to be the strongest man in Kerry. What he did was to go down to the nearest farm and lift a newborn calf. He'd do it the next day and the next and every day until the calf was a grown beast. And when some of us doubted it could be done he simply said 'You wouldn't be fool enough to imagine I could lift an animal one day and not the next, would you?' Where most people make their mistake, he said, was trying to lift a full cow the first day. Do you have a wee girl yourself, Peter?"

"Yes," said the boy. "She works with me in the kitchens."

Finn raised an eyebrow. "Oh you work here, do you? I was wondering how you managed to fix me up with the proms over there. And is she nice?"

"I like her," said the boy.

"Can you take advice?"

"I think so."

"Well Peter, hang on to her. Cling to her as your own . . . your own age group. But listen. If you should go down to the kitchens one night and find a big tinker man with his hands in her basin, strike him straight between the eyes with your cigar hand. Anything he does to you after that won't be half as painful, do you hear me now?"

"You can keep it if you like," said the boy. "The cigar."

Finn shook his head as he handed the cigar back to him. "I'm not sure I'm big enough for it either," he said.

He waved a parting hand behind him as he walked out. In the foyer he ignored the waiting lift and climbed the nine floors to the room.

Finn pushed the door open and saw the bedroom was almost in darkness. The only glow came from the lamp beside the bed, where the tilted shade was sending a circle of light across the thick blue carpet.

Mallowry was standing in the centre of the circle. She was completely naked, the glow from the lamp bathing her smooth skin into a bright ivory sheen.

Almost in a whisper Finn said, "In Granchester their skins are white."

"They bathe by day," said Mallowry looking intently into his face, "they bathe by night."

"And Ditton girls are mean and dirty," said Finn, his voice sounding stronger, accusing.

Mallowry smiled and held out her arms. "And there's none in Harston under thirty."

He undressed silently, leaving his clothes in a heap at his feet. "Why is it," he said, "that when you need a taxi in these parts you can never find one?"

Walking quickly over to her he lifted her easily in his arms and carried her to the bed, his own body following her down to the candlewick bedspread, as his lips pressed into the dark brown of her hair.

"And things are done you'd not believe," he said, his hand reaching upwards for the lampcord above the bed before switching off the light, "At Madingley . . . on Christmas Eve!"

"Griff, if you were going out for the night why did you have to come to my place to get ready?"

Dando glanced away from the wall mirror towards Jo Tiffin, who was sitting beside a small table spread about with pieces of a jigsaw puzzle.

"You mean our place," he said.

"Yes I forgot. There's your place and there's this, isn't there?"

"And this is on the way to where I'm going," he said, pulling up the knot of his tie.

"I might be going away myself soon, Griff."

When he made no reply she looked up from the table and repeated herself. "I said I might be going away myself soon."

"I heard you," said Dando jerking his neck round.

"Don't you want to know why?"

"These bloody shirts are like cardboard," he said. "All right, why?"

"My father's not very well."

There was a momentary silence as Dando thrust both his hands down beneath the neck of the blue shirt and gave it a violent tug.

"Did you hear that, Griff?"

"You're lucky to have a father to go to," he said, looking back into the mirror.

"You've got one yourself."

"I had one. He was a mute," said Dando, scowling into the glass, "a capitalist mute."

"You didn't tell me that before."

Dando swung round to face her. "Oh, he could speak when he wanted to. The only time I ever heard him speak at a union meeting was to support the bosses. He was a lackey for the coal barons, the ones who owned the valleys but never lived there except when they wanted a weekend retreat. He was a walking apology. I was ashamed of him."

"You don't seem to have liked any of your family much."

"Only one," said Dando, digging the brush into his thick, black hair.

"Your mother?"

"It was James Griffith Dando, my uncle. He was the only one with sense in the whole brood."

"What did he do? said Jo yawning. "Come to England?"

Dando turned on her angrily. "He didn't. He loathed the English. He reckoned England only wanted Wales for its cheap coal and so that they could dip in their straws, suck out the water and pay peanuts for it."

"And what did Uncle James do about it?" asked Jo lightly.

"He told all of us what we must do," said Dando, throwing down the brush and walking over to the fire. "Do you know what he once told me? He said 'Individually, Griff, our sort are always going to be small. But one day we are going to be so big in a bunch that the bosses will see us marching down the road and think it's a giant coming.' He said 'It only needs a few of us to make a big enough noise to get to the top and they'll pull the rest of us up with them.' "

Jo looked across at him as he moved back to the mirror. "Is that why you make use of them?" she asked.

He made no reply as he smoothed his hand along the line of his strong dark jaw.

"It's a woman you're seeing, isn't it?" she asked.

Dando smiled into the glass. "You wouldn't want me to be so much a male chauvinist I couldn't admit women were useful too. Have you seen my coat?"

She picked up the heavy black overcoat from the chair beside her and held it as he climbed in to it. "Oh . . . er Tiffin?" he said. "About your going away? To see your father?"

"Yes?" she said, looking directly into his face.

"See The Slasher about the time off, will you? He's your section leader."

Mallowry Bain slowly parted the front of her magenta silk housecoat and looked at herself in the tall oval mirror on her dressing table.

Smoothing her long fingers upwards over the cups of her black bra and up to her neck, she suddenly saw something which made her lean forward with a concerned look on her face.

She frowned and reached for a dark, smoked-glass jar and began pressing some white cream in a circular motion over the giant patchwork of lines at the side of her neck.

After examining her face in the mirror once more, she got up and walked barefooted across the thick blue carpet, passing the silent, seated figure of Fergus Bain who was staring at her over a large whisky.

Mallowry took a black sweater from the wardrobe and slipped it over her head as she went back to the dressing table. Pulling the high polo neck close to her chin she sat back, brushing her hair with long, aggressive strokes of a silver hairbrush.

"Do you have to go out?"

She looked round as Fergus spoke for the first time in fifteen minutes. He had crossed his short, stumpy legs in his fawn cavalry-twill trousers, and even though his green patterned cardigan was meticulously buttoned to the top his face above it was pink and flushed.

"We agreed Gus, remember?" she said quietly.

"Which of our agreements was this?" he asked, looking down at his heavy well polished brogues.

She made two more sweeps through her hair with the brush. "That we wouldn't be each other's keepers," she said without changing her expression.

"I'd hoped," he said blankly.

"Hoped what Gus?"

"That we might talk."

Mallowry got up from the dressing table and walked over to the tall, cane-backed chair where Gus was sitting and removed a pair of black ski pants.

He watched as she slipped her long legs into them. "We've never been able to talk much," said Gus taking a sip from the glass before spluttering it back in again. "Correction," he said, holding up a finger, "I've never been able to talk much."

Mallowry went back to the dressing table and picked up the hair brush again.

"It's 'the same down there," said Gus. "You find yourself talking about people, at people and never really with people. And they wonder why things go wrong."

He put his drink down on the carpet and began chuckling quietly to himself.

"What's the funny?" said Mallowry, glancing across at him.

"It just reminded me of the American who ran the world's worst orchestra and he got so uptight that he. . . ."

When Mallowry looked round she saw he had lifted his glass again and seemed to be laughing at it.

"He did what?" she asked.

"He killed the first violin. It's all right, it's not a violent story. Anyway they sent him to the electric chair and pulled the switch and nothing happened. And when they said it must be a bum chair he said 'No, it's me, I'm a lousy conductor.' "

"That sounds like one of Liederman's," said Mallowry.

". . . a lousy conductor," repeated Bain as he burst out laughing again. "The only difference between him and me is that he had to find out the hard way. I've always known it. I'm a lousy conductor and I'm a lousy communicator."

He walked over to the dressing table, picked up the half-empty whisky bottle and carried it back to the chair before refilling his glass.

"That's a joke in itself, isn't it?" he said, slurring his words. "Me a lousy communicator and here I am building roads, motorways, bridges for the biggest C.E. outfit in this country, all so that everybody else can go around communicating with each other. And I can't do it myself."

"You're communicating with that bottle pretty well," said Mallowry, attacking her hair fiercely.

Bain took another drink, pretending not to have heard her. "Did you know that there's a whole sect of people who talk to walls? Apparently they started by facing a blank wall and just chatting to it. They say things like 'You are a wall and I am a person. I can do quite a lot to you, I can touch you, paint you, I can even knock you down. You can do nothing to me but because I can do everything to you I have responsibility for you i.e. I am a responsible person even to things which have no feeling for me and therefore you should not be able to hurt me!' "

Mallowry put the hairbrush down aand reached for the lipstick, making impatient stabs at her wide puckered lips.

"I think I might join them, the wall-talkers," said Bain, swirling the whisky round in his glass. "I quite like walls anyway. I build walls and houses and motorways and the jolly old dams. Walls are really rather pleasant things when you get to know them. Did you know that apart from a few rabbits I'm a wall's only natural predator. Because any time I like I can send round a dozer driver and wipe it off the face of the earth."

"What do the rabbits do?" called Mallowry without looking round.

"The rabbits? Ah now they're quite different. They come up from below. They only have to burrow under the poor old wall and down it falls and the effects are just the same, achieved without all the expense of buying brains. Sometimes I feel they're down there right now, burrowing under me. I half expect them to come popping out of the ground some days."

"Perhaps they're all fed up with being rabbits and they want to be the Shout instead," said Mallowry.

Bain stared drowsily into his whisky. "The Shout?" he said. "Yes, I'm the great Shout. Do rabbits go away, I wonder, when the great Shout shouts? It's funny you know, I never really liked to hear shouting. I loathe noise. I always used to think that most of the things in life that needed to be said could be said quietly."

Mallowry Bain was standing looking down at him beside the chair. "Perhaps it depends on what you say and how many people you want to hear it," she said.

"You see," said Bain, "it was so quiet once. Things were different. You could get your pencil out and sit down and draw up marvellous schemes, wonderful plans. And if they were good enough you handed them in, knowing that all your shouting was right there on that piece of paper. It told them everything they wanted to know just the same as if it was standing up and bawling its head off."

Mallowry touched his shoulder gently. "Don't let that stuff have too much of a say, will you? I'll be back, well . . . not too late."

Gus looked up from his glass. "I've been waiting for you to come back for more than a year now," he said softly. "I can wait one more night."

She walked over to the bedroom door and paused before looking back at him. "Don't stay up too late, Gus," she said, closing the door behind her.

Mallowry had never been in the Black Lion at Whithope before. She hesitated for a moment in the musty entrance lobby before going into the first room on the right, where a group of men standing at the bar looked up as she entered.

"Will I do, love?" called a tall spotty youth, who wiped his hands down his dirty blue dungarees and offered himself.

She turned back and glanced both ways before opening the yellow-grained door on the other side of the corridor. She saw there was only one man in the room. It was Dando. He was leaning, almost sprawled over the small cocktail bar, whispering to a blonde girl behind it.

He straightened as Mallowry came into the room before turning back to the girl. "Well goodnight, Angel. You've got that sizzling, soldier-boy love letter to read, haven't you? Read it slowly, O.K.?"

Dando waved Mallowry towards a small copper-topped table. "Just a minute before you go," he said to the girl. "I'll have another of these and. . . ." He looked at Mallowry, "you'll have a gin, won't you?"

"Snowball," she said.

He smiled slowly. "Of course. . . ." He stood over the girl until the drinks were ready before putting two pound notes in her hands. "Never mind the till, Angel. By the way I take it no one's likely to develop a sudden need for the snug for some time, are they?"

The girl looked at Mallowry and back to Dando. "It's O.K. by me," she said. "We often close it midweek anyway."

Dando closed the door behind her and turned to face Mallowry. "Love from Belfast. That's a joke, isn't it? Never mind, she still manages to get by locally."

"No doubt she does," said Mallowry, as Dando sat down at the opposite side of the table. "But you haven't asked me here to look at your trophies."

"Her?" he said, raising his black eyebrows. "She's no chance."

"All right, so Dando's not screwing the barmaid," she said impatiently. "For all anyone cares. What do you want, Griff?"

Dando sipped from his glass, closely watching every movement of her face. "Do you believe the possession of knowledge is important in this world, Mrs. Bain?" he asked quietly.

"I suppose it depends how much you know and how often you meet anyone who knows more," said Mallowry glibly.

"I know about Teg's Head."

"Full marks for local topography," said Mallowry quickly. "Teg's Head, a rocky outcrop afforested in parts with spruce, Scots pine; then there's The Faunes country park, with pine tables with fixed benches you can't steal and don't let's forget the old lovable river Corbar, home of the grayling and the gentle brown trout and the black toad. . . ."

"I know about Teg's Head and you and Rafferty," said Dando,

looking directly into her face.

Mallowry went silent as she stared into the glass in front of her. "You've been taking up nature rambles?" she said finally.

"Gans has."

"I can't quite picture Gans with a butterfly net," she said with a forced laugh. "Have you got a cigarette?"

"I don't but I'll get you one," said Dando, walking over to the rear of the bar and taking a new packet from the shelves. Without speaking he took out a cigarette and handed it to her, watching her eyes as the flame from his lighter lit up her face. "You don't deny it, then?"

She blew the cigarette smoke from her lips quickly. "Look Dando. I know you well enough to know that if you'd said this much, you could probably tell me where I've been and with whom since losing my gymslip. But where does that get us beyond the fact that you mix with some pretty seedy Peeping Toms?"

"Good," said Dando. "Well that's got that bit out of the way. I thought it might have been a bit tougher but I'm not complaining. Now of course I know, but wouldn't it be more interesting if a few other people knew?"

"What have you got in mind?" said Mallowry. "A poster on the works notice board?"

"Oh no, nothing quite so public."

"Who then?"

"Well perhaps someone on the Board. Perhaps our ancient and venerable Sir William. Perhaps even Mr. Bain. A P.M. always likes to know what's going on on the site."

Mallowry drew the ashtray towards her and stubbed out her half-finished cigarette. "And you would walk into the office and tell Gus all about it, would you?"

Dando stretched out an arm and stroked her chin, slowly moving his finger along her cheek. "My lovely, lovely Mallowry," he said smiling, "you are . . . damned right I would."

She brushed his hand away and glared at him, her lips tight against her teeth.

"You must appreciate, darling, that a man in my position has to maintain a certain sense of duty, loyalty, call it what you will. It's hardly fair that I should be in a position of trust and yet walk around carrying such a dreadful secret with me. Of course some of the actors on our little stage might come out of it worse than others, who knows?"

"Like who?" asked Mallowry.

Noticing his glass was empty, Dando walked to the bar, deliberately delaying his answer until he had filled his glass. "Well now, Irish gangers haven't a particularly high survival record when any sort of squeeze has been on. Not even stone gangers."

"You'd sack Finn."

"Me?" said Dando with surprise in his voice. "Oh no, I wouldn't need to. Rafferty would be up the road and off into the great unknown like a sacrificial sheep. Let me get you another of Angel's drinks."

Mallowry waved him away from her glass. "And what makes you think that that wouldn't please me? After all, if you've done all this nature trailing over the past months surely you've learned enough to know that what's happening between Finn and me isn't any of your one-off quick bash affairs. What if I actually wanted Finn to give all this up so that I could eventually join him somewhere else?"

Dando laughed. "My delightful Mallowry," he said, "I know you but I know Rafferty better. You'd kill him if you took this away from him. Muckshifting's all he knows, all he'll ever know. I believe the bugger even loves it. Look. He's had his Siberia. They don't send you there twice. The second time you're out and for good. Once the word gets around there won't be another P.M. in the country who would take him on unless he had a horse for a wife. And even you wouldn't find much fun in the arms of a redundant muckie."

As Mallowry ran her hands from her forehead down her face Dando saw that her eyes were moist. "All right," she said quietly. "What do you want, Dando?"

The big Welshman stood up, glass in hand and looked down at her with a slight smile on his lips. "You can put your knickers back on for a start, Mrs. Bain," he said.

"I wasn't going to take them off," she said coldly. "So what do you want?"

"I want him out."

"Finn?"

"No, Gus."

Mallowry stared at him in disbelief. "What do you mean? Look, I don't get this. You know about me and Finn, and yet you want Gus to go?"

Dando walked slowly over to the bar and returned with a small bottle of American Dry, which he decanted into his whisky glass. He placed the drink in the centre of the table. "I'll tell you why Gus," he said. "Now if you imagine this as the great Clandy organisation, your ganger boyfriend is down here in the basement, the thick bit where nothing ever moves." He slid his finger up the glass. "But once you reach about here, you see the bubbles starting to rise. That's me, about halfway, maybe two-thirds and going up. And once you're that far there's only one thing to stop you hitting the surface. The froth at the top. And that's your man."

"What makes you think you'd make it even then?" she asked.

"Bubbles always rise."

"So does the scum on the bath. Anyway, what makes you think I can get Gus to leave?"

Dando took a gulp from the glass and examined it mockingly. "He'll let you take him. Look mate, everyone knows he's cracking. It's just a matter of time. And yet no one wants to give him the Clause 16. Look, you could help us all out by taking him on an extended holiday, maybe a couple of years. You'll know how to do it."

"And you want me to remove Gus and myself from the Clandy scene so that little bubbles can get to the top?"

"It's the only way he'd go. He wouldn't do it by himself. You won't have any money worries. Big Clandy's always good at looking after sick generals, and anyway he likes you."

"What about Finn?"

Dando reached out and patted her hand on the table. "Rafferty will be all right. He won't know a thing about it. He'll shovel on regardless. In fact he could do very well out of it. After all, soon we're going to be looking for a new G.F. too, and some people may be in a position to put it his way."

"And that would be part of the package, would it?"

"It could be."

"You're not going to tell me you expect to get P.M.?" asked Mallowry tiredly.

"No. Just Number Two. To Caswell."

"Is Caswell in on this too?"

"Caswell is never in on anything. He's a pieman. But we have a working arrangement."

"And if I choose to go to Gus or Sir William with all this, instead of doing a deal with you?"

Dando poured himself another drink at the bar and returned, towering over her as he smiled down. "It's your choice, kiddo. But if you go to them, I'd say you're out anyway. Gus has already the skids under him and Rafferty, well . . . he's no chance. There's really only my way left. The sad bit, of course is that you have to lose either way."

When she looked up at him he saw her face was quite calm. "All right," she said, "I've had enough of you for one night."

"You'll do it then?"

"I'll give you your answer later, perhaps tomorrow. I'm sure that even you Dando, wouldn't expect all your bubbles to rise in one night."

She stood up from the table, at the same time brushing her hands down the front of her black ski pants, almost unaware that Dando had his arm around her.

"Mallowry my lovely, you've really taken it all very well," he said, a smile breaking across his thin lips. "I suppose that's what they call class? . . . the ability to stay cool in adversity."

He was still looking for a reaction in her eyes when the door suddenly burst open and Finn Rafferty came in. The Irishman's face scanned the room before settling on the couple with a long, disbelieving glare.

"And just what the hell's going on here?"

Rafferty's face was red, scowling as he took a few paces towards them.

Dando released Mallowry and reached for his glass, draining it in one swift gulp. "If you've any thoughts in that thick Irish skull of yours at this moment, Rafferty, you can toss them out. Mrs. Bain will tell you all about it. Anyway one of us is about to leave."

Rafferty moved towards him, his large hands twitching at his sides, "Wait a minute Dando, what's this all about?"

Mallowry held a handkerchief to her face as she leaned forward in the chair. "Leave it, Finn," she said. "Please. Come and sit over here and leave it."

"But Jesus, will somebody give me a bit of sense. . . .?"

"Finn please! Look! For me! Just come over here and sit down."

The Irishman gave another glare in Dando's direction and walked slowly over to Mallowry's table.

"Beautifully done, my dear," said Dando, clapping his hands silently. "Delilah couldn't have handled her brute better." He reached into his inside pocket for his wallet and took out a five pound note before walking over and placing it on the table in front of Mallowry. "Give this to Angel when she comes back, will you?" he said. "Tell her it's her service charge."

Only when Dando had left the room and closed the door behind him did Mallowry start to cry. Sobbing bitterly, she buried her head into the broad shoulder of Finn's cord jacket.

Finn pulled her damp face towards him. "What did he do, Mal? Why are you here? Look, he's still out there!"

She dabbed the handkerchief against her cheek. "No, Finn," she said. "There's nothing you can do. Look, can you just get me out of here? Anywhere will do. I just want to get out of this place."

Finn walked from the room, leaving her to follow him.

Mallowry's red sports car had been following the fast-moving tail lights of Finn's Ford for a good twenty minutes before she saw him pull into a dimly lit tarmacced clearing off the Haltbriggin road.

Opening her door she saw they had parked in front of a low, wooden building. Loud music could be heard through the open window below the green neon sign which read "Dusty's Place".

Even though the big silver juke box at the entrance was thumping out "Everybody's Talking About You", when they walked in they could see immediately that the cafe was deserted.

A cracked glass coffee percolator was gurgling unattended on the black formica-topped counter, and the shiny plastic chairs round the bare, wooden tables were all empty.

Finn spread his arms apologetically. "It was the first place I saw. I was never here before."

Mallowry's eyes searched the room. From the red puffiness around them it was obvious she had been crying in the car. "Never mind," she said. "It's lovely. But first I must spend a penny."

Competing with the noise of the juke box, Finn was banging a soup spoon against an enamel mug when a thin, blonde woman came in through the front entrance. "Oh!" she said as though his great size had surprised her. "Sorry to keep you, love." She moved behind the counter. "I've just been phoning my friend."

She picked up a half-smoked cigarette and lit it, glancing at him before turning away to do up two buttons on her white nylon coat and flick her hands through her short, wiry hair.

As she turned to face him she gave Finn a flashing smile which stopped the juke box. "Transport are you, love?"

"Does it make any difference?"

"It does for overnights. We have rooms at the back, you know? For transport. Sleeping and that."

"Are they very big?"

"No, er, small you know. But very nice. For transport."

"No thanks," said Finn. "You wouldn't get mine in there."

The woman giggled before putting her finger in her mouth and sucking it thoughtfully. "What are you going to have, darling?" she asked.

"Coffee, love. Two coffees."

"Two?" she asked loudly just as Mallowry came through the door of the ladies. The woman looked stiffly at her and repeated the order. "Cups or mugs?"

"Mugs," said Finn.

"Finn, I've been thinking," said Mallowry. "How did you know I'd be at the Black Lion?"

"I saw your car outside as I was passing. Maybe it was a good thing I came when I did."

She saw that his eyes were cold, challenging. "What do you mean?" she asked.

"I mean that if I hadn't, it might have been you and Dando in here instead of you and me."

"Shall we go and sit down?" she said, moving over to the table furthest away from the counter.

Finn paid the waitress without a word and carried the mugs down to the table. He passed one over to Mallowry and sat opposite her staring down at his own.

She reached out a hand toward him. "You don't have to worry about Dando," she said. "Not in the way you're thinking."

He looked up slowly. "But what were the pair of you doing there, twenty miles out in the shaugh together all neat and cosy?"

"Look I wasn't going to tell you, Finn," said Mallowry, raising her voice as the juke box started up again. "But I suppose you'll have to know now. Come here where I can hear you above all this racket."

Finn sat down beside her. "O.K. tell me." he said.

"It's Dando. He knows about us."

"He knows what?" he shouted, scowling over his shoulder in the direction of the music.

"He knows about us, about Teg's Head. He knows everything, Finn."

Finn slid back his chair and walked over to the frizzy blonde behind the counter. "That row!" he yelled. "It seems to keep racketing away even though there's no-one feeding it."

The woman looked at him without interest. "I can't do anything about it, love," she said airily. "Some bloke put a pile of coins in around nine and since then it sounds as if it doesn't want to stop. It's done it before."

"What do you have to do to stop it? Shoot it?"

"Well you can buy silence, of course."

"What do you mean?"

"Well," said the woman, "there's a button on it which gives you three minutes of peace and quiet, the same time a disc takes."

"And what does that cost?"

"5p, the same as a disc. But it might take some time to get through, of course. It depends when your time comes up."

The Irishman dived into his jeans pocket, picked out three 5p pieces and fiddled with the shuddering silver box for several seconds, returning to the table. "How can you be sure?" he said.

"Gans told him."

"Gans wouldn't know a straight fuck if he fell over one. Anyway knowing and telling are two different things."

"He's not going to tell."

"Well that's all right, then." He raised his voice as he saw the woman trying to eavesdrop on them. "Will you have another coffee?"

Mallowry shook her head. He could see she was pale, unsmiling. "Wait a minute," he said. "Why isn't Dando going to tell?"

"Because he's agreed not to," she said limply.

"Christ Almighty!" bawled Finn. "There's only one price a man like Dando would ask if he had a goose like that in his hand."

"What do you mean, Finn?"

"You," he said, getting to his feet and shouting at the top of his voice before realising the juke box had suddenly gone silent. "You," he repeated in a hoarse whisper.

Mallowry pulled him gently back to the chair. "Finn!"

"And why not," said Finn, his voice coming over almost in a hiss. "He's always had the heat for you. His eyes have never been at peace the whole contract while you've been around."

"Listen," said Mallowry. "He doesn't want me. He wants Gus out. He thinks with him out of the way he can get a bit further up the Clandy ladder."

"And how are you expected to help him do it?"

"The way I shall have to," she said calmly, "by suggesting to Gus he needs a good, long break, and knowing how he's feeling at the moment, he'll probably agree to it."

"And he'll go, then?"

"He will if I go with him."

Across the room the juke box suddenly erupted into another blast of pop rock. Looking over at Finn's face Mallowry could see his lips opening rapidly with no words coming from the. Finally he pitched his voice above the music. "You're not going," he yelled. "I'm not letting you. Dando's driving nobody out any more."

"What would you do?"

Finn looked down at the white knuckles of his clenched fist on the table. "I've used my hands most of my life. I could do a useful shift on him."

"And what would he do?" she said. "Just pick himself up and lick his wounds in Gus's office. That's no answer."

"I'll tell you what I'll do," said Finn, squeezing the mug between his hands. "I'll go to Gus myself. . . ."

"You'll what?"

"Yes that's what I'll do. I'll go to Gus and tell him the lot, man to man. Have it out there and then."

"What would you tell him?"

"The truth of course. I'll tell him we've been mixing, that we've been seeing each other for a long time now. That I'm sorry it's had to happen like. . ."

"Finn darling, we're not at school any more," said Mallowry, lifting her voice above the jangling music. "It's not owning-up time and a pat on the head and fifty pence in your pocket for being honest. He wouldn't want to hear what you've got to say."

Finn's right hand was tapping the table unconsciously in beat with the music. "But it would be better to hear it from me than bloody Dando."

Mallowry smiled despairingly. "Sometimes I envy you, Rafferty. You're always wanting to do what you feel is the right thing for everybody. You've got a sort of aggressive, inbuilt innocence in you. But it went out of fashion, Finn, a long time ago, everywhere it seems except inside your head. You're still cruising along the open road not noticing that the rest of the world turned off at the last lay-by."

"But Gus doesn't care for you in the same way as . . . well I do."

"He does, more than you think. He certainly cares what other people think. That's why he could never come to terms with you. You'd be bad for his image."

“His image!” shouted Finn, fractionally after his three minutes of paid silence started on the juke box. He thrust his head close to the table, deliberately keeping his voice low. “So if it had been fat Caswell who had been rummaging you in the hills you think Gus might be prepared to discuss it over brandy and cigars?”

“He would have found it easier to understand,” she said.

“I’ll bet he would,” grunted Finn. “It would be like keeping it in the family. We’ll all row together boys, even if it means sharing the same oars.”

“You’ve been drinking, haven’t you?”

“Not nearly enough!”

He picked up the mugs and went over to the blonde woman at the counter. “Two coffees with milk and quiet,” he said. Noticing a half-filled bottle of brandy between the open, sliding doors of a cupboard beside her he called the woman over. “Is that your private bevvy down there?” he asked softly.

She looked quickly behind her and closed the cupboard door. “No, that’s Beattie’s,” she said starchily. “She gets a bit faint if she’s on her feet a long time.”

Finn put a five pound note into her hand. “Tip it in a tea mug and tell Beattie to re-stock in the morning,” he said.

The woman looked towards the doorway and quickly bent down and emptied the brandy into a mug. Looking down at the fiver in her hand she said, “That willbe 12p, for the lady’s coffee.”

“No milk this time?” said Mallowry when he put his mug on the table.

Finn picked it up and took a deep draught of it before smacking his lips. “It’s black, hot and sweet,” he said, “like the Bradford virgins.” She watched him take another long swig from the mug. “Well now, Big House Girl, what can we do for your image?” he asked. “Sign the visitors book and stay?”

“What do you mean?”

“Well Elizabeth over there, Taylor that is, says they have kip bins at the back for the weary traveller. For anyone who wants to doss down for the night. She thinks I’m transport: we might get special rates.”

Mallowry looked over at the blonde, who was pouring tea for two men in brown dungarees. “She thinks you’re a lorry driver?” she asked.

“Mock her not,” said Finn mischievously. “She also probably thinks you’re a roadie. A lot of them wear black you know. Night birds, ready to drop their pants for the first long-distance lover who pulls in. Shall I tell her you’re on?”

“Now you’re being ridiculous,” said Mallowry.

Finn nuzzled into his brandy mug as the juke box came to life again with a strident, ear-splitting chord. “Not at all,” he shouted at her. “It’s extremely class conscious in these places. They even have their own pecking order. Right down from the big brass boys on the Saudi run to the M.1 cowboys. They say the juggernaut boys won't even touch a bird unless she's at least one 'O' level, preferably oral. And it doesn't even stop there. Down below you find the real salt of the road, the mates, the fitters, the legmen, right down to the grease boy who's lucky to end up even with a coffee grind most nights. There they are, all waiting for birds like you to ask them what school they went to so that the winner can shout 'Bingo'."

"Grow up Finn," said Mallowry as the faces of the two lorry drivers turned towards them. "Please grow up."

Finn raised his mug to her. "I think Mrs. Bain, I shall grow up to be a long distance, Big House, buck lorry driver. I will punish my candle into the small hours nightly, working at my books, gorging into the great truths of the world and then I will build the biggest lorry in the world and traverse this globe offering the greatest ride since Mazeppa. And when I have run my course . . . then I shall drive off into the shining deserts of Saudi, saviour and friend of the oil-sucking great Western er. . . ."

"Railway?"

"Civilisation," said Finn. "And there in the clean heat of the cradle of humanity I will fold my. . . ." As the music from the juke box came to an abrupt stop Finn leaned towards Mallowry until their faces were almost touching. "Tent," he whispered.

"Finn?" said Mallowry softly.

"Hello?"

"Let's go home."

Finn looked at his coffee mug which was now empty. "I was thinking."

"What were you thinking?"

"I was thinking perhaps Dando should have come after all. He'd make a good transport. The only trouble is he would always want to be owning the truck. And he'd be wrong. If you took count out at the back there and saw how many lorry owners there were locked in the arms of long-distance Venus he'd stay in the cab. Owners only get fun with racehorses. Things which are forced out into a field to do things for a carrot. What would you be prepared to do for a carrot, Mrs. Bain?"

"Finn, I've told you."

"I know, I know. But I've been trying to put myself in Dando's position, if a pick would ever get me that far down. Now the way he would see it is that all this would disgrace Gus and rather than see Gus's shame and your shamelessness in the eyes of the mighty Clandy Board he would give you the choice of shopping you or bedding you. And if I was Dando down there in his stinking subsoil, I'd settle for the sheets and count it a good night's work."

"It wasn't like that," said Mallowry as the juke box came to life again.

"Well, didn't he even mention me, then?" shouted Finn, his eyes blazing. "I suppose I was considered such small meat in this bloody marital mix-up that it didn't matter what I felt."

"Finn!"

"Well he didn't, did he?"

Mallowry felt her eyes filling as she looked deeply into his face. "No," she said quietly, "he didn't mention you."

"You're damn right he didn't," he bawled. "He was after the bigger fish. The ones who could do him a bit of good. I was just the pantry boy who got caught stealing the mistress's cakes."

"Finn, I must go home," she said rising to her feet. "It's getting late."

Finn stood up and replaced his chair against the table.

"It already has," he said.

Mallowry was half a dozen steps ahead of him as he passed the frizzy-haired woman at the counter.

"Would you like some more silence, love?" she said with a sarcastic smile.

Finn took out a pound note from his wallet and slapped it in front of her. "No," he said. "Let's have some decent, honest, rip-roaring noise. Feed the bugger! All night!"

Sir William Clandy was seated behind the large polished oak desk in the project manager's office when Bain and Mallowry came into the room.

Putting down his glass of sherry he came forward smiling, to shake Bain's hand. "Good to see you again, Gus." He turned to take Mallowry's gloved hand, raising it to his lips and kissed it. "And it's always a pleasure to see the lovely Mallowry."

When neither of them spoke he looked swiftly round the room.

"Here, let me get you some chairs."

"No it's quite all right, I'll get them," said Bain, walking towards the window.

"Of course," said the Clandy chairman, "I was almost forgetting. You know this room very well, don't you?"

When they sat down in front of the desk, Clandy was refilling his sherry glass. "Will you join me, Fergus?" he said briskly. "No, of course you can't can you? How about you, Mallowry?"

"No thank you, Sir William," she said.

"Tea, that's it," said Clandy snapping his fingers. "Hot, sweet . . . tea? You'll have tea, won't you?" He pushed up the switch on the desk intercom. "Send in tea for two er Tiffin," he said before turning to Bain and Mallowry. "That sounds rather odd, doesn't it? Tea for two Tiffin. She's the sort of odd-job girl. Standing in for Daphne. It means food I think, doesn't it? Tiffin? Some sort of

Indian connection I believe. Mind you she's quite a tasty little . . . girl, eh Gus?"

Neither said a word as he leaned forward, spreading his hands on the desk. "Well . . . er . . . so you've decided to leave us, then, Gus?"

"We fly out tomorrow," said Bain.

"Yes, well, what can I say to you, Fergus? We've known each other a long time. You wouldn't want me to hand you any of the usual sentimental claptrap. But you know when things start to go wrong with a man, often the last person to know is the man himself. But you've shaped up to it Gus. I think you've made the right decision. Where was it you decided to go in the end?"

"The Canaries. Gran Canaria actually."

Clandy put his sherry glass down loudly on the desk top. "Old Gran Canaria, eh?" he said. "And very pleasant too. I was once there on holiday with my dear, late wife. If I remember, the bloody porters were on strike the whole fortnight and we had to shift for ourselves, which was a bit inconvenient, especially at thirty quid a week each. But that's not likely to worry you, is it now?"

"We've bought a villa at Vagueta," said Mallowry.

"Good. Good!" he said. "And I'm sure you haven't found Clandy's ungenerous in your present situation?"

Bain looked round as Jo Tiffin came into the room before turning back to Sir William who was waving the girl towards them. "No," he said, "you've been most generous."

"I should think so too," he said shaking his head. "We look after our walking wounded at Clandy's, you know. Always have done. We've appreciated all you've done for us here Gus. Well everywhere. It's been a long campaign and not without its triumphs, eh? We've . . . er . . . shifted some stuff as they say, haven't we?"

"Yes," said Bain, sipping his tea.

"Of course we have." Clandy rubbed his hands together. "And now like me, you're taking your beautiful wife to the Canaries with you. You're still a very lucky man, Fergus Bain. You know that, don't you? We can't all have our health but some of us can still be blessed with a lovely and understanding woman by our side. That can't be bad, eh? She's been a pillar of strength to you Gus. I hope you appreciate her."

When they did not reply the Clandy chairman sipped from his glass and began tapping his hand on the surface of the polished desk. "Yes, well, should you ever want to come back. You're a young man still, Gus, you know, fifty-two's no age. I could give you a few years in this business myself."

"You always could," said Bain.

"Hmmm, yes, well if you should feel like taking up the old gauntlet again. When you're perfectly fit again, of course. We'll er . . . well we'll talk about that when it happens, shall we, Gus?"

As the intercom on the desk began buzzing, Clandy reached across and depressed the switch. "No, that'll be quite all right," he said. "Send them in."

The door behind Bain and Mallowry opened almost immediately. Looking round Bain saw Caswell and Dando come into the room.

"Sir William," said Caswell, bowing slightly before noticing Bain in the high-backed chair. "Hello, Gus old chap. How are you feeling now?"

"Fine," said Bain nodding to him. "Just fine."

Dando came up slowly and stood beside Caswell, ignoring the contemptuous gaze Mallowry was giving him.

"Well now, Vince," said Clandy, looking directly at both men. "You know what all this means, I mean Gus Bain being here in these circumstances?"

"Yes, Sir William," said Caswell.

"Well if you do, you know more than I do," said Clandy. "All I know is that my Number One here is having to leave me for an unspecified period and that means the most ambitious and prestigous civil engineering contract in Europe is without a Number One. Are you ambitious, Vince?"

He broke off as Mallowry and Bain stood up and placed their teacups on the desk. "I think it's time we were leaving Sir William," said Mallowry, offering him her black-gloved hand. "You know what it's like, packing and everything. . . ."

"Of course," said the Clandy chairman, kissing her glove again. "Do you know, my dear, all the time I've known you I've never seen you wear gloves before."

She flashed him a smile of pure radiance. "When we've gone you must get your knowledgeable Mr. Dando to tell you about the value of protective clothing," she said, "particularly on the dirtier sites."

Clandy gave her a puzzled glance and offered his hand to Bain. "Well good luck then, Gus old chap. Look after him, Mallowry. He will be missed you know. He'll leave behind a very big hole to fill."

Caswell was already chuckling even before Bain and Mallowry had left the room. "I couldn't have put it better myself, Sir William," he said.

"No, Vince," he said tiredly as he returned to the desk, "I don't suppose you could."

He sat down and took another sip of his sherry before turning to Caswell again. "However, Vince, there's certainly a hole in this particular seat to fill, be it temporary or permanent, and since you're Number Two the natural thing to do in the circumstances is to offer it to you. Are you prepared to accept it?"

"I am, Sir William," said Caswell reverently.

"Well that's settled then," said Clandy. "Now as for you Dando . . . Griff. In comparison with your friend here you're being given an even bigger leg up. It's not often we have a field promotion in Clandy's but then it's not every day we get a campaign like this on our hands. I'm making you Number Two. It's no favour. But it seems you've earned it. We haven't had everything going for us this last year, what with the weather and other holdups, but I understand you've kept your end of things going pretty competently. We've had no labour disputes, for one thing. It's probably cost us, no doubt, but at least it's helped to keep us reasonably up to schedule. Caswell seems to want you as his Number Two. I know he's had to take the tiller quite a lot in these past few months and I'm sure he knows where his strength comes from. So we'll see how the new team works out, shall we?"

"Thank you sir," said Dando.

"Good. Well how do you propose to get us back up to schedule and get this show cracking again, then, Vince?"

"We need more men, basically," said Caswell. "It's as simple as that."

"More men? How many have we arsing around on site already?"

"Just over 900 including outside contractors."

"Look I want to solve this problem, Vince," said Sir William, "not outnumber it."

Dando stepped forward, smiling at the Chairman's quip. "What Mr. Caswell means, I'm sure," he said, "is more man-hours."

"Overtime you mean?"

"Exactly," said Dando. "You see we hit twelve hours a day in late spring and summer, but winters it's down to eight. I think we could get them to put in a twelve-hour day all the year round."

"And how do you propose asking the good Lord to give us all that daylight?" said Clandy.

"I don't," said Dando. "We'll provide our own. With floodlights and more floodlights. I'd like to see that dam lit up every night like the Crystal Palace."

Sir William looked at him closely. "Would the men go along with it?"

"They would if the terms were right."

"You mean the cash?"

Dando smiled slowly. "There's never been a stone lifted without it since the Pharaohs," he said. "Look, if we can guarantee them a nine-hour day all the year, basic, and double pay for the extra three they'll bite your hand off. Your dam gets finished on time for Queenie and you'll not need to spread the payroll."

Sir William finished the note he had scribbled on the desk pad and looked up. "All right, I like it. What else have you got, Vince?"

"Intercoms on the site," said Dando.

"We've already got intercoms," said Clandy.

"Only on the safaris and a few on the Range Rovers," said Dando. "I'd like to see two-way receivers and transmitters in every mobile piece of muckshifting hardware on the entire site."

"What's the point of all that?"

"It will save time and money by the simple rule that when every machine is linked with the central system you'll always know at any one time where they all are."

"I don't quite get this, Dando," said Clandy, scratching his ear. "Are the muckies not always where they're supposed to be or something?"

"Not always the non comms.," said Dando. "Sometimes it's as much as you can do to get hold of some brass hats when you need them. And if you can't there are holdups, time wasted and that means money."

"How far have you gone into this idea, Dando?"

Dando reached forward and put a green folder on the desk in front of the Clandy chairman. "It's all in there," he said. "There's also a quote from an electronics firm prepared to carry out the whole job within a fortnight."

"All right, leave it with me, then, Dando," said Clandy, putting his hand on the closed file before looking up at Caswell. "Was there something you wanted to say, Vince?"

Caswell took a pace forward. "I just wanted to congratulate you on the way you've made the changeover so smooth and well . . . informal. The king is dead, long live etc."

Clandy smiled at him. "Well we must remember we have rather a large kingdom to run. And kingdoms, of course, tend to last longer than kings. Thank you gentlemen. That will be all for now. Archbold is taking me down to the site, so may I take it I'll see you both there?"

"Do you want me to accompany you in the . . . old Kingmaker, Sir William?" asked Caswell.

The Clandy chairman looked up at him. "No Vince, that won't be necessary. Take your own transport, will you? You may be called away before I am."

Caswell made to leave the room but turned back to face the Clandy chairman. "I was thinking, Sir William. This getting back to schedule is all a matter of rational approach. Having a definite policy in mind and being decisive about carrying it through, knowing that the men are looking for positive direction, a leader who, well, leads."

"Thank you Vince," said Sir William, smiling. "Just let's get the dam built, hey? Just get the right results. For me too."

Caswell was about to follow Dando through the door when the Clandy chairman called him back. "Vince," he said quietly.

"Yes Sir William?"

"You know, Vince," he said, "I've got people breathing down my neck too."

Mallowry Bain carried the red tartan rug from the boot of the car and placed it round Bain's knees as he sat in the passenger seat.

Even though it was quite warm up on the plateau in front of the Clandy offices he seemed to be shivering inside his thick, green tweed suit.

She got into the driving seat and glanced across at him, noticing how pale his face was against the greying dark of his hairline.

"Are you all right, Gus?"

"Let's get home," he said without looking at her.

For a moment she stared through the open window towards the thin ribbon of white stone below them in the valley. Already the men working up on the rim were more than fifty feet above the ground and being pushed daily to the sky by the swelling structure beneath their feet.

They had gone barely half a mile along the new road towards Todholes when Gus raised a gloved hand. "Stop the car, will you?" he said, putting the other hand to his mouth and making a gulping noise in his throat.

Mallowry brought the car to a halt on the grass verge.

"What is it, Gus? Aren't you feeling well?" she said, watching him closely.

When he didn't reply she touched his arm. "Can I do anything?" she asked.

He shook her hand away from him. "Just leave me," he said, "I'll be all right in a minute."

"But what's wrong?" she asked with a concerned look on her face.

Bain turned to her tetchily. "Look just leave me alone for a while. Get out and have a walk or something. Just leave me to myself for a few minutes, will you?"

"If you're sure you'll be all right."

"Yes, go on, off you go!"

Mallowry got out of the car, looked back for an instant and began slowly walking up the grassy ridge in front of her.

When she reached the top she 'looked down across the white wall of the dam to where the whole sweep of the Corbar Valley stretched out before her.

Suddenly a movement on her left made her glance back towards the rising ground beneath the Faunes.

She didn't know if she had simply missed him before or whether he had just come over the rise, striding in a strong yet casual movement across the coarse turf, his divining twigs thrust out before him in his huge outstretched hands.

They saw each other almost at the same moment, but it was Mallowry who began walking to him, her steps quickening as she came nearer to him. When she stopped Finn was still moving towards her, staring at the ground beneath him.

"Hello," she said.

"I thought you'd gone already," he said sharply.

"We've just been to the crowning. Of the new Gus."

"Caswell?"

"Yes."

"You're wearing a dress," he said, examining her closely for the first time.

Mallowry smiled. "You make me sound as if I always go around in a uniform or something."

"Just lately it seems to have been always catsuits you were jumping around in."

She eyed him curiously. "I didn't think you'd been near enough to notice what I was wearing."

"You suit a dress," he said. "You've got the legs to go with it."

"Well thank you."

Finn looked down at his boots. "How did your friend make out in the re-shuffle?"

Mallowry gave a deep sigh. "By my friend you're going to mean Dando, aren't you?" she said. "And if you're going to mean Dando and you're asking how he's done, he's Number Two."

"Christ! Number Two!" said Finn, drawing in his breath. "That's even higher than he must have hoped for."

"Not quite," said Mallowry.

"So you've both done pretty well, then?"

"How do you mean, both?"

"Well as I see it your deep devotion has paid off in the end."

"Devotion?"

"Yes, to Gus," he said. "It's all worked out rather well, at least it has for you and Dando."

"I don't understand."

"Well you handed Dando the ladder, you've got the ticket to go shake the mud off your feet and lord it up in a place in the sun with the martini set. The only loser is Gus because he doesn't know. . . . That's where all the great losers come from, you know, the ranks of the 'Don't knows'."

"I love you, Finn," she said softly.

Finn stooped and lifted up a stone before hurling it towards the dam. "Of course you do," he said. "That's why you're going off to the Canary Islands with a fellow you hardly know."

"He's my husband."

"You haven't always remembered that," he said.

She bent down and picked a bunch of daisies from beside his boot. "That depends on whether you prefer to remember the summers or the winters," she said.

He looked at the flowers in her hands. "Well at least we summered well," he said.

"When I'm over there," she said, "in exile, I shall be just like your war poets. I shall think of the fields. I'll remember the fields most of all. Only I shall remember them for a much more beautiful reason."

Finn ran his hand through the thick tangle of his hair. "There were some days up there when we almost burned the grass bare. Lying back with the sun floodin' over us like a big soup. And the cold days when we just walked, and even then you were for stoppin'. Remember that day when you got me to go for the coffee flasks and when I came back you were cryin'. Why did you ask me to get coffee?"

She smiled at him. "Perhaps it was after you'd put your clothes on I couldn't think of anything else to get you to do?"

"Did you ever take him up there? Gus, I mean?"

"Gus would have had to hang flypapers on all the trees before he'd ever make love in the open," she said. "He has a thing about flies."

Finn smiled. "We saw the fields and the flies. I think we saw everything barring the wheatflash."

"What is that, Finn?" she asked.

"The wheatflash is the moment once every summer when the wheat flowers. It's as though every stem has a built-in alarm clock to tell it when to do it. At one moment the field's green and the next it's a mass of tiny yellow flowers across the whole surface and it's all over in a few seconds."

"If it's that special, surely lots of people would see it."

Finn shook his head. "I've known even farmers wait all their lives and never see it," he said. "Perhaps that's why the wheat does it that way. If too many people saw it it wouldn't be special any more. . ."

Mallowry searched his face as he tried to look away. "Do you think that's what happened to us, Finn?" she asked.

"Not really," he said. "You see, a lot of people have tried to see the wheatflash. But I've never heard of anyone before who ever tried to sell the wheat flowers. They die, you see, before you can gather a bunch in your hand."

She looked down at the daisies in her hand. "You don't know me, Finn Rafferty, do you?"

"I know a bit about the folks you mix with. And I see one of them going off to the sun and the other trying on hats. And you seem to have made it all happen for them."

She was about to speak when he reached towards her pressing his fingers gently against her mouth. "Please. Don't make it worse. Goodbye Big House Girl, go to your man if you know who he is."

Mallowry took his hand away before letting it fall. "Finn," she said. "I had to do it because you see, this is his whole life."

"But what's the point of shutting yourself away on some island if he doesn't know what you're doing for him?"

"Because I know," she said.

"Where is he now?" asked Finn.

"Gus is in the car, he's not feeling well."

"Don't keep him waiting."

"Finn?" she said.

"Hello."

"I will be back, you know."

She saw the knuckles of his hands were white as they gripped the hazel branch against his blue denim shirt. "You'll have your own reasons," he said.

"Goodbye Finn," she said, her eyes staring at the ground between her feet. When she looked up she saw he had stretched his hand out to her. Above it his face was urgent, uncertain as a boy's, searching for something in her own.

"They always say people who look back come back," he said.

She squeezed the hand tightly and turned to walk quickly back up the slope.

Before she had gone ten yards her face was wet with her crying. Several times she almost looked round, knowing that his eyes were gazing up at her from the field, watching her, willing her to turn round.

At the top of the slope she paused, imagining for a moment she had heard her name called. She turned her cheek, listening into the wind which was gusting into her long black hair as though inviting it to dance. But when the sound came it was a sudden, violent choking noise from the road in front of her.

When she got to the car Gus Bain was hunched over the grass verge. He was being sick.

Even though it was only 9 p.m. in the small red-carpeted Grouse Bar at the George, Finn was already drunk.

"Hey, have you ever been on holiday, feller?" he bawled as he clutched the white sleeve of the bald man with the camera slung around his neck. The man pulled his arm away just as Finn slapped his own hand down on a pile of glossy, coloured brochures on the table in front of him.

"I'm going on holiday," he announced, his eyes searching the room for an audience. "I'm f . . . f . . . f . . . off to the Canary Islands. 'Isles of joy and enchantment. And steep sea cliffs and sandy deserts and golden beaches washed by the blue Atlantic and plantations of sugar-cane, coffee and bananas, vineyards, pine forests and date palms,' so it says here."

He gave the bald man a jab with his elbow. "Look, I'm going to . . . where is it now? . . ." Picking up a brochure he held it close to his eyes. "Page eight. That's the place. The flight for page eight is about to depart from Gate 15. Please have your reading glasses and bookmarks ready."

He thumbed clumsily through the brochure before finally holding it up for everyone to see. "There it is," he yelled. "Lanzarote."

Above the top edge of the booklet he could see Dando looking across at him from the bar. Fasman and Gans were beside him.

"Lanzarote," said Finn, reading loudly from the brochure, "is black, volcanic, barren and infertile. Now where would you find anything like that around here? Never mind though. Lots of people have to go away sometimes. Why not go to black, volcanic, infertile Lanzarote, the rugged, rancid, Rhondda of the Martini set."

"What seems to be the trouble, Mr. Rafferty?"

The Irishman looked round and saw that Sara Dacre had slipped into the seat beside him.

"Well if it isn't the darling girl from Care," he said, trying to put his arm around her. "Nothing's wrong with me, Miss Teacher. I'm going on me holidays."

Sara evaded his clutch and took hold of his hand on the table. "Look Finn, I don't know what's happened but something will if you keep this up," she said. "I heard Dando and his friends talking about you at the bar."

"If they gave cups for talking about Rafferty they'd win 'em all," he muttered. "Will you have a drop of the creature with me?"

"You've had enough for the whole room by the look of you," she whispered.

He tugged at his forelock. "Yes Miss," he said obediently. "Certainly Miss Dacre. Do you know, I used to have a teacher once called Miss Dacre. She was little and fat and she was worse shod than the shoemaker's wife and she was married. Are you married, Miss Dacre?"

"Keep your voice down," she said. "No, I'm not."

"Let me counsel you," he said. "Don't get married."

"You're not married either."

"No, but I can tell you more about marriage than most married people and I'm mostly single." He leaned back against the blue bench seat. "Yes, that's me, mostly single."

Sara leaned over the table and picked up one of the brochures in front of them. "What have you got here then, Mr. Rafferty?"

"It's my p . . . p . . . passport to paradise," stammered Finn. "It's the warm, fragrant, balmy. . . ." As he spoke he stabbed the adjectives with his finger. "Canary Islands, where they grow tomatoes, w . . . w . . . wallop down the wine and breed beautiful women." He noticed Dando was staring at him again. "But the Canary Island's greatest contribution to civilisation is that they give the world roomfuls of little birds. Little birds who sing. Sing, sing, sing all day, do those little birds. Can you sing, Miss Dacre? Mr. Dando can sing. Can't you sing, Mr. Dando? Of course you can sing! All bloody, rotten, God-licking, chapel-queueing Welshmen can sing! And some of them sing so soft and subtly that only the sweeter birds can hear them."

"Get him out of here," snapped Dando, nodding to Fasman and Gans, who began moving towards Finn.

Finn was singing even before they reached him. "Nymphs and Shepherds come away," he sang lustily, beckoning them forward with his left hand, leaving the other to raise his pint glass above his head.

Sara Dacre waved them back and pulled the still singing Finn to his feet. "It's all right. We were just going. Come along, Mr. Rafferty, I'll take you home."

"Come along, come, come, come," sang Finn, imitating her before slumping across the table, sending a stream of stout fizzing across the surface.

He righted himself and stared down at his feet as though he was surprised they were moving.

"It's only a few steps," Sara was saying several miles away.

"Just a few short steps for a man," said Finn putting on a deep American accent, "but a great leap," he yelled, taking off into a sudden jump which landed him within a few inches of Dando's face, "for Lanzarote."

Without a word Dando took a bar towel from the counter and placed it over Rafferty's head, causing Gans and Fasman to burst out laughing. "Time gentlemen, please," he called, producing more laughter in the room.

Finn lifted the towel from his head slowly as though it were a ceremonial unveiling. The Welshman saw that below the dishevelled mop of blond hair Finn's eyes were calm and motionless.

"No, Dando," he said finally, "I'll tell you when it's time."

"I think it's your round, Gans," said Dando, ignoring him. "I'm skint."

Finn tore the brochure into two pieces and slipped them into Dando's top pocket. "Never mind, boyo," he said, swaying gently. "I'll see you in Rhyl."

Finn felt a hand on his shoulder and found himself being slowly but firmly led away by Sara Dacre. She stopped at the door.

"Just wait here and behave yourself for a minute," she said. "I've just got to have a word with someone."

As he pressed his back against the door-jamb Finn could see Dando, Gans and Fasman sniggering at him at the bar. Down the passage Sara was speaking urgently to a young, intense-looking man with a brown goatee beard. The man was pointing agitatedly in his direction as if he didn't like him. He was about to wonder why when he felt Sara's hand again reaching for him, gripping tightly into his forearm, leading him haltingly out towards the lights of the car park. . . .

Finn had to lower his head to get through the cottage door. It was a tiny room, barely ten feet square. Even the light shiny Ercol furniture seemed to have been scaled down to fit the smallness of the place. There was a low, black digital clock on the white-painted wrought-iron mantelpiece below a Boots Degas which stood out brightly against the white anaglypta walls.

"You'd better take the big chair over there," said Sara, easing him forward. "My visitors don't often come in your size."

The Irishman eyed the white-washed wooden beams of the ceiling warily as he lurched towards the chair and flopped into it. "This isn't home," he said. "I live in a Big House."

"You've got a bigger family," she said.

"How did you get yours in here," he asked, "with a shoe horn?"

Sara smiled. "Oh, you mean father and Donald? They're in the house. This is my place; it used to be the shepherd's cottage but I use it as a sort of flat."

Finn looked quickly round the room. "Either your family must have gone in for small shepherds or you were saving on the pies," he said.

He burrowed into a flattened cigarette packet he took from his back pocket and put a cigarette to his lips. Without lighting it he said, "Come here, Miss Teacher."

She put down the heap of records she was holding and went over to him. "What do you require of me, Mr. Rafferty?" she asked busily.

"Come here and tell me why you did this," he said, patting his thigh. "Are you a sort of unofficial street cleaner or do you just go around collecting stray dogs."

She ignored his invitation. "You looked to me as if you needed a back door," she said, looking at him closely, "and mine was as near as anybody's."

Finn lit the cigarette and watched her sit down on the edge of the hard-backed cottage sofa. "I didn't think you'd be one for the pubs" he said.

"I was in there with a friend, if you're fishing. He's a lawyer. I decided that in your condition you needed me more than he did at the time."

"But why me? You could get a busload of drunks there any weekend."

Sara saw that he was looking down at her legs, and slid her hands slowly down her thighs until she smoothed the dress over her knees. "Maybe I was making sure the taps run on time," she said in a teasing voice. "After all, how would we get the benefit of all this lovely water without you and your little twigs urging it along?"

"It seems a hell of a lot of trouble for a bath," grunted Finn.

He was silent for a moment before turning to her with a serious look in his face. "The drink's not a permanent fixture you know.

I mean with me. It's a fleeting sort of thing like . . . like a bird's flight. The time to fret is when you can't get a grip of your hands. Tonight was sort of special. Not to worry, there's nothing in a rake of beer that you can't shake off with a bit of honest demolition, preferably on a big Welsh skull."

"There is another way," said Sara softly.

"What's that?"

"Food," she said briskly, getting to her feet. "It will give your stomach a base to work on."

"Food?" protested Finn as he watched her put a record on the player and set off through the low door into the kitchen. As the twin speakers erupted into a tumultous burst of Mantovanni she ran back to turn the sound down so softly that the silver strings seemed to be sensously stroking the white anaglypta walls.

"I won't be long," she called as she left again. "It only needs to warm up."

Even when she had gone Finn could hear her voice calling him from the kitchen. "How's your dam coming along, then, Mr. Rafferty?"

He stubbed out the cigarette in the polished stone hearth and brushed the remains under the black metal gas fire.

"They reckon they'll be up to the milecastles in two years."

"Will you make the deadline, then?"

"You should know Clandy's by now. I should think we'll be giving it the last lick of paint as H.M. gets to the tape."

He tapped his fingers against the thin wooden arms of the chair and looked impatiently at the open door. "Come out of the kitchen, woman," he shouted, just as she appeared holding a tray of food.

"How's that for timing?" she said, bearing down on him with a smile.

"You reminded me of my mother in there," he said. "At home farmhouse women stayed in the kitchen. They even used to eat in the kitchen while the men had the trough to themselves."

Sara placed the food on the small table and pushed against his outstretched legs until he was forced to draw up his knees.

"What's this?" he asked suspiciously, prodding the plate with a knife.

"It's Quiche Lorraine. Eat it up, it's nice."

"It's bacon pie, isn't it?" he asked, dissecting a piece he had dragged to the side of the plate.

"It's good for you," she said, handing him a small china cup and saucer.

As she bent from the waist to fill her own cup from the percolator in the stone grate, she was aware that Finn's eyes were watching her legs beneath her slowly rising dress.

"How am I supposed to get my finger in there, then?" he said.

Glancing round quickly, she saw he was trying to force an entry through the ridiculously small handle of the coffee cup. She raised a chiding fist at him. "Now drink this and eat your Quiche! It will make you feel better."

"I feel lovely."

"Well go on then, eat it!"

"I don't want food," he said determinedly.

"It's the Quiche, isn't it? You don't like it?"

"I'm not . . ."

"Yes it's the Quiche. It's too rich for you."

"It's not the bloody pie, woman!"

Taking the fork from him Sara knelt down beside him and put some of the Quiche in her mouth. Finn stroked his hand gently against her cheek. "Look love," he said, "if I'd come for your cooking I'd sleep in the pantry."

She replaced the fork on the tray and sat on the Ercol sofa. "I wasn't planning for you to sleep anywhere," she said coolly.

"That sofa," said Finn, finally putting some pie in his mouth and pointing the fork towards her, "if you call it that. That sofa is the most platonic, passion-crippling article of modern living I've ever seen."

She looked down at the pale green covers. "It's part of a cottage suite," she said.

"It looks to me as if it came from a Wendy House sale."

"If it was any bigger it would swamp the place," she said. "Anyway in the state I found you, you wouldn't need anything else to cripple your passion."

Finn snorted into his coffee. "I've been known to consume fifteen pints of the black draught in a night and still produce a grateful gasp."

"Look Finn," said Sara leaning towards him, "just because it all began with Nymphs and Shepherds, that doesn't mean to say it's going to end up with sport and play."

Finn drew up his foot and slowly pushed the food trolley away from him with a chuckle which developed into a wide yawn.

"Teacher," he mumbled from behind his closed fist," I could teach you such a hell of a lot. On a good night when the brain's in, I could teach all the teachers."

She walked to the fireplace and began pouring herself another coffee. "About what, Finn?" she asked brightly.

"Apples," he said, yawning again. "Apples and things. . . ."

When she turned to look at him she saw that he was fast asleep.

Donald The Donald Dacre was lying back in the bed, propped against five large pillows.

Through the thick blue haze of his pipe smoke he could just make out the faces of Sara and Finn as they sat on either side of the white linen eiderdown.

"Would you bring a saucer or something so I can clear this thing out?" he said in a gruff, cracked voice. "I'd best leave a tidy house."

Sara Dacre took a saucer from a tray on the dressing table and put it on the bed. "I'll do it," she said quickly, "and watch your tongue, you're not going anywhere for a good long time yet!"

"What's wrong with it?" said Finn, walking round to Sara's side of the bed.

"Och it needs a de-coke," said the old man coughing loudly. "Just like me, we've both got clarted up a bit."

Sara had her father's tobacco knife in her hand and was scraping out black ash and waste from the bowl of the pipe onto the saucer. As she went to replace the pipe on the bedside table Dacre leaned towards her. "The pouch is under the pillow," he said with a wry grin. "Perhaps you'll be filling it up."

"Daddy," she chided, "do you think you ought to?"

"Pack it well, love," he said. "Nice and firm, not too loose. Have you ever used the pipe, Mr. Rafferty?"

"No sir," said Finn.

"The trouble is the tobacco's not what it was. I can remember when the veins used to be full of juice. A smoke was as good as a meal, you could taste it so much. I think the leaves have all the life squeezed out of them these days."

Sara handed the pipe and held a match for him as he sucked it into life. "Well I'm not leaving you much lass," he said. "Less still for Donald. You can't graze the sea. I should think the old shielings are just about drowned now. The funny thing was that before this came along the only thing which got this valley into a fret was when they brought the railway in. Some folk said Corbardale would never be the same again. They reckoned they'd build houses and roads and trippers would come in their thousands. But it never happened. And when I told The Donald I was going to work on the railways as a guard you'd have though I was selling my soul to the Devil."

"Are you all right, father?" asked Sara as Dacre closed his eyes and let his pipe fall slowly down the bedcover.

He opened his eyes and looked at her. "A guard was a good job in those days," he said in a deep monotone. "He used to guard the chickens and the sheep and the beer barrels for Haltbriggin. And when you were on the beer run it meant you had just thirty minutes between Kelsey and Haltbriggin to tap the barrels, top them with water and record them before you pulled in. For years they said you never got a decent pint in Haltbriggin, but they never knew why. . . ."

Sara put her hand on Finn's arm. "Close the window, Finn," she said. "I don't want him to feel the cold."

"Come here a while, boy," said Dacre, calling him back,

"There'll be no need for windows where I'm going."

"You're staying here, Mr. Dacre, with us," he said, shaking his head at the pale, beaky-nosed man in the bed.

"Rubbish, Rafferty," said Dacre, reaching for his arm but withdrawing it as another cough racked his body. "It's you who'll be staying, folks like you and Sara. It's you who'll have to speak up for what's going on out there. And if it's going to bring some good it's best you say so and defend it. I'm not against change, Finn, as long as it's for the better. But we've had such good ways here in the past it would be a pity to lose them for something you wouldn't give tuppence for. You know we've an old saying up here, 'Never swap your fiddle for a googar'. I hope it won't come to that, boy. Now you'd better see to your window. She's right, it is getting a bit cold."

Dacre closed his eyes and when he opened them Sara saw they were as blue and bright as a child's. "Is that you, Sara?" he said.

"Yes, I'm here, Daddy," she whispered, edging towards him.

"Will you dance for me, Sadie?" he said softly.

She took his hand into her own, soothing the rough knuckles with her fingers. "Daddy, I can't. . . ."

"You were always the great dancer of the family, Sadie. On your feet at birthdays and Christmas and parties. There were days when the room would fairly shake with your wee feet. Even at funerals sometimes. You danced for The Donald you know, when he left us. You won't remember it because you were only three at the time, but there you were in front of all the black mourners, lifting your skirts and dancing as though it was the most natural thing in the world. I remember thinking at the time that that's the way a man would want to be remembered. If a wee girl like you could dance at your going, there's not a stonemason in Corbar could match it. . . ."

As The Donald's eyes closed again she gripped tightly to his hand.

Hearing a sudden movement behind him Finn turned from the window and saw Sara Dacre staring forward at the black pipe which was smouldering against the white eiderdown.

There were seven in the large, low-ceilinged living room when Finn followed Sara down the stairs. As they looked up at him he felt his face being searched by all but the boy at the table.

The two women on the sofa in waiting grey were the two surviving Dacre sisters, although there was little in their appearances to suggest it. Cora Fairhurst was thin, sharp-faced, with her brother's beaky nose. Emma Glynn was rounder, greyer, more homely-looking. Ken Dulcey, the bookmaker, had been a surprise visitor, since he had rarely seen the place since the death of his wife Nesta, who had been the third of the Dacre sisters. Jack Fairhurst, red-faced and portly, came only when Cora came. On each side of the blazing log fire sat John Jennings, the Dacre's shepherd, and his wife Edna.

Cora was the first to make a move towards the stairs, reaching for Sara's hand as she came.

"Sara, my poor wee child," she said. "Has he. . . ?"

"The Donald?" cried Finn heartily. "The Donald never dies! He's right here look, nosing into his pop bottle!"

He walked quickly across the room to a small table where Donny was looking up from his book.

"I'm sorry, Donald," said Finn, laying a hand on the boy's shoulder as Emma Glynn suddenly burst into tears on the sofa and followed her sister up the stairs.

"Ah dear," said Jack Fairhurst, levering himself up from the sofa and grabbing the whisky bottle from the mantelpiece and refilling his glass. He poured some into Dulcey's glass which had quickly appeared under his nose and both men went to join Sara.

"Will you have one yourself, girl?" grunted Fairhurst. "Look, I'll get you a glass."

"No thank you," she said.

"Oh," said Fairhurst sucking his teeth noisily. "Then come over here and sit down. You've had a bit of a shock, old girl, we all have."

"No," said Sara firmly. "You sit down. Go on, both of you."

She looked over to where Edna Jennings was standing at her husband's shoulder and quietly sniffing into his handkerchief.

"You sit down too, will you, Mrs. Jennings? And you, John."

John Jennings led his wife back to the armchairs. Finn reached for a chair beside Donny and looked across at Sara as if expecting her to make an announcement.

Instead she walked to the centre of the room, and with her eyes gazing with a strange, fixed stare towards the oak chiming clock on the mantelpiece she began to dance.

At first the slow, almost shy movement of her hand feeling for the hem of her plaid skirt as her other arm rested against her hip gave Finn the impression she was performing the dance in slow motion.

But beneath the extended skirt her slim, lithe legs began criss-crossing in delicate undulating patterns, and already she seemed to be listening to a music which was only in her mind.

Finn noticed that Jack Fairhurst was coughing violently, not so much out of his obvious surprise but because he had gulped his whisky down too quickly.

Ken Dulcey was goggling too, as though he had suddenly been taken aback by Sara's decision.

Edna Jennings had an attentive, sad look on her face as she gazed towards the girl.

It was a silent, pretty dance, the dance of an unsmiling doll whose hands at times seemed to press close to her waist as if trying to still a body which was fretting to be free.

Even though there was now a litheness in Sara's steps it was not as spontaneous as Finn had expected.

As the small feet pointed their intricate paths he could not escape the thought that they were playing out a controlled and well rehearsed ritual.

The silence in the room had brought Cora and Emma to the bannister, where they watched with a look of utter disbelief on their faces. Cora's eyes were darting in turn from the top of the stairs to the dancing girl on the carpet below her.

Finn had made his way over to the drinks cupboard under the stairs, and without taking his eyes off Sara he poured out two glasses of whisky.

As she ended her dance he took his glass from his lips and vigorously slapped his hands together in applause.

For a moment he thought he was the only one to do so, until the bulky Jack Fairhurst brought his own hands together in a few tentative slaps before catching the frosty look in his wife's eyes and dropping them quickly back to his knees.

"Get Dr. Gowdie, Jennings," said Cora loudly as the big man got to his feet. "Sadly we'll now only be needing the man's pen."

"You'll be needing this now," said Finn, carrying the glass to Sara and leading her to a chair.

She sipped the drink silently.

"You mix your legs well when you dance," he said.

"Did I?" she said, avoiding his gaze.

"It's a pity your man couldn't have seen it. He'd have been first with his hands at the finish."

Cora and Emma had suddenly appeared in front of them. It was Cora who spoke. "Are you feeling better now, dear?" she asked icily.

Sara cradled the glass in her hand as she looked up. "Yes, fine," she replied.

"It's good to see you back in your chair. You should rest, you know."

Sara looked up at her but said nothing.

"A death in the family is never easy to take, I always think," said Cora coolly.

"I'm sure you're right, Aunt Cora."

"Yes well, if you need any sort of advice . . . as to what's the best thing to do at times like this, perhaps I can. . . ."

"The best thing to do, Aunt Cora, is to follow this feller in here," said Finn digging his finger into the left side of his chest. "We've all got one. And the daft thing is that sometimes they're more right than watches."

Cora looked at him narrowly. "And I'm sure they all came from the same place which also issued us with heads, didn't they, Mr. Rafferty?"

Finn smiled. "It's not so much where heads come from as what you fill them with."

She waved aside her husband, who was holding out a glass for her which he was trying to fill with whisky. "I come from Edinburgh, Mr. Rafferty. I take it you've heard of Edinburgh?"

Finn nodded.

"It is, of course, the Athens of the North," she said, "a leading centre of Scottish and English culture. What had you heard about Edinburgh, Mr. Rafferty?"

"I heard it was all pies and pianos up there."

Cora took the glass from her husband, who was still hovering beside her, and motioned him to fill it. "In fact, Mr. Rafferty, should you have ever wished to educate yourself in the cultural affairs of Scotland you would have discovered Edinburgh is a great seat of thought. . . ." She broke off, noticing that Finn was grinning at her. . . . "Do I amuse you, Mr. Rafferty?"

"No," he said. "It's just that we had one of those on the site. They can be very uplifting sure."

Cora refused to let him destroy her own thought-stream. "Yes, thought, art, music, great architecture and noble sculpture. Do you happen to know Rodin's 'Kiss', Mr. Rafferty?"

"Not at all," said Finn. "He only shook hands with me." He looked down and saw that Donny had burst out laughing between them. "That's how a Donald should look," he said, shaking his head, "laughin' and livin'."

Cora was unmoved. "All in its time, Mr. Rafferty," she said, "and all in its place. We know how to let our hair down ourselves, you know. Once a year of course, we have our own Edinburgh Festival. Music and drama and dancing. . . ." She glanced at Sara, who was still in her chair staring at the floor. "Yes, people come from all over the world to see our Scottish dancing and marvel at the great discipline and organisation that goes into it. The whole city stops for a fortnight, while we show them the fruits, so to speak, of our traditions. Where do you come from, Mr. Rafferty?"

Tossing his head back Finn raised his glass to her. "Me, Aunt Cora?" he asked. "I come from Ireland, where we've never needed an excuse for a dance. Good Health!"

When he looked across at Sara he saw she was already walking slowly up the stairs.

In death, as in life, there was always an order for things in Corbardale, thought Finn as he shuffled through the deep puddles along the churchyard path of St. Cuddy's.

Through the heavily falling rain, between the wet backs ahead of him, he could see the old brown raincoat which the Rev. James Churnside had slipped over his surplice to lead the small procession to the graveside.

Behind the vicar and the stooping, black-hatted Mr. Robson, the undertaker, came the simple oak coffin with the drenched red roses and Michaelmas daisies trailing down the sides and borne by six of the flockmasters and shepherds who had shared the slopes of Corbar with The Donald.

The new Donald, his long black hair flattened to his young face by the rain, followed on the arm of Sara Dacre, who was leading him with the concern of a shepherdess.

Cora Fairhurst was wearing a dark veil which obliterated the sharpness of her face as she walked beside her husband.

Behind them came Emma Glynn on the arm of her late sister's husband, Ken Dulcey the bookmaker, who nobody expected to turn up.

Finn himself had been allotted the plump, homely-looking Mrs. Jennings the housekeeper, whose husband Jack was at the back with the young man from the "Black Faced Sheep Breeders Association".

"Ashes to ashes, dust to dust," boomed the Rev. James Churnside like an impatient cannon even before the last of the mourners had pulled up round the coffin, which was still on its way down to the water-filled hole in the ground.

"There won't be much dust down there to bother his chest," said Finn, peering over Ken Dulcey's shoulder into the grave.

"It's a good day to be inside," said Dulcey sniffing loudly.

"Not inside one of those things," muttered Finn, turning up the collar of the dark grey raincoat he had borrowed from The Goose. "Mind you, if it's a choice between the mud sandwich and being cooked round the back and ending up three ounces of salt and 130 pounds of water vapour, I'll take this way."

When the coffin disappeared beneath the muddy pool, the Rev. James Churnside brushed the last of the dry earth he had brought from the box in the vestry onto the rain-pitted surface of the water and began guiding the new Donald back to the warmth of the porch.

After a moment Finn noticed that Sara was standing at the end of the grave alone.

At the house the black bouclé wool coat had seemed to suit her, emphasizing the pale yet strong lines of her face. But here at the graveside it had the effect of making her look smaller, even vulnerable.

She looked up when he went over to stand beside her and he was surprised to see she was smiling at him.

"What would they be saying in Clooney, then?" she asked, "at a time like this."

Finn looked into her eyes as he took her hand. "They'd be saying that when it rains on a coffin it's only the dews of Heaven droppin' on a good man."

She smiled again. "Thank you, Finn," she said. "He would have liked that."

As he raised his elbow, offering her an arm for the walk back to the porch she shook her head and reached for his hand.

Together they walked hand in hand back to the church where the vicar, dry and beaming, came forward to greet them.

"Will you have some more cake, Donald?" said Cora Fairhurst, pushing one of the best willow-patterned plates into Donald Dacre's face. "We'll be needing to build you up you know, now that you're The Donald."

When the boy refused she put the plate beside the buttered scones on the heavily laden table. "Well you know best, Donald, but remember you've some awfully large shoes to fill!"

"You won't forget to save some for the vicar, will you now Cora?" said Emma Glynn, wiping her hands on a teacloth. "He'll be here shortly."

Cora looked sharply at her sister. "I shall be amazed if he has the appetite for it," she said. "He's had more seed cake this last year than he has stomach for. I could have told you as much last Christmas when it was so mild up here. A green Christmas makes for a fat churchyard they say. At least it was green then. I think our Mr. Rafferty has been taking some of the greenness away since then, has he not?"

Finn looked up from the fireplace. "Some of it's filling up naturally with all this rain around," he said. "There'll be more when we get the aquafers flowing."

"And what to a plain, ordinary country-woman would an aquafer be, Mr. Rafferty?"

"It's a sort of big underground well."

"Artesian, would it be?"

"Same thing."

Cora Fairhurst sipped from her teacup and smiled sweetly. "But of course there are so many ways of saying the same thing. Such as what the doctor said about the poor Donald's demise. Pleural effusion he called it. Do you know what pleural effusion is, Mr. Rafferty?"

Finn loosened the knot in his black tie. "No madam. I don't," he said.

"Well now, it's fluid on the lung. Water in the breathing spaces you might say. The Donald, you see, drowned in his bed, poor man. . . ."

"Aunt Cora, please!"

Finn noticed that Sara had stood up, leaving Ken Dulcey talking into his glass.

"It's quite all right, dear," said Cora, waving her down. "It was all there on the death certificate, as I'm sure you know. Of course his er . . . cardiac condition greatly assisted the eventual conclusion, as the doctor fully expected. And even Mr. Rafferty with his vast knowledge of the effects of water can appreciate that an excess of it can weaken the strongest of hearts. And there has been a considerable weakening of local hearts in recent years, as we saw only too clearly in the churchyard. I think it's all to do with a relaxing of the will. They've fought the good fight, poor souls, until they saw it could only end up in a somewhat watery grave. When is your good fight expected to come to an end, Mr. Rafferty?"

"Don't worry your wee self, Aunt Cora," he said. "When we open you'll be the first to know. Is it tickets you're after?"

"I attend funerals, Mr. Rafferty, albeit sadly," she said. "I have no desire to be present at a wake. Any more ham anybody? Perhaps a wee slice of gammon for The Donald?" she said, advancing on the boy, who had retired to the stool beside the fire.

"No thank you," replied the boy.

"Let's see, what age would you be now, Donald?"

"Thirteen."

"Thirteen is it, and you're refusing good meat? I've seen your late grandfather tackle half a dozen rashers of back bacon and three eggs for his breakfast before the sheep even had their eyes open," she said.

"Donald used to eat like a horse," agreed Jack Fairhurst, who was looking for more whisky at the drinks table.

Cora Fairhurst glared her annoyance at his unsolicited opinion. "Big men, of course, such as the late Donald, always appreciate the value of good, solid food. He always used to say that your deeds always matched your appetite. And after all, he did such a lot for Corbardale. Don't you agree, Mr. Rafferty?"

Sara Dacre looked up and caught her aunt's eye. "Mr. Rafferty didn't know father all that well," she said.

"Of course, my dear," said Cora. "He hasn't been here all that long, has he? Well if you won't have the ham, Donald, I will. The Donald never approved of waste. I've known the time when he opposed even the building of a car park because he said it would take away good grazing land. Ah well, he's gone now to where all the good men go to. What a pity it is that it takes such a sad occasion to bring all the family together."

The "family" seated in the Dacre living room was almost entirely the early fruits of Cora and Jack Fairhurst's once earthy union which was now patently fallow. Their elder son Malcolm, a thin studious man, was wedged in the centre of the big sofa between his wife Morag and his brother Dirk, who was reading a book. Dirk's wife Joan, who had the red cheeks of a country girl, was over at the table playing cards with Emma's daughter Jean and Cora's three small grandchildren.

"Are you still at that wee local girls' school of yours, then, Sara?" said Cora, as Jack Fairhurst leaned over to offer Sara a drink.

"Yes Aunt Cora," she said tiredly, "I'm still at the Belljohn."

"Oh dear," said Cora. "You know I had great hopes for you, Sara. With a brain like yours I even harboured thoughts that you might teach at Edinburgh one day. Malcolm's at the Academy now, you know, aren't you Malcolm?"

Before Malcolm could reply there was a sudden noise from the fireplace where a plate of jam sandwiches which his ten-year-old daughter was trying to force on Donald Dacre had crashed to the stone hearth.

"You did that deliberately!" shouted the girl.

"No I didn't!"

"Donny!" called Sara from the other side of the room.

"Never mind, don't chide the boy," said Cora. "What's a little home-made jam on our own hearth. After all we're all here together under the one roof and we are family. Well perhaps with the exception of Mr. Rafferty, but then I'm sure he's quite used to getting his feet dirty."

Finn walked over to the whisky bottle, pausing on his way to face Aunt Cora. "You should have seen where my hands have been sometimes," he said.

Cora looked at him icily. "What I meant, Mr. Rafferty, was that there's an awful lot that can be excused if it's family. There are so many things that strangers might find difficult to accept, but it's quite acceptable when it's in the blood."

"Most fellers I know have seen more prizegivings outside the family," said Finn, returning with a full glass.

A burning log fell from the fire behind her and Cora turned to see Donald attempting to return it with a poker and tongs. "Well Donald," she said, "and what are you going to do with the rest of your life now that you're The Donald? Will you be rebuilding the flock?"

Donald patiently levered the flaming log up the grate until it rolled over the top bar into the fire. "I think I'd like to go in for construction work," he said.

"Construction!" said Cora shrilly. "You mean roads and drains and things?"

"And bridges and motorways. Anything that needs to be built."

Cora stared at him in complete disbelief. "And you want to go in for muckshifting? Isn't that the vernacular expression for your occupation, Mr. Rafferty?"

Finn put a peanut in his mouth from the heap he had in his hand. "The shifting's our work," he said. "The muck's always other people's.

"He's hardly had time to make up his mind what he's going to do," said Sara quickly. "It'll be years before he has to decide."

When Finn looked at the chair where Sara was sitting, he saw that she had left it and had walked quietly up behind him. "How are you doing?" she asked softly.

"If it goes to extra time I'll play for the draw," he said.

Moving close to him she said, "I'm going over to the cottage, Finn. Give me five minutes and then come over, will you?"

He made to reply but she was already walking towards the door. But as she opened it the only sound came from Cora's wide-open mouth beside the roaring fire. "Have you no normal ambitions, Mr. Rafferty? Have you always been a muckshifter? Have you had no real drive. . . ?"

Finn couldn't remember whether he had, and as Aunt Cora's strident voice rose and fell beside him he decided she didn't really want to know anyway.

He gently opened the door of the cottage and saw immediately that the small living room was empty. He glanced around at the pint-sized suite, the black digital clock on the mantelpiece and a vase of freshly picked crysanthemums on the sideboard. Walking over to the tiny pine-walled kitchen he found a single cup and saucer washed and waiting on the shiny metal draining-board.

Finn came back into the living room, picked up the still folded copy of the Daily Telegraph from the top of the record player and held it out, his eyes aimlessly drifting from wall to wall.

There was something about the size and neatness of the room which made him feel like an awkward, unwelcome giant.

Finally he walked across to the brown-painted door leading to the stairs. He lifted the latch and peered into the darkness, calling her quietly.

"Are you there, Sara?"

There was no answer. Noticing the bedroom door was partly open he climbed slowly up the stairs and opened it just enough to enable him to look into the room.

Even though the curtains were drawn and the room was quite dark he could see the shape in the bed.

"Is that you, Sara?" he asked in a whisper.

He saw a movement in front of him. "Of course it is, yes," she answered. The loudness of her voice surprised him.

"Are you not feeling well?"

"Come here silly," she said.

Finn tiptoed over to the bed and sat down uneasily on the pale blue duvet.

"Not there," she said, "inside. With me."

He saw she had raised herself up on her elbow and was turned to him.

"Look, are you sure?" he asked.

"Go on, Finn. Get undressed."

"You mean just like that?"

"Well you don't normally go to bed in your suit, do you?"

"I didn't come dressed for this kind of thing, you know," he said, looking straight into her face as his eyes became accustomed to the small amount of light which was diffusing through the blue curtains.

"Finn, just take off your clothes and come to bed. With me." The last two words were spoken in a flourish as she threw back the duvet. She was completely naked, lying on her side, her knees slightly bent towards him. Her hands were beneath her high, firm breasts. She seemed to be offering them as if they were a tribute.

He undressed quickly, leaving the black suit in a heap on the floor as he slid into bed hauling the blue duvet over himself. "Are you sure about this?" he said, before her fingers pressed his mouth into silence.

"Don't say anything," she whispered. "Just hold me, Finn. Really tight."

"But all those people? The Vicar's just arrived, did you know that?"

Before he could say more she flung herself across him with a suddenness which surprised him. Releasing a short, muffled cry her lips sought out his mouth, her hands were plunging among the soft blond hair at the back of his neck, pulling his head up towards her, and as their bodies met he felt the hard buds of her nipples biting into his chest. As her lips went slack against his mouth he could feel the tips of her teeth pressing into his own lips. For a moment her hands were gently beneath him stroking, soothing the rough corrugated flesh into a hot pumping tightness. When she lay back she opened her arms to him gazing up with an intense innocence as his huge body loomed over her. Taking his hands she firmly guided them to her breasts, murmuring as he accepted them with a warm tenderness. Even as he lowered his head gently between them he could sense her moist skin swelling with the closeness of his body. Beneath him she was trembling with an impatient, almost desperate eagerness to give herself to him. Thrusting his hand down to the thick curling hair between her thighs, Finn could feel she was already wet, her loving lips parting easily beneath his fingers as they entered her. Groaning, she withdrew them almost fiercely, her hands feeding him swiftly into her body before gripping tightly to his buttocks and making violent upward thrusts towards him with her feet. He came quickly, alone, the giving continuing beneath him . . . paining him . . . like an enormous greed.

After he moved away he looked down at her. He could see in the dim blue light which was coming through the curtains that her eyes were wide open.

"Did I shock you, Mr. Rafferty?" she asked.

The duvet had fallen to the floor and he saw that her legs were still parted on the purple sheet. "I'd expected having to lay my stall out a bit," he said.

She smiled. "You really are a beast, Finn Rafferty. A nice sort of beast, I mean."

"I'm a beast?" he said loudly. "There was me in my funeral suit not fifteen minutes ago down there with a tie to my throat and playing the dutiful sad man and you whisk me up here and squeeze half the life out of me. And you say I'm a beast?"

He reached down to the pocket of the black suit and took out a cigarette. As the match lit up the room he felt her eyes searching his face.

"Do you love me, Finn?"

"It's too soon to tell from a spar in the sheets," he said, drawing on his cigarette. "You're a remarkable woman, I'll give you that. I should wonder at your timing, that's all."

"Was I good for you, Finn?" she asked, sliding her hand along his thigh.

Finn placed his hand over hers, completely covering it. "You don't have to ask that," he said gently.

"I'll be better for you next time. You said you were going to teach me."

He got up from the bed and retrieved the duvet from the floor, placing it across her. He watched her intently as she drew a corner of it close into her neck, nursing it against her cheek.

"You will teach me, won't you, Finn?" she whispered. "You see I'm not tall and beautiful and elegant and . . . I'm not the sort of girl that men hold horses for. I don't have the hair for riding or the long, fantastic fingers for slipping round cocktail glasses. But I can be quite strong really. Inside. And I'm reasonably good at cooking. And I like children. And I . . . and I feel very, very alone."

Finn leaned across the bed and kissed her gently on the forehead. "Miss Teacher," he said softly, "one day I'm going to teach you how to cry."

Finn lifted the brass fox's head on the front door of the Wise Woman's cottage and banged it down firmly. The sudden noise disturbed the bees in the flame-red Virginia creeper beside the porch and he fended them away with his hand as they buzzed around his head.

"Vina said we were to go in and wait for her if we got no answer," said Sara, opening the low, white-painted door and walking through into the living room, which had a log fire burning in the grate.

"And she's supposed to be the wise one?" said Finn, following her into the house. "For all she knows we could be here filling our pockets with her best bats' eyes and hemlock before she surfaces from her crystal ball."

Sara sat down at a small round table which was covered with a heavy, green velvet cloth. There was a single rose in a narrow glass vase carefully placed on the white crochetted centre-piece.

"I hope you're not going to make fun of her," she said "She's not a crank, you know."

Finn pulled out the chair beside her and sat down. "Oh, she's a genuine, registered Wise Woman, is she? Licensed to peddle the wisdom of the world at a price."

"I think, Mr. Rafferty," said Vina Tredger, appearing at the door in a swirl of long blue flowing robes, "you'll find me very reasonable."

They both looked up as she entered. She was a tall, striking-looking woman with dark piercing eyes and long, blonde hair streaked with grey and held close against her head by a red patterned band.

Even beneath the thick folds of her dress Finn could see she was limping slightly on her left leg as she moved to the table. He felt sure he had seen her before.

"Stand up, Mr. Rafferty," she said in a deep, commanding voice. "Come on, up, up! It's all right, it's not for reasons of politeness, I can assure you."

As Finn rose awkwardly she walked round behind his chair, examining him closely before finally looking up into his puzzled face. "Yes, you're a Sagittarian, aren't you, Mr. Rafferty?" she said. "I just wanted to see your thighs. I can usually tell a Sagittarian by his thighs."

"Christmas Eve!" said Finn, protesting.

"A lovely time of the year," smiled Vina. "Sit, Mr. Rafferty. No, just here, so that I can have a good look at you."

"I thought you just did," said Finn, easing himself into the chair beside her.

Vina Tredger stared directly at him. "Yes witty," she said, "witty, sporting, restless, good starters, poor finishers. Yes you're a Sagittarian. Well what's it to be then? The Tarots? The cards? Or the hands?"

Finn thrust out both hands towards her. "Try these fellers," he said brightly. "You should scrape a bit of life out of those."

"Just the left one," said Vina Tredger, taking the hand but looking only at his face. "Now what do you want to know?"

He blinked with surprise. "I don't want to know anything," he said curtly. "I came with the friend here."

Vina Tredger smiled again. "Of course you did. All the men do.

Now let me see what we have here."

She held Finn's hand between her own and gazed down at it. When she spoke, her voice rose and fell as though she was mouthing an incantation. "This is the hand of a man who has the use of a rare and singular measuring rod," she said.

"You've told her about the twigs," whispered Finn to Sara, who shushed him, nodding towards the Wise Woman who was about to speak again.

"It's the hand of a man who has a passion which seizes him and is peculiar without him knowing it is so," she said, gazing at the ceiling. "He has almost a frenzy, a feeling of heat in things which feel cold to all other persons. He has the power of divining values for which scales have not yet been invented. A bravery without the desire for honour, a self-sufficiency which has a superabundance and imparts itself to all men and to all things."

Noticing that Vina Tredger's eyes were still transfixed to the ceiling Finn slipped his hand from her grasp and stared into it. "Christ, you didn't see all that lot in there, did you?" he asked.

Vina Tredger lowered her eyes and shook her head as if she was emerging from a trance. "I'm sorry," she said. "They're trying to push nobility again." She glanced angrily at the ceiling. "Twenty-five million lives painted out in one generation and who's noble?"

When she looked back at him she was smiling but there was a tightness in her lips. "Do you have nobility, Mr. Rafferty?" she said.

Finn stirred uncomfortably in his chair. "I haven't thought about it," he said. "It doesn't wake me nights."

"Ask," commanded Vina Tredger suddenly.

Finn glanced across at Sara for guidance. "What does she want me to ask her?"

"Ask her a question, silly," she said in a hiss.

His mouth spread in an uneven smile as he tugged at the thick blond hair at his neck. "When's the world going to end?" he said.

Vina Tredger placed her hands together and stared at the ceiling. "We have a saying up here, Mr. Rafferty, that the world will end when the cuckoo dies of the cold in May. Do you know about cuckoos, Mr. Rafferty?"

He made no reply.

"Did you know that cuckoos are unique in that they always feed off the flashy, brightly-coloured insects and caterpillars the other birds avoid? Particularly the red ones, always a danger signal in nature. But the cuckoo seems to find a particular delight in tasting what is taboo to others. Did you know that in wartime when it was obvious we were going to be short of food, the Food Ministry conducted an experiment into how many varieties of wild birds' eggs we might be able to eat should it become necessary. And do you know what they discovered?"

"I'm agog with indifference," said Finn, scratching his forehead in irritation.

"They found that the more brightly-coloured the bird the more bitter the egg. The only palatable eggs were those from the plain, inconspicuous birds."

"So how did those . . . er . . . the cuckoos make out, then?" said Finn, yawning.

"They didn't," said Vina. "No one could find their eggs. But then cuckoos don't build nests of their own, of course, do they Mr. Rafferty? They make use of other birds' nests. What do you think?"

Finn took away his hand abruptly. "I think you're a very wise and very nosey old woman," he said bluntly.

"I use my eyes."

"They say the only reason people watch is because they can't play themselves."

"Maybe the spectator always sees more of the game," she said. "Are you not a spectator yourself, Mr. Rafferty? I didn't see a marriage in there."

Finn looked down at his hand. "That's because there's been none," he said. "The wise women where I come from always reckoned it was always better to have one plough going than two cradles."

Vina put her hand gently over his arm. "And your mother wasn't one of them?"

"She was one of the most cleanly and notable women in the parish; good with the needle. She kept a solid cottage."

"Was there a lot of love in the house?"

Finn felt his cheeks reddening. "Too much sometimes," he said. "It was never out of the place. You don't get seven children by playing snakes and ladders. They used to make them behind the curtain, bumping and boring like it was some sort of baby factory they had in there. Labour-intensive. By the time they got the seventh off the production belt the rest of us were wedged so tight in the bed at nights we had interlocking arses."

"Your mother's no longer with you, is she?"

"No," said Finn, his face colouring.

"What happened to her?"

"She died."

"Of what?"

"Of a surfeit of babies. On the job you might say. They said it was consumption. I thought it was more like saturation."

"Did you blame your father for it?"

"Christ no," said Finn. "To him it was just like going to church. The door was always open and no one ever told you how to close it because they never really wanted you to know."

"So they weren't wrong?"

"Not wrong but. . . ."

"But what, Mr. Rafferty?"

"They were so bloody indiscriminate! Lying sprouting babies in the dark without thought about what they were getting."

"So you had a lot of brothers and sisters."

"We had a tribe. I used to wish something would happen to stop it all, like they'd find out what was doing it. But no. The kids used to come pinging out of that great aching cavity as though she was trying to people the world."

"So you hid, Finbar, as children do?" Without waiting for a reply, Vina Tredger took a few swift undulating steps towards the open fire, staring into it for several moments before she turned to him again. "Mr. Rafferty, when adults find themselves over-burdened with possessions they tend to push them away into a hiding-place, don't you find? Somewhere out of sight. Like a cupboard under the stairs. We used to call it the glory hole, a place where you could put away your past, your present, even those things you think might be of some use in the future. The junk of living, I think you'd call it. Did you have a glory hole, Mr. Rafferty?"

Finn took out a cigarette from the front pocket of his blue denim jacket and lit it slowly. "Sure we had a cupboard under the stairs," he said. "I used to use it to get away from the tribe. Some days it seemed to be the only place in the house you could go where they wouldn't be reaching in and fingering you."

In the glow of the fire Vina Tredger's eyes seemed to be shining, almost burning into his own. "And you'll have found what you were looking for, of course? That's the great charm about glory holes, Mr. Rafferty. You see adults like ourselves fill them but only a child can strip it bare at a glance and tell you what's really in there."

Finn looked down at his hand and saw that a piece of the white crochet cover had come away in his fingers. He was surprised to see how brittle and fragile it had been.

"I found a stuffed bird in there once," he said. "A wee, small thing like a snipe that looked as if it ought to be up dartin'. Then I found an old oil lamp, little but heavy as lead and I rubbed it to burst for weeks, squattin' there like Aladdin and wishin' that the bird would fly up and come to life again, but it never did."

"But the cuckoo flew, did it not?"

When he turned to face Vina Tredger he saw she had a finger pointing at him. As he stared it appeared to reach across the room at him, thrusting nearer and nearer until it seemed to be stabbing into his chest. "Leave it!" he said.

"You couldn't, could you, Mr. Rafferty?"

"You're wrong," he said standing up and looking anxiously round the room. "That's all tucked away now."

"In your glory hole, Mr. Rafferty?"

"I'm going," said Finn. He threw his car keys on the table in front of Sara. "You have the car! Go to your hairy friend! I'm taking the fresh way home!"

Vina Tredger's eyes had never left his face. "You're leaving us, then, Mr. Rafferty, are you?" she said. "Spreading your broken wings again?"

He turned to her. "Look I don't know who you are!" he said angrily, "but you're wrong! The wings didn't give out! The bloody nest flew away!"

Vina Tredger lowered her eyes down to the thick band of gold on her finger. "Go then, Mr. Rafferty," she said softly. "Go to your glory hole. But go as a child."

When the two women looked up Finn had already gone.

Finn strode angrily down the steep slope from the Wise Woman's cottage heading for the forest path which plunged down through the Cockwood towards the huts of Clandy below in the valley.

The air was close as the bracken and dry twigs, parched by the recent dry spell, cracked beneath his boots.

Inside the wood the hot afternoon sunshine was diffusing thick shafts of yellow light down between the elbowing oaks and sycamores.

He had always felt strangely at home in the Cockwood. Unlike the artificial, man-made woods of Corbar, which he called the great Undead, the Cockwood was a living forest. Each year it lived in a style of its own, a kind of bustling grandeur, and each year it died. The Cockwood was dying now. Splendidly.

The only things which looked at their best when they were dying, thought Finn, were the leaves of the trees.

Death had come to them in a glorious splurge of reds and golds and yellows and rich browns as though it were offering them one final statement before they fell to the forest floor to become part of the flesh of the earth.

Like everything in nature it had a purpose. The trees, unable to afford to lose moisture during the winter, were shaking off their leaves, sealing themselves for survival. Before the first cold snap came there would not even be a trace of the previous season. Come spring the roots of the tree would suck once again deep into the mountainside to nourish a whole new generation.

The heat of the forest was heavy against Finn's coarse denim shirt as he unknotted the blue and white spotted belcher from around his neck.

Unable to escape the searing bombardment of the sun, the air beneath the trees was musty, overpowering. He felt as though his legs were burdened down with weights.

Already he wished he'd taken the car back to the camp with that skinny slip of a schoolteacher who had got her sums wrong.

He wished he'd pushed the Wise Woman's words up her arse like a devilish pessary and he longed to be up at the Lough, soaking the sweat of the day out of his skin in the ice-cool water.

Squeezing the blue neckerchief into a tight, hard ball he flung it petulantly at a sycamore and watched the red and gold leaves float down like parchment to the forest floor.

Worse than the heat was the silence. The only sounds of the wood were coming from the thick soles of his boots crunching against the dead leaves.

For a moment he did not notice the rain.

The first drops pattered gently up among the tallest branches, sounding no louder than the soughing of a soft wind. Too close to death for succour, the fragile faces of the leaves bowed to allow the water to slide down them. It was several seconds before Finn felt the first drops on his bared head. Grunting with annoyance he increased his pace down the forest path.

The sun had now disappeared behind the black raincloud which was spitting freely into Finn's face, causing him to haul his blue denim shirt over his head to keep dry.

Deep in the darker interiors of his mind he had just cut a fresh wooden stake from the thicket, fastened the Wise Woman to it and after heaping hazel twigs around her shins was fumbling in his pocket for matches. Around him the rain was pounding the leaves and branches into a spontaneous burst of applause.

Elated by the response Finn wrenched the shirt from his shoulders and waved it vigorously above his head. It was now completely soaked and useless as a shelter against the downpour.

At first he had been agitated by the rain. All he had wanted had been to sprint down the mountain to the safety of the Clandy encampment.

But now he had stopped running and was standing bare to the waist, the rain jetting into his exposed skin and making the unexpected discovery that it was not unpleasant.

All the earlier discomfort had gone now and there was something soothing, almost exhilarating about the sharp spurts of cool water pricking his flesh. Releasing a gigantic whoop from his lungs he hurled the sodden shirt high into the trees and set off running, zigzagging his way in jerky leaps, his big face grinning up at the louring heavens.

The first boot came off barely twenty yards from the track. The second, wrenched free of its dripping sock, was raised momentarily, like some unwanted trophy, before being dropped into one of the deep puddles the storm had already made in the path.

A sock went over his shoulder as he made off again, breaking into a canter before hopping briefly to jettison the final sock.

Even before the two massive rainclouds collided above him, releasing a further deluge on the already drenched mountain, Finn's hands were at the belt buckle of his jeans, tearing the zip apart before forcing the wet cloth down from his legs.

Breaking free of them, Finn hurled them back to join the rest of his debris littering the forest path. Then solemnly, like some bizarre king rewarding his subjects, he bowed low and slowly and deliberately offered his underpants to the teeming sky.

He began to run again, pounding through the puddles like some great, ground-devouring stag, trying to keep up with the boy who was bursting within him. But every movement he was making seemed to be in slow motion. The trees beside the path appeared to pass him so slowly he could see the rain channeling down the grooves of the trunks and instead of becoming blurred and indistinct the bright reds and golds of the leaves were sharper than before.

Free of their clothes his wet limbs were moving effortlessly now as his body eagerly accepted the sudden lustration. Finn could no longer feel the rain against his flesh. It had become part of him, an overwhelming communion of water and body blending in a harmony which was both heathen and exhilarating.

There was no longer even a forest. As he raced downwards, taking long, giddy strides in his euphoria, the trees seemed to turn into waves rushing to engulf him, their cold cleansing fingers purging his body with every thrust as he breathed in the drunkenness of the great deep. Looking up through the water he let out a loud, throaty roar, a shout of joy and greeting which seemed to gush up from within him as he closed his eyes in ecstasy. . . .

When he opened them he saw he had left the forest two hundred yards behind him and he was standing in an open field. The rain had ceased, the sun was back and he suddenly felt the need to cup his mansflesh in his hands.

Below at the Clandy huts he fancied Brown Windsor would be trying to puzzle out what a naked Irishman had been doing leaping like a big white eejit down the High Meadow.

The Italians were waiting, huddled in small groups around the two stone lions as the yellow Land Rover swung into the forecourt.

As Griff Dando jumped down from the passenger seat Gans and Fasman appeared from the rear of the vehicle and stood two paces behind him. They fixed their eyes on the men, who instinctively moved together until all forty of them were in a tightly packed circle.

Dando walked over to where the two lorries were parked beside the high pillars at the main entrance of Hesters Hall, their engines running.

"All right, what's the trouble, Gates?" he snapped.

The driver shrugged his shoulders. "They say they won't go on shift. They reckon they want more money."

"Are they Caws?"

"Eyeties? You must be joking!"

"Wait here," said Dando, "and keep your engine going."

He walked back to Fasman and Gans, who were staring at the silent Italians as though they were trying to mesmerise them. After whispering to Fasman, who nodded his head in reply, Dando walked slowly towards the Italians until he was only fifteen feet from the nearest man.

"O.K., who's your spokesman?" he asked, reaching for the black leather gloves from his back pocket and slipping them over his fingers.

The Italians looked at each other, murmuring among themselves before staring back into Dando's glinting sunglasses.

"Come on, boyos. They tell me you're not very happy. Now who's going to tell me about it?"

The chatter broke out again, stopping only when a tall, raw-boned youth was pushed out from the centre of the group. For a moment he glanced back at his colleagues, seeming reluctant to leave them. Then he shrugged his shoulders and turned to face Dando.

"You're the mouthpiece for these men, then, are you?" inquired Dando.

The young Italian brushed back a lock of black hair which had fallen across his forehead and nodded uncertainly.

"Come here then," said Dando. "We can't start to settle anything from this distance."

The youth walked slowly forward until he was in front of the tall Welshman.

"So you're the leader, are you?"

The boy frowned as though he was not sure of the question being asked but slowly his large lips broke into a broad smile which revealed two perfect rows of white, even teeth.

Dando's fist hit him in full smile, the bones of his knuckles thudding against the boy's teeth with such force that the blow pitched him backwards against the gravel.

For a moment the Italian lay motionless on his back staring upwards. Then with a gurgling noise in his throat he slowly spat out a stream of white-flecked blood before his head finally flopped against the black surface.

When Dando looked across at the rest of the group they had all gone silent. It was several seconds before two of the biggest of them stepped forward.

Dando felt his fists hardening at his sides as they took a few paces towards him, relaxing them only when the Italians veered away before leaping on the back of Gates's truck. The rest followed them, slowly shuffling past the big Welshman until both lorries were full.

He looked back, exchanging a grin with Fasman and Gans before shouting up to the men in the first truck. "Here! You'd better take your spokesman with you!"

Two of the Italians jumped down and carried the unconcscious youth back to the lorry.

The trucks were just leaving Hesters as Liederman's white T.R.7 pulled into the drive. The American looked back at the departing Italians as he walked over to Dando.

"Well they seem to be happily on their way, then, Griff," he said breezily. "No sweat, then?"

"Not a scratch on me," grinned Dando.

"You fixed a deal all right?"

"Let's say we now understand each other."

Liederman looked quizically at him. "From what I heard I thought you could have been in for a tricky time," he said.

Dando put his hand on the American's shoulder. "Bob," he said, smiling broadly, "whatever made you think it would be the Italians who would let you down. After all they're the fellers who built your friend Hadrian's Wall, aren't they?"

Part Four

SAMAIN

SAMAIN *Winter* – 'The slaughter of the old beasts and the seeding of the young.'

SAMAIN

The Rev. James Churnside leaned over from his pulpit and set the hour glass moving on its black wrought-iron stand.

"Before I announce my text for this day," he said, removing his spectacles and pressing his fingers against each of his eyes in turn, "I would like to mention with deep regret the passing this week of a dear and greatly respected member of our community. Much of what this fine man did for this valley of ours, which he loved so well, went unnoticed, as is often the case with truly noble men. For this, of course, was the nature of the man, a gentleman of great wisdom and inner strength and also a humility which served as a lesson to us all. He was a man who, by his dedication to work and his generosity of spirit, held this valley in the palm of his hand, a hand which reached out and touched each one of us with its warmth and friendship. . . ."

The sudden, loud sniff below the vicar came from Latice Gillibrand who shot a dry-eyed glance at the Brigadier before staring across to the other side of the brass section.

Edna Bennett was dressed in black, a dark veil partly concealing her face, but not sufficiently enough for Latice Gillibrand to notice she was gazing towards Cuddy's Wall beneath the pulpit where the final plaque, a square of new, gleaming brass, was already in position.

"John Osborne Bennett set an example in this valley," said the vicar," by his great and positive contribution to both church and community, which will be remembered as long as his name is remembered. And as he leaves the Corbar Vale which he loved so dearly, we are left not the poorer but the richer for his having been amongst us. My text this morning comes from Revelations, chapter twenty-one, verse six. 'A draught from the water springs of life will be my free gift to the thirsty.' "

His eyes made their customary sweep of the Norman vaulting above his head, but it was a hasty gesture as if he was assuring himself they were still there, rather than a profound, spiritual pause. When the lenses of his spectacles flashed down to the congregation again there was an urgency in them, an anxiousness to get started.

"Now those of you who read your newspapers and observe your television sets will have noticed an increasing use of a certain word just recently. . . ."

"Sex," whispered the small owl-like boy, choking almost immediately as the collar of his cassock was pulled tightly against his throat. He glanced nervously round as Donald Dacre's face appeared over his shoulder from the front row of the tenors.

"Mandate," said the Rev. James Churnside. "Union leaders, politicians, even Prime Ministers seem to be constanly asking each other whether or not they have a mandate to do this or that. In other words they are looking for reassurance that what they are doing is right. Now we parsons have a mandate too. I have one. It comes, it is fair to say, from a rather loftier direction, but it is a mandate none the less. And what does the Lord's mandate instruct me to do. It says 'Feed My Flock.' Now that doesn't mean to say that I'm expected to go around with a big bottomless purse to buy and hand out food parcels. In fact, by the end of the week we parsons get closer to the bottom of our purses than most of you do. No, what it means is, I am here to point the way to the table which the good Lord fills. Feed my flock, He tells me and without putting too fine a point on it, He is also telling me to water His flock. And when I look around my parish today, set in this beautiful Valley of Corbar, He tells me He is about to keep His promise. The water springs of life, He says, will be my free gift to the thirsty. . . ."

Although Donald Dacre's strong, square face seemed to be staring intently at the vicar, he had a pencil in his hand and an almost complete cartoon drawing on his knee. It revealed the Ark bobbing on a stormy sea and the dove of peace returning with a large bag in its beak. On the bag he had printed the word "Gold" in large letters, and behind the bird a small sprig of olive was falling gently into the water. His Noah was a balding, bulbous man in a surplice and dog collar and he was wearing spectacles.

"The gift of water, the springs of life, is one of the greatest boons which can be bestowed on mankind," said the Rev. James Churnside. "To the thirsty man the gift is all the greater. And I think many of you here will agree with me that we in Corbardale have been too thirsty for too long. Thirsty for jobs, thirsty for trade for our shops and businesses, thirsty for the sort of amenities enjoyed by so many of our fellow men in the richer corners and conurbations of our land. But now, after centuries in the wilderness, you have only to look around you to see it all happening for us. The very spotlight of civilisation has been switched on to this once sadly neglected nook of England, to lighten our darkness and to bring us great joy. It was St. Eustace who once said 'Never look a gift horse in the mouth.' If the horse is free why look at its teeth, he is telling us. And the very same is true when it comes to the mandates of both God and men. For here in Corbardale we have living proof of the joint success of a mandate shared by man and God. It is our duty, therefore, not to question that mandate but to give thanks for the water springs of life, springing from that great power and love which passes all understanding. . . . We will now sing Hymn No. 587 in the English Hymnal. And I would like the second verse of this fine hymn to be sung by those for whom we are building this great bounteous future of ours . . . our little ones."

At the first rousing notes of the organ Donald Dacre's head jerked up towards the vicar who was descending from his pulpit on a golden carpet, his face serene and composed, like an enormous, celestial emperor.

As his swaying stomach appeared behind the opposite choir stalls it hovered momentarily over a second gold carpet which stretched from the Saxon quarter along the entire length of the aisle, obliterating the brass memory of Sir Henry Hesters and rclling like a broad, bright yellow motorway to the steps of the altar.

With a majestic left turn the Rev. James Churnside coughed softly against his sleeve and began cruising up to his collecting base.

Donald could see the thick yellow embroidered stole glistening against the starched white of his surplice and behind him the corded edges of the new yellow hassocks in the openings of the pews. It seemed to him that every seat in the church had been taken. Seven of the rows were filled with Clandy men so tightly packed and regimented it gave the appearance of a legion which was about to march over the Gillibrands in the front pew. He noticed the dignified, silver-haired figure of Sir William Clandy in the van, flanked by Caswell and Dando. Tina Padgett was bringing up the rear of the force, goggling like a camp follower, the small boy at her side peering up at the giant, out-of-season daffodils trumpeting down at him from the lucies window.

The choir and congregation were almost at the end of the first verse of "All Things Bright and Beautiful" when Donald suddenly remembered to sing. The Rev. James Churnside was right in front of him now, kneeling beside the yellow-curtained altar, staring not so much at the tall, golden cross but into the burnished plate beside it which had an image of a vicar in it, a vicar who was smiling. . . .

Over at the wall seat the little ones of St. Cuddy's were on their feet now, the necks of the congregation twisting round to watch them piping their way through the second verse, urged on by Sara Dacre.

"Each little flower that opens,
Each little bird that sings,
He made their glowing colours,
He made their tiny wings."

Donald could see there were seven of them singing for Jesus. Six boys and a girl. He could almost feel the joy and gratitude in their round, urgent faces. And behind them, all was being revealed, as he caught a glimpse of the long, yellow cushion spreading the whole length of the cold seat in cosy, bum-warming benefaction.

"Nice to see you here again, Sir William," said the Rev. James Churnside, reaching across Larky Challon and offering a hand to the Clandy chairman at the porch.

Clandy nodded. "Always a pleasure, vicar. And a rather good sermon, if I might say so."

"Well it's nice to have so many of you here to listen to it," said the vicar, beaming. "Before your people came we were rather thin in the aisles some days. My sermons were a bit like your water, Sir William, falling on stony ground."

"I see what you mean, my boy," grinned Clandy. "Well I hope your numbers keep up. We won't be here all that much longer now, you know."

"Yes, I suppose you're almost finished, Sir William," said the vicar, looking down beyond the lych-gate to where a glistening sheet of water was covering the valley floor.

Clandy glanced at Caswell and Dando, who were standing on each side of him. "Well as far as the dam's concerned we're on the short stro . . . we're almost ready. We're now trying to get the thing filled up as soon as possible. Could do with one or two of your springs of life perhaps vicar, eh? That reminds me, I must have a quick word with the chappie who's supposed to be coming up with our springs." He wagged a finger at him in mock reproach. "Your man's been a bit slow with the rain just lately, you know."

"Your rain will come," said the vicar, shaking his hand once more. "The Lord will provide."

"I hope so," said Clandy. "Unfortunately, however, he's not on the payroll, so I can't gee him up at all."

Finn was perched on the churchyard wall as the three men came up to him.

"Now then, Rafferty," said Clandy. "Have you found me any more water yet?"

"I got a fresh one up at Hounshale yesterday," said Finn, chewing as he spoke. "You could sail a fleet down there already."

"I know," said Clandy. "But that's mainly from the Nauny and Erianne. We want those aquafer sources you told me were there."

"And they are," said Finn. "Once I can get out into the fields a bit more I'll entice them up. I'll give you an ocean by opening day."

"You had no joy over at Blackbog, then?"

"No, it was all surface water. Nothing underneath."

"Let's see, that's where you had your trouble with the D.8s, wasn't it, Dando?" said Clandy. "Bogged down for half a week, weren't they?"

Dando curled his lip. "We whipped it. I got the idea from Rafferty."

"How do you mean?"

"Well I used divining rods, a few thousand or so hazel twigs piled up on top of the bog and the machines used them for a raft."

Finn jumped down from the wall as they burst out laughing.

"Will that be all, gentlemen?" he asked, looking at Sir William. "It's just that I'm waiting for a friend."

"Well, hello, Sir William!"

The four men turned to see Pearl Liederman bearing down on the startled Clandy, leaving her husband to follow behind her.

"I have just had the most tremendously exciting idea for the opening, Sir William!" she yelled, clutching the Clandy chairman's arm, "something that the womenfolk can do as a real, meaningful contribution."

As Clandy was plucked from the group, Dando shook his head towards the rapidly departing chairman and turned back to Rafferty. "What's all this friend business?" he said. "I heard you were running out of them."

When Rafferty made no reply he looked back towards the porch to where the Irishman watched Sara Dacre leaving the church before lowering his eyes quickly.

"I didn't mean the birds, exactly," said Dando smiling. "Although you're not doing so great with them either, I understand."

"What are you trying to say?" said Finn.

"Samson and Liam."

"What about them?"

"Oh, you haven't heard, then?" said Dando, leering at him. "They're leaving you too. As a matter of fact they're leaving all of us."

Finn looked at him sharply. "What's happening to them?"

"Keep your keks on," said Dando, patting the charged air between them with his hand. "They've got good jobs, both of them. Well there wasn't much left up here for blokes like them, except a few scrag ends and. . . ."

"Coaling?"

Dando's face lit up. "Coaling yes, there's always coaling. And that's not a bad sort of open-air occupation for a growing lad, as you know yourself."

"They've gone to a Caw site? They've joined your lot?"

"Paid up," said Dando. "They left this morning for a nice easy motorway number in North Wales. They knew at least twenty-four hours ago; funny they didn't tell you, Finn."

Rafferty ground his boot into the gravel on the path. "Bloody Samson and Liam? That little bugger!"

"Oh Finbar," said Dando, putting his hands over his ears, "remember where you are. That's no way to talk about your friends, old chap, is it? Anyway, when can we expect to start enjoying your company?"

"Dando," said Finn, thrusting both hands down into his jeans, "the day I become one of your lousy, poncing Caws it'll be the day they have to carry me in feet-first to your meeting."

Dando shrugged his shoulders. "I'll look forward to your coming," he said, "either way."

As Rafferty turned to go, Dando called him back. "In the meantime I want to see you stretching your legs filling this place. Full time! Out with your bloody fancy sticks poking up those aquafers! I'm not bringing Queenie all the way up here to open a bleeding puddle! I want to see that water so deep the sodding corgies will be on stilts. Get it filled, Rafferty, even if you have to spend your breaks pissing in it!" He reached into his inside pocket, pulled out a form and stuffed it in Finn's top pocket. "You might need that too," he said. "In case you change your mind."

Rafferty took out the form, read the first line and slowly tore it up into several pieces, letting them drop on the ground.

Dando grinned at him. "Litter can cost you £25 these days, did you know?"

Finn tried to smile. "It's still cheap," he said, "for that rubbish."

Over Dando's shoulder he could see Donny sitting on the wall in the same spot where he had waited for church to come out. The boy leapt down to greet him as he went over.

"Hello Mr. Rafferty," he said, his face polite and unsmiling.

"Oh, Mr. Rafferty is it?" said Finn. "Now that you've been away with the posh people? Schooling, weren't you?"

"They sent me to boarding school. I'm just here for the holidays."

Rafferty grinned. "So that was a guest appearance in there, was it? I could hear you from out here."

"Aunt Sara said it would be best to keep up my choir singing."

"And so it is, boy." He looked closely at Donny, shaking his head in surprise at the height he had grown and the width of his strong, broad shoulders. "Christ, you're spreading like a tree! You're a bit strapping for a treble, aren't you?"

"Tenor," corrected Donny.

"Tenor is it now?"

"My voice broke in a rugger scrum."

Finn smiled. "That's the man shovin' his way out. Course, you'll be a good big sensible age now?"

"Nearly fifteen."

"Lord, you're motoring. And was it your Aunt Sara's idea to have you go to the sleeping school?"

"I think it was Aunt Cora's, actually. I heard them talking about it."

"More praise to her head then. She did rightly. Do you still take gum?" He held the packet out to the boy.

Donny took a piece and thanked him. "Do you think she was right, then?" he asked.

"Right? Sure she was right. O.K. I know she's not always, but sense sometimes shows up in the unlikeliest places. You'll get a good grasp of the knowledge down there, and it keeps you clear of

the big mucky men like me."
"I've missed you, Finn."
Finn punched him lightly on the shoulder. "Sure you have son. But then you'll be a mite too big for the old fish now, won't you?"
"Do you still go for the apples?"
He laughed and shook his head. "The old bitch woman has a padlock on the tree sure," he said, glancing round before whispering in the boy's ear. "Mind you, I had the odd pound or two off her last summer."
The boy's sudden laughter came out so loudly that Latice Gillibrand and the Brigadier had to break off their conversation with the vicar to glare across at him.
Finn coughed and put on a serious face. "Well now Donald," he said. "Now that you have all this great age under your belt have you decided what you are going to do with the rest of your life?"
Donald brushed a strand of black hair across his forehead. "My father already had his first flock of sheep when he was fifteen," he said.
"He didn't get a great deal of use out of it, though," said Finn. "God rest the man."
"He never really wanted to be a farmer anyway according to Aunt Cora," said Donald. "And I obviously wasn't meant to be one either. Perhaps our sort have all had their time and we should be out building things instead of messing about with sheep."
The Irishman clicked his teeth. "Now what sort of talk's that for a Donald?"
Donny threw up a hand. "Well The Donald had a farm and believed in it. And his fields are down under the water."
"And I did it, you mean?"
"No, I'm not blaming you, Finn. It's just that it seems pointless, that's all."
"Do they encourage a feel for the land down where you are? At the boarding school?"
The boy giggled and put his hand across his mouth. "It used to be an agricultural college when it first started. But the farming part got pushed out until now there's only one house for farm students in the whole place."
"Where does the fun come into it?"
Donny laughed and Finn could see his face had reddened. "No, it's just that they reckon they can tell a boy from the farming house because of the pong from his boots."
"Do they call them names?" asked Finn.
"Yes."
"What do they call them?"
"Stinkies."
"And you're not a Stinky, then?"
"Christ, no."

Finn drew in his breath quickly. "I take it you're in the language department?"

Donny smiled at him. "No, I'm just feeling my way around a few things. I'll know what I want to do when I see it."

"That's the best way, boy," said Finn, starting to walk towards the gate, nodding to the leaving churchgoers as though he had known them all his life. "In the meantime, son, since you're in my highly disreputable company, I'll do a deal with you."

"What's that, Finn?" asked Donny.

"I'll do the cursing if you'll do the learning. That's fair, isn't it?"

"It's a deal," he said.

"Good, that's that settled then," said Finn. "Now we'll start in your department. I'm now going to show you one of the great wonders of the world."

"The dam, you mean?"

"No, lad," said Finn. "Just a wee piece of it. The draw-off tower. You'll see a drum of men living on a floating disc of liquid concrete, pushing its way up 400 feet to the sky like a great spear with no visible means of support. Christ, if we could find the recipe for ourselves we could build a bloody nation out of it!"

Together they crossed the road, leapt the low stone wall and began running, the boy racing ahead of the man long before the field plunged down to the great, white dam of Corbar.

Finn slipped the Land Rover into second as the vehicle emerged out of the dip and began snorting its way up towards the high plateau of Hengendelly.

As he glanced up towards the low row of white buildings on the summit he saw the yellow safari leaving to begin its descent into the valley.

Recognising the driver as Jo Tiffin, he stopped halfway up the hill and waved her down, watching her closely as she halted the truck beside him.

"You're still here, then, girl?" he said, pushing his cap to the back of his head.

"You're still building, aren't you?" she said.

"Open your door, Jo."

When she opened it he saw she was wearing a blue smock dress with a bulge beneath it which reached almost up to the driving wheel.

"You're still carrying, then?" he said.

"They don't go away, Finn. They don't arrive either for nine months. I'm not eight yet!"

Finn threw his cigarette end out through the window. "You should be at home with that feller by now, you know."

She laughed. "At 120 quid a week and all supplied? Including the babies? You must be joking! Where are you going anyway?"

"I'm just rubber-necking," he said. "I'm up to see that big ashtray in the sky they're building, the observation cabin."

"I've just driven your friend Keen up there."

"Hmph," he muttered. "He should complain about the service round here."

He leaned out of the window towards her. "Look Jo, keep an eye on that calendar. If you leave it much longer you'll be drawing two wages."

As she waved and drove off he watched her for a few moments through the rear-view mirror and then started up his engine.

When he walked in between the glass doors of the observation tower Finn found himself in a long, broad room which looked like a conservatory. Seeing nobody about he pushed his way through the double swing doors ahead of him and found himself in a large, semicircular bowl. There were tiers of yellow plush seats plunging down to a curved balustrade at the front. Above the rim of the balcony there was a matching stone cowl jutting out from the roof. Between them, on what looked like a cinemascope screen, Finn could see the bold white slash of the dam across the only dark part of the valley unreached by the advancing water. The tesselated walls and milecastles, a thousand feet beneath him, were pointing skywards in a gleaming and breathtaking display of power.

"I'll have one ticket for the circle," he bawled out. "Sally The Cat can pay for her own!"

When he got no reply he looked towards the back seats on his right and saw a heavily built man asleep in the corner, his head lolling over his upturned helmet. Another was sprawled out beneath the balustrade, snoring against the heaving, prostrate stomach of a red-faced mucky who was trying to take a wine bottle into his dreams. When two heads popped up from the front seats over to his left it was only a token gesture before the coins started jingling down on the cards.

Hearing footsteps behind him he turned and saw Keen coming through the swing doors.

Finn glanced at his watch and blew air out of his mouth. "Michael, what the hell is this? The Noddy Hour? You can almost see the dead lice droppin' off them!"

Keen gave him a thin smile. "Perhaps the heat's got them," he said.

"Heat? It's as cold as a stepmother's breath up here! We could just as well be on the sodding moon. Look, where's the bloody ganger while all this is going on?"

"They'll sleep it off in a minute, Finn."

"They'll dream it off in their own time, then. Who is he? I'll have a word in!"

Keen shrugged his shoulders. "There's no need, Finn," he said.
"Like Christ there isn't! Who is the ganger here, anyway?"
"I am."
"You?" said Finn narrowing his eyelids. His face slowly broke into a grin as he thumped Keen on the rump. "You're a dark horse, aren't you, boy? Why didn't you tell us you'd had a lift up? We'd have had so much booze under your belt we'd have made this lot look like pixies!"
When the youngster's face showed no emotion Finn stood back and glared at him. "Just a minute," he snapped. "Who gave you this leg up?"
"Dando," said Keen, looking at the floor.
"Dando personally, you mean?"
Keen saw that the Irishman's face was reddening. "Look Finn," he said quickly, "I may as well tell you. I've joined the Caws."
Finn snatched the cap from his head and hurled it on the ground. He looked up slowly. "You took the soup mix, did you, then, boy?"
"I had to. It was the only way up."
"Up?" said Finn gazing towards the parapet. "Aye, you've come quite a way, son, on such a small piece of paper."
"It's the system, Finn," said Keen. "You can't pick your bosses any more. No more than you can pick your parents."
The Irishman flicked a finger towards the dam and faced him, smiling. "Did you know, the bosses who built the original of that couldn't pick their fathers, either? But they used to do a funny thing now. The used to pick their sons, adoptin' 'em, just going and choosing the sort of kid who might want to carry on where they left off. Mind you, they needed to be a pretty good judge of a lad."
"I wanted to get somewhere, Finn."
"Christ," said Finn, looking round the tower, "if you go any higher than this you'll be a bloody astronaut!"
They looked at each other and smiled.
"Why did you do it, Michael?" said Finn softly. "We were getting a good scene going. I'd heard tell even Clandy had got the scarers on because of the way Dando's closing in. He was just looking for him to make one slip before using it as an excuse to send him down the road."
Keen shook his head. "Clandy's an old man. And Dando knows it. All this means everything to Big Clandy. They say he's quietly hoping to become the first muckshifting lord before he checks out. And he knows only Dando's methods will get him there."
"And you're weighing in with Dando?"
"If you have to bet on a horse you need to choose a winner."
Finn ran his hand through his hair. "Michael Keen," he said. "If you'd been in Clooney you might never have seen a circus in all your days. They always passed us by because we could never have scraped a tentful to watch them. But there was a wee man there in

the back bar of Breen's place, all boney and straight and sweatin', and he would dance them round us. The big white Liberties and the bays and the black, bouncing mares rearin' up on their hind legs and the wee dodger ponies so small the whip would hardly move in his hand for fear of hurtin' them. And we could see them all, you see. We could even feel the hot breath of their mouths rushin' past our cheeks and all galloping out from a man who never saw a circus in his life. And when some tourist woman once asked him where he kept them all, he turned to her and said, 'Madam, they're the ponies of the mind, the most beautiful ponies of all'. . . ."

He slapped Keen on the shoulder as he began climbing up the stairs. "And do you know, Michael," he said, "I never heard of any one of them ever winning a race."

Keen glanced up. "How do you win, then, Finn?" he asked.

Finn stopped and turned back to him. "You win by taking," he said. "Taking just as much as you deserve and no more."

He was almost through the doors when he swung round again to look at Keen, who was staring down at the dam.

"Don't fuss yourself, son," he said. "There'll always be plenty who think they're winning. You'll be in good company. You haven't done so bad yourself so far, for a circus boy. You've got your own Big Top and you've got a ringside seat for the greatest show on earth. But Michael, I wouldn't have your ringmaster for a tent of gold!"

When Keen looked for him he had already gone through the door.

Finn was in the mulberry bushes.

He had parked the Land Rover up on the coal road, its passenger door still swinging open in the stiff breeze as evidence of the suddenness of his whim.

The bushes were banked closely together in a dark green sprawl which spread almost up to the dam wall itself.

From where he was standing he could see the brown backs of the men catching the afternoon sun as they worked on the merlons and embrasures along the turreted rim of the wall. They were lined up like midget cooks, laying the icing on a long white cake which had been laid across the whole width of the valley.

He knew from experience that mulberries never survived far from water.

Below them the bowl that Clandy's were bringing to them was already more than half full. He knew, though, that mulberries had been there long before men had decided to drown Corbar.

As he took the hazel rods in his hands a sudden swishing movement in the bushes below him made him turn quickly.

Peering down in the direction of the noise he saw a low branch swinging gently as though someone had just passed close by.

He walked briskly to a gap between two bushes where the branch was still twitching. Suddenly he caught a glimpse of an orange kagoul disappearing between a clump of hawthorn.

"Hey, who's that there?" he called, waiting for the kagoul to reappear, but there was only silence from where he had seen the small shape.

Pushing his way through the thick hawthorn barrier, he tore the leg of his trousers in his haste to reach the fleeing figure, but when he burst through to the clearing the man had disappeared.

As he stared round him a high, bleeping sound started up from the slope to his right.

It took him several seconds to realise it was coming from the intercom buzzer in his parked Land Rover. He scratched his head, took a final look back to the clearing and began running rapidly back to his vehicle.

"Rafferty to base. Come in. Over!" he barked into the transmitter.

"Rafferty, there's a call out for you!" said the voice. "They want you at Baskey's. The tea hut, they said. Reckoned it was pretty urgent! Over!"

Finn gave the button a sharp dig with his finger. "Tell 'em I'm on my way! Over and out."

He put his foot down hard on the accelerator, glancing once at the slope on his left before the vehicle lurched him forward.

Finn pushed open the door of the cabin, slamming it into the heels of Dick Dancer, who moved aside to let him through. As he glanced round the dimly lit room he could see that almost the whole gang was there. When Dancer nodded to him he saw that he had a towel folded over his arm. Beside him Chauncy Bawn was sitting cross-legged on the wooden floor holding a grey blanket in his hands. Balzac, the old stone-facer, was squatting on the floor too, a black kettle suspended between his knees. Both Gomer and Sykes from the Ripper team had tin mugs shelved in their open hands, and Jimmy Bree, the young cableman, was staring down at a small, yellow teddy bear. On the far side of the improvised bed of donkey jackets and parkas were three men standing silently with what appeared to be gifts in their rough, outstretched hands. Brown Windsor, serious and still as a mahogany statue, was offering out a large, white enamel bowl of water as he gazed down on the bed. The Goose was scratching his long red nose thoughtfully as he held out a nappy, and beside him the lean, stooping Tully had both his hands upturned, revealing the silver glint of safety-pins beneath the glow of the single light bulb above the bed. On the walls the smiling, naked girls seemed to be pushing their fleshy breasts and thighs out from the bright glossy pictures towards the bed where the taut, frightened face of Jo Tiffin was tossing behind her high, splayed legs. Tucky the cook was kneeling beside her, his sleeves rolled high on his fat, hairy arms, which he was thrusting gently between the pale jerking thighs. Without looking up, as though sensing Finn was in the room, he said, "I asked for some help and they all came." When he raised his head the fat cook had the same sweaty, totally contented look on his face which they had seen when he had first stuck his fork into the hot, tangy flesh of the spit pig. "She's ready," he said, licking his wet lips. The scream which came almost at once from Jo Tiffin's wide, distorted mouth compelled Finn to turn his head away. He closed his eyes to escape from the pain of the sound. Opening them, he found himself staring stupidly at the picture of the enormous, naked black girl on the wall, who was smiling at him with white, even teeth and offering him a large, half-peeled banana. When he looked back to the bed John Christopher Tiffin, who had been a fish in the warm, dark waters of the womb, was being pushed out between the sore blood-flecked legs of his mother into a dry, dazzling heat which was forcing its way into his fresh, wet lungs through a tiny mouth which was opened only to release a long, agonised scream. Finn thought for a moment it sounded like a cry of terror.

"So there I was, wedged under this big 6 feet 10 inch copper, helping him with his enquiries like. . . ."

Dick Dancer broke off talking to the small, hatchet-faced man and glanced back as Finn Rafferty appeared behind him.

"He's gone a bit further down since then," said Finn "Haven't you, Dancer?"

"What do you mean, Finn?" said Dancer, leaning back against one of the deep embrasures in the castellated rim of the dam as a truck passed them on the road.

"I hear you've taken the bait?"

Dancer tried to smile. "Oh, that? Yeah, well er. . . . It's a bloody good number, you know. Guaranteed work for a year and a pick of the sites afterwards."

"North Wales, isn't it?"

"Yeah. Look I'm not the only one you know. He's going. Two fellers down there signed up last week. It's . . . er . . . spreading like. . . ."

"So's the pox in some places."

Dancer put down his mortar knife and rubbed his hands. "Look Finn, it's not just Clandy's, you know. Dolan's are in, A.R.L.,

McGibbons, it's a sort of umbrella over just about the whole industry, shielding its members. It's not like the old days, you know. This lot covers you from head to foot for just about everything."

"You make it sound like a cocoon."

Dancer grinned. "Well it is in a way, I suppose."

Finn reached forward and fastened Dancer's shirt button just below the red neckerchief and stood back. "Dancer, the best lookin' cocoon I ever saw only had a worm inside it. Who else is joining from our lot?"

"Windsor's going."

"Christ, not Brownie! Where is he?"

"Up at the first milecastle."

Rafferty started to walk away.

"Finn?"

Finn turned round and saw Dancer's face straining to get the words out. "Finn," he said finally, "it's got to be better, you know. For all of us. When you and I were first mucking we didn't get sick pay, disturbance money, we didn't even get pensions!"

Rafferty smiled. "We never had free dentists, either," he said. "But we could bite, Dancer! By Christ we could bite!"

Brown Windsor was polishing the round brass handle in the oak door of the milecastle tower when Finn came up to him.

"Shine it well, Brownie," he said. "You're going to have the hand that holds up Britain fingering that soon."

"Hello Finn," said Windsor looking up. "What's the word today, then, boss?"

"Turncoat," said Finn. "It means someone who swaps his uniform."

"What sort of people do that, then, boss?"

"They tell me your sort, Brownie. I hear you've joined Mr. Dando's army?"

Windsor shrugged his shoulders. "He reckoned it would be best in the long run. He said the Caw fellers would look after people like me."

"So that people like you could look after people like him?" said Finn.

"Mr. Dando said we were part of a tradition. A reminder of our once great past and that Britain needed to show the world that she could still be understanding and tol . . . tole. . . ."

"Tolerant, is it?"

Windsor nodded. "And apart from that, Finn, he said that I, that's me, will be allowed to read out the aims and policies of the Caws for the next year at the annual meeting."

"Oh Brownie," said Finn putting a hand on the little West Indian's shoulder. "But do you think he'll ever let you write them?"

When Finn got back to Dancer he saw there was a short, broad-backed man standing beside him with a stone chisel in his hand.

"Chauncy Bawn," said Finn. "Christ, don't tell me you've gone over?"

Bawn turned round and Finn could see his face was drawn. "I was telling Dancer, Finn," he said. "I can understand it in a way. Look at them, they're sick with striving, they've had enough. The crack's cat – dead rotten. They've had the screws on them too long."

Finn looked hard at him. "And you Chauncy, are you going too?"

"I'm going," he said. "But not to the Caws. I'm getting clean of the place."

"You're packing it in, then?"

Bawn breathed out slowly. "A feller can fight too long," he said. "But when he knows he's losing it doesn't mean to say he has to join the opposition. A winner like Dando would have the eyes out of your head and still come back and spit in the holes."

"Where will you go?" asked Finn gently.

"I'm going where these things can still earn me a living I can look at," he said, staring down at his rough, brown hands, "I'm going to be a stonemason. Back home, where they still give people a bit of earth to their backs when they go to rest. It'll be just a yard in the old village where I can tinker around and carve out a shape of stone to say they've been here." He laughed and tapped the chisel against the merlon on the wall. "It's funny, after all that mucking, I should get the taste of the idea from old Hadrian here. He must have been a good stone man himself."

"He was," said Finn.

"Perhaps I could call my place after him. Hadrian Enterprises, do you think?"

Finn picked the chisel up from where Bawn had left it on the dam wall. "Call it Bawn," he said, "Bawn, Mason. Well Chauncy, I can't promise you an order but I'll take your hand, you bugger! And I'll give you a word of advice."

"What's that, Finn?" said Bawn, still holding his hand.

"Go to your stone, Chauncy Bawn. And carve out a good name for your folk. But if you should happen to see a wee slip of a girl come dancing into your yard, competin' with your stones, put your hand to her arse and show her the gate. Will you do that?"

"I'll try to remember it," grinned Bawn, as Dancer watched their hands finally go down.

"There's fellers I've known closer than you, Bawn," said Finn, turning away to look at Dancer. "Some so close when the going's been tough that they were pigging together in the same bed even though he'd come home all hours smelling of ladies bicycle saddles. And then you find out you don't know them at all."

"Where are you going now, Finn?" said Dancer as Rafferty started to leave.

"Me, Dancer?" he said. "I'm going up on that mountain. And

I'm going to cut me a hazel switch and I'm going to coax up a sweet, fresh, mountain stream. And I'm going to roll up my sleeves. And then I'm going to dip my hands in it."

Jo Tiffin had been walking along the Gamelpath road towards Todholes for more than ten minutes when the yellow Land Rover overtook her and screeched to a halt twenty yards away.

She looked back, shifting the baby to a more comfortable position on her arm and resting her small brown travelling case on the pavement.

"Is that you, Jo Tiffin?" shouted the blond-haired driver, sticking his head out of the window.

"Yes," she called back.

"Hang on there!" said the voice. The vehicle began backing until it was level with her.

"Oh, it's you, Finn," she said as the driver leaned through the passenger window.

"Where are you going to, in Heaven's name, with your child and things?"

"To London."

"Well you're going the wrong way, it's down there," said Finn, pointing back.

Jo Tiffin shook her head, "I'm going for the bus, silly, and catching the train from Haltbriggin. Home."

Finn peered into her face. "You mean you're going for good? You're pulling out?"

"That's right. I'll be on the 2.15 from Haltbriggin, then it's goodbye Corbar."

"Get in, then," said Finn, flinging the door open.

"But you're going down to the site, aren't you?"

"Get in!" he said. "Here, throw me up your case! You can't trust the buses anyway. We'll get there quicker in this thing."

They had already gone through the village when he glanced across at her. "What's all this about, then, Jo?"

"It's quite simple," she said. "I've got my cards, that's all."

"You mean as safari driver?"

"I mean as everything. As a woman. As his woman."

"He gave you the clause 16 then? Pitched you out of the house?"

Jo smiled. "The two of us were never really far enough in a house together for him to pitch me out," she said.

"He paid you off?"

"He gave me some money."

"Was it on account of the kiddie?"

"Partly."

"The bastard!"

Suddenly the red light on the control panel began flashing, accompanied by a high, loud bleeping which stopped when Finn depressed the switch.

"Base to 149 Rafferty!" announced the voice over the intercom. "State your position! Over!"

Finn pressed the second of the two buttons in front of him. "I'm down at the culvert at Hounshale. Over," he said hastily. "Did he give you enough money, Jo?"

"The union minimum for redundancy, what did you expect?"

The bleep began again as the red light flashed. Finn pressed the button and whistled softly through his clenched teeth.

"Base to Rafferty," said the voice. "You are not at Hounshale! State your position! Over."

Finn stabbed impatiently at the transmitting button. "Well, if I'm not there I must be in the canteen. Try there. Over."

"Where are you, Rafferty?" said the voice as Finn answered the bleeper a third time.

"I'm glad you've asked that," said Finn, responding quickly, "for now I've squirted my windscreen I'm able to give a much more precise indication of my whereabouts. I'm just at this minute going into the quarry at Baskey's. Over."

"That's funny," said the voice. "I'm just going into Haltbriggin and you're in front of me, Rafferty."

Finn glanced into the rear mirror and saw the black eye-patch of The Slasher above the driving wheel of the Land Rover behind them.

"Listen, Slasher," said Finn, winking at Jo as he pressed the transmitting button. "If you can see my Landy and there's a big good-looking fellow and a beautiful girl in it, you've caught up with the people who just stole it. I think they're an eloping couple so don't let them out of your sight. Over."

"Right now, Jo, hang on to your wee one," said Finn calmly, "we're just going to execute a few manoeuvres."

Even though he could already see the station ahead of them in the main street, Finn suddenly swung the Land Rover into a left turn, revving quickly down the side street before turning left again down a cobbled alley, narrowly avoiding a vegetable cart before making another tight left turn which brought them back up to the High Street. Completing his fourth left turn in less than a minute he looked in the mirror, smiled as he noticed the road behind was clear and pulled into the station forecourt.

"Slasher never was much good at left turns," he said, helping Jo and the baby down to the pavement. "When He gave him the blinker I think the good Lord intended him for a Tory. Do they have a bar in this place, do you know?"

When he had found her a seat in the small, green-painted refreshment room Finn took off his donkey jacket and hung it on the wooden coat-stand beside the table. As he did so a thin, elderly man in a dark business suit removed his black crombie from the next peg and placed it two spaces away from the donkey jacket.

"Now, how long is it till your train?" said Finn, slapping his hands together and eyeing up the bar counter.

"About half an hour," she said. "We're early."

"Right, we could use a few while we're waiting."

"What about the dam?"

"The dam's been waiting four years. It can wait another half hour."

When he returned from the bar he placed a brandy and a whisky in front of Jo and sat down behind his own whisky.

"Anyway there's only Dando on and a skeleton staff." He bent down and lightly chucked the baby's cheek with a fist which covered the child's head. "That means he can't be feeding 'em right, doesn't it? Eh, young 'un?"

"Who are all these for?" asked Jo.

Finn grinned at her. "There are three of us here, aren't there?" he said. "If we're going to wet this feller's head we can't let him go without a bit of strain under his belt."

Jo sipped from her glass and when she put it down Finn saw she had an anxious look on her face. "Finn, be careful, won't you? I mean with Griff. He's determined to be it, you know."

"Be what, by Christ?" said Finn.

"The Shout. He's had his mind set on it ever since I've known him. He's not going to let anyone stand in his way."

Finn drained his glass and reached for the other whisky. "Perhaps there's still a few that won't be just standing," he said.

"He says he can take Caswell any time he wants to, Finn. He's told me that. He reckons he's there for the picking."

"Sure Caswell wouldn't take much plucking, that's for certain," he said, finishing off the baby's drink before leaning over to the child. "Did you enjoy that, then, John? Christ I did too, Finn; let's have another! You're welcome."

When he came back he again placed three whiskies and a brandy on the table. "Come on, you're falling behind, child," he said. "Here's one for yourself, one for your wind, one for your nappy and one for your mum who has to shovel the thing out."

"Should you be drinking like this on duty, Finn?" asked Jo, looking concerned.

"I'm always on duty," he said, downing his own drink in one, "so I always drink. That's why I never became a parson. They can't drink on duty!" He took another glass from the baby and stared across at Jo. "So it didn't add up, then?" he said. "You and Dando."

She pulled the shawl closer to the baby's head. "Whichever way Griff adds things up it never quite comes to two," she said. "Three was an impossibility. You know, somehow, Finn, I can't see Griff ever needing anyone, a woman I mean. Even at the end, if he's ill or something, I don't think there will be a woman with him."

Finn was now on the third of the baby's drinks. "I wouldn't blame the feller for that," he said slowly. "Lovely people that you are, who'd want a woman clinging onto them when they go? You see the Heaven bit falls down when it comes to matching the men and the women. If it's supposed to be true love and you've had a few birds in your time, which one do you meet up there? Is it the last one you see, do you think?"

Jo put her hand gently on his arm. "Perhaps it's the last one you think of, Finn," she said.

"I'll let you know," he said.

"I wish I'd known him earlier, Finn. Before he was away, I mean."

"Away where?" said Finn, staring over his glass.

"I was talking to Curran. He says Griff changed a lot after that year he had off."

Finn stopped drinking and glared up at her. "What year's this?" he asked.

"Well about seven years ago he was given a twelve-months sabbatical to study earth-moving techniques abroad. You knew that, didn't you?"

"Where did he go?"

"Bulgaria."

Finn slammed the glass down noisily. "He went to Bulgaria to study muckshifting?"

Jo could see the Irishman's face colouring. "He never talks about it. Not even to me. He got quite angry when I mentioned it once."

"I'll bet he did!"

"What are you thinking about, Finn?" she asked.

He took the last of the baby's whiskies and sipped it slowly. "I'm thinking that the Bulgarians, unlike Dando, don't do anything for themselves. Not even muckshifting. They have their advisers, you see. They're like the Romanians, they're quiet people. They let others do the calling. I know one thing about muckshifters in Bulgaria, though."

"What's that, Finn?" she asked.

"Every man jack of them's a Party member."

"Where are you going?" asked Jo, as Finn got up from the table.

"I'm fixing us one for the train," he said.

"Not for me, Finn, I'll have to be getting ready."

"All right," he said. "I'll have one for your train."

When he came back Jo was already standing up.

"Your feller will make a good little Londoner," he said. "Look, he's fast asleep, just when it was his shout."

Jo looked closely into his face. "Are you sure you're going to be all right, Finn?"

"He's heard me, look, he's smiling," said Finn, looking down at the child. "You know, where I come from if a baby smiles in its sleep they say the angels are whispering to it. I hope he has some good dreams!"

He drank the whisky on his feet and carried the case to the platform.

The passengers were already entering the train when Finn bounded aboard and placed the suitcase on the seat next to the window. Helping Jo and the baby up the step he closed the train door and faced them through the window.

"I hope you find what you're looking for, Jo Tiffin," he said gently.

She tried to smile. "All I wanted before I came up here was a good job and a room with a key," she said. "I suppose it's a bit late for that now."

"Get that key, girl," he said. "But next time only open the door when you want to." He kissed her softly on the lips.

"Hey, what about your drinking partner?" she said.

Finn kissed the baby on the cheek. "It's been a long time since I kissed a feller," he said. "The difference is that you're just startin'."

When he looked back at her he saw Jo's eyes had clouded up. "Jo Tiffin!" he said gruffly, wagging a finger towards her.

Suddenly she forced her lips into a smile. "You see, I remembered, Finn," she said. "Wherever you go, go smilin'."

"God bless you, girl," he said, as the sudden movement of the train pushed him back down to the platform. He was still waving when she finally closed the window.

"Where's Dando?" yelled Finn, thrusting his head through the small, open hatch of the reception office at Clandy base.

A dark, bespectacled woman looked up from her desk. "Mister Dando's up at the Erianne, just above Hounshale Bottom," she said in a clipped voice. "If you. . . ."

When she came to the window Rafferty had already left, leaving the front door swinging behind him.

Finn leapt into the Land Rover and headed for the dam. Turning right with a loud screaming of tyres at the Todholes entrance he slotted the truck between the "No Entry" signs and followed the white castellated wall towards Calcherside. He had flashed past the five completed milecastles in as many minutes before he turned north on the coalroad, sending one of the "No Entry" signs careering against the parapet behind him.

For the first six miles the coal road was deserted, enabling him to touch eighty miles an hour in places. He passed a line of idle excavators parked on the grass verge, standing like sleeping giants.

Before he crossed the makeshift bridge over the Erianne he looked down to his left, where Baskey's place was now the biggest water meadow in Europe.

He was nearly at Baskey's when he spotted the tall, spindle-legged figure in the top hat walking towards him carrying a haversack.

The hat lifted slightly as Finn stopped the vehicle, but the man's mouth remained silent.

"You look like a man flittin', Tully," said Finn.

Tully put the haversack down. "Ach, it's just a change of sky sure."

"A Caw job is it?"

"It is, yes, er . . . you see. . . ."

"Dando talked you round then?"

"Well it's the new missus, you see, Finn. She has this place down at Stevenage, near her folk, and there's mucking going nearby if you have the card."

"And you have?"

Tully ferreted into his inside pocket. "Yes, it seems such a small, insignificant-looking emblem but they tell me it can give a man job protection."

"It's all right, I've seen them," said Finn. "And who protects you Tully, from yourself?"

Tully gave him a thin smile. "They say nearly the whole of the South's one shop now. Closed, of course. But if they need to lock you up I suppose you're better off inside then out. My problem at the moment is a slight matter of the fare, having no vehicle you see."

Finn drummed his hand against the passenger door. "It never used to trouble you in the past, Tully. I remember when we landed up at that key party in Staines. And when all the fellers threw in their keys I thought that would have sunk you. But no. You tossed in your bloody bus pass, didn't you? And you still pulled that old charity bird. And she was only there for the collecting tin."

Tully grinned. "I think I went for the feel of a good bed more than anything," he said. "But the train fare, Finn, do you think you might see your way. . . ."

"Here," said Finn handing him a fiver. "You can get the rest down at the Tup where you left your pay packet."

The battered top hat left Tully's head just long enough for him to stuff the note into his top pocket. "I'm obliged to you, Finn, Lad," he said. "Mind you, it appears I'll still need to sell something of value to achieve the balance. What do you suppose I might get for my old fiddle?"

"Probably a googar," said Finn.

"And what might that be?"

"Never mind," said Finn, starting up the Land Rover. "Sleep warm, Tully."

Ahead of him the coal road faded out into a flat clearing of gritty, almost grassless soil. On one side the Forestry Commission had planted Austrian pines which were now maturing in a copse which spread to within twenty yards of the lip of the valley. On his left the ground fell away three hundred feet to the dam water in the deep gorge of Hounshale Bottom.

When he drove into the clearing he could see the black silhouette of Dando standing on the edge of the slope gazing through his dark sunglasses at the valley beneath him.

He coasted past the two D.9 dozers which dwarfed the yellow Land Rover parked behind them and pulled up beside Dando.

"So there's two more going, then?" he said, jumping down from the cab. "Three, counting Tully."

Dando dropped the corners of his mouth as he spoke. "I don't know what you mean," he said.

"Let me remind you, then," said Finn. "They were Number 374, Jo Tiffin, and John Christopher Dando Tiffin. He wasn't here long enough to have a number, God help him."

Dando removed his sunglasses and smiled. "Oh those?" he said. "How did you get involved, Rafferty?"

"I've just been doing your job, haven't I?" said Finn. "Seeing them off. Giving them the warm, big-hearted handshake at the station."

"They left today, did they?"

"Oh, don't worry yourself," said Finn. "They were quite reasonable about it, especially the lad. We wet his head and he drank your health in a British Rail teabar and he said 'Remember me to me dad, won't you, next time you have a free fist!' "

"You're pissed, Rafferty," said Dando.

"I'm banking on it."

Dando shuffled on his feet. "What are you doing up here anyway? There's no drought up this end."

"I told you," said Finn. "I've come to pass on their messages, to say their goodbyes. There's been a few goodbyes from here lately, hasn't there?"

"The dam's almost finished," said Dando. "What do you expect? They've shifted to other sites."

"Was that why Dancer went and the Cock Lodger and Liam The Liar? There's hardly a man left on site who isn't one of your Caws. They tell me even Caswell's one now. What sort of bloody workers set-up is that?"

Dando grinned and turned away. "The best sort, Rafferty," he said. "It's like your water down there, it's vast, it's all-embracing, it runs smoothly and it fits anything you choose to pour into it."

"It covers it, you mean," said Finn. "It's an easy way of drowning out anyone you don't want, like Bain. Or Caswell? Tell me, if he's a card-carrying member of your red monkeys and you run them, that just about makes you the Shout already, doesn't it?"

"Not me, Rafferty," said Dando. "We all are. There'll be ten thousand of us soon. Big men, little men, birds too, and each one of us is the Shout."

"But it's handy for you that they'll still need someone to pull the strings, isn't it?"

Dando grinned. "There will be a difference," he said.

"What's that?"

"I mean that at least the men will know they're dealing with a muckshifter and not an office boy. I can handle every machine on this site as well as they can and they know it. I don't have to read the books. When was the last time you put your sticks down and drove a D.9, Rafferty?"

Finn looked across at the two giant tractors. "I was driving one of those jokers before you were . . . a twinkle in a Bulgarian's eye," he said.

Dando peered at him closely. "What are you getting at, Rafferty?"

"We all know how accomplished the Bulgarians are at muckshifting," said Finn. "Surely that's why you went there, wasn't it? To learn?"

The Welshman's eyes narrowed as he looked across to the clump of pines away to their right. "I'll show you what I've learned, Rafferty," he said quietly. "You see those trees? Well, they've got to come down, haven't they? Can't afford to have gash trunks rolling down into our nice, new pond, can we? The Forestry people are coming tomorrow but we can't wait quite that long, can we? So perhaps we'll give them a little bit of help."

Dando leapt onto the high caterpillar tracks of the D.9 and into the cab. Within seconds he had the giant tractor moving forward towards the line of trees.

Rafferty was standing beside the second of the D.9's when Dando's machine hit the first pine. The tree cracked apart with a loud snapping noise and toppled slowly beneath the tracks as the D.9 moved on to the next pair of pines in its path. Both surrendered at once, groaning as their roots were torn from the ground, the dozer arching above their prone trunks before continuing its path of destruction through the copse. Finn could see that the dozer was now clinically cutting a broad swathe through the whole wood. Only when the carnage was over and the D.9 turned to come back could he see the full effect of the most powerful bulldozer in the Clandy fleet.

Dando had left behind him a 16-foot parting in the forest, stretching for more than a hundred yards. The Irishman could see the pale sunlight pouring in through the lifeless gap, onto the corpses of the stricken trees.

As Dando returned Finn could see him smiling in the cab,

glorying in the instant power that the 48-ton dozer, with its pushing force of 50,000 feet pounds, was giving him. The dozer was only thirty yards away from him when he realised it was not going to stop.

He leapt on the tracks of the second D.9 and through the sliding doors of the cab seconds before the blade of Dando's machine struck, sending sparks flying above the steel tracks.

When Finn looked back he saw Dando had driven only a few yards and was swivelling the machine in a full circle to prepare for another run at him.

He glanced down quickly and pressed the starting button, decelerating with his right foot pedal, pushing the forward lever to the full three notches, giving the machine maximum throttle as it roared to life. Tugging at the right-hand slewing clutch he sent the vehicle scudding sideways just as Dando's machine came at him, cannoning off his rear towbar.

The deafening noise of both engines made him reach for the heavy metal ear protectors on the front panel. As he clasped them over his head he could hear Dando's voice shouting at him.

"That was just a warm-up, Rafferty. The next one's for you!"

For a moment Finn wondered where the voice was coming from. Then he realised it was being relayed through the back-to-back transmission, the "talkthrough" the Welshman had had installed in every piece of muckshifting equipment on site.

Looking up, he could see the red Clandy letters clearly on the side of Dando's tractor as it twisted round to face him yet again.

He strapped the black leather speaker across his mouth. "All right, Dando," he said quietly. "I can hear you now! There's no need to shout. There's only the two of us here."

"At the moment," said Dando, revving the big dozer and pushing it into third as the four-foot-high tracks bit into the ground, eating the distance between the two machines.

"You're a fool, Dando," called Finn. "That's £200,000 worth of tractor you've got under you."

"How much are you worth to me, Rafferty?" came the reply, as Dando's D.9 headed once again straight for him.

Finn flung his own forward lever into third, taking up the line of the oncoming machine. For a moment it seemed that both tractors would collide, until at the point of impact Dando slewed his machine sharply to the left, avoiding Finn's blade by a few inches.

"What's the matter, Dando?" yelled Finn. "Worrying about the Clandy hardware now it's yours?"

When Dando brought his machine round for the fourth time he saw that it was Rafferty who was waiting for him fifty yards down the clearing.

"You made a mistake, Dando!" roared Finn. "The rest don't scare you! They need you! You've soup-mixed 'em. You've given 'em so much they won't lift a finger to you because they've got too much to lose. I've got nothing to lose, Dando. We're the ones to worry about now."

Finn depressed the decelerator and calmly pushed the forward lever up through first, second and third, throttling forward in noisy snorts until the big D.9 was moving at top speed.

There were barely twenty yards of daylight between the two tractors when Finn took the hydraulic lever in his right hand and slowly raised the heavy steel blade eight feet into the air where it jutted menacingly from its trunnion arms.

Dando just had time to lift his own blade when the Irishman's dozer piled into him, sending a spray of bright white sparks over his cab as the two steel scimitars crashed against each other. The force of the impact threw Dando to the floor of the cab, his machine recoiling on its tracks, pursued by Finn's searching blade.

"All right, if you want games, Dando, let's try a few!" bawled Finn, releasing the hydraulic lever with a sudden movement which sent the blade crashing down on the metal driving sprocket at the rear. Watching Dando struggle to get back into his seat, Finn broke off the action. But it was only a brief gesture.

Dando's voice was taunting him over the transmission. "Come on, coalie! What are you waiting for?"

"I'm not," bawled Finn, lashing his D.9 into top gear before charging like a war tank. Just when it seemed he would slice through the Welshman's cab, Dando suddenly slewed his tracks at a right angle, crushing his blade on to the right trunnion arm of Finn's dozer, snapping the steel elbow at the joint. Immediately the useless blade slumped down on one side, clattering limply against the tracks of Dando's machine.

When Dando looked across at Finn's cab he saw the Irishman was no longer in the seat. He leaned forward, craning his neck to search for him among the twisted interlocking blades. Only for a brief instant did he see the fist which hit him, sending him sprawling across the cab as the Irishman came hurtling at him through the door.

Before he had time to recover, Finn's hand was at his shirt hauling him up and striking him again. The force of the effort threw Finn back across the seat. He felt his hair being grabbed violently as Dando swung his face against the forward lever arm.

Wrenching himself free Finn reached for the Welshman's waist, grappling with him until a fist came up almost from the floor into his face, pitching him back towards the open door.

Dando was on top of him in an instant, his hands around his neck, forcing his head out of the cab and down towards the churning caterpillar tracks.

The two bulldozers were now locked together in a test of strength which was sending both of them spinning round, gouging out a deep, circular hollow in the dry ground.

As Dando raised his fist like a hammer above him Finn caught it and hauled the Welshman over his head and down onto the moving tracks.

When he looked down he saw that Dando had been stunned by the fall and was being carried by the belt towards the advancing tracks of the second dozer. At the last moment Finn flung himself down, snatching the limp body from the grating metal.

They were five yards clear of the duelling machines when Dando opened his eyes and lifted himself to his knees. As the Irishman's face came into focus he raised his elbow, crashing it against Finn's cheekbone. Finn scrambled to his feet, ducking only just in time as another raking fist passed over his shoulder.

"You bastard!" he said, lifting his hand to his cheek and whistling slowly to himself as he stared down at the blood on his fingers. "Look at it! Tosspot!" Dando looked down as Finn's hand came up, swiping across his face, sending him staggering backwards.

"All right, if this is how you want it, Dando, here's something from the others too," he yelled, sinking his fist into the Welshman's stomach. "That's from Jo!" As Dando doubled up the second blow burst against the bridge of his nose. "That's from Tully. And these are from John! . . . Christopher! . . . Dando! . . . Tiffin!" bawled the Irishman, slapping Dando's head from side to side with every name. "He hasn't grown fists yet, lucky for you! And this one is from Dancer!" he yelled again, ramming a fist into Dando's eye, feeling the blood spurt against his knuckles even before he had time to withdraw them. "Chauncy Bawn coming up," he shouted, aiming a straight left at the reeling Welshman's jaw. "He's a gentleman, Chauncy!" The last punch hit Dando in the soft of his stomach just above the groin, felling him to his knees as a sudden gush of blood came up from his mouth. "That was from Liam The Liar!" snarled Finn. "He isn't!"

When Dando raised his head his eyes were dark slits between the swollen flesh. "You can't stop us, Rafferty," he said, trying to smile. "You know that, don't you? We've got Dolans, more than half of A.R.L. and we're close to taking McGibbons! We're growing, you see, because we've got a reason to! Only people like you stay the same. You're dead, Rafferty! All your sort are!"

Finn glared down at him. "You don't have to tell me where you poison's working. You send some of your monkeys out to breed. And ditch the rest because they won't. And either way you win. Why did you keep me, Dando?"

Dando wiped his arm across his lips and spat another stream of blood onto the ground. "Clandy wants you here till the tub's filled," he said.

"It's you and Clandy running things now, is it?" said Rafferty, breathing heavily. "What happened to Caswell? Have you got a nice sunny isle picked out for him next?" You're a bloody Goth, Dando, a barbarian breathing down the boss's neck until you decide to take him over."

"You know nothing about me, Rafferty."

Finn leaned forward and pulled the Welshman's head up by his thick, black hair. "The only thing I don't know about you, Dando," he said, his jaw trembling, "is what she saw in you."

"Who?"

"Christ, you've even forgotten her name. Mallowry. Mrs. Mallowry Bain, the wife of the feller who used to be the Shout, remember? The pair of you seemed to have had that worked out pretty well, didn't you? How did you do it, Dando?"

"Perhaps she just fancied me," said Dando, smiling through his raw, bleeding lips.

Finn brought his fist up to hit him but changed his mind and pushed the Welshman's head down, watching him slowly slump helplessly to the ground. "The truth, Dando! None of your bloody Welsh lies! Give me the truth!"

Dando raised himself up on one elbow. "You always wanted the truth, Rafferty," he gasped. "That's your weakness. All right then, I'll give it to you. She wanted a winner, Rafferty! Not someone like you! Just look at yourself, gloating like a big kid because you think you've won a fight. You charge on, head down, living from day to day as though you invented freedom. You had the drive, boyo, but you never had the ambition and without it all you've got is useless blather. That's why your sort always lose. Anyway, the fight's not over."

"What do you mean?" said Finn, glaring down at him.

"Look behind you, Rafferty."

Finn swung round and saw that the abandoned D.9s were still locked together in battle, their tracks slipping in the churned-up ground as they fought to the death. But it was already obvious that Finn's tractor, weakened by the fractured trunnion arm, was getting the worst of the struggle. Inch by inch Dando's tractor was pushing it back until it was poised on the rim of the plateau, threatening to plunge at any moment into the yawning crater.

Rushing forward, Finn sprang on the tracks of Dando's D.9 and dived head-first through the open door of the cab.

The giant tractor shuddered to a halt. But the Irishman had not been in time to save his own machine. Giving one final token shove against the immovable bulk in front of it, the dozer reeled back from its efforts and slowly slid into the gorge.

Finn and Dando reached the edge of the clearing just as the dozer hit the water three-hundred feet below them, parting the still surface of the lake, sending ripples dancing out towards the Faunes on the opposite shore.

"How do we explain that little toy going when they check the plant list, then?" said Finn.

"We, Rafferty?" said Dando. "You were doing the driving. But don't shit yourself, as Form 190 should clear it. Especially since I sign them all."

"What are they for?"

"Damage by vandals."

Finn shook the hair out of his eyes. "You've got a form for just about everything, haven't you, Dando? Mind you, this one doesn't surprise me. You can put it down to family."

Dando ran the back of his hand across his bloody face, leaving a broad, white streak where it had been.

"No, Rafferty," he smiled, "you've got the wrong mob. I'm a Goth. Remember?"

The man and the boy walked side by side down the slope, their gumboots leaving a trail of deep indentations in the snow stretching back to the coal road where the yellow Land Rover was parked.

They stopped, staring out together across the black lake which had immersed the valley to within fifty feet of the white rim of the Corbar Dam. To their left the dam, majestic, imposing, seemed to be rising out of the water in a gesture of aloof defiance. Ahead of them, even through the heavy drizzle pitting the surface of the reservoir, they could see over to Todholes where, as though by divine insistance, the waters had halted just below the stubby, stone tower of St. Cuddy's.

"There you are, then, Donald," said Finn, turning to the boy, "she's ready."

"You filled her in the end, then?"

Finn pulled his cord cap closer to his eyes and winked at him. "To be honest, I had a wee bit of help from the fellow upstairs. It's rained buckets here for a good two months. Snow too. Mind you, I did manage to sniff out a good fourteen aquafers and a string of streams with the old sticks. And we borrowed a few gallons from Ullswater. These things work both ways, you know."

Despite the rain, Donald had the hood down behind his blue anorak. "You must be very pleased with yourself, Finn," he said.

"Let's say there's a good few more people who are going to be even more pleased when this stuff starts flowing," said Finn. "Even your college mates down in Hampshire. Just think, in a couple of weeks' time, when you all get back, you could be dousing yourself in the shower and flushing out your evil thoughts with Corbar water. What do you make of our wee dam, then?"

Donald glanced up at the great white wall. "It's a bit like a castle," he said. "It looks as if it's come here expecting a fight."

The Irishman laughed. "She's a fighter all right and she'll need to be! She's the biggest competitor against nature we've ever built. They had to weigh up everything that could be thrown up against her, water, wind, waves, the lot, and she'll hold them all, they reckon." He looked into Donald's face. "You're not so sure about her, then? I thought youngsters always went in for the forts?"

The boy screwed up his face. "No, she looks strong enough all right. . . ."

"What then?"

"It's just that . . . well, everything used to fit in this place. Even the houses and farms they built seemed to look as if they'd sort of grown here."

"And this doesn't?"

"Well, it is a bit arrogant-looking, isn't it? As if it's saying 'I'm here and to hell with you'."

"Donald Dacre," said Finn loudly. "Here I am dripping in the rain, furthering this great college engineering career of yours and you're rabbitting on like an old conservationist! You're not aiming to be a bloody rebel, are you? And another thing, you're cursing again."

When Donald looked up at Finn he expected to see him angry but instead he saw the Irishman's eyes were twinkling. "No, it's impressive enough, Finn. Beautiful in a way. But it couldn't compete with seeing the first sun come up over the backs of a cut of sheep. When I was young there were so many sheep here that if you closed your eyes, they looked like a sea themselves."

Finn wrenched off his cap and scratched his head pointedly. "Fifteen years of age and he talks about when he was young!" he yelled. He suddenly looked across at the boy and snapped his fingers, "I've got it!" he said. "You've become a Stinky!"

"Yes I have," said Donald blushing.

"Well I'll be a monkey's eejit! And you with all the talk of building things. 'I want to be useful,' didn't you say?"

Donald grinned. "Farming's useful."

"So you've joined the wee Stinkies, then?" said Finn. "Christ, I should have had you smelt when you came in. Mind you, The Donald would have taken your hand on it. I think after you'd ganged up with me, he had you marked down for some sort of future water hooligan, going round floodin' folk's gardens before they could reach for a crop."

"I'd be happier digging with them," said the boy.

"Just a minute now," said Finn. "I suppose with you being the big farmin' man you'll be saying we were all wrong to toss the old sheep out and bring in the tub?"

"Not at all," said Donald. "We were wrong too."

"How's that, son?"

"We were wrong to sit here for centuries and accept that this place was only fit for hill sheep. If the land was poor we should have given it something."

"Like what?"

"Shit," said Donald.

"What?" shouted Finn.

"Shit! Nitrate! What this valley always needed was cow muck, horse muck, pigshit, anything to jerk some life into it. We should have had herds of them up here, shitting knee-deep as far as the eye could see, getting the green up again. The buffalo would have been even better, but we lost them, didn't we? And when we'd got the soil breathing agin we could have packed this place so full of crops and cattle and sheep they wouldn't have let you near us with that thing."

"Hold on there!" gasped Finn, raising his hands. "Hold your whisht a minute!" He let out his breath quickly. "Christ, Donald, I'm glad you're not a fightin' man too!" Donald smiled and pushed aside the fringe of long, black hair across his forehead just enough for the Irishman to see the dark swelling over his left eye.

"Jesus," said Finn, grinning as he shook his head in disbelief.

"Augh, it's only a scratch sure," said the boy.

"I'd hate to be that feller's ward attendant," said Finn. "Please God you won't pick an argument with me."

"Finn . . ."

"Christ, he's going to," said Finn, tossing his head.

"Are there a lot of wells and streams and things?" asked Donald.

Finn sighed. "Now that I do know a bit about," he said. "The country's teeming with them. You only need to fart in some places and they'd come sprouting up."

"And can most people find them?"

"It's supposed to be a gift, but if you need 'em bad enough you can find 'em."

"Then why are you fussing around like a big wet nurse, bringing all this to us in a bowl and treating everybody as if they're helpless. Let 'em find their own wells. At least give them a chance to try to find more of what they need in life than they think they can. People used to look for their own wells, didn't they?"

When the boy looked up at the Irishman he saw that even though he was smiling his face suddenly looked quite old.

"They did too, boy," said Finn. "I used to know a feller like that myself once." He glanced up at the sky, which was darkening again over the Faunes. "Look, it's cutting up a bit rough over there. We'd best get on up to that sheep-slaughtering castle of yours. I want you to meet a feller who's the king of that castle."

The rain was already turning the deep snow to slush as they started back up the slope to the coal road.

As the gathering wind bit into their faces Donald rubbed his fingers against his swollen eye. "Did you do a lot of fighting, Finn?" he said. "I mean when you were as old as me?"

Finn put his hand on the boy's shoulder and stared up towards the Land Rover. "Donald," he said, "I'm wondering if I was ever as old as you."

"Starkers she was," said Dando, smiling into the telephone on the polished oak desk. "Stark bol . . . just standing there without a stitch on her and with her hand on it. . . ."

Without removing the phone from his mouth he motioned the busty, bouffant-haired woman hovering in front of him to sit down.

"Are you there, boyo?" he said into the phone. "Well she just stood there and said 'It's a bit high up to eat grass so you'd better feed it, . . . FEED IT!" he repeated, raising his voice. As he listened to the caller, Dando's face broke into a thin smile. "What do you think, boyo?" he said. "Anyway, I'll call you back, we've got a dam to open."

He put down the phone, winked at Ken Challis who was in the chair beside him and turned to the woman.

"What's your job, then, Mrs. Collins?" he asked, smiling up at her.

"I'm second cook in the canteen," she said. "You should know that, you've seen me in there often enough."

His smile froze. "Well I'm promoting you, Mrs. Collins. . . ."

As the light on the desk intercom began flashing red Dando flicked up the switch impatiently. "Birmingham's been on again, Mr. Dando," said a girl's voice. "They are rather concerned. . . ."

"Not now! No calls!"" snapped Dando, switching off before turning to the cook. "Yes, you're going up in the world, Mrs. Collins. You're going to be the Queen of England. Only for a few hours, of course. We need you to stand in for her at tomorrow's dress rehearsal for the opening."

"What do I have to do?" she asked.

"Not much. Just be here at ten sharp with your scissors. You'll be up in the observation tower next to Gans, who'll be standing with his hands behind his back trying to look useful. O.K., you can go."

"What do I wear?"

Dando grinned at her. "Either a tiara or a headscarf, whichever's handier," he said. "And if the weather stays like this, you'd better bring a mac too."

As the woman left the room he leaned over and spoke into the intercom again. "Send in the other one."

"Ah, Mrs. Gray," said Dando as a straight-haired, heavily built woman stamped across the red patterned carpet to his desk. "Now you're going to be our Mrs. Sally Gwillym at tomorrow's dress rehearsal, aren't you? Have you thought about it? Never expected to be Prime Minister, did you?"

The woman put down her shopping bag. "Well, I'm not really sure," she said. "I've always voted Conservative myself, you see."

"Mrs. Gray," said Dando tetchily, "There's an extra four hours on your time-sheet which says you're going to be Sally The Cat tomorrow, O.K.? . . ."

As the red light on the panel flashed again Dando depressed the switch.

"There's a call. . . ."

"I told you. . . ."

It's Kinmannack, Mr. Dando."

"Oh," said Dando, winking across at the bearded R.E. "This should be interesting. All right, put them on. Through the phone!"

Dando slowly tapped his fingers on the desk-top, raising his eyebrows and smiling occasionally as he listened through the yellow telephone. "O.K.," he said finally. "Tell him we're very happy with him, will you? And another thing. Tell him we appreciate all he's done for us, won't you?"

He put down the phone and turned to Ken Challis. "Kinmannack will be ready in two days," he said. "They're linking up tomorrow, the rest is just routine testing."

"That's Caswell's patch, isn't it?" said Challis, sucking on his pipe. "Is it important?"

Dando grinned at him. "It's a power station in the north east of Scotland, if that's important," he said. "More important to us is that when Kinmannack links up, U.K.A.P. will have 18,000 miles of pipeline and waterways serving the whole country. And on Wednesday they'll all be waiting for us to switch on."

He looked up quickly at the large woman standing in front of him as though he had suddenly remembered she was still there.

"Oh yes, Mrs. Gwillym," he said, ". . . Mrs. Gray. Well, all you have to do is talk in a big, deep voice and look as if you could play flank forward for Neath and we'll expect you at ten. Right?"

The woman left the room as a tall, dark-haired man walked in.

"Yes, what do you want, Keen?" snapped Dando.

"Sir William says that if you're ready, Mr. Dando, he wants to go up to the tower now."

"Tell him O.K., Keen, I'm coming," said Dando, as he reached over to answer the intercom again.

"Birmingham's still worried," said the girl's voice. "They want to know what will happen to them if anything happens to us?"

"Tell 'em we'll build them a pier!" said Dando, switching off as he sprang to his feet.

Sir William Clandy was waiting in the back seat of the Rolls with a green and blue rug across his knees as Archbold ushered Dando inside the vehicle, leaving Challis at the door.

The gleaming beige Kingmaker glided down from the Clandy base, turning right into the Todholes entrance just as two muckshifters dragged the "No Entry" to one side to allow it through.

They were almost across the dam when Dando saw the Land Rover parked against the parapet with a man and a boy standing beside it.

For a moment the blond-haired man's eyes seemed to bore deeply into him. But as he passed the Irishman had turned his face as he stared with a look of resignation at Keen in the front seat.

"Is that the king?" said Donald as the Rolls passed them.

The raindrops fell around Finn's face as he shook his hair quickly. "Christ no," he said. "That's just a works outing. The real feller has a castle over his head, I told you."

He looked along the line of milecastles behind the boy's back. "Do you see all the fancy flags, then? It'll be like the League of Nations up here on Wednesday. There's your Stars and Stripes see, for Liederman's lot, the Union Jack, the old Saint Andrews, there look, to please the Scots Nats. And the Welsh dragon, Dando's dishrag. And Saint George fluttering after it. I don't know what the twelve hands are, gropin' each other."

"That's the new European flag," said Donald. "For the E.E.C. members."

Finn sniffed. "Well I suppose they've a right to crow a bit. They paid for most of them. They've shoved everything up except the Tricolour."

"The Irish flag, you mean?"

"That's the feller."

"Why don't they put that up, then?" said Donald. "Especially since most of you seem to be Irish."

"Donald," said Finn, frowning mischievously at him, "did you ever hear of a prospective English lord who went around with a Tricolour on his bonnet?"

He looked out to where the wind, freshening from the north, was rucking the surface of the lake into white-edged patterns.

"Mind you, if this lot keeps up," he said, "they'll be lucky even to have the poles up there by Wednesday."

Archbold brought the Rolls to a halt on the black tarmacced forecourt of the observation building.

As he walked back in a slow, measured pace to open the rear door for Clandy and Dando another car pulled up and a tall, beautiful woman came out from the taxi and stood watching them.

Despite the rain which was now dropping heavily, she was hatless, her long, black hair falling across the white collar of her raincoat, which was hanging loose around her elegantly tailored black catsuit.

"Mallowry my dear," said Sir William, smiling as he walked

forward with his arms outstretched. "How very nice to see you again."

She kissed him on the cheek. "You almost sound as if you never expected to see me again," she murmured.

"Nonsense my dear, you're always welcome, you know that," he said taking her arm. "You know Griff of course, don't you?"

"Mallowry," said Dando, nodding towards her.

Mallowry Bain glanced at him quickly before looking back at Clandy. "The last time I saw Mr. Dando he seemed to be looking for something. It seems as if he found it."

"Griff's the P.M. here now, Mallowry," said Sir William.

"So I gathered," she said, staring at Dando, who was wearing a black Crombie overcoat and standing slightly ahead of Keen, Fasman and Gans. "And he's looking well on it already."

"How's Gus, my dear?"

Mallowry shook her head. "Not quite as well as Mr. Dando, I'm afraid," she said.

"Yes, well er . . ."' said Clandy, moving her firmly towards the building. "You won't have seen our little masterpiece yet, will you? You must come and look inside. It really is a beautiful view up here, you know."

As they passed between the tubs of yellow chrysanthemums in front of the tall, sliding doors he glanced back at his chauffeur. "Archbold, see to Mrs. Bain's taxi driver will you? You didn't bring him all the way from Gran Canaria I hope, my dear? You know what the accountants are like these days."

"That's very kind of you, Sir William," said Mallowry as the electronically operated doors parted in front of them. "No, it was only Haltbriggin."

Keen followed them as the three crossed the flag-bedecked foyer with its tubs and hanging baskets of flowers, before stepping down into the large, semicircular observation room. On either side of the white balustrade the flags of Britain, America and Europe were fluttering in their stands. Between them the line of bunting was already soaked with rain.

"It's like the royal box at the theatre," said Mallowry, looking round admiringly.

"That's exactly what it will be on Wednesday, my dear," chuckled Clandy. "The only problem is we're having to try to squeeze half Europe in here as well."

As they walked down to the balustrade, Mallowry saw there were only two other people in the box: Liederman in his familiar white safari suit and Ken Challis, who both stood up to greet her.

Mallowry gasped with surprise as she looked down on the dam a thousand feet below on the swirling water.

"It affects everybody like that, Mallowry," said Liederman. "It really is staggering, isn't it? I think even Griff realises now why I wanted this baby to be something else. Doesn't that Hadrian stone really get you?"

"It is rather imposing, isn't it?" she said, turning to him.

"No other dam in history was ever seen in this way, so it 'had to be special," said Liederman.

Mallowry looked across at Sir William, who was gazing across the dam through a large pair of binoculars. "So you finally finished it then, Sir William?"

He smiled at her. "We finished it, my dear, not me. I'm only the old office boy," he said. "Liederman, Griff here, Mr. Challis the R.E. They did it. It was a team job."

Down on the dam close to the Calcherside entrance Mallowry thought she could see two figures standing against the stone parapet, staring across the lake.

"Is there anybody working down there at the moment?" she asked.

Dando looked across at her. "No, she's all ready for unwrapping. There's only one of the muckshifters down there showing a college kid around."

"Do you think I might borrow your binoculars for a moment, Sir William, just to see a few of the finer details?"

"Certainly you may, my dear," he said, looping the strap from over his head and passing them to her, watching her as she trained the glasses on the white wall.

Raising the binoculars until she had the two figures clearly in focus, she saw the boy was sitting on the stone parapet, his legs dangling over the water which was pushing gently against the wall beneath him. The man was beside him, grinning at him, his yellow hair flattened too his head by the falling rain.

"You like it, don't you?" said Liederman, leaning towards her.

She smiled at him as she handed back the glasses. "Yes," she said, "I like it very much."

When she looked up she saw that Dando was smiling too. "I'm sorry Gus wasn't well enough to come and see all this," he said.

"I don't think he really wanted to," said Mallowry.

"Oh, I think Gus would always want to come and see us if he was able to," said Sir William.

Mallowry stared down the row of faces without looking at any of them. "Gus died two weeks ago," she said.

"My dear Mallowry," said Clandy, putting his hand on her arm, "I am sorry. Why diddn't you let us know?"

"Oh, don't worry, he thought about you," she said. "He thought about all of you. In fact you were the last people he must have had on his mind. Just before he died, you see, he wrote five words on the back of an envelope. It was the only time in his life I've ever known him to write on the back of an envelope. He wasn't the type."

"What did he say, my dear?" said Clandy gently.

"He said 'Don't tell them at Corbar.' So you see he was probably even thinking about you too, Griff."

Dando grimaced and made no reply. It was Liederman who spoke. "Then it wasn't natural? Gus I mean," he said hesitantly.

Mallowry turned to him slowly. "It was about as natural as that toy fort you've stuck up down there, Bob."

"My poor dear," said Clandy. "I suppose it's too early for you to know what you're going to do now?"

When he looked into Mallowry's face he was surprised to see that she was smiling. "No it isn't, Sir William," she said. "I know exactly what I'm going to do. And this time I don't care who knows it."

"What plans have you made, my dear?" he asked, his voice softening.

As she turned to him, the wind gusting up from the great lake caught her hair, blowing it out dramatically behind her. "I'm coming back, Sir William," she said. "I'm coming back to one of your muckshifters. He doesn't know it yet but I'm here anyway, if he'll have me. You see, I'm going to marry him. Or if he prefers it, I'm going to live with him. But either way I'm going to be with him."

Sir William Clandy's mouth, which had remained open all the time Mallowry had been speaking, closed as she finished. "Well goodness me, my dear," he said, his eyes twinkling, "May I ask which one it is?"

"You can indeed," said Mallowry, laughing as she looked down at the dam, "it's that one."

She had scarcely got the words out before five pairs of eyes swooped down to the dam, where only the Clandy chairman with his binoculars was able to pick out a large blond Irishman, who had his arms raised wide as though he was telling a boy about the big fish he had caught.

"And this great pike, you see," said Finn, spreading his arms as far as he could reach. "It came puffin' and snortin' up from the deep of the pond to get after this ball of meat."

He flung his arm over the parapet pointing to the bubbles rising against the side of the draw-off tower to the right.

"Just like that gush of air bursting up from the draw valve there," he said. "Anyway, up it came, grasped the meat in its jaws and fixed itself on Wingy's hook. Now do you know how long it takes to haul a strugglin' pike ashore? It took him two hours. Playing with it and coaxing it, until the thing was at his boot ends, three foot long and weighing a stone or more!"

"Did he eat it then?" asked Donald, staring down at the bubbles.

"He did not!" said Finn. "Nobody eats pike and that's the point of the story. The pike was already being eaten you see. Alive. Because when Wingy was putting his toecap to the creature's head he saw something moving in the fish's side. And do you know what it was? It was a vole! Inside the fish's stomach! And it was alive, eatin' its way out. He must have snapped it up from the bank a good bit earlier."

Donald winced. "That must have been painful," he said.

Finn shook his head quickly. "That's just it. It can't have been. Because if you had a big-toothed rat in your stomach you wouldn't carry on eating your breakfast as if nothing was happening. And Wingy, you see, used it ever after as proof that fish feel no pain. It's on account of them being cold-blooded, and even if they had any nerve endings they'd all be covered by the scales."

"They have pike in the church, you know," said Donald. "Up at St. Cuddy's."

Finn looked up in surprise. "They do not?" he said. "In a tank you mean?"

"No," said the boy, "In one of the windows. Lucies they call them."

"Ah, the silver lucies!" said Finn.

"But it's funny, Finn. . ."

"How do you mean?"

"Having fish in a church."

The Irishman scratched at his cheek. "Perhaps it's even stranger to the fish," he said. "I mean them being up there and having a church built over them. The fish were there first you see, like your farmers. Did you know we used to go around with fish in our coats long before anyone thought of hanging a cross round their necks?"

"And you think fish never feel any pain like we do, Finn?" said Donald.

"I think there's a chance," said Finn. "Do you know, I've heard say that if you can get down deep enough in the ocean you can hear the whales singing. Now those fellers wouldn't be celebratin' if there was nothing to sing about, would they?"

He gave the boy an enthusiastic shove towards the Land Rover. "Now let's show you the Queen's tower. It's the one she's going to visit on Wednesday, so I expect they'll have the flags flying there, inside and out."

Finn pulled up outside the second milecastle and led Donny through the narrow, arched doorway into a small room where the lion flag of Hesters and the Union Jack had been set into a circular glass table. Six royal blue armchairs were arranged around it, one of them with a white crochetted cover on its back, emblazoned with the yellow initials E.R. Although the walls were entirely faced in pine panelling, there was hardly a space where photographs, drawings and plans of the dam had not been displayed in their shiny gilt frames. As they stared round the room, a tall, bulky man came slowly down the circular stone stairway.

"Goose," shouted Finn, rushing forward. "What rank have they given you now?"

"I'm a castel . . . something or other," he muttered. "Looking after the place for a week."

"Castellan, eh?" said Finn smiling. "Very fancy. That's a move up anyway. Donald!" he cried, pushing the boy forward. "This is the king of the castle I promised you. Kings go back so far in this feller's family he's forgotten a good half of them."

The Goose shook Donald's hand. "I'm just the caretaker, lad, really, until all the fuss is over," he said. "They didn't want to risk anyone breaking in and messing up the place until she sees it."

"Terrorists, you mean?" said Finn. "Christ, they would need to pack a punch to get past that stomach of yours. The Donald's come to look at your castle. He fancies it for a shippon when we've finished with it."

The Goose nodded to the boy. "There's not much to show you apart from all the stuff down here, but there's a tidy view from the top."

"They've given you some home comforts," said Finn, spotting the paraffin stove beside the table.

"You need it up here some nights," said The Goose.

He led them up the circular stairs where they passed three rooms on the way before stepping out into an open rectangular turret surrounded by a three-foot wall of castellated stone.

Finn hauled up the high collar of his donkey jacket as he looked out along the reservoir. "Weather's closing in, Goose," he said. "It's coming down quite fierce now."

" 'Twould loss you out there," said The Goose. "It's just like a wind tunnel. It comes through that gorge and really whips up the water some days. If it keeps up like this I reckon we'll get waves up here just like the west of Ireland."

"You're still gripping on, then, Goose?" said Finn, looking into the old muckshifter's face. "To the old ways? Dando hasn't got at you yet?"

"Dando's got at me all right," he said tiredly, "he hasn't got me and won't. I think we're about the last, Finn, aren't we, you and me?"

Finn nodded as The Goose turned quickly to the boy. "Well have you seen enough, then, son? There's no sense in getting drowned."

Finn held up his hand. "There's one thing I want him to see while we're up here. Look down there, boy," he said, pointing to where a round, blackened piece of metal was fixed to the Hadrian stonework ten feet down the tower.

"What is it?" said Donald, peering down.

"It's the bird of Rome, boy!" said Finn, looking intently into Donald's rain-streaked face. "The eagle! It was left in Corbar by the fellers who fought on the Roman wall."

"Who put it down there, then?"

Finn smiled. "Someone who thought that while we're busy celebrating our Western Empire we shouldn't lose touch with those who built the first," said Finn, gazing out through the swirling rain towards the Calcherside entrance to the dam.

"It's like a peel tower up here, isn't it?" said Donald. "The sort of place where they used to stand on the top and pour boiling oil on their attackers."

Without taking his eyes from Calcherside, Finn said, "with The Goose boy, it's more likely to be chip fat."

Suddenly, something he saw high up near the mulberry bushes below the coal road made him swing round to face The Goose. "Can I have your eyeglasses a minute?" he asked.

The Goose handed him the binoculars. "It's cutting up a bit rough now," he said. "It's brewing up like a sea storm."

"I wasn't looking at the water," said Finn, scanning the bushes in the distance. "Anyway, that open valve bubbling up down there isn't helping any."

"What open valve?" said The Goose, giving him a curious look. "They've opened nothing on here today."

Finn pulled the binoculars away from his face. "Sure there is," he said. "Over at the draw-off tower there. It's bursting up like a drain."

"Look, I'd best be getting on the blower to base," said The Goose quickly. "There's no activity due here today."

As the caretaker turned to go down the stairs, Finn raised the glasses again and focused sharply on the slope below Calcherside. He could see it clearly now, a small orange kagoul bobbing in and out of the mulberry bushes. He could even pick out the sparse, untidy grey hair of the man wearing it, his face pale yet urgent as he stared ahead, certain of where he was going. Even as Finn watched, the man vanished as a bush appeared to grow from the spot where he was standing.

Finn let the glasses fall to his chest as he clutched his forehead with both hands. "Christ!" he yelled. "What's he done, the bloody old fool!" He caught the boy by the arm. "Look son, I don't know what's going on but there's something wrong. Now listen. Go to The Goose, tell him I'll be away a few minutes and tell him to jump in his Landy and get both of yourselves out of here! O.K.?"

What's happened, Finn?" said Donald.

"Don't ask because I don't know myself," he said. "There's plenty of time but just get clear of here, both of you. Understand?"

The Irishman leapt onto the stone steps, gathering speed as he rushed down the circular stairs and out onto the roadway, not stopping until he was in the driving seat of the Land Rover hurling the gearstick into first.

Spray was already splashing up from the wall against his windscreen as he drove furiously along the dam, slewing the vehicle left up onto the coal road.

After travelling only twenty-five yards he swerved off the road heading towards the reservoir, taking an erratic zig-zag course down the hill. With each change of direction the rear wheels of the truck skidded on the wet grass as he plunged lower, aiming the vehicle between the bushes in his path. Finally he stopped, jumped down from the cab and ran towards the mulberry where he had last seen the man in the kagoul.

The shrub came away easily in his hands. When he looked down there was a small two foot square hole in the ground where the bush had been.

Finn slithered down, feeling the ground firm beneath his boots only when he had lowered himself a good four feet inside the hole. As he dropped to his knees he could see the beginnings of a tunnel falling away to his left. Sliding forward on the seat of his jeans he steadied himself by digging into the slimy earth with the heels of his boots.

After a few yards the tunnel levelled out, and although it was pitch dark around him he could now stand up without any difficulty. Even the ground seemed more solid as he kicked at it with his metal toecap, and he realised he was standing on stone slabs which were descending in a regular pattern of steps.

He could now hear the water clearly. When he had first entered the hole it had been a strange, muffled, swishing sound. But now he seemed to feel it all around him, rushing downwards to a point below him in the distance where a faint bluish light could be seen at the end of the tunnel.

The large, uneven stone steps beneath his feet were now plainly visible as he hurried towards the light along a short stretch of flattened rock which ended in a pair of six foot high stone pillars which had more steps leading down from them.

Beyond the pillars Finn found himself gazing disbelievingly into a large chamber where he saw eight more stone pillars set in two rows of four. Even through the jiffling surface of the pool which covered the entire floor as water cascaded down from the ceiling, he could see the vivid reds and blues of the mosaic tiles beneath. For a moment he felt as though the light in the temple was flooding up from the tiles themselves, so brilliant were the hearts and swastikas and dolphins gleaming up from the floor. But the only light was emerging from the torches burning in the hollowed-out sides of the stone altars on his left.

Curran was at the far end of the chamber. He was kneeling in a foot of water, staring up at a square stone plinth on which had been placed the white carrara marble head of a woman.

Water was streaming down the perfect, regular lines of her face from a large, gaping hole in the wall above her, where more sounds of water could be heard rushing along the back of the chamber.

"You bloody little fool!" shouted Finn in an angry, despairing voice. "You've done for us all!"

When Curran looked up there was no sign of surprise in his grey, tired face. Instead his eyes had a strange light in them as he reached out the palm of his hand towards the marble bust. "I found her, Finn," he said quietly. "I told you I'd find her."

He got up slowly and walked towards him, wading through clear water which seemed to dance around his feet. "She's yours too, Finn," he said, smiling. "You helped me to find her."

"Christ, I had nothing to do with this bloody madness, Curran!" yelled the Irishman. "Do you know where we are?"

Curran smiled again, a controlled, unconcerned smile. "It's the temple of Duturna," he said. "Remember the Dutton, Finn? The stream I couldn't find because they diverted it with a plastic pipe? Well, it came back, you see, back to its original course, the same spot it must have been when the Roman legionaries who built this place found it."

He started shuffling back to the marble bust. "Look, come over here, Finn," he beckoned, reading the Roman letters in the centre of the plinth as if he knew them by heart. " 'DVTVRNA – PRO SUO AMORE.' 'Duturna,' it says, 'For her love.' Jupiter himself made her a goddess, you see, the goddess of the most precious commodity of life. Water. He did it for her love, you see, her love for him. . . ."

"Curran!" bawled Finn as though he was talking to a deaf man. "We're directly under the dam! This is Corbar water coming through your roof, and as for that mountain torrent back there, God knows how much of that there is heaped up under the foundations!"

"Oh, we're quite safe in here," said Curran with a distant look in his eyes. "It's a cave temple you see, carved into the rock like the Mithraic temples the legionaries found in Persia. There must have been a landslide in the valley soon after it was built, which sealed up the entrance and preserved it. It was as though the valley wanted it to survive as a place of secret worship."

"So this is where you were making for that day when I thought I spotted you up here?"

Curran nodded. "That was the closest I came to losing her," he said. "The only other person who could have stopped me was the first Shout."

"Bain?"

"Yes, Bain. If Gus had had his grout curtain, as he wanted to do, this place would have been pumped full of concrete in a matter of seconds, but perhaps it was all meant to happen this way."

Finn suddenly took hold of the man, shaking him violently by the shoulders. "Listen to me, Curran! Get out! Get out with me now! There isn't much time!"

When he released him he realised Curran was completely unmoved.

"Finbar," he said gently. "My good friend. Do you really believe I could leave now? She belongs here, you see. And besides, I've nowhere special to go."

The rising water was now two feet deep around his legs as Finn waded over the floor of the temple back to the tall pillars at the entrance.

When he looked back for the last time he saw that Curran had knelt down into the water again, facing the marble goddess with his hands cradled against his chin.

"For Christ's sake, Curran, come with me! Now!" he yelled. "There's no bloody time!"

Even after Finn's feet could be heard racing back up the stone steps Curran's face was at peace.

"You go, Finn," he said softly. "You have all the time in the world. You've got sixty million years of it."

When Finn's Land Rover screeched to a halt on the dam road, another Land Rover was parked in a pool of water beside the wall.

Donald and The Goose were staring down into the lake, which seemed to be trying to reach up and grasp them as it buffeted against the dam.

"They don't know what the hell it is, Finn!" shouted The Goose. "But they're getting a bit jumpy about it up there. Look at those waves building up! I told 'em we'd get waves if it cut up rough."

"Look, Goose," snapped Finn. "There's no time to explain. Just get the lad into that Landy and get to hell out of here!"

He bundled the boy towards The Goose's vehicle, hurling him into the passenger seat as the old muckshifter hobbled round to the other side.

"Where did you go to, Finn?" he said.

"I went to see a feller."

"What did you find out?"

"That Hadrian was right," said Finn, spitting into the road. "We're not ready yet. There's still too much stirring in the roots to put a uniform on this place."

"You coming too, Finn?" said The Goose as he started up the engine.

"Not yet," said Finn. "Drive like hell up to the tower. It's the safest place for miles. I'll follow you later. There's something I must do first. It won't take long."

"Be sharp, then," said Goose, leaning out of the open window. "By the way, Finn?"

When Finn looked up, The Goose was holding out a bottle of

champagne and grinning at him. "I rescued this feller. Just in case the queen woman doesn't get to opening it on Wednesday."

Finn shook his head and blew out fiercely. "Christ Goose, the future's not what it used to be!"

He waited until they moved off before jumping into his own Land Rover and headed through the pelting rain to the show castle.

The oak-panelled door was locked when he tried the handle. He scowled for a moment, before taking five paces back and rushed it with his shoulder, bursting it open with a loud, splintering sound. Pushing past the blue chairs he ran up the circular stairway and disappeared just as one of the chairs toppled slowly down against The Goose's paraffin heater.

When he broke through onto the open turret he began searching around frantically before wrenching open a door and emerging, carrying a coil of rope.

Breathing heavily he tied a large double loop on one end of the rope, playing the other end around his waist before knotting it tightly against him.

He slipped the loops over one of the jutting merlons and launched himself backwards, digging his boots against the outside of the wall as he lowered himself down on the rope.

When he was ten feet down the wall he paused, arching his back out as he swung on the rope, watching the black shield in front of him.

Reaching forward he ripped the shield from the wall, stuffed it inside his blue denim shirt and hauled himself back up to the parapet.

Smoke was already pouring through the doorway as he leapt onto the stairs. He ran down the steps, choking as the smoke swirled up from the lower floors.

When he reached the ground the room was a mass of flames. Fire was licking up the pinewood walls. The flagpoles were lying charred and smouldering across the blazing chairs. Clutching the eagle to his chest he ran through the flames and out into the dark, roaring air.

He had gone barely five-hundred yards in the Land Rover when he heard an enormous, sickening crack. With a deep shudder the road ahead of him collapsed, sending the waves jetting into towering spurts as they swooped through the sudden opening.

When Finn pulled up there was a thirty-foot gap yawning across the road, through which a sea shrieked as it came seeking its freedom.

Beyond he could see the outline of the arch of the first milecastle above the jagged edges of the collapsed wall. There were two figures in the centre of the arch, their arms thrusting the air, pushing him back.

"Christ, are you buggers still here?" he bawled. "Get out! Now!"

"Get back, Finn!" yelled The Goose. "Go back over Todholes. You'll never get through this stuff."

As Finn looked back there was a loud explosion as the royal milecastle, with red tongues of fire spurting from its windows, slumped across the road, settling into a wall of flame.

"Go back to where?" said Finn.

"Don't mind yourself," yelled The Goose. "We'll get you out, if there's a rope or something."

"That was the rope."

The waves pounding across the parapet were almost obliterating Finn's face as he cupped his hands and shouted across the gap. "Can you hear me, Goose?"

The Goose's face appeared again between the arch. "I'm here."

"Listen then, Goose!" called Finn, sweeping his wet blond hair from his eyes. "There's nothing you can do here! Get the boy safe! Get him up to the tower while there's still time. Is he there with you?"

"Yes, he's here, Finn," said The Goose, bringing the boy forward.

"Is that you, Donald?" bawled Finn, searching for his face through the spray.

"I'm here, Finn," Donald shouted.

"Well listen, son, I've got something for you."

He flung the shield across the gap, watching as the boy caught it easily.

"That's it, catch the bird, boy!" shouted Finn. "Nail it to your farmhouse door and don't join anything unless it's a fair fight! Do you hear me? With that feller in your hand you might even win the world back. Are you still there, boy?"

"Yes, I'm still here, Finn."

Finn smiled as the boy's face suddenly appeared again, peering at him urgently through the spray. "Then listen well, son!" he yelled through his cupped hands. "This is important! I want you to go up there, to that big ashtray and talk to those tall people up there! And when they ask you who lost the big dam of Corbar for us, boy, you tell them! Tell them Finn Rafferty said it sank for the want of a grout curtain and he was never a man to lie, will you tell 'em that?"

"I'll tell them, Finn," said Donald, the tears from his eyes joining the rain which was streaking down his cheeks.

As the boy turned away Finn saw The Goose staring at him helplessly across the chasm.

"There must be something I can do, Finn, surely to Christ?" he shouted.

"There is too!"

"What's that?"

"Throw me the bottle, will you?"

For a moment The Goose disappeared behind the wall of spray, reappearing with the champagne in his hand. "Here it comes," he said, tossing the bottle across the gap, watching as Finn plucked it out of the air.

"One more thing, Goose."

"What's that, Finn?"

"Look after the boy, Goose. It's him, you see! He's the one! He's your egg!"

When The Goose looked back at the Irishman he could see even through the driving rain that the tears were pouring down his face. "Finn," he yelled. "Your face . . . I can't do this. . . ."

Finn jerked his sleeve angrily across his cheek. "Shut up, Goose!" he yelled. "I'm just a bit rained up, that's all. Now get lost, the bloody pair of you! Get out! Or I'll scramble your brains."

As Finn watched them run to the Land Rover he was suddenly aware of a voice from high up in the observation tower.

"This is an emergency! I repeat! This is an emergency! Will all personnel evacuate from the vicinity of the dam!"

Finn glanced up to the tower where he knew The Slasher would be standing with his electric loudhailer. He would be wearing his fawn trenchcoat and the black eyepatch.

"Christ, Slasher," he muttered, "you could always be depended on for the useless words."

He bit on the hard cork stopper, spitting it out just in time to send it bursting from his thumb end as the champagne cascaded into the churning waters below.

"Are they all off now?" said Dando, craning forward as The Slasher scanned the dam with his field glasses.

"Goose and the kid have just left," he said, lowering the glasses. "Rafferty's still on the dam."

"I must go to him," said Mallowry, trying to push through the crowd of men who were pressing forward against the balustrade.

Dando turned sharply. "Get hold of her, someone," he said quickly. "Keen, can they get that helicopter up yet?"

Keen looked up from the telephone on the floor. "Not a chance, they say," he said. "They reckon they couldn't even send a pigeon out in that!"

"But they must!" cried Mallowry, breaking away from Gans. "I need him! I need him!"

She struggled as both Fasman and Gans caught hold of her.

"I want to be with him," she shouted, as the two men held her arms tightly to her side. When she saw her struggle was useless she threw her head back and let out a long, agonised scream, her face distorted, unrecognisable in her despair.

"She was so beautiful," said Liederman, looking down as the

Hadrian stone facing on each side of the widening gap began peeling away from the dam and plunging into the advancing water.

Mallowry's screaming went on until Dando stepped forward and slapped her hard against the cheek.

"Listen to me, Mallowry," he said. "There's nothing any of us can do. She's going any moment. Anyone who goes out of here now's a dead man."

The rain was lashing straight into the windscreen of the tiny Land Rover as it raced up the mountain road.

The Goose could see the lights of the observation tower as he swung the vehicle hard to the left to begin the final ascent.

"Soon be there now, boy," he said, ramming his boot hard down on the accelerator and reaching for his pipe.

He spotted the sheet of water lying in the hollow only a split second before the truck met it. He struggled to regain control of the steering-wheel, but the Land Rover was already planing helplessly into the grass verge.

The front offside wheel hit the winrow at sixty miles an hour, pitching the vehicle high into the air before it fell into the field and began plunging sideways down the slope.

Turning over and over as it slid into the dip, the Land Rover finally came to rest on its roof, its wheels spinning crazily above it.

Only when the moving wheels stopped did the silence begin. . . .

"Is he still there, Slasher?"

"He's there."

"What's he doing now?"

The Slasher dropped the field glasses against his chest and looked round with a puzzled look on his face. "I can't make it out," he said. "He seems to be drinking to us."

"Give me that speaker," said Dando, snatching the loudhailer from his hand.

Finn had taken his jacket off. He was leaning back against the parapet, holding up the champagne and pouring it over his lips, flinging his head back to allow the driving rain to wash it from his face.

The sudden noise from the tower made him lift his other hand to his forehead, brushing away the limp hair from his eyes before peering up to the tower.

"Rafferty? This is Dando speaking!" announced the voice. "Raise your hand if you can hear me!"

Finn took a swig from the bottle, bowed slightly and raised two fingers in the air.

Above him Dando leaned over to The Slasher for confirmation.

"He can hear you, Griff," he said.

"Now listen to me, Rafferty!" shouted Dando. "We have to know what happened! Can you tell us what went wrong?"

Finn grinned up at him and raised his hand about five feet from the ground. Suddenly he shot his finger in the air, pointing it up as far as he could reach.

"What's he trying to do?" snapped Dando.

"I think he means the boy, Griff," said The Slasher, "the college kid! He's trying to say the boy knows what went wrong!"

"Look, he's just moved! What's the bloody water witch doing now?"

The Slasher took a long look through the field glasses. "Yes, he's up on the wall now. He's standing on it. He seems to be trying to tell us something. . . ."

Finn was standing on the parapet barely ten feet from where the dam was breached. Beneath him the waves which The Goose had predicted were already hurling themselves against the stone wall.

"Yes, Shout," he said quietly, "the boy will tell you what went wrong. All the boys will tell us one day. When we're fit to listen."

The white ashtray in the sky was only a blur above him as he turned to face it.

"And if you had an ear in your hand, Griff Dando, instead of a stretched mouth, I'd tell you too," he shouted. "You're a big man, Dando! But you were never as big as what these people had going for them here! Before you came! There were giants here, Dando! Fellers big enough to stick their necks and their heads up through the sky if there was a chance of seein' a fresh look at things! And if they got singed on the sun a bit, there was no crying because it was their choice, their necks. But you, Dando, you took them and cut them down to size, you tried to make them all the same. All smaller than you. And just to make sure they were smaller than you, you built yourself a house on a bloody mountain. But you needn't have bothered, Dando. You don't have to worry any more about the ones you can see coming. From now on fellers like you have to worry about the other sort. The ones you can't see. That's where you made your mistake, boyo. You forgot about them, Dando, the ones who only look small. But the seed is there, boyo! The giant seed! That's still there! There's only one way for them to go, Dando, and that's up. And when those fellers start burrowing up after you, there's not a tower in the world tall enough for you! . . ."

The wave hit Finn with a force that pitched him down to the road, washing over him as he struggled to get to his feet.

As he did so he felt the dam shudder beneath him as though the currents were already forcing their way under the foundations.

He staggered back to the parapet as three chunks of Hadrian stone tore themselves away, taking the coping with them as they crashed down in the water.

Away to his right the first milecastle succumbed, collapsing into the chasm with an awesome groan.

Almost at once a new breach appeared on his left, as a huge section of the dam slid into the waves, carrying with it the blazing royal milecastle which lit up the darkening sky before it plunged five hundred feet down to the swirling lake behind him.

Finn was now on a stone island surrounded by two swollen channels of water which were already closing in, the tips of the waves creaming over the parapet, reaching for him, fingering him. . . .

"Mr. Dando? It's Lossiemouth! They say they can get a helicopter up! If we still want one."

"Christ, Keen, what is it? Supersonic?" said Dando. "All right, let 'em try!"

He glanced across at Sir William Clandy, whose face was set in a grey mask. "I'm surprised anyone can move in Scotland," he muttered. "They reckon the M.6 is a racetrack. All six carriageways on the move. All going north!"

There were now more than two-hundred people packed into the cabin behind him, but not one of them spoke.

"Keen," said Dando, as the youngster looked up. "How far is Lossiemouth?"

"About 250 miles sir."

Dando ran his hand through his thick, black hair. "Ah well," he said, "there's always the pigeons!"

The bird was a bright blue speck above his head.

For a brief moment Finn thought it was flying to him. But it was going away.

Suddenly it was flying not over a raging torrent, but the smooth, silver pool at Charlton. He saw a boy's eyes, bright and wide, as he beckoned him down to the water.

"Today, Donald Dacre, I'm going to make you a man of fish!"

When Finn looked up again, he was in the small low-ceilinged cottage at Falalee.

"Miss Teacher," he said softly, "one day I'm going to teach you how to cry."

Finn stared ahead, willing the waters to dissolve into a new picture. But all he could see was a swirling cauldron and the rain beating down at him as he lowered his head.

When he looked up again his lips slowly parted into a smile, as the grey of the waves suddenly transformed themselves into the brilliant green of the forest clearing, and there was Mallowry standing before him, her eyes greener even than the glade and her long, black hair sweeping down her beautiful face.

"You're the one they call the diviner, aren't you?" she asked, smiling at him through her soft, moist lips.

As his fingers gripped the edge of the parapet Finn was nodding to her, half crying, half laughing as he braced himself for fresh waves which were belling their arrival.

But when he looked again they weren't the waves of Corbar at all.

They were the Atlantic rollers bursting into the beach at Ballybunnion, with the sun burning down from a clear blue sky on to the firm yellow sands.

He watched as the small boy broke away from his parents and raced down to the water's edge, flinging off his white shirt as he addressed the waves. "I've come back, sea!" he was calling. "Just as I said I would!" Finn stretched out his arms, his mouth joyously raised as it roared into the rain. "I've come back!" he cried. "I've come back."

Out through the mist he could now see only the boy's back and the pale white of his legs as he ran back up the beach, pausing as if measuring the height of the sea wall before leaping upwards. . . .

When the broad back in the blue denim shirt swung round, the face was Finn's, laughing as he raised the overflowing champagne bottle, watching it splash over his boots as he stood with his legs apart, gazing down from the table in the Great Hall of Hesters.

"Do you taste my love in every glass of wine?" he was singing, tossing his head back until his hair danced yellow beneath the chandelier. "Do you touch your heart and feel the best of mine?"

"Please tell them for me I still remember them," he sang, watching the quick fingers of Tully jinking across the fiddle strings as his eyes darted out from under his creased top hat. Dick Dancer was there too, plastering his black hair close to his head with the drips of the spilled champagne on the table. And Chauncy Bawn, nodding his white head thoughtfully before going to his stone. And Liam The Liar, arguably the most notable and accomplished liar of his time, had a headful of Guinness. And Brown Windsor, the Keady man, beating out the music with hands the same as the oak on the table. God, they were Paladins then. Mountainy men. You could almost feel the juice in them. Samson was scratching at his gaping shirt as though there were six men bursting to leap out of him, and young Keen was there too, with a toast at his lips and his cheeks glowin' and Christ, you've never seen so much promise in a boy! The Goose was at the end of the table, for a reason which escaped him, for it was his seat. But The Goose it was, grinning enough to part his face and he, the bugger, sitting there with a crown the colour of butter on his head.

"Christ, he's a big un!"

Dando was pointing up the valley to a wave larger than all the rest which was forming half a mile from the dam wall.

The Slasher blew fiercely through his teeth as he trained the glasses into the rearing waters. "One more will just about do for him, Griff," he muttered.

"What's he doing now?"

"He's back on the wall again," said The Slasher. "Yes, he's standing on the wall and . . . just a minute . . . he seems to be going to meet it. And . . . he's laughing!"

"Laughing?" said Dando.

The Slasher shook his head and flicked the black eyepatch up over his forehead before peering into the field glasses again. "Oh no," he groaned. "Now he's singing! . . . He's a crazy man!"

Dando smiled. "Oh, I don't know, Slasher," he said. "They tell me he always liked choirboys."

Finn Rafferty didn't feel the last wave which took the Hadrian Dam of Corbar. His arms were open, waiting for it, embracing it. The eyes were dry now. Brown, trusting and fantastically alive. And there was a song in his smiling mouth to which a sea was listening. "Along this darkened roadway, our love will always shine. For today is the highway and tomorrow is the time. . . ."

He knew what the sea was now. It was only lips. It was all the lips, the lips which brought him and the lips which would accept him back. The lips which had loved him and the loving lips, beckoning him, sucking him into a rebirth which had its stirrings in the warm, teeming belly of the world itself. It was the lips of calling giants, down where the great whales go, where the pain ends. And somewhere, sometime in the soft murmuring of the ocean would be the lips of Mallowry, down there with the reaching creatures, among the singing things. She would be singing too. He knew that would go on. The singing would always go on.

Michael Keen peered down at the wreckage of the Land Rover lying upturned in the hollow beneath him.

"Is there anybody down there?" he called.

For a moment not a sound came from the buckled heap of yellow metal. Then a quiet, scratching noise could be heard coming from the inside of the vehicle as the door cracked away from its hinges and fell back against the wet grass.

Donald glanced down once more at the dead face of the bulky

muckshifter and, satisfied that there was nothing more he could do for him, he scrambled out, limping into the daylight.

Looking up he saw that the rain had stopped.

He began walking, his feet quickening as he climbed up the hill in the direction of the Shout.